Mandy Magro lives in Cairns, Far North Queensland, with her daughter, Chloe Rose, and their adorable toy poodle, Sophie. With pristine aqua-blue coastline in one direction and sweeping rural landscapes in the other, she describes her home as heaven on earth. A passionate woman and a romantic at heart, Mandy loves writing about soul-deep love, the Australian rural way of life, and the wonderful characters who call the country home.

Also by Mandy Magro

Rosalee Station
Jacaranda
Flame Tree Hill
Driftwood
Country at Heart
The Wildwood Sisters
Bluegrass Bend
Walking the Line
Along Country Roads
Moment of Truth
A Country Mile
Return to Rosalee Station
Secrets of Silvergum
Riverstone Ridge
The Stockman's Secret
Home Sweet Home
Savannah's Secret

MANDY

MAGRO

Road to Rosalee

First Published 2021
First Australian Paperback Edition 2021
ISBN 9781867223559

Published by
Mira
An imprint of Harlequin Enterprises (Australia) Pty Limited (ABN 47 001 180 918),
a subsidiary of HarperCollins Publishers Australia Pty Limited (ABN 36 009 913 517)
Level 13, 201 Elizabeth St
SYDNEY NSW 2000
AUSTRALIA

A catalogue record for this book is available from the National Library of Australia
www.librariesaustralia.nla.gov.au

Printed and bound in Australia by McPherson's Printing Group

For Helen Parker Dixon
My dear friend, fellow dream-chaser, awesome business partner, and an all-round inspirational woman.
I'm so thankful we crossed paths. Xx

True love can work miracles on a shattered heart.
When given unconditionally, it can be the thread
that helps to stich the broken fragments back together.

PROLOGUE

The fresh scent of the thousands of eucalypts the Blue Mountains were famous for lingered upon the air as dust-speckled dawn sunlight was snaking its way across the timeworn timber boards of the one-bedder farmhouse Lucy Harrison had called home for almost seven months. Her job as cook at the roadhouse out the front paid the rent.

She knew eighteen was too young to have a baby. She also knew she should have thought of that when she'd fallen into the charismatic stockman's swag at the B&S ball, a virgin and more drunk than she'd realised, but clued in enough to lie to him, both about her age and the fact that she wasn't on the pill. It wasn't his fault she was in this predicament. She'd wanted him to want her, had spent half the night trying to woo him. If he didn't live thousands of miles away, she might have told him she was pregnant. In hindsight, she should have, but it was too late to harbour those kinds of regrets now. She'd made her decision and now she had to follow through with it. She just wished she had someone to hold her hand right now, to tell her everything was going to be okay. But she was very much alone, and terrified of what lay ahead.

Hopefully, the ambulance she'd called would be arriving soon because the contractions were coming faster, detonating inside her like fireworks. With each wave of primal pain, a deep intrinsic need to protect her baby grew, to the point that she knew now she couldn't put the child up for adoption. Her innate need to raise this child was almost overwhelming, ridding her of all her worries about not being able to handle motherhood.

Caressing the mound of her belly, she took in deep lungfuls of air, vowing to make her baby girl her life's purpose. Her girl would know nothing like the hellhole she'd grown up in, with a drunkard father and an absent mother. Her baby deserved the best life she could give.

With the next swelling contraction seizing her, she bent forward and gripped the verandah railings so she didn't buckle beneath the pain. After eight months of pretending, of covering it up with oversized clothes, it was really happening – she was going to be a mum. A single parent.

One day she would move to the big smoke to be reunited with her best friend, Sally, and start a new life. But for now, this ramshackle house was her home, and would soon be her baby's home too.

One step at a time.

CHAPTER 1

Melody Harrison hated the fact that today was her twenty-third birthday.

She didn't want anyone to say the word 'happy' to her. She wasn't happy, not in the slightest. Her mother was dying, her marriage was in ruins, she'd lost contact with her closest friends because of her insufferable husband and she was so bone-tired, she felt like curling into a ball and sleeping for a year. But she had to soldier on. One step at a time.

Finding a free seat amidst the chaos of commuters, she sank down and blinked back another onslaught of tears. Where had the strong, confident, happy young woman she'd been when she'd met Antonio four years ago gone? She'd give almost anything to find her again.

She was having a really hard time coming to terms with what the marriage counsellor had told her after their last session, on the quiet.

'Even though he's denying it, Antonio is a covert narcissist, Melody, and a very clever one. So don't blame yourself for not seeing it earlier, or for his cheating. I know you're hoping for a miracle, but he won't change. They never do. Even when they say they will. It's all a ploy to keep you tangled in their web. You can leave him, if that's what you feel you want to do. You're a strong woman. You can do this.'

Even though she'd lived through it, day in, day out, the words had been overwhelming in the moment. What was she meant to do with such information?

Once the fog had cleared, Melody had got to work. With a clinical diagnosis, she started researching on the web for countless hours. Now she was starting to very clearly understand the demise of her marriage … and of her self-worth. The intense love bombing, the devaluing, the breadcrumbs of false 'I'm sorry's and 'I promise to get help's, blow after blow to her trust, the crushing heartbreak, confusion, self-doubt. Then, when she was at her lowest point, manipulating her to believe in him again.

Even the fact that he had declared his love so quickly, and they'd married within months, only for him to change tune the minute she moved in, going from 'I love you' to 'I choose to love you because you're hard to love'. Now she saw the pattern so very clearly.

Her heart had been crushed when she'd discovered that her husband wasn't the big romantic at heart he'd led her to believe he was. As a young married woman, she'd still held on to her high hopes for a happily-ever-after, even though a big part of her had screamed to run for the hills. So she'd stayed in the hope the romantic man she'd met would resurface. And here she was, years later, still waiting.

Golden sunlight and engulfing darkness mingled as the Sydney metro train sped through a maze of graffitied tunnels intermittently broken up by flashes of wintery fog, banked-up traffic and high-rises. Turning up the bluegrass melody playing from her AirPods, she sighed wearily. If only the view was instead of the endless countryside in which she'd spent her childhood. Her days spent exploring the wilds of her backyard, the Blue Mountains, on foot or horseback had been filled with so much happiness. She and her mum had spoken about moving back there one day, if she ever unravelled herself from the clutches of Antonio and her beloved café, but then, in the blink of an eye, everything has changed. Her mum had been given the devastating diagnosis and everything in Melody's world had been tipped upside down and inside out. How was she meant to get through this? How could she come out the other side unbroken? The world was going to be a very lonely place without her mum to turn to.

She twisted her wedding band around her finger, and then, as she had many times the past couple of weeks, almost slipped it off. But as it wedged on her knuckle, she stopped herself. The thought of the mess that would follow if she asked for a divorce stopped her – she didn't have the strength for such turmoil right now, nor did she want the weight of it on her mother's already heavy heart. There were way bigger fish to fry in her turbulent life.

Melody was well aware that her focus needed to remain on her mum because as much as she didn't want to believe it, she knew they didn't have long left together. With that timely reminder, she found herself choking back sobs again. She'd made a promise to herself that she wasn't going to cry today, and a stickler for never breaking a promise to herself or anyone else, she had to try and hold it together. She owed herself that much.

Feeling as if the weight of the world was upon her small shoulders, she breathed in deeply then sighed it away. She'd never taken so many desperate deep breaths in all her life. Having sardined herself between an elderly lady with her nose buried in a book and a clean-shaven man in a suit whose attention was held fast by the glow of his laptop, she felt safe enough to allow her heavy eyelids to drop. She recalled Aunt Sally's advice and did her best to envision lying on a white-sand beach, the rolling waves ebbing and flowing, seagulls floating on the gentle breeze above her. As nice as that fantasy was, it was tough to remain in such a beautiful place for long when her mother was living in a daily hell of pills and chemo and the spectre of imminent death.

With her heart squeezing tighter, she tried to ignore the almost unbearable weight of fear and heartache. How she was going to handle the next chapter of her life was beyond her comprehension, but her mother had taught her from a very young age that it's one step at a time. That's all she could do.

Opening her eyes, she realised they were almost at her station. Standing, she tossed her handbag over her shoulder and, reaching up on her tippy toes, steadied herself with an overhead handhold as the train screeched to a halt. With the morning rush hour at its peak, as soon as the door slid open, she was propelled forwards. Elbows out to protect herself, she squished out among a sea of commuters. Then, one foot after the other, she turned left and strode towards the stairs that led up and onto the street. Racing up the stairwell and into the mayhem of Sydney's CBD, she glanced skywards as another crack of thunder reverberated off the skyscrapers engulfing her. After weeks of tempestuous weather, she yearned to feel the caress of sunlight against her skin. As if mimicking her tortured soul, the slate-grey sky was heaving with ominous black clouds aching to dump their heavy load. She sympathised with Mother Nature's need to unleash her vehemence, because she too felt like she was a pressure cooker about to explode. Or implode. She wasn't sure which would be worse.

The past three months had been her worst nightmare, and still, the worst was yet to come. She dared not focus on it right now. That would come in the dead of night, when she lay awake, staring at the ceiling through teary eyes.

Frenzied people brushed past her, almost all of them walking blind with their gazes glued to their phones. If she had a choice, she'd toss her mobile in the bin – in her opinion, it had taken away people's need to really connect, eye to eye, heart to heart, soul to soul. The only reason she had the damn thing was for important calls, and to keep up with the social media avenues she used to promote her gastronomic masterpieces, or food porn, as Marianna, her business partner and mother-in-law, liked to call it. Posing and taking selfies for all the world to see to then tally up how many likes she got was worse to her than cutting off a finger. There was more to life than what other people thought of her. As long as they felt her emotion in the food, that was all that mattered. She'd made a name for herself in foodie circles, and people came from far and wide to taste her culinary skills – ones she'd first learnt from her mum, then finessed in the years of her apprenticeship.

Antonio was well aware she was the reason their café was so successful – it was her only saving grace according to him. Whenever anyone asked what her secret was, she always said it was the love she poured into everything she cooked, and she firmly believed that, because in the grand scheme of things, love was what made the world go round.

As if on cue, her phone chimed her message tone – *The Dukes of Hazzard* horn. Had her mother taken a turn for the worse? Her heart leaping into her throat, she yanked her phone from the depths of her handbag, relieved to see it wasn't a message from Aunt Sally – not her real aunt but her mother's best friend – but from Antonio.

Hey, Lorenzo has called in sick and we're run off our feet. You were meant to be here already. Are you far away? See you soon?

Melody quickly checked the time. She was barely running five minutes late. *Far out.* She gritted her teeth and groaned. No 'hope you're okay' or 'how is your mum?' No, even though she didn't really want to hear it but it was the principle that he'd clearly forgotten *again*, 'happy birthday'. Antonio Calabrese could be so damn selfish. The man she knew now was a far cry from the one she'd fallen for as an eighteen-year-old. Young love was so hopeful, so heedless. *So naïve.*

Strutting faster now, she shoved her mobile back into the seemingly endless pit of her handbag. Stuff him, she wasn't writing back. She was only minutes away and trying to walk and text would only slow her down anyway.

Her boots feeling as heavy as the eyelids she was fighting to keep open, she jiggled on the spot while waiting for a crossing to give the green go-ahead. After a sleepless night spent by her mother's bedside, she really didn't want to be doing this today, but she didn't have a choice. Her share in the café was the only thing keeping her sane, as if life could somehow continue on through the hardest of times. She needed the distraction of it to ground her. As her beautiful mother would say, you got this, my darling.

But did she?

Her hurried footsteps echoing off the sidewalk, she took the corner, barely avoiding a head-on with an equally frazzled-looking man. She was about to apologise when he glared at her. Argh! Stuff him too. His fault as much as hers. She resisted giving him a piece of her mind as she stormed away. Whatever happened to common decency, compassion, empathy? To make matters worse, half a block from her workplace, the heavens opened up like god was emptying his bathtub. The rain lashed down by the bucketful, instantly soaking the ill-prepared through to the skin. People ran this way and that, hands and newspapers overhead, as if the water would somehow make them shrink. Her umbrella was swiftly overhead, and her somewhat rainproof jacket was pulled in tighter; Melody had always been taught to be prepared for anything. But she sure as hell hadn't been prepared for the devastating news delivered by the family doctor, and definitely wasn't ready to say her final goodbyes. No twenty-three-year-old should be. *Cancer is an absolute bitch.*

Reaching her destination, she breathed a sigh of relief. She'd made it – one hurdle down – and now she had to try to get through the day without crying or losing her already very thin patience with Antonio. Glancing to the stone plaque beautifully etched with *Café Amore*, she pulled her brolly down and shook the droplets of water off. With floor-to-ceiling glass walls and a deck that was used in the summer months, the eatery had stellar views of Sydney Harbour and the iconic Opera House. Not that she got to enjoy the view much. Her place was at the back of house, pouring her passion into the dishes – cooking was her way of escaping from everyday life, and boy oh boy, she needed that right now.

She heaved the door open, the tinkle of the bell lost amidst the chatter of the breakfast customers and the drone of traffic behind her. The scent of strong Italian coffee lingered, and she breathed it in – she couldn't wait to enjoy a double-shot latte. Making a beeline for the back, she avoided Antonio, weaving his way through the tables, collecting plates and schmoozing the clientele – he was a master at winning people over, especially women.

Tucking wisps of hair that had escaped her plait behind her ears, Melody headed into the heart of the hip eatery – the kitchen. A huge pot bubbled on the stove, the scent of her famous oxtail and pork-mince bolognese sending her tastebuds dancing, an impressive feat when she couldn't recall the last time she'd had an appetite. She and Marianna had spent countless hours perfecting the recipe, and now it was close to perfect. Grabbing the wooden spoon, she gave it a stir, the bubbles of rich tomato goodness still not dark enough in colour, nor thick enough – it would be another hour before it was ready to be cooled, the oxtail plucked from the bones, and then served over freshly made pasta for the lunch rush. She was in the mood to make pappardelle today. The thick egg pasta would be perfect slathered in the rich sauce and topped off with some freshly grated pecorino, possibly a little chilli oil, depending on the diner's palate.

'Thank god you're here, Melody.' Appearing out of nowhere, Antonio dumped a tray of dirty plates and cups into the sink then spun to face her – clearly they were extremely busy because he rarely got his hands dirty. 'Oh, man, you look like death warmed up.' He bustled over, leaning in to kiss her. 'Did you get any sleep at all last night?'

'Gee whizz, Antonio, don't go sugar-coating anything, will you.' Rolling her eyes at his lack of tact, Melody turned her cheek to his inbound lips, deflecting his kiss to somewhere more platonic. 'Unless you count a couple of hours with your eyes closed as sleeping, no, I didn't.'

Sighing, he rested against the bench, his dark eyes on hers. 'So how is she?'

'Not good, but you know Mum. She refuses to have me sitting at her bedside all day long, waiting for her to die.' She half shrugged and smiled sadly. 'Her words, not mine.'

Antonio shook his head. 'I don't know how you do it, sitting with her most of the night then coming in here six days a week.'

'I do what I have to.' The shattering image of Antonio lip-to-lip with some girl from his gym flashed through her mind and she blinked back the threat of tears. She wasn't going to break down at work again. She'd done that too many times lately, and she'd made a promise to herself not to. Besides, he didn't deserve any more of her heartbreak. 'As you know.' She shot him a look.

'Come on, Melody. When are you going to stop being so pissed at me for my stuff-up?'

She and Antonio had been having this same conversation over and over since she'd caught him red-handed three weeks earlier, making out with some buxom blonde with lips bigger than hot-air balloons and boobs to match. It made her wonder how many times he hadn't been caught. Melody was relieved of the need to reply as Marianna Calabrese bustled into the kitchen.

'Oh bella!' Marianna said in her sweet, singsong voice, thick with an Italian accent. 'You made it, my precious daughter-in-law.' Her long dark hair, threaded with streaks of grey and tied back into a tight ponytail, swung to land over her shoulder when she skidded to a stop. 'And the happiest of birthdays to you, sweetheart. Your present is still on the way. It got held up in the post, but it's coming.'

'Thank you, Marianna. Sorry I'm a little late.' Ignoring the panicked look on Antonio's face, Melody unwound her scarf and dumped it, her jacket and her handbag into her staff locker. 'I missed my first train by seconds and had to wait for the next one. Talk about frustrating.'

Wiping her hands on the starched-to-a-crisp red and white polka-dot apron tied around her generous hips, her megawatt smile radiating the genuine warmth she was renowned for, Marianna tutted as she closed the distance between them. 'Shush now, there's no apology needed.' She cupped Melody's cheeks, her big brown eyes filled with compassion. 'Because you, tesoro mio, are a blessing to me, to my son, and to this kitchen. I appreciate you being here with everything you're going through.'

Emotion lodged in Melody's throat, making it impossible to reply. Instead, she smiled and nodded.

Marianna had always had Melody's back, and if she knew her son had been making out with another woman – just like Antonio's father had done so many years before, sending Marianna running all the way across the oceans to her family who had emigrated to Sydney – she'd lose it. That was why Melody had decided to keep her lips zipped. Marianna hated infidelity of any kind, and Melody didn't want a rift between mother and son on her conscience right now.

With his mother bustling back out of the kitchen, Antonio cocked his head as if pondering something. Melody could almost hear his brain ticking from where she was standing, putting her apron on. What the hell was he scheming now?

'What is it, Antonio?' She kicked off her boots and pulled on her chef's clogs.

'I know what you're thinking and no, I haven't forgotten your birthday. I actually planned to get your favourite from that little Lebanese place tonight, so would you mind if I called over to Sally's with it?' He took a tentative step forward. 'We can celebrate together with takeaway and a bottle of wine.'

'It's probably not the best idea.' She took her spot at the bench, eyeing the array of fresh ingredients she'd had delivered from the markets first thing this morning – a daily ritual.

'Please, Melody. It's been almost a month and I don't think I can say sorry any more than I already have.' He stopped on the opposite side of the bench, tipping his head to catch her eyes. 'Are you ever going to forgive me, pasticcino?'

'Please don't call me cupcake. You know I hate it.' Sighing, she brought her weary gaze to his. 'Honestly, Antonio, I don't know if I can ever fully forgive you, and if I do, I'm not sure I'll ever forget what you did.'

'But I've told you, it meant nothing and—'

She held her hand up to stop his excuses – she'd heard enough of them. 'I know, I know. It was just a stupid kiss, and she kissed you, not the other way around, yadda, yadda, yadda.' She met his gaze, hers fierce now. 'And like I've told you, it didn't look like that to me.'

'I know it didn't.' He regarded her like a wounded puppy. 'I've gone and stuffed everything up, haven't I?'

She offered a regretful smile. She almost wished that she could just magically forgive him. It would be simpler, easier. 'It's proving way tougher than I thought it would be, to forgive and forget, especially right now. All I want to do is focus on my mum.' Her hands went to her hips. 'You need to give me space, like I asked you to after our last marriage counselling session. You can't just push me to act like everything's going to be okay, because I honestly don't know if it will be.'

Antonio's mouth opened to say something, but then closed, as if he thought better of it. He regarded her for a few long moments, his gaze narrowing. 'I can't blame you, I suppose, but just know I'm here, waiting for you to love me again, like you should as my wife.'

'Mm-hmm,' was all she could muster for the raw anger rising in her throat.

Marianna's head popped through the doorway, a pen tucked above her ear. 'Antonio, we need you out here, pronto.'

'Coming.' Antonio turned and wandered back towards the hub of the café, his sway as cocky as ever.

His body language infuriated Melody, as did his expectation for her to believe his BS and simply get over it. Who did he think he was, making her feel bad for his selfishness? If she hadn't been his wife for four long years, she wondered if she'd have even tried to forgive him, or whether she'd have run for the hills the second she'd caught him – like his mother had from his father. And through it all, she had to admit to herself that she felt cold, almost cut off from feeling the emotion she usually would with such a betrayal, a by-product of what she was enduring with her mum. Numbness was way easier to handle than crying all the time.

Turning her attention to the vine-ripened tomatoes, purple garlic and bunches of basil, she decided to make some bruschetta topping, along with a Caprese salad. After that, the fresh pappardelle. The lunch rush would be upon her before she knew it, so she needed to get cracking.

CHAPTER 2

Squeezing some soothing cream onto his hand, Zai Wellstone gently rubbed it over the intricate tribal design of his latest tattoo that reached from just above his elbow to his shoulder and over the left side of his chest. It had taken a total of sixteen hours over two sessions to complete, and although it had pushed him past his pain threshold, he was thrilled with the result. Every one of his five tattoos meant something; he didn't get them just for the hell of it. This one embodied his connection to the Maori culture, the design he'd chosen in remembrance of his late grandpa, or koroua, as he'd always called him. It represented the tribe his ancestors had come from. Having been born in Australia, his father thought it unnecessary to focus on their heritage, but his koroua, god rest his traditional soul, would have admired the deep spiritual connection behind getting it permanently inked onto his skin.

Grabbing the Western button-up shirt from the end of the bed, he tugged it on, but left it open as he finished packing. Making sure his favourite boots were among his possessions, he then slipped on his thongs, startling when his phone rang.

'Talk about give a man a heart attack,' he muttered as he snatched it from his back pocket, smiling when he spotted who the caller was before wedging the phone between his shoulder and his ear.

'Hey, my brother from another mother, how goes it?' He started to do up the buttons of his shirt.

'Hey buddy, really good, you?' The sound of a motorbike revving to life reverberated down the line.

'Yeah, can't complain.' He could – about a lot – but he wasn't about to spew all his dramas on Patrick, his good mate and, essentially, his boss.

'Are you looking forward to getting back out here?'

'Sure am.' Zai felt a rush just thinking about being back among the dust, flies and genuine company of Rosalee Station. 'Even though it's been nice to spend a bit of time with Mum and Renee, and be able to dunk myself in the ocean whenever I like, I wish I could click my fingers and be back there right now. The city just doesn't suit me.'

'After growing up in Mount Isa, can't say I blame you for feeling like a fish outta water in Brisvegas, Zai,' Patrick said before bellowing a 'Come on!' in cattleman tone. Clearly, he was moving a mob. 'So, I know you don't like to talk about it much, but tell me, how's it been, being back home for the break?' Patrick's Irish lilt was still strong even after years of being in Australia. 'Did you get a chance to sort it all out with your father?'

Pulling the bedroom curtains aside, he watched his father stride towards his Porsche Cayenne SUV and hop behind the wheel. 'Yeah, not really.' Zai's heart sank as he watched him reverse out and then disappear down the long gravel driveway. 'We almost came to blows a couple of times.'

'Shit, that bad, hey?' Patrick heaved a sigh. 'He's a stubborn bugger, your old man. Even the father-in-law reckons so.'

'You can say that again. And Steve would know.' Turning away from the window, he collected the last of his things from the bedside table and shoved them into his travel bag, along with his phone charger and the biography he'd been engrossed in the past couple of nights. 'I don't know why I expected otherwise when I told him about being offered the manager's position out there alongside Slimbo.'

'I'm sorry, bud. I really thought it might change his mind about it being a dead-end job for you, especially knowing you'd be the man in charge while Georgia, li'l Donny and I are over in Ireland for Liam's wedding.'

Zai shrugged. 'Stranger things have happened, I suppose. Dad's always seen me as the disappointment of the family. Even when I became a fully fledged chopper pilot, he was pissed off. It's not like it's going to change anytime soon, if ever.' He ran a hand across the stubble he knew he should shave but couldn't be bothered to. It wasn't like he had anyone to impress. 'I've just got to find a way to let my need for his approval go and get on with my life the way I want to live it.'

'Too right, even though that's much harder said than done.' Bellows of cattle echoed.

The sound was music to his ears. Zai tried to shrug his despair off. 'Them's the breaks, Pat. At least I feel at home when I'm out there.'

'Well, if it's any consolation, Judy and Steve are ecstatic you took the job. They were going to put the brakes on their retirement caravanning trip round Oz if you didn't accept. We all love having you out here, Zai. You're an asset to the place and a treasured part of our family.'

Zai sank down on the corner of his bed. 'Thanks, mate, that means a lot.' After two outstanding years mustering at Rosalee Station, Zai couldn't wait to make it three, now his goal of making it to head stockman was coming to fruition.

'Just speaking the truth, Zai. Now get your butt back here, because Slimbo is going to need you more than ever with Georgia and me gone.'

Zai smiled from ear to ear at the very thought of hanging out with one of his favourite Aussie larrikins – Slim was an absolute classic to work with. 'Ha, yeah, he and I are going to drive each other nuts.'

'I bet, but you both love the banter, because it keeps both of you on your toes.' Patrick said between chuckles. 'Mind you, Showbags and Tumbles do a damn good job of it too, I might add. Which we need with Hasselhoof's grumbling, which honestly is getting worse by the day.'

'Ha, true that. The motley crew are getting back together. Look out.'

'Yeah, lord help us. And speaking of that, are you still good to grab Matt on the way through Mareeba, bud? He's just going to oversee things for a couple of weeks, you know, get the muster on the go and the crew in line before heading back to his place. Poor bugger is spread so thin, thank god he's got Sarah holding the reins for him.'

'Yeah, of course, and damn straight, Sarah is a top chick. It's totally understandable he wants to make sure Rosalee is running like a tight ship while you and Georgia are gone.'

'Thanks mate, really appreciate it. I know Mareeba is out of your way a bit.'

'Nah, not at all, I'd rather go the coast road anyway, there's more to see, and it'll be nice to catch up with Walshee. I haven't seen him for ages.'

'Yeah, neither have we. He's been real busy at his new place the last year, getting it all set up. It'll be good for him to pop his head in here for a couple of weeks before getting stuck back into training his bucking bulls.' The whirr of the generator that powered the cattle station got louder. 'Anyway, enough yabbering, I gotta run. I'll be back just in time for Slim's big day. Catch you then.' Patrick's voice was almost drowned out by the hum of the diesel motor.

'Yup, for sure, we'll all be there with cowbells on.'

'Good, catch ya, bud. Drive safe.'

'Will do. You three have fun in Ireland.' The call ended and Zai slipped the phone back into his pocket.

It was nearing the end of April, with the mustering season about to begin for the year, which meant a couple of months of incredibly hard yakka. The unforgiving yet breathtaking countryside he'd longed to lend his hand to was finally calling him back to his real home. He couldn't wait to leave the trail of traffic Brisvegas delivered and instead see the familiar trail of dust in his rear-view mirror. His six-month stint at the racing stables, both to pass the time and to put more money in his bank account, had been feasible, but certainly not his thing. It didn't flop his mop, as Slim would say.

Thoroughbreds were a whole other kettle of fish to stockhorses, as were the people that bred them. There was only so much of the hoity-toity horseracing lifestyle Zai could take. Give him dirt and dust over airs and graces any day of the week. If he could, he'd stay out at Rosalee Station permanently, but a seasonal stockman's work just didn't allow for such a luxury. Slim was the only person that got to stay out there all year round, the larrikin's job as an all-rounder rare as hens' teeth – and Zai had a feeling that Slim, after almost thirteen years of calling the place home, wasn't going anywhere soon. Unless Slim and Sherrie, his wife-to-be, had plans none of them were privy to yet.

Slinging his bag over his shoulder, he took one last look around what used to be his bedroom. The memories he had of his childhood in this place were not the best. Most of the time he'd spent in here was tucked away from his father's snide remarks and his mother's looks of disappointment, all of which were only exaggerated by his younger sister's need to do everything necessary to win her father's love. Now morphed into a massive guest room with an ensuite bigger than most people's kitchens, and a walk-in closet to boot, it resembled nothing he remembered. Not one for extravagance, he was going to be glad to see the back of it. Give him his swag beneath the stars over the grandeurs of his parent's oceanside home any day.

Wandering down the hallway, he stopped short of his younger sister's bedroom, and popped his head round the doorway. 'Hey, little blister. I'm off.'

'Ahh.' Her nose buried in a medical textbook, Renee had a concentrative frown that gave way to a mischievous smile as she brought her glasses-framed gaze to his. 'I thought something stank.'

'Oh hardy-ha-ha.' He strode over to where she was sitting at her desk, sticky notes strewn from one end of it to the other, scribbled with words almost too long to pronounce. 'How's the study going?'

Rolling her eyes, she groaned. 'I swear my brain is about to explode.'

'No way.' He gave her shoulder a squeeze. 'Your brain is huge and can fit a lot. You got this, sis.'

'Ha.' Renee glanced up at him. 'I hope so.'

'You have, and you watch, you'll end up top of your class, I just know it.' He offered her a confirming nod. 'At least one of us is going to make Dad proud.'

'Oh, Zai.' She took her glasses off. 'Please stop being like that. Dad does love you, a lot.'

'Is that so? Well.' Zai's brows shot skywards. 'He has a real funny way of showing it.'

'You were always meant to be a stockman, bro, it's in your blood, just like it's in Mum's, not that she wants to admit it.' She spun her desk chair around to face him. 'I still remember the day you went galloping bareback down the street on one of the horses from old Ray Reynolds's place.' Laughing, she snorted a little. 'Dad almost had a fit and Mum almost had a coronary.'

'Yeah, it wasn't one of my finest moments, hey?' He grimaced then grinned. 'Or was it?'

'I can still hear Mister Reynolds, when he was trying to calm Dad down.' She tried to pull a poker face, but her lips were lopsided. '"You know what, Christopher, riding a shod horse down a steep bitumen hill bareback is a real show of true horsemanship."' Her ability to mimic Ray Reynolds's voice was uncanny. '"So, in my firm opinion, you should be mighty proud of your son."'

Zai cracked up. 'Yeah, and even with that, Dad still couldn't see how I was nothing like him.' He shook his head. 'I mean, he wouldn't be caught dead anywhere near a horse, let alone riding the thing, and I wouldn't be caught dead with a scalpel in my hand, let alone slicing someone open with it.' The very thought of it made him shudder.

'Ha ha, fair point.' Renee smirked playfully. 'I wouldn't like to be the patient on the operating table. With you at the helm, I might go in for a heart transplant and wake up with a lobotomy.'

Zai chuckled. 'Geez, thanks for the vote of confidence, sis.'

Renee shrugged. 'Just saying it how it is.'

'Yeah, true. I just wish Dad could see it how it is.'

'Yeah, well, you know Dad, he's not an easy one to sway once he's made his mind up.'

'You got that damn straight.' He breathed a sigh. 'Anyways, I gotta head, so get up from that god-awful desk you tie yourself to and give your brother a farewell hug.'

'Aw. I don't want you to go.' Renee leapt up and threw her arms around him. 'I'm going to miss your larrikin ways around here. Mum and Dad are so serious all the time. '

Zai held her tight. 'I'm only a phone call away.'

Renee held him even tighter still. 'Yeah, I know, but it's not the same.'

Before he shed a tear, Zai untangled and stepped back, but kept hold of Renee's hands. 'Love you heaps, my little blister.'

'Love you too, bro, like shit tons and then some.'

Zai mocked shock. 'Don't let the old man hear you use language like that beneath his roof.'

'What he doesn't know won't kill him,' she said, wiping a lone tear from her cheek as she sniffled.

'On that note.' He wiped the next ones that rolled from her eyes. 'I'm outta here.' Departing before his resolve broke, he made his way downstairs, to where his mother was enjoying her routine cup of tea and bowl of muesli at the kitchen bench at the same time as she did every day. Everything worked like clockwork here, day in, day out – it drove Zai nuts.

'Hi, love. Sleep well?' she asked, like she'd said every other morning he'd walked in here.

'Yeah, can't complain.' He leant in to brush a kiss over her cheek. 'How about you?'

'I tossed and turned all night long.' Her eyes filled with sadness as she brought a hand to his arm. 'I wish you weren't going back there. I hate having you so far away.'

'Oh, come on, Mum, it's not like you're never going to see me again,' he said gently.

'I know, but it's always so long between visits.' She blinked faster, her sky-blue eyes a mirror of his.

'This is the life of a stockman, Mum.' Disregarding her look of indignation, he shrugged. 'I have to go where the work is for as long as I can, and I'm okay with that.' He wished to god she and his dad were.

'Mm-hmm.' She dropped her hand and turned away from him, focusing back on the home and design magazine she got delivered each and every month – renovating the house countless times over gave her a sense of usefulness.

His patience wearing thin, Zai drummed the counter. 'Come on, I can see there's more you want to say, so spill.'

She heaved an almighty sigh, resting her forearms on the breakfast bar, and turned to face him again. 'It's just, you could have been anything with that high IQ of yours … the world could be your oyster.'

Doing his very best to remain poker-faced, Zai breathed in deep, willing himself not to say anything he'd regret – it would be a while before he could make it up to his mum if he did. 'I'm just following what's in my heart.' It was said candidly, with an undertone of annoyance.

Her lips pressed into a thin line as she took her sweet time answering him. 'In my strong opinion, and your father's, you should learn to follow your head. Your heart will only get you into strife.' She eyed him, as if waiting for the match she'd just tossed to ignite into something far bigger.

'We'll see.' He shrugged her gaslighting off as he headed over to the fruit bowl and grabbed an apple. 'Dad's already left?' He took a bite, enjoying the tangy crunch, a small distraction.

'Yes. He said to say goodbye.' She sat up straighter.

'Couldn't pop upstairs quickly to say it himself?' He took another bite, eyeing her as he chewed.

'He was running late for surgery,' she said a little defensively.

'Pull the other one, Mum.'

'Oh, Zai, please, not now,' she huffed. She closed her eyes and shook her head. 'I really don't want you leaving on bad terms.'

She can talk. 'Sorry, Mum, but it's no wonder I feel like the black sheep of this family when you carry on like this.' He strode towards her. 'I've been super patient, the entire time I've been here, but enough's enough.' He paused to find the right words. 'So how about you tell me, when are you and Dad going to accept this is what I want for my life?'

His mum regarded him with wide eyes. 'Most probably never.' Reaching out, she patted his cheek. 'So how about you tell me, when are you going to accept that your father and I are just looking out for you, and only want the best for our only son?' With that, she stood and headed to the fridge, daring a challenging glance over her shoulder when he didn't respond. 'Fair enough, Zai, but let me tell you, you'll understand one day, when you're a parent.'

Zai bit his tongue, hard. He knew from experience that self-justifying with his mother was not going to get him anywhere, but he had to at the very least say his piece. 'I reckon I'll accept my kids for who they are, and encourage them to do what makes them happy because you only get one shot at life, so why waste it doing something that isn't feeding your soul?'

Jacinta Wellstone's eyes almost rolled back in her head. 'Oh lord, here we go again with the hoodoo guru stuff. Life isn't all about fate and destiny and following your path, my boy. It's about hard work and dedication and doing everything you can to be the very best you can be.' Her manicured brows bumped together, and she folded her arms. 'We all make choices, and you've chosen a path that's not going to bring you any form of security. What kind of woman is going to marry a man who can't provide for her, let alone a family?'

Zai had heard this a thousand times before, from both his mother and father, and he'd had a gutful. 'Mum, please. Just drop it.'

'Okay, I'll sweep it back under the rug we all tiptoe over.' Almond milk in hand, she padded back towards him, then wrapped her arms around him. 'We do love you. You know that, right?' she said into his chest.

Zai gently hugged her – she was only doing what she thought was best, but he just wished she understood that wasn't his idea of living. 'I know you do, but I'm not so sure about Dad.'

She stepped back and met his eyes. 'He loves you. Maybe a little too much.'

'I'll take your word for it.' He leant in and kissed her cheek, needing to put a stop to this conversation. 'Anyway, I have to head. I'll call you when I'm there, okay?'

'Yes, that would be good.' She stepped back and watched him wander out of the kitchen. 'Please be safe,' she called after him.

'Always am,' he replied matter-of-factly.

Heart heavy from the heated chat – not what he wanted right before he left, but inevitable – Zai headed out the front door. Without looking back at the grand two-storey home, he strode to his trusty four-wheel drive parked in the shade of a big old mango tree. With B&S stickers covering the tailgate, enough aerials to make contact with the moon, and a pair of massive spotlights bright enough to blind an alien, his LandCruiser looked so out of place here. Then again, preferring jeans, a Bonds singlet and a pair of roughed-up boots to metro-man clothes and sneakers, so did he.

Climbing behind the wheel, he dropped his bag on the passenger seat, packet of Minties at the ready, and turned the key. Revving the engine to life, he switched the stereo on and chose one of his favourites to keep him company – good old Waylon Jennings. He reversed out and turned down the drive, resisting the urge to put the pedal to the metal to get out of there faster. With a twenty-five-hour drive, broken up by an overnighter at Sarah and Matt Walsh's place in Far North Queensland, he had a long trip ahead of him. The sooner he got to where his heart was sated, the better. He didn't belong in this synthetic world. Never had. The outback was where god intended him to be, and he was going to fulfil his calling as a stockman, come hell or high water. One day, he might even be lucky enough to own his very own property, where he could live off the land he so loved with a like-minded woman by his side. His parents were going to have to find a way to accept him exactly how he was, or risk him drifting further away.

CHAPTER 3

If Melody had thought herself weary in the morning, now she was beyond exhausted. The café had been filled to capacity most of the day, and after missing one of her trains, again, and then having to wait twenty minutes for the next one, it was close to eight-thirty when she finally arrived at Aunt Sally's place – her home away from home.

In the past, she'd been terrified of train stations after dark, but now she dared anyone to try and attack her. She had so much fight in her, she'd be glad to take it out on some thug.

Climbing the back steps of the cottage, she slipped off her boots and stepped inside the chocolate-box house her mother had called home the past two months. With a background in nursing, Aunt Sally was an absolute godsend.

As she dropped her key into the bowl on the entrance table, a bell jingled as her black cat, Magic, met her, wrapping himself around her ankles and meowing a warm welcome. Smiling, she bent and scooped him from the floor, cuddling his hefty six kilos to her. Having rescued Magic from being put to sleep almost three years earlier after she'd found him in a bad state in a back alley behind the café, she'd done her best to curb his big appetite, but had come to accept he was just big-boned and needed more food than most felines did. The loving tomcat was her most loyal companion. She'd brought him, along with a bag of clothes, to stay here three weeks ago after catching Antonio cheating.

'Hey, buddy, I missed you today.' She buried her face into his silky-soft fur, and he purred louder.

As she wandered through the kitchen, the scent of toast wafted along with the lingering of countless incense sticks that had been burnt over the years by her boho aunt. The house was quiet as she tiptoed through the lounge room, where the television was on but the sound muted. *The Bachelor* was playing – she could not for the life of her understand how any woman believed she could find true love on such a show. It took time to fall in love, to get to know someone – hell, after four and a half years she was still learning things about Antonio, things she wasn't sure she could live with, or truly forgive. But leaving him wasn't so cut and dried. There was their house, then the café, and the division of finances and furniture – she just didn't have the strength to deal with it, not with Mum at death's door. And then there was the fact that she did still care for him and love him – she was married to him for Pete's sake. And it hadn't all been bad.

Sally met her in the hallway, looking as tired as Melody felt. 'Hey, you.'

'Hi, love. I hope you got to find some enjoyment in today, seeing as it's your birthday.' Melody shrugged and Sally placed her hands on Melody's shoulders. 'I got you one of those little Black Forest cakes you like. We can have a slice of it later, with a glass of wine.'

'Okay, thank you.' Melody smiled and brushed a kiss over her aunt's cheek. 'How is she?'

'Your mum's had a really hard day, sweetie.' She looked to the open doorway, then back to Melody. 'I had to up her morphine so she could get some rest.'

Melody nodded. 'I thought you'd have to, seeing as she was in a fair bit of pain this morning.' With Magic keen to hop back down, she unravelled him from her arms, and released him to the floor.

Walking side by side, they stopped and peered into the bedroom where shimmering stars danced upon the walls and ceiling. It had been an idea of Melody's, to bring the outback sky her mother had always loved into the room via a projector. Her mum had been beside herself when she'd first switched it on. Now it was more for the sake of normality.

They went to the bedside, where Melody saw the fading shadow of the strong, vibrant, effervescent person her mum used to be. Skeletal, with drawn cheeks and only tufts of hair; the cancer was eating her alive from the inside out. It tore Melody apart knowing how much discomfort she was in. If only there was a way she could save her, but no amount of research she did, no amount of medical advice she sought, both clinical and natural, was proving helpful. She'd reached a dead-end – acceptance of the fact was so very confronting.

Placing a gentle hand over her mum's, she looked to Sally. 'Did she eat or drink anything today?'

'She's refusing to eat,' Sally said sadly. She cleared her throat. 'But I held some ice to her lips, and she had a few tiny sips of orange juice.'

Emotion strangling her, Melody bit back tears. 'She's given up, hasn't she?' she finally choked out.

'I think so, sweetheart.' Sally rushed to her side, and wrapped an arm around her, pulling Melody close. 'I know you don't want to hear this, but it'll be better when she's gone, my love, because then she'll be in no pain and finally at peace.'

Allowing herself to finally break down, Melody wrapped her arms around Sally, and quietly wept. She knew her mum was on her deathbed, but still, some part of her didn't want to believe it. She kept trying to fool herself into thinking she would wake up one morning to find this was all a bad dream, or that her mother would be miraculously cured. It was all part of the process for loved ones, apparently – that's what Sally had told her on many occasions.

Her aunt allowed her the time to grieve, silently comforting her by stroking her hair, bangles jingling as she did. Eventually, with her tears all but dried up and her head throbbing, Melody untangled and stepped back, sniffling.

Sally tenderly wiped wisps of hair from her face. 'Would you like something to eat?'

Melody shook her head. 'I'm not hungry, thank you.'

'Come on now, love, you have to have something. You're losing weight, and you need your strength.' She offered a kind smile. 'How about I make you your favourite?'

'Which one?' Melody smiled a little.

'A bacon and egg sandwich with my garlic aioli. And a nice hot chocolate to go with it. Then we'll follow it up with your special cake.'

'That sounds lovely, thank you.' She appreciated her aunt so much.

Sally patted her arm. 'You go and have yourself a nice long shower and I'll have it ready for you when you're done, okay?'

'Okey-dokey.' Melody's forehead puckered. 'I honestly don't know what we would do without you. Thank you for loving me and mum like you do.'

Blinking faster, Sally drew in a breath. 'Ditto, sweetheart. You and your mum are the closest to family I have.' Her bohemian skirt swished at her ankles as she turned to head out the doorway. 'My blood relatives aren't worth my time or energy,' she added before slipping away.

With Sally gone, Melody took a moment to lean in and softly kiss her mother's forehead. Lucy Harrison stirred just a little, but the drugs kept her in their grasp. Dragging herself from her mother's bedside, Melody padded to the shower, considering the fact that her aunt was in the same boat as her. She felt bad for not having thought too much about how hard it would be for Sally, nursing her childhood best friend to her death. It hadn't been from ignorance that she hadn't stopped to really think about this until now, but more because she hadn't wanted to accept her mother's cancer was terminal. The comprehension that all of this was truly happening, and that nothing was going to make her mum better, tore at her already tortured soul.

How was she going to say goodbye to her mum forever?

An hour later, showered, fed and fighting to keep her eyes open, Melody hugged her aunt goodnight then headed back to her mother's bedroom. Lucy was still sleeping and Magic had taken his usual post at the foot of the bed. Curled up, he too was fast asleep.

Unfolding the blanket she'd left on the dresser that morning, Melody pulled it over herself as she got settled into the recliner. It didn't take too long for her eyelids to drop closed, and for the next few hours she slumbered fitfully, jolting awake with fright after fright, each time bringing her cheek to her mother's face so she could feel that she was still breathing.

Wide awake just after midnight, Melody finally saw signs of movement. She sat up straighter and took her mother's frail hand in hers. 'Hey, Mum, can you hear me?'

'Of course I can, love.' Lucy blinked heavy eyelids half open. 'I'm not dead yet,' she mumbled with a hoarse chuckle that promptly had her coughing and gasping.

Plucking a tissue then putting it to her mother's lips, Melody helped to prop her up a little. 'Please don't talk like that, Mum. It's not funny.' With a heavy heart, she noted the splatters of blood on the tissue as she tossed it into the little bin.

Lucy looked to Melody through hollow eyes. 'I'm sorry, darling, you're right. It's not funny in the slightest.' Her lips quivered as she smiled. 'I suppose I'm just trying to make light of an awful situation, that's all.'

'I know you are, but …' She tried to meet her mum's smile but failed miserably.

'Oh, my love, I'm so sorry. I know this is hard for you.'

Melody couldn't believe her mother was the one apologising. 'Please, Mum, I'm okay. You don't need to worry about me.' Sinking to the side of the bed, she gave her hand a gentle squeeze. 'I'm tough like you, remember?'

'That's my girl.' Lucy held her gaze, her mouth opening to speak again, but then closing. She did this a couple of times.

'What is it, Mum?'

'I have something I really need to tell you.'

Melody nodded. 'Okay, well, I'm all ears.' She stood, coming closer to her mum so she didn't have to project her voice.

'I don't know how else to tell you this …' Lucy's lips pressed into a thin line as she took a few lengthy moments. 'You know how I've always told you that your father didn't want anything to do with us?'

'Yes.' Melody's heart stalled and she unconsciously held her breath.

'Well, it was because he didn't know about you.' Lucy's eyes filled with tears.

Tears prickled Melody's eyes too. 'What do you mean?' Leaving hers, she wiped at her mother's with a fresh tissue.

'I never told him I was pregnant.'

The room felt as if it were closing in on her. Melody sank down to the chair before her knees could buckle. She took her time to catch her breath and to rein in her anger – she could not, would not, yell at her dying mother. Gathering what she could of herself, she took a deep breath then blew it away. 'Why would you do such a thing?'

'I was young and stupid and didn't want him to think I was trying to trap him. Nor did I want him to talk me into having an abortion, if that was what he decided was for the best.' Lucy paused, taking little gasping breaths.

'It's okay, Mum. Take your time.'

Even though she had a million questions and her mind was spinning, Melody couldn't believe how calm she was being. But with her mum so close to death, nothing else mattered as much.

After a few minutes, Lucy had regathered herself enough to speak again. 'I kept telling myself once you were born, I'd tell him. Then when you turned one, I'd tell him, then … well, you get the picture. And here we are.'

All Melody could do right now was nod. As she cast her gaze to the floor, tears welled and trickled down her cheeks and she roughly brushed them away. She was so tired of crying, especially knowing there'd be plenty more to come.

'I'm so sorry, sweetheart. I shouldn't have kept this from you,' Lucy sobbed. 'I'm such a failure as a mother.'

'Oh, Mum, no, you're not.' Melody shot to her feet, pushing her own turmoil to the side, as she plucked two tissues – one for her and one to wipe her mother's cheeks. 'You've always done what you thought was best, and put me before everything else in your life.' Leaning in, she kissed her mum, their tears mixing. 'I forgive you for not telling me.'

'Oh, my beautiful girl, thank you. You've always had a kind heart, and a gentle soul. You're going to go so far in this life.'

'One step at a time,' they said in unison.

Feeling as if she were about to shatter into a million tiny little pieces, Melody carefully climbed in beside her mum, and draped an arm over her chest. 'I love you so much. I don't want you to go.'

'You're going to be okay, sweetheart. I just know it.' She turned to face Melody, their noses touching. 'And when you're missing me, I want you to look up at the stars and know I'm looking down on you, loving you from the heavens.'

'I promise I will.'

'Good. That's all I need to know.' Lucy's eyelids began to drift and flutter.

'Thank you for telling me about my father.'

'Of course, love. You deserve to know.'

Melody felt compelled to know more. 'What's his name?' She couldn't make a decision now, but at least she'd have the option to google him later.

'Matthew Walsh. As far as I know, he works on the family station. Rosalee Station.' Lucy's words were beginning to sound as if she were drunk.

'Okay.' Melody pulled the sheet up and over both of them.

'If you find him, please tell him I'm so sorry.'

'I will, Mum. You sleep now. I can see you're exhausted.'

'You too. I love you, my Sweet Melody.'

Closing her eyes, Melody said, 'I love you, too, Mum, with all my heart.'

* * *

Sunlight poured through the parted curtains, stirring Melody from a bad dream, one where she could hear her mother's hysterical screams from her freshly buried casket. She was down on all fours, raking at the earth with her hands, her fingernails lifting with her frenzied digging, but getting nowhere fast. She could hear her mother gasping for air, suffocating, and she couldn't get to her quick enough.

Waking with a fright, Melody quickly realised she was in her mum's bedroom, still lying alongside her. She looked to her mum's face, only inches from her own. She held her breath, listening for her mother's. She couldn't hear it but maybe it was just soft and faint. Sitting up a little, she took her mother's hand in hers. To her horror, it was cold, limp … lifeless.

'Mum?' She sounded as tiny as a mouse.

Silence.

Leaning in, she rested her ear up against her mother's lips. There wasn't a breath.

'No,' she sobbed. 'Please lord, don't take her from me. I'm not ready to say goodbye yet.'

Staring into her mum's face, now so peaceful, so free of pain, like a glass dropped from a great height, her heart shattered into a million tiny pieces.

And without her mother by her side, it was going to be almost impossible to put herself back together.

* * *

'Ashes to ashes, dust to dust …' The priest's words sounded as if they were being said beneath water.

It was an offensively sunny day – stormy weather would have suited the sombre occasion much better. The funeral was a small affair, just how her mother had wanted it to be. Standing at the graveside, Melody stared into the dark oblivion that would be Lucy Harrison's final resting place. Aunt Sally stood beside her, holding her hand so tightly, she was essentially holding her up. The casket began to sink so slowly, lower and lower, taking with it the roses they'd all placed upon it, and taking her mother further away. Then, hearing her aunt's heartfelt sobs, she dared a look at her grief-stricken face, the shadows of pain in her eyes mimicking her own. They'd both lost the person most precious to them, and now the hard road was about to begin. They no longer needed to be strong for her mum's sake and now, both of them were breaking. Needing to look anywhere else, Melody took her gaze to the bright blue sky, the few listless clouds. With the sun on her face, she imagined climbing aboard one of the cottony puffs, and floating away to a place where her heart no longer ached; to a place where her mother was still alive.

With Antonio clearing his throat, she looked to where he and his mother stood on her other side. His fingers were also entwined with hers, but unlike her aunt's touch, she didn't gain any comfort from his. He wasn't crying, but Marianna was shedding enough tears for the both of them. A tissue to her eyes, she tried to offer Melody a comforting glance. Melody was too numb to know how to receive it. Nor did she feel a thing for this man standing beside her, the very one she'd imagined her whole life revolved around only a month ago. Right then and there, she knew she couldn't stay here, pretending to be something she wasn't, surviving one day to the next.

She needed a break from her tumultuous life with Antonio, to work out if he was the one she wanted to call her husband. Or not.

And she needed to know who her father was. She needed to stand in front of this Matthew Walsh and tell him to his face that she was his daughter. She needed to see, either way, if he wanted her in his life.

First, though, she would give herself some time to truly grieve. Then, one step at a time, the rest would follow.

Back at the house, the onslaught of unwanted hugs began, given by women who meant well but who would never fill the gaping hole her mother's death had left. Melody slipped away from the small huddle of mourners, then outside. Magic followed her. As if on autopilot, she kicked off her shoes, padded down the steps, walked across the back lawn, and sank into the swing chair suspended beneath the big old oak tree. Magic settled himself not far from her. With a little shove, she started swinging, her feet brushing against the ground. To and fro, to and fro, the squeak of the chains strangely comforting. This had been her mother's favourite spot before the cancer had left her bedridden. In the early stages of the melanoma, they'd welcomed quite a few days out here, cuppa in hand, both of them hopeful for a full recovery, and then at night, in this very spot, side by side, staring at the stars and making wishes upon any that would shoot through the blackness. A fat lot of good all that wishing, hoping and praying had done. The world sucked, and so did hope and dreams and optimism.

Closing her eyes, Melody grabbed hold of the chains and tipped her head backwards, so she was hanging. Her head woozy from the rush of blood, she watched the sky come closer and then fade, the tempo of it soothing. She allowed it to carry her back in time, to the Blue Mountains, where her mother's spirit had been alive and so very free.

'I love you, Mum,' she whispered, looking to the heavens. 'And just so you know, I'm going to find my dad and make things right.'

CHAPTER 4

It was the very first day of winter in Australia and as the weather was growing colder, so was Melody's heart. She didn't want to feel so closed, so cut off, but for so long she'd had to contain her emotions to be able to function and sadly, that meant shutting off her usually passionate nature. She'd gone from living on a high before her mother's diagnosis to surviving through a constant low since her death. Her world wasn't what it used to be. Even her cooking had been lacking her love. So she'd made the tough decision to have a break from working at Café Amore, and from everything else in Sydney. Leaving Magic behind had been hard but it wouldn't be for too long. Besides, she knew her Aunt Sally would spoil her feline mate rotten.

Looking to the sea of clouds outside her plane window, she found it hard to believe it had been almost two months since her mother had passed. For the first few traumatic days after the funeral, she'd thought about her body, buried beneath the earth, and cried enough tears to fill the ocean. She hadn't been able to sleep or eat, or even think.

Then she'd learnt that life was going to go on regardless. And her grief had mixed with fear and anger, and time had blurred from one day into the other, the next week into the following, and she'd done all she could to immerse herself back into her life, maybe a little too quickly. The routine had given her some kind of strange purpose, a reason to get out of bed every morning, but had she given herself enough time to grieve? Was there ever enough time for such a thing? Or was it like her Aunt Sally said, that eventually she would just learn to live with the permanent hole her mother's untimely death had left in her aching heart?

Then there was the matter of Antonio and their rocky relationship. He'd been understanding of her meltdowns and detachment at first but had lately become impatient and snappy. And so had she. He'd even had the gall to complain that his primal needs weren't being met, and that making love to him would make her feel better. Yeah, right. It was all about him, as always. Sex was the last thing on her mind. He'd appeared shocked two weeks ago when she'd told him she was going away for a little while, to meet her biological father and to get her head straight – but she also detected that he was relieved too. Maybe he was beginning to see what she already knew – they weren't meant to be together. Maybe there was more to it and he was starting to think more about the buxom blonde she'd caught him kissing? The massive mistake she'd somehow forgiven him for but hadn't forgotten.

Marianna had been supportive of her extended leave, encouraging her to take all the time she needed. It gave her comfort to know her beloved café was in good hands, with

Marianna at the helm and the new chef Melody had handpicked manning the kitchen.

One foot in front of the other, she was going to do her best to find some stable ground so she could make smart decisions, not emotionally messy ones. For now, it was all in the hands of fate, or god, or the universe … whichever one it may be. Or maybe it was all three?

Plucking her iPhone from the seat pocket in front of her, she left it on aeroplane mode and went to the screenshots she'd taken of Facebook and LinkedIn. It had taken her all of half an hour to find all she needed to know for now about her father. Matthew Walsh was married to a lady named Sarah and they owned a property in Mareeba called Diamond and Dust Stud, where he bred and trained bucking bulls and held bi-annual bull-riding schools. Their place was picturesque. Sarah was very pretty, Matthew was very handsome, and their little boy, Beau, was adorable – the perfect little family with a seemingly perfect life. And here she was about to possibly upend it. But what was she meant to do? It wasn't like she could keep this to herself and move on, especially now her mum was gone. She wanted to meet her father, to get a sense of who he was so she could get more of a sense of who she *really* was. Maybe that was the solid foundation she'd been searching for her whole life.

She sighed. There were so many maybes in her life right now …

A high-pitched squeak was followed by a flight attendant's nasal voice. 'Ladies and gentlemen, we are about to make our descent into Cairns, so can you please bring your seats to the upright position, secure your tray, slide your window shades up and make sure your seatbelts are secured. We will be arriving to a beautifully sunny day, with a temperature of twenty-six degrees, so if you are visiting, have a wonderful holiday, and if you are returning, welcome home.'

Melody pondered this as she got ready for landing. Was she holidaying, or arriving home? Her heart suddenly raced as she deliberated what she was about to do. Arriving here unannounced was a ballsy move, but she didn't want to risk contacting her father only to have him hang up on her, or ignore an email or message, or deny what she was telling him. She needed to put him on the spot and to see his face when she did. After what Antonio had put her through, she was having a hard time trusting people.

The window shades being lifted, sunlight flooded the cabin. Trying to calm her nerves, she pressed her face up against the oval peephole to a totally different world, watching in awe as it tilted beneath. She'd never been this far north and she didn't know what to expect. A lush green rainforest canopy met deserted palm-lined white-sand beaches with only a handful of mini high-rises, all of it surrounded by a sparkling aqua-green ocean. Aunt Sally had warned her of the crocs up here, so there was no way in hell she was putting a toe in any of that water. Suddenly, rows of houses were whipping past, so close she was surprised the aircraft's hull wasn't thumping the tall antennas. She imagined people in thongs, shorts and sundresses enjoying beers and barbeques in the big backyards, some with pools, some without. Then the city was upon them, the chequerboard of blocks neat and tidy, the roads virtually empty compared to Sydney traffic. The wheels dropped and skidded as they hit the tarmac at wind-force speed. Her teeth almost rattled as they thundered to a halt. The flight attendants firmly reminded those already standing to remain seated with their seatbelts buckled. Some people had no patience – it wasn't like they were going to get to the terminal any quicker.

Looking to her folded hands, Melody finally did what she'd thought about the past four months and slipped her wedding ring off. She really didn't want to explain her messy love life to every Tom, Dick and Harry – nobody here needed to know she was a married woman. Unzipping the little compartment inside her handbag, she popped it in for safekeeping and zipped it back up. Looking to her oddly bare finger, she rubbed where the ring had been for the past four years. It was freeing, like she was already embracing a newer part of herself – a noteworthy sensation.

The vibe of the domestic airport was as relaxed as the laid-back people wandering about. It took Melody all of an hour to grab her suitcase, pick up her rental car, and start heading up the winding Kuranda Range towards Mareeba. The temperature had already dropped a couple of degrees, though the tropical scenery accompanied her on her hour's drive west. From sugar-cane fields to cascading walls of tree ferns to rows of mango trees to paddocks dotted with healthy-looking livestock – all of it did something extraordinary to her weary soul. It was as if she could finally take a deeply satisfying breath and let go, if only for the drive. At some points, the Skyrail Cableway soared above her, the gondolas taking tourists from Cairns up to the hippie-style village of Kuranda. The passengers must have had an eagle-eyed view over the mountains and all the way out to the glimmer of the Great Barrier Reef.

A sign caught her eye: *Welcome to Mareeba 300 sunny days a year … a great place to live!* What a treat that would be, she thought.

Suburban cars began to become few and far between and dusty four-wheel drives and bumper-stickered utes became the norm. The Mareeba township was a little bigger than she'd expected, with almost everything anyone would want for – butchers, pubs, bakers, beauticians, hairdressers, clothing stores, and loads of different food outlets, along with a massive Coles and IGA, and that was just the shops she noticed. She also couldn't help but notice how manly the men looked in their wide-brimmed hats, fitted jeans and boots. There was just something about a country bloke that got her libido all fired up – a man who knew how to fix things, wasn't afraid to get his hands dirty and had a physique to match the hours spent labouring the land. Very different to the majority of men back in Sydney, where suits and clean hands prevailed.

As she left the hustle of the main street and headed past the cemetery then Mareeba Rodeo Grounds, the voice from Google Maps alerted her to the fact that she was almost there. Fear walloped her fair and square in the chest and she almost hit the brakes. But it was now or never – and she'd come this far. She'd coped with way worse, losing her mum – she had this. She heard her mother's voice in her head. *One step at a time, my Sweet Melody.*

Indicating right, she turned down Brookes Road. Rows of fruit trees appeared, all huddled beneath an endless stretch of white nets. It all looked familiar thanks to her time spent perusing her father's business's Facebook page. She slowed as she passed a two-storey weatherboard Queenslander, recalling a photo of her dad and his family on Christmas Day, standing out the front of it. An ornamental windmill circled among blooming rose bushes and a sign hung from the front fence: *Clarkes' Farm.* From what she and Aunt Sally had worked out over countless nights spent at the laptop with countless glasses of wine, her dad and Sarah's place was a little up the road from here. She reminded herself to keep breathing as she headed up the road. She could do this.

Another sign came into view, the stained timber plank hanging from chains – *Diamond and Dust Stud, Matthew and Sarah Walsh*. Thank goodness the front gates were wide open, almost as if welcoming her in. If only it were so.

She came to a stop, drawing in a massive breath, followed by another, then turned and bumped over a cattle grid. Vibrant green paddocks stretched out on either side of the long driveway. The glint of a corrugated roof was just up ahead, around a small bend. A muscular bull glanced up as she rolled past, a long stalk of grass hanging out of his mouth. He eyed her, his pointed horns lethal. Three calves frolicked further down, chasing each other through the longer grass, one of them bucking as if had a rider upon its back. Just past them, two older cows moaned low bellows, as if telling their youngsters to quit playing around and join them. The calves heeded their calls, bounding towards what Melody assumed to be their mothers. She couldn't help but smile – it was endearing.

The dirt track dipped down and over a gully where a shallow creek rippled beneath a little timber-planked bridge. Then the newly built house came into view, low-set and sprawling. It had shady verandahs stretching all the way around it, with views to die for. Windchimes dangled from the corners – the sound melodic as the gentle wind played them. Lush green gardens popped with tropical gingers and birds of paradise, and the lawns were trimmed to perfection. Someone clearly had a green thumb

– unlike her. She had the ability to kill a cactus – apparently from over-watering it, but still.

Beside the house was a round-yarded paddock with two horses on the farthest side – a bay and an Appaloosa. On the other side of the house, just past a huge water tank, a Toyota Prado was parked in the shade of a carport beside a LandCruiser old enough to be classed as a relic. Up a little farther was another trayback LandCruiser, this one more modern. She wondered which one, if any, was her dad's.

Her heart beating fast, she parked beneath the shade of an old gum tree and, after taking a moment to pull herself together as much as she could, stepped out. An old dog hobbled over to greet her, his muzzle silver-grey. Trying to decipher whether he was more border collie or kelpie, she warily reached out to pat his head. Panting like he'd just run a marathon, he pressed into her, his tail slapping the ground. All her attention on him, she didn't see the incoming furry missile until it rolled to a stop at her feet. The puppy would have been no older than four or five months, and by golly, it was absolutely adorable. She scooped it up and it licked her face. The slap of a flyscreen door grabbed her attention and she turned to see a petite woman with curly blonde hair step onto the verandah, a little boy around three wrapped like an anaconda around her leg. Melody knew it was Beau, and he was even cuter than his pictures. And the striking woman was undoubtedly Sarah.

'Hi there,' Sarah called, her smile warm and welcoming.

'Oh, hi.' Placing the wriggling bundle back down then straightening, Melody shaded her eyes as she took steps towards the house, meeting Sarah.

Sarah patted the dog now basically sitting on her feet. 'I see you've met Dukey boy. He's not the best guard dog in his old age, but I'll allow him his retirement. He's earned it, haven't you, buddy?' She smiled towards the old dog then searched around behind her. 'And this is his scoundrel of a granddaughter, Duchess.' She drew Beau into her arms, balanced him on her hip, and then tipped her head to the side. 'Can I help you with something?'

'Oh, yes, sorry. I was sidetracked by how cute the puppy is.' Melody swallowed down her nerves. 'Does Matthew Walsh live here?' She knew he did, but she had to start somewhere.

'Yes, he does. I'm his wife, Sarah. And you are?' With Beau wriggling, she placed him back down. He flopped onto the floor to be slobbered all over by Duchess, giggling madly.

'I'm Melody Harrison.' Noting where Sarah's hand now rested tenderly upon her belly in the way only a protective mother's would, she realised Sarah was possibly pregnant. Swallowing down an emotion she wasn't sure what to make of, she tried to offer her sunniest of smiles. 'My mother was a friend of Matthew's, and I wanted to pop by to let him know that … she has passed away.' Her voice broke and she choked back a sob – so much for holding herself together.

'Oh, love. I'm so sorry.' Sarah quickly closed the distance and reached out to touch Melody's arm. 'Matt's not home but he shouldn't be too much longer, so please, come inside.'

'Oh … it's okay. I can come back another time.' Melody sniffed back her need to cry. 'I don't want to bother you.'

Sarah waved a hand through the air. 'It's no bother whatsoever. Matt's just down the paddock, showing off his newest addition to the motley crew to his mate.' She offered her arm. 'Come on, I can make us a cuppa while we wait, if you like? And I have a couple of pieces of my mum's famous lemon meringue pie hidden in the fridge, just waiting to be devoured.'

Melody couldn't help but like Sarah immediately. She was a genuine person with the kindest of eyes. 'Okay. Thank you.' She cleared the ball of emotion jammed in her throat. 'That sounds lovely.'

Sarah turned to her son, laughing at how Duchess had him pinned to the floor. 'Come on, Beau. Mummy will make you some fairy bread.'

As if she'd just said magic words, Beau shot to his feet and ran to her side, Duchess hot on his trail. 'Yummy!' He looked to Melody with big brown eyes – very clearly his father's. 'Hello,' he said a little shyly.

'Hi,' Melody said with a little wave. Heading into the shade of the verandah, she caught sight of something weirdly funny. She blinked as she slipped her thongs off at the door, wondering if she'd just lost her marbles. 'I have to ask – am I really seeing a chicken riding bareback on the bay horse out there?' She pointed in the general direction.

Sarah followed her gaze. 'Ha. Oh, yes, that's Chilli. She's an absolute scallywag. And that horse, he's my boy, Victory. He's almost at retirement age now, too, the darling. He and I have shared lots of adventures together.' She pointed to the horse stood beside him. 'The Appaloosa is Matt's, her name is Marshmallow, our little girl named h—' She stopped short of ending the sentence, instead offering a contrite smile. 'Our darling Eve named her Marshmallow, before she went to heaven.'

Melody's hand went to her chest as she sucked in a breath – she'd had no idea they'd lost a child. 'Oh, Sarah, I'm so sorry.' She felt complete empathy for the pain in Sarah's emerald green eyes.

Sarah's smile was sad now, and she was blinking faster. 'It's okay, it's been almost five years now since the accident, not that it gets any easier.' She shrugged as she tugged the flyscreen open. 'You just get better at dealing with the loss and heartache, I think.'

'I couldn't imagine what you went through,' Melody offered by way of condolence as she followed Sarah inside. It was open-plan living at its finest, the lounge room, a chef's dream kitchen and dining room all rolling into one big space, with wall-to-floor windows to allow the majestic views in. 'How long have you and Matt lived here?' She really liked their choice of timber and neutral coloured furniture.

'Oh, about a year now.' Sarah headed over to a floating island bench with copper pots and pans hung above the six-burner stove. She pointed to a row of stools opposite her. 'Please, pull up a seat, Melody. Make yourself comfortable.'

Melody could tell by the appliances and layout of the kitchen that Sarah was a passionate cook. 'Where were you before this place?' She slid onto the saddle-style seat.

'We were at our previous property, Tranquil Valley, in Malanda, which we both loved, but we sold it because I wanted to be nearer to my family now I've got this little rascal to contend with, and now another on the way.' She patted her stomach. 'A girl, this time round, apparently.'

'Oh, how wonderful, a little sister for Beau.'

Beau screwed his face up. 'Girls stink.'

Melody chuckled, as did Sarah.

Sarah shook her head, rolling her eyes skywards. 'He'll love her when she's born, I'm sure.' She busied herself making fairy bread while the kettle boiled. Then, plonking the plate down at a little kids' dining set near the window, she got Beau settled with a chocolate milk, then wandered to the fridge and dug out the most delectable-looking pieces of lemon meringue pie. 'I have to hide the last bits or Matt will eat it all in a heartbeat.'

Melody watched her place it down in front of her. 'I can understand why. It looks amazing.'

Serving them generous slices alongside mounds of whipped cream and a freshly brewed cup of coffee each, Sarah dragged a seat round the other side of the bench and sat opposite Melody. She pushed the sugar bowl towards her. 'Help yourself, love.'

Melody plonked a teaspoon of raw sugar into her cup and stirred. 'Thank you for this, Sarah. It's very kind of you.'

'No worries at all.' She offered Melody a kind smile. 'I always enjoy another woman's company, it gives me a break from all the boys' chatter about tractors and bulls.'

They ate in virtual silence, their little moans and groans all that was needed to convey just how moreishly delicious the sweet tart was. 'This truly is the best lemon meringue I've ever had, and that speaks volumes considering I'm a chef.'

'Oh my gosh, you are?' Sarah looked impressed.

'Yes, I am,' she said, proudly.

'Wow, that's fabulous.' Sarah sat up straighter, her eyes wide. 'I have to say, I'm so envious. That would've been my dream vocation if I hadn't chosen to be a cattleman's wife which, take my word for it, I'm certainly not complaining about.'

'I can tell you like cooking.' Melody eyed the impressive kitchen, with its Caesarstone benchtops, gourmet appliances and sweeping views out the bay-style windows. 'And I have to say, I'm extremely jealous of your kitchen.'

'Yes, my biggest stipulation when we built the place was to have the kitchen I'd been dreaming of, and I have to admit, Matt was happy to give me free creative expression in here. It's turned out even better than I envisioned.' Sarah sighed, smiling as she looked around as if seeing the space for the very first time. 'I love it so much in here. It's where I spend the majority of my time.'

'I would too, if I were you.' Melody nodded. 'The kitchen is the heart of any house.'

'It sure is.' Sarah drew in a slow breath, allowing a few moments to pass, before turning her full attention back to Melody. 'So, when did your mum pass, love?'

'A little over two months ago.' Melody quickly looked down at her coffee, now cradled in her hands, the warmth of it bringing her comfort. 'But it feels like it was only last week.'

'It's really tough losing someone you love, especially before their time.' Sarah reached across the table and placed a hand on Melody's arm. 'Time will help ease the heartache, sweetheart, I promise you that much.' As if sensing Melody's impending tears, or possibly some of her own, she grabbed a box of tissues, plucked one out, and then pushed it over to Melody. 'Please feel like you can be yourself, and if you need to cry, do.' She dabbed the corners of her eyes. 'Trust me, I'm speaking from experience. It's best to let it out when it comes, otherwise you'll go and bottle everything up and that's no good for the soul.'

Unable to hold back her emotions any longer with Sarah's heartfelt words, Melody plucked a tissue from the box and wiped at the tears that continued to fall. 'Thank you for being so nice to me,' she said between sniffles.

'Of course, why wouldn't I be?'

Because I'm your husband's long-lost daughter …

'Because you don't know me from a bar of soap,' Melody said quickly before she said what was really weighing on her mind. She wanted to break the news to Matthew first, just in case it went sour, or in case he wanted to keep it from Sarah – whatever the case, it was his right to hear what she had to say first.

Sarah regarded her for a few lengthy moments, her gaze kindly sympathetic. 'No, you're right, I don't know you, but I have very good intuition, and I can tell you've got a heart of gold, Melody Harrison.'

Melody didn't know what to say to that, so she didn't say anything at all – she didn't feel the need to fill the silences with Sarah. It was strangely comfortable between them. She wondered if that energy would shift once Sarah learnt the truth of who she was.

The crunch of tyres on gravel pulled their attention out the window. 'Here he is, right on time for afternoon tea,' Sarah chuckled, and rolled her eyes. 'They say the way to a man's heart is through his stomach, and Matt is no exception.' She stood and wandered over the kettle. 'I tell you, that man of mine eats like a horse.'

Beau jumped up from where he'd been colouring. 'Yay, Daddy's home.' He ran to the flyscreen door and pressed his face up against it.

Like a horse let out of the gates at the Melbourne Cup, Melody's heart took off in an eager gallop as she watched the tall good-looking man she'd stared at on her laptop over the past couple of months alight from the LandCruiser. His dark hair was more a gunmetal grey in the sunshine, and the sound of his deep laughter carried on the breeze that shifted the sheer curtains. He tugged an Akubra on with one hand and held a bunch of wildflowers in the other. His extremely masculine passenger unravelled from the other side and joined Matt on the trek over to the house. The men's cheery voices travelled into the kitchen. Melody felt as if she was trembling from head to toe while her heartbeat became frantic, as if fists were pounding against her chest from the inside.

You can do this.

The unknown man was younger and taller, with broad shoulders that looked as if they could carry the weight of the world. His dark short-cropped hair intensified the ruthless cut of his jaw and cheekbones. And in his cowboy get-up, with a dimple-encrusted smile that would buckle most women's knees ... far out, he was drop-dead gorgeous. She darted her gaze from one to the other, both making her heart race, though for entirely different reasons. She suddenly felt extremely nauseated. This was too much. The room started to spin. The floor wavered. Melody hoped and prayed she could at least get through the moment she'd envisioned countless times without making a complete fool of herself.

Matt stepped inside first, scooping Beau up and leaving the younger guy to pull the door closed behind them. 'Hey buddy, have you been good for Mum?' He kissed Beau's cheek twice.

'Yuppidy,' Beau said, nodding his head. 'Mummy has her friend visiting,' he added, pointing to Melody.

'Oh, hey.' Matthew's smile widened, deepening the dimple on his chin as his piercing brown eyes met with Melody's before travelling to Sarah. 'These are for you, my lovely wifey.' He held the flowers out.

'Aw, thank you, darling.' Taking them, Sarah leant in to give him a kiss. Smiling like a woman head-over-heels in love, she turned back to Melody. 'Matt, this is Melody, she said you know her mother.'

'Oh, hi Melody.' Balancing Beau under one arm, he held out his hand and shooks hers, all the while considering her curiously. 'So, who's your mum?'

'Lucy,' she stammered. 'Harrison,' she added, her voice quivering.

'Lucy Harrison? Hmm.' He scratched his head. 'Doesn't ring any bells.'

Oh god. She hadn't expected this – he didn't even remember her mum. Talk about throwing her in the deep end. The room fell very quiet and time seemed to slow, or maybe Melody just imagined it. Sarah looked to her husband, her expression one of confusion. It was as if nobody knew what to say. The arresting guy met her gaze, locking piercing blue eyes onto hers. And then, his smile, as sexy as sin, pinned her to the spot. His energy was a heady mixture of charming, and a little dangerous. Her breath caught. Her head spun. She didn't know if she returned his smile or not.

'Did I go to school with your mum?' Matt's voice drew her attention back to him.

'No.' She shook her head.

'So how do I know her?'

Blinking as if startled, Melody suddenly felt trapped and her fight-or-flight instincts kicked into full force. 'Oh, maybe I had it wrong.' She shot to her feet, the chair tumbling behind her. She righted it then grabbed her handbag. 'I'll let myself out, sorry to bother you all.' Before anyone replied, or could stop her, she ran past the fetching giant of a man, who was looking as speechless as she felt, and out the back door. Her feet couldn't carry her to her hire car quick enough.

'Melody, please. Wait …' Someone called. Heavy footsteps raced after her, stopping her just before she got into the driver's seat. Matt's hand going to her wrist, he pulled her back to face him. 'I think I do remember your mother, now I've had a minute to jog the cogs.'

'You do?' Hope filled her heart.

'Yes. If my memory serves me right, she and I met at a B&S ball. I think I was about seventeen.' He half chuckled. 'And she was the best damn dancer this side of the equator.'

Her hands clasping, Melody smiled a little. 'She did like to dance.'

Matt met her smile. 'How is she?'

'She, um …' Melody looked down at the ground. 'She passed away.'

'Oh shit. I'm so sorry.' Matt shoved his hands into the pockets of his jeans. 'Can I ask how?'

Melody dared to meet his gaze again. 'Cancer. Melanoma.'

'I'm real sad to hear that.' He drew in a breath, and slowly blew it away. 'Do you live around here?'

'No, I'm up from Sydney.'

Confusion mixed with his look of genuine sympathy. 'You came all this way to tell me about your mum's passing?'

'No. Yes. No, I, uhh …' Her breathing became even more erratic and she suddenly felt like she was about to pass out.

Moments lengthened. The silence between them stretched.

'How old are you, Melody?'

She gasped for a decent breath. 'Twenty-three.'

As if putting two and two together, Matt's expression shifted and his sharp eyes regarded her.

A wave of nausea gripped her tight and she fanned her face. 'I'm sorry, but I feel like I'm about to be sick.' She spun and raced to the nearest bushes, hurling half-digested lemon meringue pie into it. Vomiting always made her cry, and this time was no exception. She remained bent over, just in case there was more to come, and to also try to hide her tears.

Matt rushed to her side. 'It's okay. Just take some deep breaths.' He placed a reassuring hand on her back. As she straightened, he led her over to a couple of camp chairs perched around a fire pit.

She slowly sat, taking deep breaths, trying to find the right words.

Matt thumbed over his shoulder. 'I'm just going to run inside and grab you some water. I'll be right back, okay?'

She nodded. The scent of past campfires lingered in the grey coals she transfixed her blurred gaze upon. Almost able to reach out and touch the kitchen window, she could hear muffled voices from inside but couldn't make out what was being said. Matt quickly reappeared, passed her a glass of cold water, and then settled down beside her. She took a few small sips. Matt drummed his fingers against his bouncing leg. The ball of emotion lodged in her throat made it impossible to speak. They sat in silence until it became too uncomfortable.

'You feeling a bit better now?' he finally asked.

'Yes, thank you.'

'Good.' Matt breathed in deep. 'So, what is it that you really came to tell me, Melody?'

She cleared her throat, wishing her head would clear as well. 'My mum asked me to tell you something important.' With her heart skipping beats, she met eyes that matched the colour of her own, and then, before she could stop herself, said, 'I'm your daughter.'

CHAPTER 5

Shocked to his very core, Zai found it hard to believe what he'd just overheard. He couldn't even begin to fathom how Matt would be feeling right now. For a few dragging moments, he was rooted to the spot, unable to move, unable to process, and powerless to help. Standing at the kitchen window with Sarah by his side, he felt as if he'd just been involved in a car crash, ricocheting from one soul-jarring impact to another – the stunning stranger's bombshell, Matt's flinch swiftly followed by a look of absolute disbelief, the extended silence as they stared at each other as if looking into a mirror, the cliff-hanging moment when time seemed to stall, suspend, stop. The silence was almost deafening. Melody's anguish was written all over her exquisitely delicate face.

Zai wanted to kiss a smile onto her downturned lips.

Matt remained speechless – unbelieving, perhaps? Blinking fast, Melody said something softly, her gaze beseeching. And then, with Matt's lack of response, as if giving up on any hope of getting to know her father, she stood, shoulders slumped, and turned to walk away. Only then Matt snapped to and leapt from his chair, hustling to grab her. She turned back to him, a look of optimism replacing the trepidation. Matt hesitatingly reached out, holding her at arm's length and staring for a heartbeat, then two, then three. She smiled awkwardly. Then, as if finally grasping what she was saying, Matt said something quietly, closed the bit of distance, and took her into his arms. Melody resisted for a second, but then her handbag dropped to the ground and she grabbed hold of him as if her life depended upon it. They clung to each other wordlessly for a few long moments, and it was only then that Zai felt able to pull his gaze away.

Sarah's desperate breaths, and Beau humming to himself as he innocently continued drawing, came into his scope.

Turning to offer Sarah support, he was met with fear-filled, teary eyes. 'Sar, are you okay?'

She nodded but continued to breathe as if suffocating. As soon as he placed a hand on her back, she broke into hushed sobs. He wasn't sure what to say, and not being a man who spoke empty words, he offered comfort by rubbing her back, waiting for her to catch her breath. As he did, the magnitude of the revelation really sank in. How was this going to affect a woman who'd tragically lost her baby daughter when Matt had rolled the ute? Would this drive Matt back to the bottle? God, Zai hoped not.

Regathering herself, Sarah finally went to say something, but then stopped short. She turned to look over her shoulder at Beau, still oblivious to what was unfolding. Clearly relieved, her hands went to protectively cradle her belly. She looked pale, unsteady on her feet. Zai placed an arm around her in case she collapsed, and guided her towards the dining table, where he sat her in a chair, then pulled one up beside her.

She brought owl-eyes to his, and he held them for a beat, shifting a little uneasily in his chair. 'I don't really know what to say, but I'm all ears, Sar.'

'I don't really know what to say either, Zai.' She slowly shook her head. 'Did that really just happen?' Her voice shook. 'Did I really just hear her say she's his daughter?'

'Yeah, crazy, huh.' He heaved a sigh. 'I take it you didn't know anything about another child out there that was Matt's?'

'No way, and neither did Matt, because he would have told me.' Her fingers came to her lips, and she shook her head again. 'I feel stunned, and numb, all at the same time.' Heavy tears rolled down her cheeks again. She half smiled, then shrugged. 'Here I am, worrying about me, but I can't even imagine what Matt feels like right now.' She dared a glance back out the window.

'Yeah, true.' Zai clasped his hands tightly. 'Me either.'

Beau's chair scraped along the timber floorboards and he ran over to his mum, climbing up and onto her lap. 'Why are you crying, Mummy?' He wiped the tears from her cheeks, his little eyes filled with concern.

'Oh, Mummy's fine, sweetie. I'm just tired, that's all.'

'Okay.' He beamed her a heartwarming smile. 'I cry when I'm tired too.'

Sarah chuckled softly as she wiped a smudge of chocolate from his cheek. 'You do, don't you?'

'Yes.' He nodded exaggeratedly. 'And when I hurt myself. And when I'm hungry.'

Beau's honesty and sweet goodness was endearing, and both Zai and Sarah couldn't help but laugh. 'You're an awesome little whippersnapper,' Zai said, ruffling Beau's already chaotic curly hair. 'God love ya.'

Wrapping his arms around Sarah's neck, Beau chortled, baring his teeth like a lion.

Footsteps sounded across the verandah and the back door swung open. Matt and Melody stepped in. Zai straightened and met his mate's unsettled gaze. Matt looked like he'd seen a ghost and Melody's mascara was smudged beneath her pretty latte-coloured eyes. Compelled to go to her, to somehow comfort her, Zai shot to his feet before sense took over and he stepped back a little, giving them some space. Beau leapt off Sarah's lap and skipped over to his dad, begging him for an aeroplane ride around the house.

Matt flashed his little boy an unsteady smile. 'Soon, buddy, but how about you go and finish colouring in first?' With Beau doing as he was asked, Matt regarded Sarah apologetically. 'From the looks of things in here, you obviously heard what was said out there?'

'Uh-huh.' Sarah stood and closed the distance, gently touching Matt's cheek. 'Are you okay?'

'Yeah. You?'

She tipped her head to the side and shrugged. 'Sort of.'

'Can you come here for a sec?' Without waiting for a response, he took Sarah by the hand and guided her out of the kitchen.

Now alone with a woman who stole his breath away, Zai caught her darting gaze, momentarily locking it to his so he could offer her some silent consolation – he may not know this exquisite looking woman, but he knew exactly what it was like to feel as if you were a superfluous cog in the workings of a close-knit family. Not that Sarah and Matt would make Melody feel like that once the news settled in; this was the just the initial aftermath of a gobsmacking situation, he was sure.

The ticking of the clock above the stove suddenly sounded extremely loud, as did the drip of the tap. Zai reached out to tighten it, but to do so, he had to brush past her. Their arms touched and something shot through him, kicking his heart rate into top gear.

The dripping subdued and he stopped short of her. 'Are you okay?' he finally asked, the strange connection he was feeling baffling him. Women, even gorgeous ones, usually didn't have this effect on him.

'Mm-hmm,' she murmured, her body language speaking otherwise. Clearing her throat, she looked at him sheepishly then, as if unable to hold his gaze, lowered her red-rimmed eyes to the floor.

'Can I get you something to drink? Water, coffee, tea?'

'You got anything stronger?' She actually smiled. 'I could do with something to take the edge off, if I'm being honest.'

'Afraid it's a dry house.'

'It is?' She finally held his eyes.

'Yeah, but it's not really my place to explain.' There'd been enough laid on the table for today, he thought. Besides, it was up to Matt and Sarah to tell her about Matt's five years of sobriety, if they chose to.

'Fair enough,' she said gently. 'I'm okay for a drink, then, thank you.'

Zai could see she needed a hug, and he had this immense hankering to touch her. Less than a metre out of his reach, he almost did just that, but then, afraid he might make her more uncomfortable, he stopped himself. Again. Leaning against the kitchen bench, he shoved his hands deep into his jeans pockets and shifted from foot to foot. There was a strong air of independence about her, despite her vulnerability right now, and he liked that about her, a lot. To be able to hold her own at a time like this showed immense courage.

He had an urge to take her into his arms, to allow her to cry the tears she was holding back into his chest. Then, like a slap to the face, his voice of reason told him to snap out of whatever was going on here. He had a reputation as a bit of a Casanova for a reason, though no one knew he kept women at arm's length because he was terrified of being hurt.

He cleared his throat. He needed to get a damn grip on whatever was going on between him and this stunning woman.

After a few hushed words in the hallway, Matt and Sarah returned. 'How about we all sit, and have a chat about …' Matt paused, as if not knowing the right words, '… this?' He gestured to the table with a tip of his head.

'Tea or coffee?' Sarah asked, looking from Zai to Melody, as if on autopilot.

'Ahh, I'm good for a cuppa, thanks Sar.' Although sympathetic to Melody, Zai felt so sorry for Sarah too – this would be a jolt to anyone's life. 'I think this might be my time to exit the building so you three can talk candidly.'

Matt offered a grateful half-smile. 'Yeah, probably a good idea, do you mind, mate?'

'Of course not. I've got a few things to do in town anyway, so all good.' Zai grabbed his keys from the bowl on the bench.

'You'll be back in time for dinner, won't you?' Sarah asked, almost pleadingly.

'Of course.' Zai beamed her a smile. 'I wouldn't miss your cooking for the world.'

The room feel unnervingly silent. 'Right then, I'm off.' He offered Melody one last look of encouragement. 'Deep breaths. You'll be right,' he said quietly as he passed her.

'Thanks,' she replied with a tiny grateful smile, one that lingered in Zai's mind all the way into town.

* * *

An hour and a half later, with the floodgates well and truly open, and once Beau was down for a nap, Melody had filled in the blanks while pouring her heart and soul out to kind listening ears. Sitting across from Matt and Sarah at the tissue-scattered dining table, with the mouth-watering scent of a leg of lamb slow-roasting filling the room, she offered a shrug to fill the tiny silence that now ensued after the lengthy, and at times very emotional, conversation. It was so strange to be gazing at her father while not really knowing much about him – but this was a good start. He'd become justifiably weary before her eyes, his clamped hands atop the table at times white at the knuckles and his jaw muscles occasionally tight, especially when she'd been explaining why her mother had chosen to keep it all a secret. Even though they had good reason to, not once had he or Sarah had a bad word to say. She admired their resolve in not hitting below the belt, but instead doing their best to comprehend why her mum had felt it best. And Sarah's subtle touches of support to him, along with her genuinely compassionate attention to Melody, revealed they both had empathetic natures. Melody counted her blessings – there weren't many people like Matt and

Sarah Walsh in this dog-eat-dog world. She could see why her mother had fallen for him, that one night. Part of her wondered what would have happened if they hadn't come from opposite sides of Australia. But there was nothing to be gained from living in the past.

Finishing the last of her glass of water, Sarah leant forwards, her sympathetic gaze fixed to Melody's. 'Why did you choose to arrive out of the blue instead of calling first? I could imagine it would have been scary for you, turning up here.'

'It was terrifying, but I was more worried you wouldn't want anything to do with me, and at least by being here in the flesh, I thought it would be harder to be avoided, or forgotten.'

'Oh, love.' Sarah's hand went to her heart. 'We'd never turn our back on family, no matter what, isn't that right, Matt?' With him staring off into space, a million miles away, she gave him a little shove with her elbow. 'Hey, love,' she said, louder this time.

'Oh, yes. I mean, no, of course we'd never kick a mate to the curb, let alone one of our own.' Sitting up straighter, he reclaimed a look of composure. 'Sorry I'm a little out of it, it's just all such a shock to the system.'

Nodding, Melody smiled for the first time in hours. 'No worries. I totally get that.'

'You know …' Sarah tipped her head to the side. 'Now I know you two are related … you've got your dad's eyes, Melody.'

'Yes, I do.' Melody had realised this the second she'd met her father's eyes. 'Mum had blue eyes.' Thinking about the last time she'd peered into the windows to her mum's soul, she thrust back the need to cry again. 'I'm so sorry I didn't say anything to you when I got here, Sarah, it's just, I didn't—'

'Please, don't apologise,' Sarah said, gently cutting her off. 'I haven't walked in your shoes, so I'm certainly not going to judge the way you handled things.' She smiled now, right from the heart. 'The way you've conducted yourself at a time like this, well, what can I say other than wow, what a strong-blooded woman. Anyone would think you're from country stock.' With that, she offered a wink and a grin.

Matt cracked a big, genuine smile too.

Doing the same, Melody felt more of the load lift from her heart. 'You're too kind, Sarah.'

'Aw, thanks, and you're a sweet girl, Melody.'

'I'm a lucky man, having a wife like you, Sarah, and …' He admired Melody like only a father would his own flesh and blood. 'Finding out I have an amazing daughter like you, well … I have no words.' He sniffed, hard, and cleared his throat. 'We have a lot of catching up to do. Twenty-three years of it.' Pointing to his glistening eyes, he chuckled. 'Look at me, going all soft in my old age.' He plucked a tissue from the box Sarah had placed between them earlier. 'My bloody eyes are leaking.'

Sarah reached across the table and placed her hand over Melody's. 'I can't even begin to imagine what you must have gone through, losing your mum and learning such news, but just know you are part of our family, okay?'

'Amen to all of what she just said,' Matt concluded unwaveringly.

Humbled and unable to form any sensible words, Melody bit her bottom lip and nodded. The swell of emotion that grew in that very moment tugged at her heartstrings. Had she been alone, she would have wept, loudly, with a combination of happy and relieved tears, but she did her very best to hold herself together.

As he rubbed his hands over his five o'clock stubble, a strangled noise came from Matt and he shot to his feet. 'I'm just going to duck to the boys' room. You two okay for a minute?'

'Yes, of course we are.' Sarah stood too, knowingness in her gaze. 'I better start prepping the veggies or we won't be eating until midnight.'

'I'll be back to help you in a sec.' And as if there was a fire, he quickly strode out of the kitchen.

Melody watched him disappear. 'Is he going to be okay?'

'Yes, he just doesn't like people seeing him upset. He feels it's his place to be the rock all the time,' Sarah said, sighing. 'Goes with the territory of being an alpha male with country blood pumping through his veins.' She turned to Melody. 'It's been a big day for us all, but we have the gift of tomorrow to start afresh.' She tipped her head. 'Would you like to stay for dinner?'

Melody didn't need any more of an invitation to spend more time with these amazing people – her new family. 'Only if I'm not imposing.'

'Of course not.' Sarah's forehead puckered. 'Sorry I haven't asked yet, was obviously a bit sidetracked with everything, but where are you staying while you're up this way, and for how long?'

Melody shrugged. 'I decided to wait until I saw my father's reaction to the news before I booked anywhere, you know, just in case I was hopping on the next plane back home.' She grimaced a little. 'And as for how long, it's kind of up in the air.'

Pausing for a few moments, Sarah drew in a breath. 'Well, that's settled then. You can stay here with us. I'd hate to think of you heading back to the city without getting to know your father, and Beau and me too.'

Overwhelmed by Sarah's welcome, Melody faltered. 'Really?'

'Yes, really.'

Melody bathed in the light of Sarah's admirable matter-of-factness. 'Will Matt mind me staying?'

'Trust me, he wouldn't want it any other way,' Sarah said with absolute conviction.

'Thank you so much, Sarah.' She gestured to the pile of vegetables on the sink. 'Would you like some help with dinner?'

'Nope, being kitchen hand is Matt's job. He'll kill me if I give it to you.' She waved a hand through the air. 'You kick back and relax, maybe have a wander around the house, if you like, to get your bearings. Once I've finished in here, we'll take you to the guest room and get you settled in.'

Matt returned, his disposition more relaxed. 'I hope you're going to be staying for dinner, Melody,' he said.

Melody nodded. 'Yes, I am.'

Sarah tossed the tea towel she was drying her hands on over her shoulder. 'Actually, I've invited Melody to stay here, with us.'

'You did?' Matt's eyes widened along with his smile. 'And did you say yes, Melody?'

'I did, but only as long as it's okay with you.'

'Of course it is. You're welcome to stay as long as you like.'

For a few moments, Melody watched Matt help Sarah with dinner preparations. Antonio had never helped her cook dinner. It was nice to witness and it made her ache for what they had – a genuine, mutual, respectful love with the firm foundation of marriage beneath their feet. Everything about them felt so calm and ordinary, and the return to routine even though their world would have been shaken was comforting for everyone. She liked to think she was part of it, but it was going to take more than just acceptance from Matt and Sarah for it to be so.

There'd been so many questions, all of which she'd answered as best she could. This all felt dreamlike – she'd never expected the meeting to go as smoothly as it had. The kitchen felt oddly different, as if a little of her was etched into it. Shifting her gaze to where Beau was pushing his matchbox car along the floor, making the sounds to go with it, she smiled – he was a cutie pie. It was a little overwhelming to think he was her little brother, yet so comforting to know she could call this beautiful family her own too.

The crunch of wheels out the front of the house made her heart flutter – Zai was back. She suddenly felt the need to escape the house for a little fresh air before coming face to face with him again. There was just something about him that made her go weak at the knees.

'I'm just going to pop outside,' she said. 'I'll grab my suitcase.'

Halfway through peeling a potato, Matt paused and glanced over his shoulder. 'Do you need a hand?'

'Nah, I'll be right, but thanks for the offer.' She slipped out to the back verandah and inhaled deeply.

Sinking into a chair to breathe, she got lost in the stunning view until footfalls sounded and she turned to meet striking blue eyes set amidst dark skin. 'Hey,' she stammered.

'Hey there.' He stopped just short of her. 'You okay?'

Sucking in a deep breath, she gave him a smile. 'Uh-huh.' She dropped her gaze from his broad shoulders to the big belt-buckle then, catching herself doing so, looked swiftly back to the dusky horizon.

'It's the best part of the day, sitting out here.' He stepped in beside her, casting a long shadow across the timber floorboards. 'Do you mind if I join you?'

'Not at all.' She shot her eyes back to his and shuffled over.

Zai sat, leaving a little bit of space between them. 'They're great people, Sarah and Matt.'

'They sure are.' Her burdened heart buoyed in agreement. 'I just hope I haven't upset the apple cart, turning up unannounced.'

'I know it must all feel really strange, but take my word, they'll make you feel welcome and do everything they can to make you feel a part of the family.'

'They've already gone above and beyond what I'd expected.' She offered a sidelong glance, totally amazed by the way this hunk of virile man cared enough to try to understand how she must be feeling. 'I'm lucky they're both so kind and accommodating.'

Telltale signs of heartache fleetingly traversed Zai's rugged features. 'Yeah, they've been there for me a hell of a lot, through all my stuff.'

Identifying with his slumped shoulders and sad smile, Melody's heart reach for his. 'What sort of stuff?' she asked gently.

He met her stare. 'I'll save it for another time.' His smile was slow. 'I think you've had a big enough day without listening to all my dramas.'

She took a mental and emotional step back. 'Fair enough.' He had a point, and it wasn't her place to pry either. 'So how do you know them?'

'Matt's dad and my dad are old mates. And I've done a bit of work out at Rosalee Station as a stockman.' He ran a hand through his short-cropped hair. 'I sometimes muster in their chopper too, when they need me to.'

'Oh, wow, how cool.' She imagined him in the saddle, and at the helm of a chopper, looking all rugged and masculine – it suited him to a T. 'You on a break at the moment?'

'Yeah, just for a couple more days. I'm heading back out there bright and early tomorrow morning.'

Liking the sound of his slow, easy country drawl and wanting to hear more of it, Melody felt a pang of disappointment knowing his time here was short. 'You driving there?'

'Thankfully not.' He stretched his faded-denim-clad legs out and crossed them at the ankles. 'I'm catching a lift with Stan. He flies the mail plane out to the station once a week.' Lacing his hands behind his head, he rested his head back.

Melody couldn't help but notice how his biceps stretched the sleeves of his T-shirt, or the way the warm glint of the setting sun made his features all the more arresting. 'Oh, cool. Do you like it out there?'

'Damn straight I do.' He shot her a disarming grin. 'All that space is my kind of heaven.'

'Hmm.' Totally at ease in Zai's company, she rested back too, finding herself engrossed in both the plush hues of crimson sky and the magnetism she felt with this compelling man. 'It'd be nice to visit Rosalee Station one day, so I can meet the family there and see where my father is from, but I'm not sure I'd be able to live all the way out there.'

'When you do, I reckon you'll be surprised by just how much you like it.' The huskiness of his voice complemented the richness of the sunset. 'So what do you do for a quid, Miss Melody?'

'I'm a fully qualified chef, down in Sydney. I part-own a hip little café.'

He turned to her, his gaze wide. 'Wow, holy heck, now that's impressive. Good on you.'

She basked in his praise, and smile. 'Thanks, but it's really not that remarkable. If I'd said I was a doctor, or lawyer, or something like that, I'd totally get your enthusiasm.' He pulled an I-don't-agree-with-you face and she sucked in a quick breath. 'Although, I do have to say, I found my calling when I decided to turn my love of cooking into a career. Food is my everything.'

'I totally get where you're coming from, because I like to eat food, a lot. Probably a little too much.' He patted his flat stomach. 'Mind you, I don't know where it all goes. Mum reckons I have hollow legs. I reckon it's because I don't sit still for long.' He offered her a cheeky look. 'Seriously, though, we need passionate cooks like you in this too-fast world filled with its fast food and microwave meals.' He shuddered. 'Which, for the record, are disgusting.'

'I couldn't agree more.' Realising she was twisting her hair around her finger, she quickly tucked the strand behind her ear. What was this man doing to her?

'So how long are you up this way for?'

Liking the way he was looking at her so intently, like he wanted to learn everything about her, she pulled her legs to her chest. 'I'm not really sure yet. I've kind of taken indefinite leave.'

'Good on you.' He nodded, smiling at her. 'We could all do with a little break from life at times, so we can figure what it is we want from it without the noise and opinions of everyone else.'

'Yeah, very true,' she said, noting the hidden meaning behind his words – he clearly had his own private battles, and that made her feel even more connected to him, in a peculiar kind of way.

His presence drew her in, somehow making the turmoil of the day fade into the background, if only for this little while. They sat quietly, contentedly, comfortably, watching the sun sink further behind the mountain range.

'I never tire of watching Mother Nature at her finest.' He spread his arms wide. 'She's absolutely stunning.' His sidelong glance lingered on her. 'Don't you think?'

Lost in his eyes, something inside her shifted, as if it had fallen into place. 'It sure is.'

It was only when the stars began to show in a twilight sky that they broke out of their bubble and wandered back inside to the warmth of family and the aroma of wholesome, delicious cooking.

CHAPTER 6

In the hour before dawn, Zai woke in the comfort of his swag to the soft bellows of fifteen hundred head of cattle in the holding yard, the crackle of campfire and the tinkering of the cook – all of which was almost drowned out by Showbags's rasping snores.

Blinking into the lantern-lit mustering camp, Zai brought his gaze from where the billycan balanced over dancing red and orange flames from a tepee of branches, past the makeshift clothesline strung between two gidgee trees strewn with clothes in desperate need of detergent and a washing machine, to the glimmer of the morning star nestled within the soft glow of the moon. Unlike the long sweltering days he spent in his timeworn saddle with his stockhorse's thudding hooves beneath him, the Aussie outback's darkness was a gift of cool crisp air, and with no rustle of leaves above him and the singsong of the native birds yet to come, the effervescent stillness was encompassing.

Yawning, he stretched his arms high, feeling as if he could almost touch the rocky surface of the moon with his fingertips. He loved this part of the day. He got to have a moment to himself, away from the banter of the men, the cracking of whips, and the whop of the chopper blades above it all, so he could truly appreciate the magnificence that was Rosalee Station. As he gazed dreamily into the nocturnal abyss, his contemplations swayed from the beauty of Mother Nature to the same pretty face that had all but possessed his mind these past couple of weeks – belonging to the mesmeric Miss Melody Harrison. Try as he might, he hadn't been able to shake her from his thoughts for too long. Which surprised him no end. No woman had ever been able to hold his attention so entirely, but she had, and without even trying. There was just something about her that got his heart racing and his libido revved up, in that order – usually it was the other way around. And it wasn't a case of him not being attracted to her good looks and voluptuous body – how could he not be? – but her combination of vulnerability and strength spoke to him on a fathomless level, making him want to know everything he could about her. The short time he'd spent with her at Matt and Sarah's place had barely scratched the surface. If only he could dive into the depths of her, what would he discover? Although, he was also acutely aware, it might be dangerous of him to make himself so engrossed, so captivated – he may not ever want to resurface from her depths. And he was fairly certain Matt wouldn't want him going anywhere near his daughter in a romantic sense. And he couldn't blame him in the slightest.

The very thought of getting romantically involved with Melody caused something inside him to somersault like tumbleweed down a dusty road. Oddly, and abruptly, he slipped into some weird place in his heart, making it skip a beat. It was an odd sensation. He sucked in a startled breath. Hot dang, what had she done to him?

'Breakfast is up, you lot, so bloody well come and get it before it's cold,' the cook bellowed, banging a wooden spoon against a pot. 'Hurry it up, would ya? We haven't got all bloody day.'

Crashing back into the present moment, Zai chuckled to himself as he watched four bewildered heads spring up from swags as if a shot had just been fired. 'Hold your britches, I'm a-coming, Pothole,' he called over the clang and clatter and mumbled swearwords. 'I'm bloody starving, Marvin,' he added, tapping his growling stomach as he sat up.

Grabbing his boots from beside him, he thumped each one upside down to make sure no critters had made home in either – a bite from a desert scorpion was not the way he wanted to start his day – before tugging them on. Rising from his swag, he unfolded his weary bones as if each vertebra was an unoiled cog. Rolling his bedding up, he sauntered over and tucked it into the tray of Pothole's dusty old four-wheel drive – the nickname of Pothole had been well-earned as he always seemed to be on the road.

Retrieving his Akubra from the branch he'd hung it on, he tugged it on, groaning every time he had to bend. It had been almost two weeks on this particular muster, and his back was retaliating against the countless hours he'd spent in the saddle, as were the insides of his thighs. Another twelve or so hours and they'd be arriving back at the homestead. Thank the lord. He couldn't wait to stand beneath the stream of a hot shower with a bar of soap so he could wash dust from places it should never be, and a feed which included ice-cream doused in chocolate Ice Magic, then crawling into his bed at the cottage behind the homestead for a decent night's sleep. The pure bliss of simple pleasures was always amplified after a long muster.

Joining the men in the makeshift kitchen while avoiding kamikaze moths, he poured himself a cup of strong billy tea, filled a tin plate with bacon, eggs, steak and baked beans, and grabbed a piece of warm damper from the depths of a cast-iron pot. Helping himself to some treacle, he made sure to put the lid back on real tight to avoid a stampede of ants – it was a sorry affair when they had to eat ants with their damper. Then, balancing everything carefully, he sidestepped Pothole and pulled up a spot by the centre of gravity – the glow and warmth of the campfire.

'G'day's and 'good morning's were mumbled between bites. It was fairly usual that nobody really spoke until they had food in their bellies and the caffeine kickstarted their wits. Never one to eat breakfast, Pothole sat on his heels right in the middle of everything, sucking on his pipe like his life depended on it. The only time he didn't have it in his mouth was when he was shaving, eating or sleeping.

Sitting on an upturned flour drum, Zai balanced his plate in his lap as he tucked into the hearty breakfast, enjoying each and every bite. 'This is an awesome, fair- dinkum bushie's brekkie, as always, Pothole.' He licked a bit of sticky treacle from his thumb. 'I honestly don't know what us blokes would do without you feeding us such good grub.'

'You lot would most probably starve to death,' Pothole said with a smirk before hooting like a hyena, his gappy grin setting the men off too.

'Yeah, fair point, Pothole.' Slim pointed his fork at the chaotic salt-and-pepper-haired man now content with blowing smoke rings. 'Or we'd be farting each other to death because we'd be living off canned baked beans.'

Grinning at Slim's shock of ginger hair, Zai shook his head. 'Only you'd come up with something that included farting, Slimbo.'

'Of course he would. He's a master at the art of butt-singing,' Showbags mumbled through his mouthful, his freckly face full of mischief. 'And butt-slinging, in the bushes, where the bears do you-know-what.' He wiggled his brows animatedly.

'Yeah, while stinking the whole damn camp out,' Tumbles added, grinning, the busted lip he'd achieved yesterday after tripping over thin air giving him a lopsided smile.

'Oi, fair crack of the bloody whip, you lot,' Slim said good-humouredly. 'I may look like a reckless brute but I got feelings, you know.'

The group of men cracked up laughing again – the caffeine was clearly starting to do its job with the mixed-up, muddled-up group of misfits. Hasselhoof's throaty mirth was the loudest, just like his constant complaints – hence the reason he was nicknamed Hasslehoof, the 'hoof' describing his horseshoe smile. Over the last couple of years, Zai had learnt to turn a blind eye and ear to Hasselhoof's daily grievances about everything from the shitty weather to the price of beer to the flies to the fact that there weren't enough hours in a day. But he had to admit, it was starting to grate on him a little this year. The old bugger was getting even grumpier in his older age.

'Nah, but in all seriousness, you really are the best cook we've had out here, Pothole, god love ya,' Slim added as the group somewhat recomposed themselves.

'Thanks, mate.' Pothole heaved a sigh. 'But I'm afraid I have some news to tell all of ya.'

Not accustomed to much conversation from Pothole, nor the serious look now plastered on the old bloke's face, the whole camp fell silent as they waited for him to continue.

Pothole stood and cleared his throat. 'I'm afraid this will be my last post, you lot. Was supposed to be my last season but my boy's just given me a grandson, two months premmie but the doc says he's going to be okay. So I'm heading back home to hang my tongs up, be by my son's side and retire by the ocean, where I can fish all day long with a beer in me hand.'

Nobody answered for a few lengthy moments.

'Oh, dang it to losing your cooking,' Showbags said, breaking the silence. 'But congrats on the grandbaby.'

'Well, bugger me dead. What are we going to do now?' Hasselhoof rambled, his frown lines deepening. 'I don't wanna have to explain how I need iodised salt to some new bastard again, or how I don't like my steak still bloody mooing.'

'And just when I was getting used to your sorry arse being in the damn way all the time,' Slim said, his usual banter lightening the sombreness of the situation.

'I think that's the fellas' ways of saying we're going to miss you, Pothole,' Zai added to the mix. 'Big time.'

Blinking a little faster, Pothole remained silent as he puffed away on his pipe.

There was resounding agreement from all, other than Hasselhoof, who was too busy complaining about how nothing stayed the same and how bad this situation was going to turn out for all of them. They might even have to start cooking for themselves, he dared to add as he stomped towards the bushes, a half-flattened toilet roll in hand.

Slim burped loud enough to send tidal waves to Japan. 'Right, you lot, enough grumbling and pouting. Pothole deserves to kick back and enjoy life now he's sixty-odd, and to spend time with his family now he's a grandad, so congratulate the old bloke and let's get this show on the road.' He grabbed his weather-beaten hat from his knee and slapped it on his head as he stood. 'And let's see if Tumbles can stay in the saddle for longer than two hours today, shall we?'

'Ha, yeah.' Showbags pointed his fork at Tumbles. 'Or maybe you can score a hat trick and knock another one of your teeth out.'

Tumbles responded by giving Showbags, and the rest of the chuckling group, the middle finger. He was met with more throaty laughter.

The men cleared their plates, making sure to wash everything they'd used in the sudsy bowl on the fold-out table, before heading off for another hard day's work. In appreciation for Pothole's many delicious meals over the past few years, Zai went the extra distance and quickly dried everything up, so Pothole didn't have to. Between gathering firewood, keeping the camp clean, packing and unpacking a new campsite each day, and occasionally tackling a drum-load of their washing in dishwashing soap over the coals, Pothole had truly earned his keep.

Dawn had just broken in golden splendour when Zai moseyed past the windmill that pumped essential water to the holding-yard troughs and over to his stockhorse, Sao – so named because the gelding was renowned for nicking the Aussie pantry staple off camp tables and out of hands, especially if there was cheese and tomato on top.

'Hey, buddy.' He gave his horsey mate a scratch on the neck. 'Did you have a good rest?'

Sao replied with a whinny and a nudge of his muzzle to Zai's shoulder.

Retrieving his saddle and blanket from the rustic timber cattle yards, much to the annoyance of a flock of rowdy galahs, which took flight, Zai got his workhorse ready. After lecturing Sao about sucking in wind when he was trying to tighten the girth strap, he hefted himself up and settled his boots in the stirrups. He enticed Sao into a canter, joining the other men. Surveying the landscape from his vantage point, a smile tugged from the inside. It was here, in the saddle, surrounded by the unforgiving yet momentous countryside and among the repartee of his fellow stockmen where the weight of his father's unfair expectations lifted from his shoulders. More than anywhere else, this place was where he felt truly home. If only his father could accept this was an integral part of him instead of being bitterly disappointed he didn't follow in his medical footsteps. He held on to the hope that stranger things had happened – that one day, maybe, possibly, Christopher Wellstone might have an epiphany and accept Zai for the country-hearted man he'd become. Then again, if Zai's experience was anything to go by, he wasn't holding his breath when it came to a change of heart from his single-minded father.

In a matter of what felt like minutes but was closer to an hour, the sun had risen to its rightful place in the cloudless azure sky, the cattle had been led out of the holding yards, and they were well on their way home. His hat brim pulled low to avoid the glare, Zai was just starting to settle into the slow but steady pace, but in true style of a muster, it only took one in the crowd to blow the amity. He felt his skin prickle with awareness a split second before a belligerent bull took it upon itself to jab his horns into a cow in front then, using the disruption to his advantage, broke ranks.

As the men snapped to attention, galloping this way and that, the disturbed mob charged off every which way, heading for the scrub or stony ridges. Some greener cows made them work for it, the less cunning ones were easier to chase and pull into line. As for the bulls, the one-tonne beasts were unaccustomed to having to move quickly and could be easily overtaken by a skilled stockhorse – the trick was to pounce on the four-legged brutes before they became too aggressive. Careering alongside the very bull that had caused the mayhem in the first place, Zai pulled Sao to a sliding stop and leapt off, landing sturdy in his boots. Now a few paces behind the fleeing bull, he gave chase – the tyrant wasn't getting away that easily. It skidded to a stop, spinning to face Zai and pawing the ground, snorting as it considered charging. Unperturbed, Zai thought on his feet and dashed to the side, coming around the rear of the beast. Grabbing it by the tail, he deftly threw it off balance and it tumbled to the ground, momentarily stunned. Zai knew he had to work quickly or risk being struck by the deadly horns. In the blink of an eye, Showbags was at his side, leather belt at the ready. Working together, both of them grunted and groaned as they secured the bull's hocks.

'Good job, boys.' Slim and his horse skidded in beside them. 'We'll have to come back in the truck to grab the bastard. I'll send Tumbles ahead shortly to go and grab it from the homestead.'

Wiping his brow with his forearm, he took off his hat and slapped it against his leg, a cloud of red dust rising. 'We ain't letting this one back in there. He'll just keep wreaking havoc.'

Zai offered a firm nod as he fought to catch his breath. 'Agreed.'

Showbags gave Zai a hefty slap on the back. 'Good work, Wellstone.'

'Cheers for the hand, mate,' Zai replied between breaths.

'You're a goer, Wellstone. Damn near had smoke coming out your butt, you were chasing this bugger down so hard.' Slim flashed a dust-rimmed smile then looked to Showbags. 'Righto. Let's get back to it. I want to reach the homestead paddock before we run out of daylight. I got me a gorgeous woman to see in Mount Isa tomorrow, so I ain't gonna be stuck here working past knock-off time.'

The next few hours went by uneventfully – thankfully. In the meantime, Tumbles collected the pick-up truck and they got the bull loaded and away. At midday, they put the brakes on and camped out beneath the shade of a couple of gidgee trees. Spam and mustard pickle sandwiches, salt and vinegar chips, packets of gingernut and butternut biscuits, and flasks of billy tea were on the menu, along with copious amounts of water. The cattle loitered nearby as Zai enjoyed the much-needed fodder and rest, while myriad relentless flies swarmed him – swatting them away was useless.

Belly full, Zai rested back against the trunk of a boa tree, clasping his hands behind his head. 'So, Slimbo, is Sherrie getting excited about your big day?'

Slim grinned like only a man in love could. 'She sure is, and why wouldn't she be, marrying a stud like me.' He held a poker face as he undoubtedly waited for the banter to begin.

'Ha, yeah right, you're punching above your weight with that one,' Showbags chimed in.

'Too right. I don't know how you nabbed her, Slimbo, she's a looker and a real nice chick to boot,' Tumbles added, grinning. 'Maybe she needs to go to Specsavers?'

'I reckon she does,' Hasselhoof said dryly. 'Or a shrink, to be marrying the likes of you.'

'Oi, lay up, you lot, or I might have to fire all your arses.' Laughing and shaking his head, Slim took the stance of a bodybuilder, but certainly didn't look like one. 'FYI, I won her over with my good looks, smoking body, and chivalrous charm.'

Snorts of laughter followed. Slim tossed them all a good-natured frown, followed by the forks.

'How many people have you guys got coming to the big day?' Zai asked when the laughter had subsided.

'About sixty, give or take.'

Zai nodded. 'That's a good number.'

'No number is a good number at a wedding,' Hasselhoof grumbled, shrugging when he was shot looks of disbelief. 'What? You're only going to get divorced eventually, so why bother getting married in the first place?'

'Far out.' Zai rolled his eyes, chuckling. 'Always the cynic, hey Hasselhoof.'

'Well, some bastard has to be a realist and talk some sense around here.'

'What are you on about?' Showbags pretended to be wounded, grabbing his chest. 'I always keep it real and I talk plenty of sense.'

Tumbles laughed out loud. 'More like you always talk garbage, Showbags.'

'Nailed it, Tumbles.' Zai loved how he could feel so light and free around this bunch of down-to-earth guys.

'Come on, you bunch of misfits. Time's a-wasting and we got work to do.' Lunch basket in hand, Slim started collecting empty pannikins and rubbish.

Zai rose and dusted off his jeans. 'Great, thanks for that Slimbo. Now I'm gonna have Johnny and June's "Time's A Wastin'" stuck in my head all arvo.'

'Oh, crap, me too now you've brought that up.' Showbags gave Zai a playful shove. 'Thanks for that, mate.'

'Pleasure,' Zai fired back, chuckling. 'Anytime.'

Their game faces on, the men took their stations in the saddle and the mob meandered down the dusty track lined by a barbed-wire fence stretching between a steady line of rustic timber posts. Sao ambled at the back of the mob, so Zai sat loosely in his saddle, the reins long. With the scorching sun belting down on his back and his mouth as dry as the desert surrounding him, he took big gulps from his water bottle. Draining it, he tucked it back into his saddlebag. As they ate up the kilometres, the clip-clop of Sao's hooves was increasingly drowned out by the bleating of calves and their mother's replies, the calls as distinctive to each other as Beau would be to Sarah. Needing to rectify the situation, Zai gently urged the calves that were trailing at the back to catch back up to their mamas. They soon found each other and order was somewhat restored until, out of the corner of his eye, he witnessed one of the mob break ranks again. Cursing the flighty micky, he locked his boots into the stirrups, whipped Sao around in a stockman's pirouette, and took off after the four-legged fugitive. For a few short seconds, everything was blinding dust and his teeth crunched down on the grit. When the dust cleared, he spotted the micky racing uphill, heading for a steep ridge that suddenly dropped thirty-foot to a gully on the other side. Little did it know it was heading for death if they didn't stop it, and fast.

Balls to the wall, Tumbles took off up the steep ridge, his mare giving it her all, but, as they almost reached the top, the horse slipped. Her back legs were sliding downwards and she was pawing with her front feet to try to regain leverage. Racing after his accident-prone buddy and the bastard bull, Zai prayed for the best, but as always, when it came to Tumbles, disaster swiftly followed. The horse grabbed ground, but at the same time, Tumbles somersaulted backwards from the saddle and rolled with increasing velocity. A human cannonball, Tumbles collected sticks and stones as he descended, coming to an abrupt stop at the bottom. While Zai's attention was on Tumbles, Showbags had come in from the other side and had saved the day, the rogue bull now under his control and almost back at the mob. Zai released his breath in a whoosh as Tumbles sat up, his hat and one boot missing, his hair in disarray, and a bewildered look on his dirt-smudged, gashed face.

'Is he alive?' Slim bellowed.

'Yeah, all good,' Zai called back.

Slim gave him the thumbs up. 'Excellent. We'll keep heading then.'

'Righto, Slimbo, we'll catch you up.'

Tumble's reliable mare bolted in beside them, prancing nervously – they were very lucky she hadn't fled the scene. With her lathered in sweat and breathing hard, Zai leant over Sao's neck and grabbed her dangling reins. 'You right down there, Tumbles?'

Eyes wide, Tumbles stared straight through him.

Disturbed by his mate's empty gaze, Zai jumped to the ground, and placed a gentle hand on Tumbles's shoulder, careful not to touch where his shirt had ripped and he was bleeding from gravel rash. 'Tumbles, mate, are you okay?'

With a deep inhalation, Tumbles blinked fast, as if coming to. 'Hey, yeah. I think so.' He felt his arms and then legs, then touched his face, wincing a little when he brushed his bleeding lip. 'I'm still pretty much all together, and I know my name, so that's a good sign, isn't it?'

'Yeah, it is.' Zai bit back a chuckle. Trust Tumbles to make light of the situation. 'Can you stand?'

'Now the world's stopped spinning like I'm in a damn dryer …' Tumbles shook his head a little, as if to clear it. 'I'll give it a shot.'

Zai offered a hand up and Tumbles grabbed hold as he rose on shaky legs. Just as he straightened, he buckled forwards, looking like he was about to throw up, but after a few deep breaths, he regathered himself. Zai checked his buddy over, and apart from some cuts and a hefty egg on his head, he appeared all right. 'I honestly don't know how you haven't broken any bones, mate,' he said, shaking his head. 'You came down that hill like no tomorrow.'

'I don't do things in halves, Wellstone.' Hands going to his hips, Tumbles grinned. 'It takes skill to be a stockman and a stuntman, I tell ya.'

Zai couldn't help but crack up laughing. 'Shit, mate. What are we going to do with you?'

'Nothing. I can do it all by myself.' Tumbles offered a cheeky grin.

'You sure can.' Zai pointed up yonder. 'I can see your boot, and there's your hat. I'll go get 'em. You wait here and regroup with your horse.'

'Groovy gravy, thanks Wellstone.'

Boot and hat recovered, Zai passed them over. Grimacing, Tumbles tugged both on and, after readjusting the saddle and girth strap, gave his horse a reassuring rub-down, talking to her soothingly as he gingerly climbed into the saddle.

Zai glanced to where the men and the mob were now way up ahead, a copper cloud of dust hovering above. 'Let's head before they leave us behind.'

'Righto. You lead the way while I recover my pride,' Tumbles said a little sheepishly.

It was late afternoon and the daylight was quickly fading as they reached the main yards of the station. Leaning over in the saddle, Zai unlatched the gates. Overhead, the blades sliced through the air as the freelance pilot swung his Robinson R22 like a dragonfly in the expanse of sky. Man, horse and chopper worked like a well-oiled machine, herding the cattle in and pulling the rogue micky bulls quickly into line, all of the livestock to be sorted and drafted at first light tomorrow morning before heading off to the meatworks, or being let back out to graze for another year.

Darkness was closing in when the men finally let their equally weary horses loose in a nearby paddock. Bidding his mates goodnight, Zai made a beeline for his cottage – a hot shower, an icy cold beer and a huge bowl of ice-cream was on the cards. Kicking off his boots at the back door, then peeling off his socks, he thought about the next muster as he stepped into the coolness of the besser-block building, and the fact that there'd be a new camp cook. He wondered who it would be, and if they were going to be spoiled or foiled. Good hearty food was so important when they were working long, hard days. And then, as it had many times throughout the past couple of weeks, her face popped back into his mind, and he had an idea – one that sent his heart into a canter. He knew exactly the right person for the job. But it depended on whether she was interested. He grabbed the cordless phone – there was only one way to find out.

CHAPTER 7

Melody had never acknowledged the deep yearning hidden away inside of her to know who her father was, to have him know her, to hear him talk, laugh, simply to see him breathe. She'd never allowed herself to imagine going fishing with him and catching mammoth mud crabs with the sweetest claws she'd ever tasted, or standing in the hickory smoke of a charcoal barbeque, watching rib-eye steaks sizzle with beers in hand, nor had she ever envisioned herself watching him train his bulls to buck like champions with such grit and determination, but also with so much kindness, gentleness and love for the cantankerous animals that scared her half to death.

This place, his and Sarah's place, was a whole other world to the one she'd grown up in, and yet she felt integrally part of it all because the blood that pumped through her veins was the same as his. Almost three weeks had passed since she'd arrived at his doorstep with her broken heart in her throat and an inability to see past that terrifying moment. Now, though still with a deep hole from the loss of her mother, she felt as if she belonged somewhere. It was going to be so tough, eventually returning to Sydney and the mess she'd left behind her there. Antonio hadn't sounded happy when she'd told him she'd been welcomed with open arms – once again, he would've been thinking of himself and the fact that she wouldn't be running back to him with her tail between her legs. Aunt Sally, on the other hand, was over the moon for her. She was glad her aunt was heading off to a mountain retreat for a while, to process the loss of her best friend. She was taking Magic, so she wouldn't be alone while she mourned.

Stretching her legs out from beneath her, her eyes were drawn to where the new day was just beginning to break on the horizon. 'It's so beautiful.' A wispy smile touched her lips as she blinked into the brightness of the first shafts of sunlight.

'It sure is, I never get tired of it.' Matt's tone was as gentle as she'd found his heart to be. He offered a sidelong glance as he took a sip from his coffee. 'It's kind of like watching Mother Nature open an awesome gift, every single day.'

She nodded, her smile widening. 'I really like that analogy.'

She also liked how she and her father often shared a cuppa on the front verandah, watching the sunrise or sunset, or sometimes, on the odd days when her dad would make it home before dark, both. She also loved how he was so keen to know and learn everything he could about her.

He cleared his throat. 'I've got something to ask you, Melody,' he said.

Staring down to where the sunlight was reaching for her toes, she wriggled the pins and needles from them. 'What is it?' she said, bringing her attention to his.

Matt took a breath, then turned a little in his seat to face her. 'Well, the cook out at Rosalee Station has resigned, and we were wondering if you'd like to take the role on? The pay is pretty darn good.' He paused, and quickly added, 'It's only for six or so weeks, while the mustering season is still going. Some nights you'll be camping out but most of the time, you'll be cooking in the communal kitchen.'

The shock of his offer had her searching for the right words, any words, in fact. Was he trying to get rid of her? Or was this his way of keeping her around longer? Could she do it? Did she even want to?

'Please don't feel pressured to say yes if it's not something you're keen on. We can always put an ad up and the job will be snapped up in a heartbeat, I'm guessing.' He glanced to the sky then back to her, his Adam's apple bobbing. 'I just know you want to get to see where our heritage lays. And Sarah, Beau and I will be out there soon enough so I can be the best man at my mate's wedding.'

'Um, well …' Rendered speechless, Melody couldn't believe what she was hearing. Her, a camp cook, in the middle of Woop Woop? They had to be kidding, right? There was no way she'd be able to handle being so isolated. She smiled and shook her head, trying to refuse his offer as kindly as she could. 'I don't think I'd last a day out there, let alone six weeks.'

A smirk tugged his frown away. 'You'd be surprised.'

She chewed her bottom lip and sighed. 'I'm not sure I should be away from the café for that long.' Her last phone call from Antonio, two days before, had been short and certainly not sweet. He'd reminded her how important it was she took her third share of the business – as well as their marriage vows – seriously.

'Yeah right, like you have,' had been her reply, one she'd instantly regretted. Being factious would get them nowhere.

Regarding her for a few lengthy moments, her dad offered a firm nod. 'It's totally understandable if you need to get back to it, but the offer is there.'

A million questions swirled through her mind, and she grabbed hold of one. 'How far is it from Mount Isa?'

'About ten hours' drive.' He half shrugged. 'Give or take.'

'Wow, that far?' She swallowed down, hard.

'Just bear in mind that in a camp, the number-one rule is to keep the cook happy no matter what, so you'll definitely be looked after by the blokes.' His expression was eager as he waited for her reply. 'Along with the fact that you're my daughter. They wouldn't want to set a foot out of order around you, that's for certain,' he added.

Some crazy part of her wanted to say yes. She didn't want this adventure into her new identity to come to an end. 'Can I think about it?'

'Of course you can. I just need an answer by this arvo.'

She blew a loud breath. 'Gee whizz, no pressure.'

Matt grinned. 'Nope, none at all.'

They returned to watching the sunrise. As she silently, frantically tried to decide if going out to Rosalee Station was feasible, weighing up all the ramifications if she said yes, Melody found herself wanting to ask her father more about what had happened the day he'd come close to dying. 'I've been meaning to ask, who was it that found you, down the mine shaft?'

'An Aboriginal tracker called Getty. I haven't seen him since that day, and have no idea where he is now, but I'll never forget him.' His expression turned sombre and the muscles in his jaw tightened, like he was holding emotions at bay. 'I basically owe my life to him.'

Melody laid a gentle hand over her father's. 'I'm thankful he found you. Otherwise I would have lost a mother and a father.'

Looking to her with all-embracing understanding and compassion, Matt took her hand in his and gave it a squeeze. 'You really are a sweet girl, Melody, and I'm so proud and honoured to be your dad. I just hope, in time, I make you proud too.'

Overwhelmed, she bit back tears. 'I'm already proud of the man you are, and I can't wait to get to know you and your beautiful little family even better.'

'That means the world to me.' Matt's eyes glistened and he blinked faster, a slight smile re-emerging. 'So, tell me, does this mean you're going to say yes to my offer?'

* * *

Waking bright and early the following morning, Melody couldn't believe she'd said yes. But bearing witness to the pleading in her father's eyes had made it impossible for her to say no. Besides, she was longing to know more about her family roots, and she wasn't ready to go back to Sydney, with the emptiness and monotonousness of the city rush, or to Antonio. She knew what she had to do regarding their marriage, but she just wasn't quite ready to face the music. Asking for a divorce was going to create a massive ripple effect – how was she meant to continue owning a business with her ex? For once in her life, she was just going to go with the flow and see where that took her. It was a liberating, if scary, feeling.

Still half-asleep, she rolled onto her side and cuddled a pillow to her. After a topsy-turvy night she just wanted another hour or two before having to make the call she was dreading. Antonio wasn't going to take the news of her extended break well, but then again, like her Aunt Sally had drummed into her on their long phone call the day before, she needed to think about herself for once. This was what she wanted, what she needed to find her feet and, hopefully, find herself. She was doing the right thing, heading out to Rosalee Station, or so she liked to believe. Only time would tell.

Yawning, she pulled a pillow over her head, closed her eyes and willed herself to stop overthinking everything – it wasn't doing her any favours. She needed to learn the art of letting go, of living in the moment, of living her best life doing the things that made her heart sing and her spirit soar. There was something about being near her father, and also sharing time with a woman as kind and thoughtful as Sarah and a child as full of wonder as Beau; something about the country air, the simpler, slower pace of life, that made her believe she was on the right path to such enlightenment.

Almost sinking into the mattress, she jumped with fright when Makka, the Clarke Farm rooster, crowed outside her bedroom window, his calls startling her to heart-thudding life. She bolted upright, sending the pillow flying across the room, almost laughing out loud when she spotted the state of her bed hair in the closet mirror.

After catching her breath, she tugged the curtains behind her bed open and pressed her face against the flyscreen, spotting the loudmouth straight away. 'You may think you're the king of the castle here, Makka, but did you also know you're a pain in the butt?'

His comb flopping side to side, Makka regarded her, cock-a-doodled again, and strutted off, as though he was diligently off to his next important job. Shaking her head, Melody laughed at the rooster's audacity – he was an absolute character.

Giving up on the notion of any more sleep, she climbed from the tousled bed, straightened her pyjamas, quickly tugged the doona up and fluffed her pillows, and headed into the bathroom. She needed to freshen up before heading to the kitchen in search of a cuppa, and a splash of cold water on her face would do the trick.

Padding through the quiet house, she strode towards the electric jug, startled once again at her father's voice. 'Morning, Melody.'

She spun to face him. 'Good morning.' It felt so surreal, to be standing in the same house, in the same room, as her biological father. She still felt like she had to pinch herself.

Seated at the breakfast bench, Matt offered a kind smile. 'Did you sleep okay?'

'Sure did.' She didn't want to complain about the fact that she'd woken countless times after dreams of being stuck in the middle of nowhere, bored out of her brain with nothing to do. 'You?'

'Yeah, like a log.' He stood, his chair scraping along the tiles. 'You ready for your big adventure in the outback?'

'Yes and no.' She shrugged. 'I'm a little worried I won't fit in out there.'

Reaching the sink, he glanced over his shoulder, brows furrowed. 'What do you mean?'

'I dunno.' She shrugged again. 'I'm worried I might be a little too city-ish with my style of cooking, and in my ways.' Duke arrived at her side and she gave his head a welcoming pat. Duchess wasn't far behind, the puppy somersaulting to a panting stop at her feet. She bent and scooped her up, laughing as Duchess tried desperately to lick her face.

'You're overthinking things, I reckon, Melody. A trait I'm accustomed to, as Sarah always reminds me.' Her father turned to face her, kindness in his deep brown eyes. 'There's no way you're too city-ish. I can see the country blood in you a mile away. Besides, the people out there accept folks for who they are, country, city, whatever.' He patted his chest. 'It's what's in here that counts, and you, my splendid daughter, have a heart of gold.' He grinned a little. 'Just like your old man.'

'Wow, thank you.' Melody had no power over the tears that sprung up and rolled down her cheeks. Wishing she could have a stiffer upper lip, she tried to wipe them away. 'Sorry, I've been really emotional since …' She sniffled. 'It's tough, knowing I'll never see her again.'

'Of course. There'd be something wrong with you if you weren't emotional about losing your mum.' He took a step towards her. 'Take it from the master of being hard on yourself – you need to stop being so hard on you and let yourself wholly and solely feel what you need to at any given moment.' He gave the bench a soft tap. 'It's what helps you to heal and move on with lighter steps and a lighter heart. Trust me.'

Unable to speak for fear of breaking into uncontrollable sobs, she nodded. 'Thank you,' she finally squeezed out.

Regarding her for a few more moments, he turned and flicked the tap on, washing his cup and plate then drying them and putting them away. 'The blokes are going to feel like all their Christmases have come at once, with your amazing cooking. '

'I hope so.'

'I know so.' It was said with absolute certainty.

With the kettle boiled, she poured a hot stream into her cup. 'Have you figured out how I'm getting out there yet?' Dolloping in two teaspoons of sugar, she decided to drink her tea sweet and black this morning. 'And when?'

'I wish I could take you myself but I just can't get away from here.' He offered her an apologetic smile. 'So, you'll be catching the plane from Cairns to Mount Isa, stay overnight at the pub, and then old Stan Loot who flies the mail plane will take you from there to the station, with a few stops along the way.' He wiped his hands on the tea towel. 'Does two days from now work for you?'

It was all really happening. It made her head spin. 'Of course it does, thank you.' She felt a rise of panic, especially as Matt wouldn't be the one to take her out there and introduce her to the men, but she shoved it back down – at least she knew Zai.

'Great. That's settled then.' Matt propped himself against the kitchen bench, crossing his mismatched socked feet at the ankles, a mischievous grin spreading across his face. 'Word of warning, though. Stan is a little bit of a wild boy in the sky, but he's super safe, I promise.'

'Oh, lord help me. I'm not good at flying at the best of times.' Melody grimaced.

'I've hitched a lift with him many times over the years, as has Sarah, and I've always arrived alive, although sometimes a little nauseated from the landing.' He offered a good-humoured wink.

'Far out, thanks for that info, now I'm crapping myself even more.' From a small plane to an even smaller one – this was going to be one hell of an adventure, she could feel it in her bones.

'Ha, sorry, but seriously, you'll be right.' He reached out and gave her shoulder a squeeze. 'Just keep reminding yourself you got this, okay?'

'Kind of like fake it til I make it?'

'Yeah, something like that.' Matt strolled over to the hook beside the back door, and grabbed his hat. With one tap to his leg, Duke hurried to his side, and Duchess half scuttled, half tripped over her floppy paws to join them. 'Sarah, Beau and I will meet you at the station in about four weeks, give or take, depending on what's happening here. We're just waiting for her parents to get back from their trip to visit some friends down in Tassie so they can take care of the critters.' He scooped Duchess up, chuckling when she sideswiped his cheek with a lick.

'Sounds like a plan.' She pulled up a chair at the bench and sat, wishing they were all heading out there together. It was going to feel strange arriving on her own.

As if reading her mind, Matt sauntered back towards her, spun a breakfast stool around and planted himself in saddle position opposite her, his forearms resting on the chair back. 'I know this is all surreal, and a little scary, but I want you to know, I'm so glad you came and found me, as is Sarah. And the extended family can't wait to meet you when they get back for Slim and Sherrie's wedding.'

Staring into her father's eyes, Melody found herself overwhelmed with emotions – what if she didn't live up to expectations? What if she didn't get along with the men or, even worse, her extended family? What if she got there only to decide she hated it and wanted to go back to the city? She desperately didn't want to let them down.

'You're very quiet.' Matt reached out and placed a hand over hers. 'What is it?'

She felt stupid saying it out loud, but … 'I'm just worried they won't like me. The men. And the family, when I meet them.'

He looked at her with genuine shock. 'How could anyone not like you?'

'You're just being nice.'

'No, I'm being honest.' His frown gave way to the hint of a smile. 'It gets me in lots of trouble, saying things how I see them, but I have to be real, or why bother saying anything at all?'

'True. And I like that about you.'

'You're going to have the time of your life out there, you'll see.' He stood and tucked his chair back under the bench. 'The outback changes a person. There's just something about being in the middle of Mother Nature's heart, where you can feel and hear her beat so very clearly. It makes you reassess everything in your life and gets rid of the limitations we all put on ourselves. In a strange way, it draws the real you out.'

'Well, then.' Melody's admiration for her father's fathomless depth intensified. 'If that's the case, I'll never want to leave.' It was said frivolously, but a part of her, a very small part, wondered if it would be so.

'Like I said, magic happens out there.' Matt gave her a knowing smile, as if he knew what she was yet to experience, or maybe something she was yet to tell him … but no. There was no way he knew about Antonio – he was the kind of immoral man that she wouldn't want her father meeting. Ever.

She took a sip from her tea. 'I'll soon see.'

'Yes, you most certainly will.' Golden sunlight poured into the kitchen when he yanked the back door open.

Watching her father disappear out the door with Duke and Duchess in tow, Melody tugged her phone from her pocket and huffed. It was now or never. She dialled Antonio's number. He answered just as it was about to be diverted to message bank.

'Hey, you.' His voice was crackly with sleep. 'What's up?'

'Hey.' Used to being up at the crack of dawn now, she hadn't stopped to think about Antonio's yearning to sleep in until midday on his day off – it had always driven her nuts. 'I'm so sorry for waking you. I can call back later if you like.'

'All good, I'm awake now.' Background rustlings sounded down the line. 'How's it going there in bumpkin town? Met anyone with two heads yet?'

Melody ignored the passive-aggressive jab. 'Yeah, it's actually going really good.' She paused, sucked in a breath, and then rushed the next bit, before she could chicken out. 'I've agreed to take on the cook's job out at the family station. For six weeks.'

'You've what?' His voice was gruff. 'What about your obligations here? To the café and to me? We need you here, Melody. You're my wife, and a good wife should submit to what her husband needs from her.'

She was about to snap back but stopped herself. 'I haven't forgotten I'm your wife, Antonio, nor have I forgotten about the café I have poured my heart and soul into the past three years. It's just … well, I need this right now. Can you understand that?'

'I don't understand what you are doing at all. You should be here, with me, not gallivanting around the countryside like some hippie.'

'I'm not gallivanting like some hippie, Antonio. I am spending time with my father.' She couldn't help the icy tone, and she wasn't about to explain that her father wouldn't be arriving at the station for a few weeks. That was none of Antonio's business.

'You've spent three weeks with him now, Melody. And besides, have you stopped to think how isolated you're going to be on some cattle ranch?' He laughed, snorted even. 'You won't last a bloody day there, let alone six weeks.'

She looked out the window at her dad racing past on the quad bike, with Duke and Duchess in a crate tied to the back, and her exasperation subsided. 'We'll see.'

There was an extended silence then an almighty huff. 'Right. Well, I suppose there's nothing I can do or say to change your mind, so I'm not going to bother. Your bad choices are not going to rub off on me any longer.'

'What do you mean by that?'

Antonio huffed again. 'I mean that I am going to do what's best for me, and for the café.'

'That café is part mine, remember.' She was being baited and she knew it, but she just couldn't break the old habit of snapping into defensive mode.

'Not on paper it isn't.' He sounded quite pleased with the power that gave him.

She gasped. 'You wouldn't.' Naïvely trusting Antonio way back when, she'd invested her savings and a substantial financial gift from her mother into the café with the promise of being a part-owner but hadn't signed a damn thing to say so.

'Try me, Melody. Your place is here, with me and at the café. If you choose otherwise, we'll see what happens.'

'Please, Antonio, don't play that card.' Melody held out the hope that Marianna wouldn't let her be ripped off where the café was concerned, if it came to that. 'Please, just try and be happy for me, that I've found my dad and everything's going better than expected.'

'I give up trying to steer you in the right direction, Melody,' he said. 'If you insist on going out to the sticks, I think we should have a trial separation.'

It was just like him to issue an ultimatum and expect her to back down. *Not this time.* 'I couldn't agree more,' she snapped.

There was a muffled sound, followed by another then the slamming of a door. After a couple of lengthy seconds, Antonio's voice came back through the phone, crystal clear. 'Sorry, what were you saying?'

Melody's instincts jerked to life – maybe he hadn't waited for her to agree to a separation before he'd started sleeping around. 'What was that noise?'

'Oh, just the neighbours wanting some sugar.'

'Our neighbours are night owls. What are they doing up at this time?'

'Who knows? I'm not their keeper,' he snapped.

Suspicion swirled in her stomach. That sick feeling returned, the one she'd lived with since he'd cheated with the buxom blonde, the one that had subsided in the weeks she'd been here surrounded by people who were genuine and loving. 'Have you got someone there, Antonio?'

'No, Melody, don't be ridiculous.'

She honed her hearing, wishing she were a fly on the wall in their apartment. 'Are you sure?'

'Of course I'm bloody well sure.'

'Okay, well, I suppose I just have to believe you, don't I?'

'I suppose you do.' His reply was terribly cold. 'Take care out there, won't you?'

'Yup, righto. Bye.' She hung up the phone, shoved it across the bench, out of her reach, thanking her lucky stars that she might have found a way out of her messy life and into a world where she felt wanted, needed, loved.

One step at a time.

CHAPTER 8

His mouth drier than the Simpson Desert, Zai emerged from where he'd been wedged between the cool concrete floor and the underbelly of the Fiat tractor for the past hour, trying to figure out why it was making noises it shouldn't be. He was pretty sure he'd worked it out, and it was nothing a bit of a service and tinker wouldn't fix. Striding over to the workbench, he sculled the remainder of his water bottle then wiped the beads of sweat from his brow with the back of his hand, no doubt succeeding in smearing grease in its place. Snatching a rag from the worktop, he rubbed off what he could – he'd get the rest later, along with the day's dirt, in a long, cooling shower. Which he'd almost give his right arm for right about now. It was just shy of lunchtime, so there was still a ways to go before he could luxuriate in one.

As he gathered the tools he needed, his stomach grumbled in protest against skipping breakfast. With Pothole leaving yesterday, it was every man for himself in the kitchen department, and he simply hadn't had the time this morning to make anything, other than chucking back a strong cup of coffee. Now he'd kill for something to eat, but he had to get this done first – Showbags needed to finish the slashing before they headed off on the next muster in a couple of days. Searching for something to drain the engine oil into, he did his best to ignore the growling hunger pains – he hadn't envisioned being sidetracked like this when he'd walked out the cottage door before sun-up with a list a mile long. He should have known something would go belly-up. Station life never ran smoothly – expecting the unexpected was a given out here. Plus, most things took longer than expected. It was usually a case of making do with what you had, or having to wait a week to get a part flown in. In this case, he didn't have the time to wait.

The tin shed was roasting beneath the sun-drenched corrugated iron roof. Zai hauled his shirt off and threw it to the side, wishing he could do the same with his jeans. If he could get the job done in his jocks and socks or, god forbid, in the nud, without looking like a weirdo, he'd damn well do it right now. But if he were caught out, he'd never live it down – the blokes would have a field day rehashing the yarn, making it more colourful with each retelling. He assessed the risk versus the gain – tempting, but no. The temperature gauge had hit close to forty degrees right before he'd stepped in here, and he knew it would still be climbing – it always did until the peak of the day at two-ish. Yesterday had topped forty-four degrees and today was probably going to be much the same, if not hotter. Hell, he'd be able to fry an egg on the bonnet of the LandCruiser.

Needing a distraction from the relentless heat and the flies that wanted to cling to him, he flicked the old radio on. It crackled to life and he turned it up. Willie Nelson's nasal voice was unmistakable, the old tune the very one his sister always told him was his theme song. He always laughed at her tongue-in-cheek comments about his bachelorhood, knowing she didn't mean any harm, but little did she, or anyone else for that matter, know how much he wished he could remove his armour and let down the walls of his fortress. He wanted to find his person, the woman that would complete him, a wife who he could make a family with. But nobody needed to know that, deep down, he desired love just like everyone else. He just didn't want the complications or the heartache of laying his heart on the line. He'd done that once, and had gotten burnt, badly – he was far better off on his own, even if it meant maintaining his wild and free reputation.

Singing along to 'Mammas Don't Let Your Babies Grow Up to Be Cowboys', he wandered back to his job at hand. Repositioning himself back beneath the belly of the tractor, he left the drip pan beside him and fumbled for the wrench he was sure he'd grabbed before sliding underneath. Realising he'd forgotten it, he cursed before shimmying out again and grabbing it from the toolbox. Then, back to it, he turned the wrench a couple of times and tossed it just in time to slip the drip pan beneath so it could catch the stream of dark oil. Now, he waited.

The sound of boot falls had him turning his head, and a pair of weathered hands appeared, bestowing a foil-wrapped parcel right before Showbags's grinning mug followed. 'Ya hungry, bro?'

The scent of bacon wafted, and Zai's mouth watered. 'Bloody oath I am.' Climbing out, he took the parcel and a can of icy soft drink gratefully. He quickly unwrapped the sandwich, chomping down on a little bit of heaven. 'I thought you couldn't cook? This tastes bloody good.'

'Correctomundo. I can't cook for shit. Tumbles made it.'

'Really?' Zai fought the vision of Tumbles somehow blowing the kitchen up. 'Good on him.'

'Yeah, says seeing he's on a day off, he's happy to strap the apron strings on,' Showbags said with a comical roll of his eyes. 'He looks like a right tool with Judy's old floral apron on, let me tell ya.' Laughing and shaking his head, he tucked into his own bacon and egg sanga, dripping at the edges with tomato sauce. 'How's it going? You fixed it yet, or what?' he asked between bites, half the sauce making it around his mouth.

'Yeah, almost. It's a bitch of a job when I can't find the right tools, but getting there, thankfully.'

'Good.' Showbags burped a beauty, then chuckled. 'Oh, before I forget, Slim's caught up so he wants to know if you can go and collect the new cook from the airstrip this arvo.'

'Yeah, of course I can.' Zai's brows furrowed. 'What's held him up?'

'He called me on the satphone about an hour ago, swearing like a trooper.' Showbags grimaced. 'Something's chewed through the wires of the pump at the third dam.'

'Oh shit. Hopefully he can fix it.' Sandwich devoured, Zai screwed the foil up, aimed, and then tossed it in the general direction of the bin near the workbench.

It hit his mark and he and Showbags both yelled, 'Shot!'

Sucking back on his can of cola, Showbags arched an interested brow. 'So, tell me, seeing as you've met her. Is this Melody sheila a looker?'

'She sure is, and she's also Matt's daughter, so keep your dirty mitts to yourself, Showbags. And make sure the other blokes keep their dirty mitts to themselves too while you're at it.' Zai realised too late just how protective of Melody he sounded.

Showbags held his hands up in surrender. 'Bloody hell, just asking. No need to get your knickers twisted, Wellstone.'

Zai was as surprised as Showbags by how quick he was to bite at such a harmless question. It was usual for the blokes to be keen when a new female was coming to the station. 'Jocks in a knot, not knickers twisted. Get it right, Showbags.' His lips twitched with the smile he was holding back, and then he laughed out loud. 'Sorry for snapping. This bastard tractor is giving me the shits is all.'

Showbags regarded him suspiciously, then his eyes widened, like he'd just discovered the pot of gold at the end of a rainbow. 'You're bloody keen on her already, aren't ya, mate?'

'No, I'm not,' Zai replied as matter-of-factly as he could.

Showbags wagged a finger in his direction. 'Yeah, right, pull the other one.'

Zai rolled his eyes, huffing. 'Whatever.'

'You're a terrible liar.' Showbags's grin was filled with playful rabble-rousing. 'And while you're at it, don't forget that the same goes for you, with the whole she's-Walshee's-flesh-and-blood thing. We all know he won't like any of us buggers getting keen on his daughter, especially the likes of you, Casanova.'

Groaning at his nickname, Zai dug his elbow into Showbags. 'Oi, bugalugs, why am I any worse than you?'

Showbags looked at him as though he'd lost his mind asking such a question. 'Come on, Wellstone. Everyone knows how much you love being a single man.' He wiggled his brows for effect. 'You get way more action than we all do, you handsome bloody bastard.'

Feigning shock-horror, Zai then pretended to be wounded. He allowed the men to think he got lots of action in the lust department simply by saying nothing and by denying nothing. The truth was he hadn't for a long while and didn't want to either – shallow hook-ups weren't fulfilling anymore.

'Zai and Melody sitting in a tree, K-I-S-S-I-N-G,' Showbags added. 'First comes love, then comes marriage, then comes Zai pushing a baby carriage.'

'Oi, fair crack of the whip, you shit-stirrer.' Zai gave him a playful shove. 'Bugger off or make yourself useful, would you?' Not understanding the clenching in his stomach, or the sudden stampede of his heartbeat, he pointed towards the bench – anything to get Showbags off his back. 'Go and grab me a cloth so I can mop the drips up and get this thing back out yonder so you can earn your bloody keep.'

Showbags huffed animatedly. 'Far out, do I have to do everything around here?'

Chuckling, Zai gave him the bird and got one in return.

As he got back to work, he had to quietly admit that he was really looking forward to laying his eyes on the mesmerising Melody Harrison again.

* * *

'What do you do if you're landing in the dark, Stan?' Her hand pressing against the dash, Melody thrust her voice over the whirr of the engine and through the headset.

'We do it outback-style.' Stan grinned like a rebellious child.

'How's that?' With the day getting away from them, Melody was keen to know.

'They soak toilet rolls in kerosene, stick each one in a tin can, position them out along the runway, and then light them up.' He looked to her with wide eyes. 'It works an absolute treat, I tell ya. Anyone would think it was daylight.'

Melody shook her head, laughing softly. 'I could only imagine such a thing happening out here.' Once again, she turned her attention outwards and lost herself in the vista that was the epitome of all she'd heard of the Aussie outback.

Now she could see it, feel it, and breathe it in … something about it filled her in a way she couldn't quite explain, or want to.

It just … felt right.

With arcs of dust on the windscreen, the mail plane heaved and pitched like a roller-coaster as it battled the thermals, the occasional tin roof beneath glinting so brightly, it was almost blinding. Having clawed into the air from the runway of Mount Isa at first light, they'd been zigzagging their way across the country, meeting all sorts of country people. White and black, young and old, they were universally generous and hospitable in a way that Melody couldn't quite believe. The pilot, the very charismatic Stan Loop, had scored himself scones and cakes and sausages and homemade beer, cheerily given to him by fierce-looking men with broad smiles shaded by their battered hats, or women almost too sweet to live in such arid land. Although, she could tell, beneath their warm and welcoming spirits these women must be built tough to call such challenging lands their homes. Along the way, they'd dodged kangaroos, sheep and cattle, and even emus. Once, they'd had to shoo a few cows from the shade of the plane's wings and now, thankfully, they were almost at Rosalee Station. She'd keenly listened to conversations about the weather, the lack of rain, the price of livestock, dingoes and rabbits, the lives and deaths of loved ones, and the struggles of everyday life out here, where the clock didn't rule your every step, but the climate certainly did. It was a whole other world – one she was about to call home for six long weeks.

The plane bucked then dropped a little. Stan whooped. Melody held her breath, and momentarily squeezed her eyes shut, waiting for the tin can they were in to settle back down. Once it had, still gripping the edge of her seat tightly, she caught her breath then once again stared out at the earth that had been scorched clean of features by the severity of the sun. Her father hadn't been kidding when he'd said the mail plane would be a ride she'd always remember. But despite the fact that this was more than a little out of her comfort zone, she found herself mesmerised by the brightness of the country sky, the copper-red of the rocky ridges that appeared as if they were reaching for the heavens, and the ever-evolving patchwork of landscape below. This was the closest she'd ever come to peering down on god's creation and it was beyond beautiful.

Black soil plains had turned red, and the running creek beds she'd spotted outside of Mount Isa were now stone dry. With barely a tree to be seen, the rusted-metal red land was vast, intimidating and striking. Dried-up river arteries sliced the land into sections and colossal ant hills were all over the place. An old four-wheel drive bonnet leaning up against a fence caught her eye, but with the sun glinting off it, she couldn't make out what it said. Then suddenly, what she guessed to be the main homestead's roof flashed beneath them and she swivelled in her seat to watch it, another couple of dwellings, and what she thought must be stables, all of it surrounded by lush gardens, shrinking behind them ever so quickly. Her heartbeat raced with the thought of finally arriving, and what she would discover when her feet hit the hard-packed earth. She also wondered who would be collecting her, and silently hoped it was Zai – she'd feel a little more comfortable with him, seeing as they'd already met. There was something about him that made her feel relaxed, and he was very easy on the eye, she had to admit. Not that it should matter. As much as she was ready to call her marriage quits, she was still lawfully spoken for until she made that information known to Antonio when she returned to Sydney. For now, she wanted to focus on the here and now, at Rosalee Station.

'Here we are. Time to get this old girl down,' Stan bellowed, swinging the plane around in a sweeping banking turn that briefly left Melody's stomach behind them.

Looking down at the mirages created by the intense desert heat, she could barely make out a landing strip. 'Where are we touching down?' She hoped it wasn't going to be like some of the teeth-chattering bone-rattlers they'd landed on earlier.

'Right here.' His voice crackling through the headphones, Stan offered a sideways glance. 'Hold onto ya britches, girly. We're going in.'

The seventy-four-year-old's horn-rimmed, startling thick glasses offering her no comfort, Melody sucked in what felt like her hundredth nervous lungful of oxygen for the day. Her breath snagged as they all but fell out of the sky. She said a quick prayer, then held on for dear life.

The Cessna circled twice and then dropped as if the engine had been cut. Anyone would think Stan had been a fighter pilot in his past life. For a few terrifying seconds, Melody actually honed her ears to make sure the engine was still running. Then she braced herself as the red dirt hurtled towards them and the wheels hit the dusty ground. Her teeth gritted tightly together as they bumped along, things flying off the dash and into her lap. She almost laughed out loud at the craziness of it all, but her racing heart prevented her. Then, mercifully, Stan brought the plane to a steady halt as a cloud of red dust engulfed them. Stillness hung for a few lengthy moments before Melody found herself breathing again.

'Thank goodness we didn't have to vie with the bloody roos today.' Stan's bushy grey brows yanked together as he flicked switches and then tugged his headset off, prompting Melody to do the same. 'Those bouncy bastards have a death wish, I'm sure of it,' he added as he slid out of his seat and nimbly clambered into the back of the plane.

Right on time, a dusty four-wheel drive came to a stop just shy of them. Melody gathered her things and climbed out to the knee-buckling sight of Zai striding towards them with a delicious countryman swagger. Even though her feet had just hit smack-bang in the dead heart of Australia, she felt as if she'd just dived off a mountaintop, and she was having trouble catching her airborne heart.

Good god, at least please let me have the ability to string a sentence together.

Reminding herself to play it cool, she couldn't help but stare at the very fetching sight of Zai in his very manly cowboy get-up. Tall, tanned and muscular, his biceps flexed and shifted as he straightened his Akubra, his dashing smile curling.

'Glad to see you made it, Melody.' His evocative grin travelled from her face, down her body, pausing on her bright-pink manicured toes, then quickly landing smack-bang on her face again.

The gesture was more appreciative than insulting – it gave her a buzz. 'I sure did.' It was all she could verbally muster right now. His clean, spicy scent drugged her senses – he was aerial testosterone at its most lethal. And the fact that he never broke eye contact sent a weird flutter through her chest.

'G'day Stan, how goes it?' Zai said, turning his attention elsewhere, much to her relief.

'Yeah, you know, can't complain, Zai, and don't really want to.' Stan reefed his shorts almost to his armpits – his knee-high socks adding to his dress sense, or lack thereof, as he looked Zai up and down, a playful grin on his wrinkly face. 'Gee whizz, Wellstone, you didn't have to go to the trouble of scrubbing up for my arrival. Bloody hell, anyone would think you had someone to impress.' His gaze darted to the left of him, landing on Melody.

For one second, and then another, they all could have heard a pin drop on the red earth beneath their feet. Looking from Stan's witty expression to Zai's flushed one – Melody would have laughed if she could rein her galloping heart in.

A mound of boxes in his arms, Stan closed the distance between himself and Zai. He passed the leaning tower of cardboard over. 'You would have thought Georgia would've had enough of internet shopping by now. She's so much like her mother,' he offered, rolling his eyes. 'We never had all this internet malarkey in my day, I tell you. And if we had, with the way the missus likes to shop, we would have been bankrupt.'

'It does make it easier, I suppose,' Zai replied as he piled the boxes into the four-wheel drive.

Leaning into the cockpit, Stan re-emerged holding a Tupperware container. 'I brought you one of the wife's passionfruit sponges. Just make sure you don't keep it all to yourself, Zai, because I know how much you love them.' The crow's feet at the corners of the mailman's eyes creased from smiling so much. 'Lesser men have been put to death for such a crime, you know?' He offered a good-humoured wink. 'Slim's always pretty keen on a hefty slice.'

'I wouldn't dare do such a thing, Stan.' Zai scrunched his handsome face up. 'That's death by hanging out here, for sure.' His expression turned to one of absolute seriousness, although the hint of a charming smile lingered beneath.

'Oh yeah, and plenty of place to bury a greedy body out yonder, too,' Stan chuckled, pointing towards the hazy horizon.

Witnessing the men's obvious respect for one another, and their delightful banter, Melody chuckled as Zai's deep baritone voice skittered over her senses and helped to warm her tattered soul. She could seriously sit and listen to him all day. And those penetrating blue eyes of his, subtly glancing her way as he and Stan yakked about the usual – weather, the cattle, flies. Oh, lord help her. Zai was the kind of distraction she really didn't need, especially out here, where everyday distractions were clearly going to be few and far between. Although, she had to admit, after everything she'd been through, Mister Wellstone was a breath of fresh air. Air she could breathe in, but not hold in for too long – he'd make her way too giddy. Already did, to be fair.

Stan took a wider stance, his hand rubbing his chin as though the conversation was becoming more serious. 'How are you and Slim going holding up the fort while Pat and Georgia are away?'

'Yeah, we're keeping all the ducks in a row, so pretty good.'

'That's great to hear.' Pausing, the two men shared some sort of silent manspeak before Stan nodded. 'Well, then, must be off. I'll catch you in a week's time.' He slapped Zai on the back much harder than a man of his age should have been able to. 'Keep on keeping on, won't you?' He looked in Melody's direction. 'And make sure you take care of this gorgeous girl. She's very precious cargo.'

'Yup, I most certainly will, old mate, you can be sure of that.' Zai shook Stan's outstretched hand. 'Safe travels.'

Honoured to feel so cared for by these two heart-of-gold men, Melody slipped into the conversation like Cinderella and her glass slipper. 'Thank so much for the lift out here, Stan.'

'My pleasure, love. Anytime.' He offered her a spirited salute, and then climbed back aboard.

Melody and Zai stood at a safe distance as they watched him get settled. Then, after a brisk wave, he taxied away from them and, seconds later, was vaulting towards the bright blue sky and out of sight.

Ear-piercing silence settled in his wake.

Melody found herself a little speechless in Zai's presence.

Zai shot her a disarming look. 'So, how was the ride out here?'

'It was …' She cocked a brow at him. 'Invigorating.' The low rumble of his responding laughter was satiating, so much so she wanted to indulge more of it.

'Ha, yeah, I suppose that's one way to put it.' He offered a knowing look, one that spoke of all the times he'd been in the passenger seat of the Cessna.

Melody laughed, then quickly swallowed a snort – there was no way Zai was going to hear that embarrassing trait of hers.

Fidgeting, her gaze fell on the faint show of tattooed chest peeking out of his shirt and she instinctively licked her lip as she imagined what it would feel like to rest her cheek there.

My god, what the heck is wrong with me?

As if reading her mind, his eyes briefly dipped to where her hand played over the curve of her breast. 'You ready to head?'

Sweet baby Jesus, were her responding nipples evident? She cleared her throat, fanning her face. 'Mm-hmm.' Dang it, why was she feeling so damn hot? It was just this heat, surely.

Zai grabbed her suitcase from beside her. 'Holy moly, you got the kitchen sink in here?'

'Almost,' she said playfully. 'Goes with being a chef.'

'Lucky us.' He winked over his shoulder before throwing the bag over it as if it were weightless. Placing it in the back of the old trayback four-wheel drive, he quickly made his way round to open her door. 'Here you go.'

Melody was not used to be looked after like this, especially by a man. 'Wow, thank you.' She climbed up, hoping she did it with a little grace.

'All part of the service,' he said, closing the door and then offering her a charming smile through the window. 'There's no aircon in this old girl, so we have to leave the windows down, I'm afraid. Just be careful with breathing in too deep, or you'll inhale half the countryside.'

Oh, she was going to struggle with being around Zai. She watched him make his way around to the driver's side, slide in and rev the four-wheel drive to life. Then off they went, bumping along the earthen track, the pile of bolts, wire and tools bouncing around on the dash. Fine red dust rolled into the cab, and she blinked against it. As she gazed out at the land she'd witnessed unfolding from the sky, they chatted about general stuff, the background music humming from the radio filling the few silences nicely. In the weeks she'd been totally focused on getting to know her dad, Sarah and Beau, she'd gone and forgotten just how alluring Zai was. His sexy scorch-her-clothes-off stare made her feel naked, and very vulnerable to his mischievous charm. Boy oh boy she needed to rein in the wild urge to dive across the seat and kiss him – it wasn't like her to be so reckless, lustful. She adjusted her v-neck T-shirt, wishing she'd chosen something with a little less cleavage – she didn't want to give him the wrong impression – and had thought about the fact that it was white amidst a sea of red dirt, and now quickly gathering sweat too.

Diverting her attention out her open window, she tucked strands of flyaway hair behind her ears as she drank in her jaw-dropping surrounds. They rolled past a holding yard chock-full of cattle, quickly followed by a huge shed jam-packed with all sorts of machinery. At the approaching vehicle, chooks dashed this way and that, and a lone duck made a beeline for the shade, turning just as the ute passed to give them the eye. She quietly chuckled with its audacity – it reminded her of Makka back at her dad's place. Weeping bottlebrush hung over the side of the dirt track, the brilliant red flowers startling against the dusty backdrop. Then she spotted the sleek bodies of five stockhorses, heads down as they grazed on paddock grass. To the right of impressive stables was a bucking arena, chutes and all – she knew it would have been somewhere her father had trained his bulls in days gone by, along with the nerves-of-steel riders keen to learn the art of staying on the bull's back. Pride filled her – her father was proving to be an awesome man, one she had no trouble connecting with, finding comfort in, loving. If only she could say the same for Antonio, but the further she got away from him, the more she understood just how far apart they'd grown.

Zai slowed as a massive two-storey red-brick homestead came into view, the shaded verandahs beckoning her to its pot plant–dotted coolness, as did the hammock strung up between railing posts. She could just imagine laying there reading or snoozing – with the uninterrupted views of untainted vastness, it was the perfect spot.

Zai parked beneath shade of a coolabah tree alongside the rustic timber fence that surrounded the house. 'Here we are, home sweet home.' He grinned and shrugged. 'For now, anyway.'

'It's really pretty,' she said with a dreamy smile. She gathered her bag from near her feet and before she could open her door, he'd gone and done it for her. 'Cheers, Zai.' She grinned as she stepped past him. 'A woman could get really used to this kind of service.'

'It's pretty common round these parts to open doors for the ladies, so you'd better get used to it.' He tugged her suitcase from the back, quickly dusting a thick layer of fine red dirt off it. 'Right then, follow me.' He tossed an arm towards the homestead. 'Your country castle awaits.'

'It certainly could pass as one.' She breathed, scanning the sprawling house. 'It's massive.'

Falling into step beside her, he pointed to a newish building leading off at the side of it. 'That there is the common area kitchen you'll be using, all scrubbed spick-and-span for you. There's a you-beaut deep freeze in there, and a massive pantry, both of them stocked full. We have to rely on frozen and canned food out here, in between our fortnightly fresh food delivery.' He turned his gaze to the left. 'And those buildings there are the workers' barracks, Slim's little farmhouse … and …' He pointed to a quaint little cottage peeking out from the behind the homestead. 'That there is my place. It used to be where your dad called home, before he married Sarah and moved to FNQ. Georgia and Pat's place is up the road a little bit.'

She nodded as she tried to take it all in. 'Cool, I can't wait to check it all out.'

'There's not really any flash gadgets in the common kitchen, well, not that you'd be used to, I'm sure, but it's functional, and the oven is huge.' He lifted his sunglasses. 'Georgia had it built about three years back, designed the layout herself, and drove Pat mad in the process, mind you.' He chuckled, shaking his head. 'Those two are hilarious to watch. Married eight years and still as madly in love as ever.'

'I'm looking forward to meeting them when they get back from Ireland,' Melody said softly. 'And Judy and Steve too.'

'You've got a beautiful family, Melody. They're the most down-to-earth, welcoming people you could meet.'

'Like Matt and Sarah.'

Zai nodded. 'Yes, exactly.'

Squawks of cockatoos resounded from the railings of a holding yard they passed, and a windmill spun lazily in the gentle breeze, throwing shadows across her face. She blinked into the sunlight glinting off the Colorbond roof of the homestead as they wandered down the pebbled pathway, past a row of citrus trees heavy with plump fruit. Reaching out, she plucked a leaf and held it to her nose, breathing in the deliciously clean scent. She'd be making use of the lemons and limes, for sure. Lemon pie, lemon butter, key lime pie – the list was endless. Climbing the front steps, she saw a swing chair hanging in the shade of the wide front verandah – she'd be reading there too, in her spare time, as well as in the hammock. Wind chimes tinkled melodiously and a sun catcher tossed rays of light over the timber planks. Bougainvillea climbed the front trellis, popping with vibrant shades of pink and purple – the lush green garden surrounding her new abode was like a tropical oasis. An enormous rainwater tank sat off to the side of the house, and a thriving vegetable path was alongside it. Someone clearly had a green thumb – she'd make sure to tend to it. How lucky she was to have a herb and vegetable garden at her fingertips.

She drew in a steady breath as they reached the front door decorated with pretty leadlight. She was expecting Zai to pull a key from his pocket, or pluck one from the mat beneath them. Instead, he simply opened the screen door followed by the timber one. He stepped aside for her to step in first.

'You don't lock up with everyone out working during the day?'

'Why would we?' He turned, as if surveying the landscape for the very first time. 'Have you seen where we are?' His kicked off his boots. 'We don't really have any problems of break-ins out here, unless you count the snakes, spiders and possums that sometimes like to make themselves at home.'

'Oh crap.' She cringed – critters terrified her. Heck, even the sighting of a spider in the house back in Sydney had her running. 'Does that happen often?'

'More often than not, especially in the summer months when everything is vying for a cool spot.' He spotted her engulfing panic and offered a gallant grin. 'But don't worry, we'll come to your rescue if the need arises.'

The outside world dissolved as she stepped into her grandparents' home. The scent of timber polish and what she could only describe as many years of memories lured her from the entrance hall and into the heart of the lounge room, where a black leather lounge chair owned the centre of the room and a huge grandfather clock ticked away. One wall was lined with shelves overflowing with books, and there were so many photos, both coloured and black and white, of days gone by – she could almost hear the faded voices of the people captured in the images. It made her feel a sense of pride, knowing she was a blood relative to the many generations that had called Rosalee Station home.

Passing photos of her dad as a boy, then as a young man, they made their way down a hallway, past a beautiful light-filled kitchen. Taken aback, Melody paused to admire the space, the butcher's block clearly having had years of use, as had the copper pots hanging above it.

'Wow,' she breathed. 'Talk about the heart of the home.'

'Ha, yeah. Kitchens always are out here in the bush. Food is what brings us all together at the end of a long hard day, or when you're looking for a caring ear … actually, anytime, to be honest.'

'I like that food is part of connecting out here.'

'I thought you would.' He pointed to a Smeg refrigerator. 'We stocked the fridge as best we could with our recent order, so anything you're missing, you can just grab it from the common kitchen.'

'Thanks, Zai, you've really gone and thought of everything.'

He looked chuffed with the compliment. 'I do my best.'

They continued on, passing an office and laundry. At the end of the hallway, Zai shoved the half-open door with his toe. 'This is your room.' He surveyed it like it was the first time. 'Not too shabby, I hope?'

'Holy … it's so pretty.' She rushed to the window, where an endless vista of paddocks met her. 'And the view, oh my god.' Her hand went to cover her open mouth. Turning, she breathed in the large room, with its four-poster bed and matching bedside tables. 'It's absolutely gorgeous.'

'Glad you like it.' Zai wheeled her suitcase near the mahogany desk. 'I'll leave you to get settled in then. I've got a few jobs to finish before sundown.' He pointed to the little cottage out back. 'As you can see, I'm just a hop, skip and jump if you need me anytime, okay?'

'Okay. Thanks, Zai.'

'No worries.' He turned and headed out the doorway.

'Oh, before you go, when would you like me to start cooking for you lot?'

He briefly considered this. 'How about dinnertime tomorrow night? Gives you the day to make yourself familiar with the place and the kitchen you'll be working in.'

She nodded. 'Perfect.'

He regarded her for a few more moments. 'Righto. Well, catch you a bit later then.' He tipped his hat and disappeared out the doorway, his footfalls quickly fading down the hall.

Plonking down on the end of her bed, Melody flopped backwards and stared at the revolving ceiling fan. She was beat, but also exhilarated. Her outback adventure had just begun and she couldn't wait to see how her time here unfolded. Although they were isolated, something told her the six weeks were going to fly by.

CHAPTER 9

The following morning, after a decent first night's sleep, Melody woke to the sound of absolutely nothing – it was almost mystical, in an encompassing kind of way. She honed her ears in a bid to hear something, anything, but it was actually so quiet, her ears were ringing. Cuddling into her pillow, she rolled onto her side and stretched out her leg, and used her toes to pull the blackout curtains to one side. Blinding golden light had her squinting. She sat up and ran her hands through her tousled hair before tugging it into a messy bun.

As inaccessible as the dark side of the moon, unless you had a you-beaut four-wheel drive and bush know-how, this place felt like a whole other universe. At the landscape unfurling before her very eyes, the spirit of adventure on the grandest of scales took over her. Something about being in the outback, where there were fewer rules, fewer people, fewer expectations … and then so much more of the good things – open spaces, genuine people, fresh air – made her feel footloose, free, and somehow more in control of her life. She suddenly felt the urge to live it to the full, for herself, and in her mother's memory.

Leaping from the bed, she stretched her arms high, pausing when she caught her reflection in the mirror on the dressing table. Without an ounce of make-up on, her freckle-dusted nose was more evident – genetics of her dear mum, as were the chaotic curls that had reclaimed her usually ironed-flat hair. Just like she had at her father's place, she would wear both curls and freckles with absolute pride. There was no need for airs and graces out here, or time-consuming hairstyle and make-up regimes. From what she could gather, Rosalee Station was all about being authentic, unlike the city vibe where you had to keep up appearances. And without Antonio breathing down her neck, reminding her of her flaws and shortcomings, she felt like a real person again, her real self, not some high-maintenance man's china doll. Looking to her mobile phone on the dresser, now useless given there was no service here, she smiled – it made her feel untraceable.

Wandering to the kitchen, she made herself a cuppa, keen to plant her butt in the swing chair on the verandah for a little while – she'd spent hours there last night, gazing at the brightest star-studded sky she'd ever laid her eyes upon, with the occasional glance to where warm light spilled from the open windows of Zai's place. Keen for his comfortable company and witty charm, she'd almost wandered over and knocked on his door, but had stopped herself – she didn't want to make a habit of such things. And she certainly didn't want to give the man the wrong impression from the get-go.

The phone rang from the hallway and she dashed to grab it. 'Hello.'

'Hey, Melody.'

'Hi.' It was nice to hear her father's voice. 'How are you?'

'Yeah, good. I just called to make sure you're settling in okay before I head out for the day.'

'I sure am.' She glanced around the massive home. 'It's very comfortable here, and my bedroom is awesome.'

'Good, great. Have the men been polite?'

'I haven't met any of them yet, other than Zai, of course. I'll be cooking them dinner tonight, so I gather we'll be meeting and greeting over the table.'

'You'll all get on like a house on fire. Just don't mind Hasselhoof. He can be a cantankerous old bugger, but he's harmless.'

'Right, noted.' Zai had covered each of the mean, and the traits that had earned them their names, on the way to Rosalee the day before.

'Okay, well, I'd best get a move on. Call if you need us, and I'll be sure to call you every day to check in on you and see how you're faring, if you don't mind.'

'Of course I don't mind. You have a good day.'

'You too, sweetheart.'

Melody felt so loved and cared for when she hung up the phone – it was a nice sensation. Stirring her sugar into her coffee, she realised she didn't even know what the time was. She looked to the clock above the stove – it was almost seven. After making herself a piece of toast, she headed out into the glorious day just as a grey kangaroo bounded across the front yard. Eyes wide as she licked the marmalade from her lips, she stood stock-still, watching it pass through with rapt fascination. She dared not move until it had vanished out of sight – the Aussie icon was even more massive than she'd imagined after seeing them on telly.

Spotting a rope swing hanging beneath a cluster of towering gums, she double-checked the coast was clear of any more roos then padded down the steps, over the lawn too lush for the likes of land so arid, and sank down on the seat, sighing in pleasure. She swung gently to and fro, the rusty chain squeaking in protest. Vividly coloured parrots squawked from the branches above, some taking flight with her intrusion. A few listless clouds drifted across the bright expanse of blue.

What a wonderful way to start the day.

Time ticked by, and ten hours later, after spending most of the day making herself familiar with her surrounds and the common kitchen, as well as having the occasional freak out because she felt completely isolated, Melody busied herself at the sink, rinsing bowls to then pack into the dishwasher. Just like she prayed she'd get over the isolation heebie-jeebies, she prayed the men would be happy with her choice for their first dinner together – beef stroganoff with homemade egg noodles and an apple pie and custard for dessert. She hadn't thought to ask if any of them had allergies or intolerances, but something told her there wasn't really such a thing when it came to the likes of a hard-core stockman, or maybe that was just her idealising the kind of man it took to be able to work in such harsh surrounds. She would soon find out.

Ducking to the staff toilets, she grimaced at the state of the seat, and the copper stains in the bowl. Why some men couldn't wipe up after themselves was beyond her. She took a double glance to make sure there were no snakes hiding within, or redbacks on the toilet seat – a gal couldn't be too careful. Ten point check done, she resolved to hover just above the seat, deciding she would give it a good going-over with bleach later on. Knickers around her ankles, and just about to do the balancing act, she spotted a flash of green jump between her legs and splat onto the concrete floor. She screamed, stumbling forwards before face-planting on the door. Rubbing her head, she turned slowly, horrified … and spotted a green tree frog sitting on the window ledge above the toilet, eyeing her accusingly.

Clutching her chest, she breathed a sigh of relief that it wasn't a creature far more sinister. 'Far out, buddy, you almost gave me a heart damn attack.'

The frog ribbeted, as if replying.

With her heart rate returning to somewhat normal, Melody chuckled to herself. Her need to pee all but gone now, she tugged her knickers back up and, after washing her hands, returned to the kitchen. Not long after, and right on time, she heard Zai's familiar husky voice approaching, along with the clomping of boots along the timber floorboards in beat with the clips of a dog's nails. Irritatingly, her stomach dropped then swooped, and as much as she fought to remain nonchalant while she stirred the boiling water into oblivion, her breath caught, just like it always did every time he was anywhere near. My goodness. What powers did this man possess?

After kindly reminding the old station dog, Harold, to stay put on his blanket by the back door, Zai's knuckles rapped against the timber door as he strode in. She turned to find him looking at her in that mischievous way he did, his blue eyes piercing. The room suddenly felt several degrees hotter. 'Hey, you.'

'Evening, Melody. Something smells bloody awesome.' With long strides, he brushed past her, the scent of leather, sun-heated denim, diesel and heavy-duty hand soap lingering. 'What's cooking, good-looking?'

She dared a sideways glance while stifling a grin. 'Bit forward for a first dinner, don't you think?'

'I always like to say it how I see it.' He shrugged nonchalantly. 'Besides, no sense in beating around the bush out here, seeing we are smack-bang in the centre of it.' His dark, cropped hair only accentuated his chiselled features and dimple-clad cheeks. Lifting the lid of the stew pot and sniffing it like it was the most amazing scent he'd ever inhaled, he flashed her a swoon-worthy smile. 'Oh my god, is this what I think it is?'

'If you're thinking it's beef stroganoff, you're correct.'

'Man, the guys are going to go nuts over this.' He plonked the lid back down.

'I hope so.' She found herself softening, relaxing in his presence. 'So, how'd your day go?'

'Yeah, can't complain.' He flicked the kettle on and turned to rest against the kitchen bench. 'How 'bout you, are you settling in okay?'

'Aside from abruptly meeting the green frog in the staff loo and being chased away from the chook pen by a very grumpy duck.' The low rumble of his voice whipped a warm sensation through her. 'I'm settling in as good as I can.'

'Yeah, Plucka is very protective of his girls. I swear, he thinks he's a chicken. But don't worry, he'll get used to you soon enough. And the smiling croaker in the loo is named Kermit. He's been residing there for the last couple of years.'

'Ha, Kermit and Plucka. Classic.' She chuckled, shaking her head in delight. 'Only in the outback would someone meet characters like that.' Her thoughts went to her cat, Magic, and her heart squeezed tight. The rise of sudden emotions shocked her. She quickly blinked back hot tears, straightening her shoulders as if it would somehow stop her blubbering.

'Hey, what's up?' Zai's hands, square and strong, came to rest against the bench as he closed a little of the distance between them.

'I'm just not so used to the isolation, I suppose, that's all.' She wasn't about to say she missed her cat, and besides, she was telling the truth – the isolation was foreign. 'I thought it wouldn't bother me, but it takes a bit of getting used to, being here by myself all day long, if I'm being honest.'

'Of course it does. You'd be used to having people everywhere, coming from the big smoke. It's the polar opposite out here.' He gave her back a friendly pat. 'Is there anything I can do to help you feel less isolated?' He dropped his hand back to his pocket.

She could think of quite a few things and immediately felt bad doing so, being a married woman. 'No, all good, but thank you for caring. I'll be right. Just gotta tough it out and get used to it, which I'm sure I will, given time.'

He regarded her as if trying to read her thoughts. 'There's nothing to be gained from trying to be tough out here, you know that, right? You can just be yourself, however you might be feeling, at any given time.'

Something about what he said, or maybe the way he said it – she wasn't sure what – got her defences fired up. 'Is that so?'

'Yup.' He slid his thumbs into the belt loops of his jeans and grinned, as if he found her anger amusing.

She looked away for a few brief moments, not even sure why she felt so challenged. 'What makes you think I'm just trying to be tough? I might just *be* tough.' She swept her hands to her hips and looked him straight in the eye, arching an eyebrow.

'Oh, trust me, I know you have a quiet strength in you, Miss Melody. I just want you to know you're not alone here, that's all. And if you're struggling with anything, anything at all, I'm all ears.'

'Well … thank you.' Feeling less defensive, she dropped her hands from her hips. 'But sometimes, we have to fake being tough to make ourselves believe it too.' As she had through her failed marriage, then losing her mum and now, finding her father.

'Ain't that the bloody truth.' He plucked a few peanuts from a jar and tossed them into his mouth.

Melody went with the conversation – it was better than an uncomfortable silence. 'So, tell me, Wellstone, do you consider yourself a toughie?'

'What you see is what you get with me, whatever that might be.'

She recalled him mentioning how Sarah and Matt had helped him through some tough times, and something inside of her wanted him to open up to her about whatever it was, seeing as he was probing her. 'So easy, breezy, would describe you, hey?'

'Yeah, pretty much.'

She looked at him with scepticism. 'So nothing ever really fazes you?'

'Nope, my life is easy come easy go.'

'You have no issues at all, with life, or friends, or family?' He didn't reply, turning his suddenly intense focus to making himself a coffee, as his Adam's apple bobbed in his throat. She'd clearly hit a nerve. She'd gone too far, all because she felt some strange defensive mechanism kick in – most likely because that was what she was used to with Antonio, or possibly it was the fact that she was keeping that part of her life hidden. She relaxed her stance and touched her hand to Zai's arm. 'I'm sorry, I didn't mean to be so direct. Are you okay?'

'Yup, all good.' His gaze met hers for a fleeting moment before he flicked his baby blues away. 'Would you like a coffee while I'm at it?'

She knew he was diverting the conversation, and that was okay – they all had their right to privacy. 'Yes, please. White with two sugars.'

'Nice, like me.' He smiled a little now.

Melody lifted the lid of the pot and gave it a stir. 'You have it the same?'

'Nope, I'm white and sweet.' He chuckled, easing the atmosphere instantly. 'I take mine black with no sugar.'

'Straight and strong, kinda like you too,' she offered, playfully.

Grinning, he passed her a steaming cup. 'Spot on.'

'Thanks.' Going to take her first sip, she accidentally spilt it, scalding herself. 'Shit.' She quickly placed it down on the bench and spun to find Zai much closer than she'd expected.

He already had the cold tap running. 'Here.' He took her hand and held it beneath the steady stream of cooling water.

Melody didn't know whether she was unsteady from the pain, or from his touch. 'Far out, it bloody hurts.' She wriggled on the spot, blinking back an onslaught of pain-induced waterworks.

'You keep it under the water and I'll go grab something more to help.' Returning from the fridge, he gently manoeuvred her and rubbed some soothing aloe vera on the red welts. Then, to her surprise, but also to her delight, he very deliberately raised her hand to his lips and blew. The coolness worked a treat, or was it just him rendering her senseless? Caught up in the moment, she went very still. Her wrist tingled where his fingers were gently wrapped around it. Flustered, she blinked faster, determined not to let him know what effect he was having on her with something so simple.

'Does that feel better?' His voice was low and husky.

All she could do was stare at his mouth. A few breath-held moments passed until she snapped back. 'Yes, thanks, Zai. I'm all good now.' He released her wrist.

The edges of the mouth she was imagining kissing quirked. 'Righto. Tell me what I can do to help you get dinner on the table,' he said.

'You don't have to help.'

'I know, but what if I want to, Miss Melody?'

Melody's heart melted, and she fought to not visibly swoon over him. 'In that case, you can set the table, if you like, and I'll get everything into serving bowls.' Man oh one hell of a man, he was a charmer – she leant back against the kitchen bench to give her weak legs some support.

He got to it. 'Make sure you let me know if you need a hand, seeing yours is hurting.'

'Thanks Zai.' She really appreciated this man for all that he was showing her he was.

Minutes later, a small wiry bloke wandered in beside a tall lanky bloke, both of them laughing as if they'd just heard the funniest thing in their lives – she couldn't help but giggle at their snorting chuckles. Slim, the man she'd heard so much about from her father, soon followed – she liked his warm, genuine energy instantly. Then in laboured the man who could only be Hasselhoof, complaining about the day. All of the men were exactly as her father and Zai had described. She was looking forward to their first dinner together, where she could get to know them a little more.

* * *

Zai couldn't stop staring across the dinner table – damn, she was gorgeous.

The day had dragged on and into forever. Dinnertime hadn't come quick enough for him, the thought of laying his eyes on Melody again making his heart race that little bit faster all day long. He enjoyed being the one to introduce the men to her, had felt a little bit more of an important part of her life in doing so, and could tell by the initial reactions of Showbags and Tumbles, and their keen interest across the dining table, that they found Melody's striking features and wittiness just as captivating as he did. And it was okay to admire her from afar, but if they tried to make a move, watch out. His protectiveness was something he tried to put down to the fact that she was Matt's daughter, and nothing more – well, nothing that he wanted to admit.

Her head tilted to the side as she listened intently, latte-coloured eyes sparkling. She entranced all the blokes, joining in on their banter and conversations. While laughing at one of Showbags's jokes, Zai watched her yank the hair tie wrapped around her ponytail free. Blonde curls fell over her shoulders, her mane so striking, he longed to touch it. She ran absent fingers through the ends before tugging it back into a knot atop her head.

With his stomach filled to bursting with her amazing food, double servings of it in fact, he fastened his fingers behind his head as he stretched his legs out beneath the table, resting back and enjoying the full-bodied, carefree sound of her laughter. The blokes' usual repartee had her in stiches, especially Slim's animated mannerisms, the energy of someone new to chat to giving a fresh vibe to the common kitchen and an added boost to the men's morale – all but Hasselhoof, anyway. Ignoring the old bugger's permanent frown, Zai focused all his attention on Melody, and the upward curve of her full, kissable lips – he wanted to do all he could to hear and see more of her merriment while she was here. This gorgeous woman deserved to smile. All the damn time. He was going to make it his mission to make sure she did.

When he'd first crossed paths with her in Matt's kitchen that fateful day, her unhappiness had hung around her like a suffocating cloak, which was no wonder given she'd recently lost her mother to such a dreadful disease. He'd watched his very own grandmother die of it a few years back – it had been heartbreaking. And a woman needed her mum, no matter how old – he couldn't imagine losing his own mum, as crazy as she sometimes drove him. Witnessing Melody's pain and fear that day, he'd so badly wanted to smooth her hair back from her tear-stained face, to comfort her, to take her into his arms and kiss her, to tell her he was going to make sure everything was well in her world again. But knight in shining armour didn't fit him, and a damsel in distress certainly didn't become her. As the song went, they were more like two lost souls swimming in a fishbowl. Heading into town had been both to give the Walsh family the privacy they needed for such a revelation, but also because he'd had to get away from her, fast. She did something to him he had never, ever, experienced until now.

'Cat got your tongue, Hasselhoof?' Showbags queried, playfulness twinkling in his gaze as he proverbially prodded the village grump. 'You haven't said a word all night.'

Removing the toothpick from his mouth, Hasselhoof frowned even deeper across the table. 'Do me a favour and shut ya trap, would ya, Showbags?'

Showbags pretended to be gobsmacked. 'Gee whizz, Hasselhoof, anyone would think you didn't like me.'

'I don't like anyone. Now eff off and leave me the hell alone,' Hasselhoof protested, adding a string of expletives beneath his breath still loud enough for them all to hear it.

'Now, now, I know the whole world is out to get you somehow, but how about some manners at the dinner table, huh?' Showbags was stirring that imaginary wooden spoon, and every man was holding back a grin. 'We have female company, or hadn't you noticed?'

'Bloody hell, get stuffed, would ya?' Hasselhoof threw back the last of his orange juice.

Showbags patted his belly. 'I already am stuffed, thanks to Melody's fine cooking.'

Glaring like a micky bull, Hasselhoof looked like he was about to detonate.

Slim and Tumbles glanced at each other, rolling their eyes and shrugging.

Zai cleared his throat. 'Come on now, lads, calm your farms, would you?' He tossed Melody an apologetic glance. 'I'm sure Melody doesn't want to listen to your bellyaching on her first night. Let her ease into it, would you?'

'Yeah, I second that.' Slim grinned. 'Otherwise she might run for the bloody hills, and after a taste of her cooking, I wanna see more of where that came from.' He tipped his head to the side. 'Actually, I better be careful, or I might not fit into my suit for my big day.'

Huffing, Hasselhoof offered a glower worthy of killing every man at the table. Standing, he rinsed his plate off, thumped it into the dishwasher and stormed out without a goodnight to any of them, or a thank you to Melody.

'Wow,' Melody said, smirking. 'Did he have a bad day?'

'Every day is a bad day for Hasselhoof,' Showbags said, standing and gathering the plates.

'Yeah, don't worry about them two, they do that all the time,' Zai offered.

Melody shrugged. 'I actually find it amusing.'

'Yeah, so do we,' Slim added, joining Showbags and Tumbles at the sink.

Melody went to stand, but Zai stopped her. 'We always clean up, seeing as you cook.'

'Oh, okay. Thank you,' she said, eyeing them a little oddly, like she'd never seen a group of men clear up before.

Fifteen minutes later, Slim, Tumbles and Showbags had said their thanks and goodnights and wandered off to bed. Zai was finally alone with Melody, in the dark, with nothing but the call of the cattle around them as they wandered towards the homestead, old Harold hot on their heels. Stars scattered the velvety black, and the half-moon's silvery light made her appear angelic – lord give him strength to resist his urges. It would be so easy right now to lean in and kiss her, to tell her how beautiful he found her, inside and out. It shocked him how comfortable he felt envisioning doing just that. The stockman lifestyle, footloose and fancy-free, had suited him down to the bone. He didn't need to complicate things in his mind – he knew this was out of his control and that she was out of his league. Here was a woman who took life seriously, and it intrigued him and, in a very strange way, intimidated him. Intelligent, sassy, witty, independent, beautiful – she was an absolute catch. Not to mention that Matt would most probably skin him alive if he tried to lay a finger upon her silky-soft skin. And with his track record, he couldn't blame his mate.

Not feeling a need to fill the silences, he quietly walked alongside her for a little while longer as she stared up at the night's extravagance, a look of wonder on her face, seemingly lost in her thoughts. It was almost as if he wasn't even there. He liked how she was so content in his company. The night couldn't get much more magical than this. But then, as if right on cue, a shooting star burst across the sky, capturing their attention.

'Oh my gosh!' She pushed a lock of hair behind her ear and turned to him, looking at him in a way that made him worry that his attraction to her was written all over his face. 'That's the very first shooting star I've ever seen.'

'Get out, is not.'

'Is too.' Her eyes were wide.

'Well, in that case, you'd better make a wish.'

For a few magical moments, she lit up even brighter. Then, her eyes fluttered closed. Her lips moved, but her words were quieter than a whisper. When she opened her eyes again, she flashed him a smile that almost sent him to his knees.

They continued on in a companionable silence. Now it was his turn to stare – down at his boots while they walked while he tried to rein in his racing heart. They reached the path that forked one way to the homestead and the other way to his cottage out back, and although he wanted to whisk her inside and send her to places he hoped she'd never been to with another man, he tucked his hands into his jeans pockets and bid her goodnight.

'Catch you tomorrow then, miss.'

'I reckon you will, Zai, given we both live round here.'

He chuckled. 'Ha, yeah, good point.'

Their eyes met. He almost felt as if he were on the very first date of his life. But this wasn't a date, and she wasn't interested in him.

'Night, Zai.' Her sweet singsong voice rippled into the darkness.

He met her gaze. 'Night, Melody. Sleep tight.'

'Will do.' She turned, offering a soft smile over her shoulder. 'You too.'

CHAPTER 10

After almost two weeks at Rosalee Station – the cliché of time flying because she was having fun becoming more applicable as the days passed – Melody awoke with an emotional hangover. It was as if someone had taken her heart from her chest and wrung it out. The deep ache of losing her mother, the sudden rise of the roller-coaster ride of meeting her father, and the dip back to earth as she'd landed herself the job as camp cook had all come crashing down like a tidal wave. She had good reason to feel so emotionally exhausted, and knew it was a sign to stop ignoring her feelings, and deal with them; the good, the bad, the ugly, and the not-so-bad too. Running from the pain of her messy life would only work for so long.

She needed to take the time while she was in the outback to regroup, redesign and restore her life back to the way she wanted it to be. And that certainly didn't include staying married just to save her share of the café. Antonio could try to bully her into remaining his wife as much as he wanted to – if she had to lose everything, so be it. Anything beyond that, though, she was still very unsure about: where she'd live, what she'd do for work. Hopefully, the right path would reveal itself.

Days had taken a familiar rhythm. Starting with waking before dawn to prepare the men's breakfast and packed lunches, to attending the chook pen and veggie patch, the washing and upkeep of the house, and venturing around the place on the quad bike with old Harold as her chaperone – the lovable old cattle dog was growing on her – and ending with the fluorescent light being flicked off as she left the common kitchen and made her way back to the homestead accompanied by Zai each and every night. Much to Melody's surprise, she felt like part of the furniture and, most fundamentally of all, part of the crew – even Hasselhoof had warmed to her, in his own kind of odd way. And the landscape that had at first terrified her with its unforgiving vastness – there was just something about the place that made her feel a part of it all, as though her heart was beating in tune with Mother Nature's rhythmic pulse, something the hullaballoo of the city drowned out. That wasn't to say she didn't miss having everything at her fingertips, but there was also something to be said for making do, for being happy with the simple things, for valuing those who valued her.

The house phone had her dashing from the laundry, just in time to grab it. 'Hello.'

'Hey, Melody. Just me, checking in for the day.' The sound of Beau's delighted squeals and the yapping of Duchess momentarily halted her dad's voice. 'Are the blokes still behaving themselves?'

She treasured that her father had stuck to his promise and called her every day to see how she was going. 'Hey, yes, they sure are …' *Dad*. She thought it but wasn't comfortable enough to say it out loud yet, and she wasn't sure how Matt would receive it either. 'They've all made an extra effort to help me feel super welcome, well, apart from Hasselhoof but I'm not taking that personally.'

'Ha, yes, he's a grumpy old bugger. I'm happy to know they're behaving themselves, otherwise I'd have to come and sort them out.' Matt chuckled. 'But seriously, I knew they'd take care of you. They're a good bunch of fellas.'

'They are.' She wandered into the kitchen to make herself a cuppa. 'How's Sarah going with her final exams?'

'Really good, she's almost finished, thankfully.' He sighed. 'She's so exhausted, the poor thing. Sitting up all hours of the night to study is taking a toll. I have to keep reminding her she's four months pregnant and she needs to rest up too.'

Melody so admired Sarah's drive to follow her dream. 'You must be so proud of her.'

'I am, and I'm super proud of you too, making a go of it out there.' The smile he would have been sporting shone through his buoyant tone.

'Thanks, that means a lot.'

'How the isolation going? Is it bothering you as much as it did at first?'

'Not as much.' Gazing out the window towards the horse paddock, she shrugged. 'The place is certainly growing on me.'

'See? I told you it would, love.'

'Yes, indeed you did.' The kettle whistled like billyo, and she plucked it from the gas stove and poured the hot water into her cup. 'Have you worked out when you're arriving?'

'We have, finally. If all goes to plan, and there aren't any hiccups with the motorhome along the way, we should be arriving there around the twenty-seventh.'

She quickly did the maths. 'Oh, a little over three weeks away.'

'Yeah, sorry it's a bit later than expected, sweetheart. We were trying to have a couple of weeks out there before Slim's big day, but looks like it'll be just under a week. I hope you don't mind us crashing the homestead once we get there.'

'Of course I don't.' Her gaze fixed on a whirlwind, tossing red dust and leaves in a spiral across the back yard – they desperately needed rain. 'It'll be nice to have some company. The homestead is way too big for one person.'

'I get what you're saying. Homesteads are notoriously built to welcome many people within the walls. I suppose you can think of it as a safe haven of sorts from the elements and to give people a chance to catch their breath with loved ones before facing it all over again.'

'Wow.' Her hand went to her heart. 'That's a beautiful way to put it.'

'Glad you think so.' There was a short pause. 'Righto, I'd better get a move on. I've got me some bulls to train. We'll chat again tomorrow?'

'Okay, will do. Have a good day.'

'You too, sweetheart, and don't go spoiling those blokes too much.' His hearty chuckle ended the phone call.

Wandering back to the hallway, she placed the phone back into the holder. Then, as she stepped out of the homestead, the flyscreen door slapped closed behind her. It was just shy of nine, and the sun was already commanding the wide expanse of blue. Padding across the verandah to where she liked to lean against the railing, she scanned the endless vista while sipping her coffee. Her father had been right – it was another world out here. A world she felt blessed to be a part of.

Swatting a fly from her face, she groaned when it refused to bugger off, and instead held a welcome party for more of its buzzing friends. Recalling the hoard of moths and flying ants she'd witnessed kamikaze into the blue glow of the zapper last night, she glanced towards where it hung on the corner of the awning. They were damn persistent and bred tougher than city flies. Just like the men, she thought humorously.

Her thoughts drifted to Zai, and the way he always made her feel so at ease in his company, as though she'd known him for most of her life. She also couldn't deny the fact that she was extremely attracted to him – what woman wouldn't be? But she shouldn't be. Her life was messy enough without adding a holiday fling to the mix.

And that's all it could be, given she'd be returning to Sydney once her stint as camp cook was over. It was easier said than done though, when it came to Zai Wellstone and his commanding presence. Even if she could ignore his soulful blue eyes, ripped body, and nerves-of-steel-with-a-heart-of-gold personality, it was the very first time in her life she'd met a man who really listened and wanted to know more, no matter how much she told him about herself. And apart from this, Zai was intelligent, and witty and interesting, and thoughtful, and … heck, the list just went on and on. But give it time, she thought. They always showed their true colours after a while. Antonio had certainly taught her that.

She turned her attention to the glint of a sloping roof just beyond the first dam. She hadn't ventured that far as yet, instead choosing to go in the opposite direction when she went for a ride on the four-wheeler – there was more life to be seen that way. But now the ramshackle shack tempted her, as did the glimmer of the body of water beside it. Finishing her coffee, she left her cup on the banister, tugged on her boots and descended the stairs two at a time. Twenty minutes later, after a brisk stroll down an earthen track while keeping her eyes peeled for snakes, she pushed her sunglasses to the top of her head and tried the rusty door handle, not expecting it to open. Nonetheless, her curiosity got the better of her.

Butting it with her shoulder, she felt it budge, and one more shove had it swinging open. She was almost too afraid to peek inside, but after a cloud of dust cleared, she cautiously stepped into the gloom. Morning sunlight spiked through holes in the high-pitched roof and struck the timber floor like spears, the dust dancing upon its goldenness. Cobwebs spanned every corner, the intricate interlacing a work of spider art. Discarded farm equipment, rusted with age, was piled along the far wall. Drums were lined up alongside it all.

She sucked in a sharp breath. An old ute was parked up in the farthest corner, the side of it crumpled in, as was the roof. Her heart skidded to an almighty stop. Was this the ute her father had rolled the day he'd hit a bull and lost his darling Eve? A young girl who would have been her sister, had she lived …

The notion was deeply distressing. It took Melody a few moments to get her feet to move, and she took slow, cautious steps towards it. A thick layer of dust covered every inch of it, though a tarp had been tossed over the bonnet. She placed a hand on the windowsill and bent to peer inside, wincing when her finger caught on broken glass. She brought her fingertip to her mouth, the small droplets of blood tasting metallic. The inside of the ute was crushed and crumpled and scattered with shards of windscreen. She could almost imagine the mayhem, as if she'd just stepped back in time, and was watching the horrific scene unfold. Straightening, she felt her heart ache for the horror, fear and heartbreak Matt and Sarah would have suffered that day, and the pain they would have endured every day thereafter. The grief with the loss of a young child, she imagined, would be something a person would never be able to move past, but only grow somewhat used to.

'There you are.'

Melody jerked out of her thoughts and blinked back tears as she spun to see Zai. 'Holy crap, you scared the life out of me.' She sniffed hard and smiled through her anguish.

'I'm sorry, didn't mean to.' He came to her side. 'What in the heck are you doing in here?' he asked, looking at her then the ute, then back at her again.

'I was just exploring and came across this.' She glanced back at the mess of glass and metal. 'I gather it's the …' She choked on the last words.

'Yeah, it is.' He cleared his throat, as though uncomfortable with the conversation. 'Your grandparents wanted to get it out of sight, out of mind.' He half shrugged. 'It's not like you can get a tow truck out here, so this was the next best thing.'

'It's so sad.' She shook her head, a well of emotions almost engulfing her. 'I can't even begin to imagine what they went through.'

'It was pretty tough.' Reaching out, Zai gave her arm a gentle squeeze. 'You right?'

'Yeah, sorry.' She sniffled and wiped her damp eyes. 'I just feel for their loss.'

'It took a long time for them to get past the grief of it, and for your dad to move past the guilt. He went to hell and back, torturing himself over it. We weren't sure he was going to make it through at one stage.' He cleared his throat again – clearly it was hard for him to talk about. 'I don't think your dad knows the ute's in here. We don't really use this building anymore, so probably don't mention it if possible, hey.'

'Oh, of course not. I never saw it.' She took steps to distance herself from it, and Zai joined her.

It felt good to step back outside into the sunshine, into the present moment. 'How did you know I was down this way?'

'I followed your boot prints.' He grinned. 'Tool of the trade out here, being able to track.'

'Wow, clever. So, what were you hunting me down for?' Tucking her hands into her back pockets, she tipped her head away from the sun.

'Oh, I just wanted to give you a heads-up that me and the men are heading out to fix a few of the fences. We'll head back for lunch around one, if that's okay with you?'

'Yeah, of course it is.'

'Righto then. You heading back to the homestead?'

'Sure am.'

'I'll walk you back then head off.'

They chatted comfortably about this and that, and before she knew it, her heavy heart had lifted and he was bidding her farewell. Climbing aboard the horse he'd left tethered at the front of the homestead, he tipped his hat, turned and galloped away. She waved him off, wandered past the sheets she'd hung out earlier, flapping in the breeze, kicked her boots off at the back door, and stepped into the welcoming coolness of the house. Enjoying the challenge of creating menus based on frozen and canned foods, with a little fresh produce thrown in from the garden, she pondered what she would make them for lunch, and then dinner and sweets – to their delight, she'd told them they'd always get dessert in her kitchen. A bushman's usual diet of steak, stew, corned beef and damper wasn't anything to complain about, but she wanted to give them food with a little more oomph, a little more pizzazz, and one very fetching stockman in particular, she wanted to sprinkle his serving with a little more … something. Deciding to make her lemon meringue pie and custard along with spaghetti bolognese made from slow-cooked oxtail and some homemade garlic bread, she headed over to the common kitchen, stopping to pick some fresh bush lemons along the way, and began gathering everything she needed from the pantry. For lunch, she was going to whip up beef and bacon pies and an apple and cinnamon teacake.

Two hours later, she'd achieved all that, leaving the oxtail to simmer in the slow cooker for the afternoon and the bread to rise. Instead of waiting around for the guys, she decided she'd do them a favour. She eagerly grabbed the two-way. 'Zai, Slimbo, anyone, do you copy?'

The two-way crackled to life at the other end and Zai's unmistakable husky voice carried to her. 'Howdy, cook. What's up?'

'I reckon I need a little adventure, so how about I bring lunch to you guys?'

'Oh, that'd be tops, Melody, but are you sure?'

'Yes, a hundred percent.'

'Righto, well, to get to us, turn down the track beside the arena and just keep following it for about fifteen clicks. Just don't turn off and you can't go wrong.'

'Okay, got it.' It didn't sound too complicated.

'Excellent, see you soon. And don't be afraid to give me a shout on the two-way if you run into any trouble or find yourself lost, okay?'

'Yup, done.' So there she had it, the rendezvous point was sorted – now, she just had to get there.

Determined to prove she could hold her own in the challenging landscape, she packed the men's lunches into the front of the old LandCruiser and headed round to the driver's side. Harold appeared from beneath the shade of the cottage and lumbered over. She gestured for him to hop in, glad for his doggy company. With him settled in the passenger seat, she climbed up behind the wheel. How hard could it be, taking the men's food out to them?

Half an hour and four cattle grids later, she felt as if she were about to drive off the edge of the earth. She was starting to worry she'd taken a wrong turn somewhere along the way, which would have been virtually impossible, but not entirely unachievable given her inexperience out here, when she spotted them over the far side of a fenced paddock. As the men spotted her too, hands shot in the air to acknowledge her, some of them holding their hats. Deciding to pull up in the shade of the only cluster of trees for miles, she climbed out and started to set the food up on a tablecloth she'd flung out on the tray of the four-wheel drive, out of the reach of the bull ants scurrying like lines of soldiers across the red earth. Harold got himself comfy beneath the LandCruiser.

The sound of galloping hooves brought her head out from the passenger-side floor where she was collecting an Esky filled with icy cans of soft drink and a basket with pannikins and a couple of flasks of tea and coffee. When she saw who was heading straight for her, her heart skipped a beat, then another. She quickly reminded herself to breathe. Zai Wellstone was impossibly handsome and, on top of that, chivalrous. Until crossing paths with him a month ago, she didn't think men like him existed.

'Well, howdy there, Miss Melody.' He pulled his horse to a stop just short of her.

If only he knew she was really a Mrs. 'Howdy, to you too, Mister Wellstone.' She wished she could see his eyes, hidden behind his sunglasses and shaded by the rim of his Akubra.

As he dismounted and his boots hit the dusty ground, she glanced to where his open-neck blue shirt was tucked into his jeans and her stomach fluttered with anticipation. For what, exactly, she wasn't sure, and she quickly tried to cover up her attraction by momentarily glancing over his shoulder to where Tumbles, Showbags, Slim and Hasselhoof were approaching on their horses.

'In all the places we could bump into each other.' Zai lifted his hat off, removing the shadows from his gorgeous smile. 'Fancy seeing you here.'

She laughed at his playful banter, her heart ramping up to a fast trot.

Joining her, he pushed his sunglasses to the top of his head. 'You're an absolute trooper, coming all the way out here.'

'You guys are busy.' She shrugged his compliment off. 'So no biggie.'

'I beg to differ.' He went to take the Esky from her. 'Here, let me help you unpack.'

She pulled it back towards her – she hadn't come this far to be fussed over. 'I got it.'

'So do I,' he said, yanking it free from her with a smirk that only deepened his dimples. 'You're just like your old man, you know that? Stubborn as a mule.'

'I kick like one too,' she said, watching how his biceps strained with the weight of the Esky.

'I believe you.'

Melody couldn't help but chuckle at the look on his face – this man was infuriatingly, captivatingly addictive.

Spotting the spread laid out on the tablecloth – buttery flaky pies, moist apple teacake, packets of salt and vinegar chips, a bottle of tomato sauce, a container of mushy peas for the pie connoisseurs – his eyes widened to saucers. 'Holy moly, you've gone to heaps of trouble by the looks of this feast.' He spun back to her, his grin from ear to ear. 'You are totally spoiling us, Melody, you know that, right?'

She half shrugged. 'Ahh, it's nothing. Honestly, it gives me something to pass the time, cooking up a storm.'

The other four men climbed from their saddles and joined them, and there was a chorus of oohs and ahhs – even Hasselhoof looked somewhat impressed, his frown lines the least creased she'd ever seen them. It made her happy to bring such pure delight to their faces with her food.

'Ladies first,' Slim said, waving an arm to her.

'No, you guys go for it. I'm just going to take a breather before I tuck in.'

'You don't need to twist my arm. This looks awesome,' Showbags said with a grin, his plate at the ready.

'Too right it does. I feel like I've died and gone to heaven,' Tumbles added, looking like a kid in a candy store.

'She's bloody awesome, hey guys?' Zai said proudly, tossing an enigmatic glance in her direction.

'Bloody oath she is,' Slim agreed, grabbing two pies then smothering them in mushy peas. 'I'm going to lose my newfound figure with you around, Melody. Sherrie's going to be right pissed off with me, but I'm a man who can't help himself around good food, I tell ya.'

A blush rose on Melody's cheeks. She still wasn't used to their effusive and enthusiastic praise. Something about their gratification as they licked their lips and filled their plates meant more than the great reviews she'd regularly got in the newspapers back in Sydney. It was wholesome food versus posh nosh – the latter was exhausting. This down-to-earth style of cooking for equally down-to-earth men was elating. Allowing the men to grab their fill, she carefully poured hot tea into a battered enamel mug, topped it off with some sugar and milk, stirred, then sighed with pleasure when she took a sip, the sweet warmth washing away the dust from her throat. With all five men settled beneath the dappled shade, she grabbed some lunch for herself and nestled down among them.

'So, tell me, Tumbles, what event earned you the nickname?' she asked, licking sauce and mushy peas from her fingers.

Tumbles took a long swig from his lemonade, burped, excused himself, then grinned waywardly. 'Well, I was riding this old nag when I was about seventeen, and this big old grasshopper smacked her fair and square in the right eye. In a split second, it was on for young and old and she reared up like a bucking bronco and sent me flying through the air like a cannonball.'

'Oh my gosh.' She tried not to laugh but couldn't help herself – the animated look on his face was priceless.

'And trust me when I tell ya, Melds, that wasn't even the worst of it,' he added with another playful grimace, the shortening of her name a first from him. He shook his head, as though recalling the very day, tutting.

She waited for a few seconds, then a few seconds more. 'Come on, don't leave me hanging.'

He snapped to, sucking in a breath. 'So, because I was trying to hang on so hard when she was bucking, I went and tore the muscles in my groin. I was hobbling around with the gait of a man who looked as though I had an entire tree trunk up my butt.'

Every man alongside Melody shuddered. 'Oh hell, Tumbles, that would have hurt like hell.' She winced.

'Tell me about it. I couldn't walk properly for almost a month.' He nodded, his expression turning grave. 'And to make matters even worse, I couldn't even you-know-what with my girlfriend for almost two months. It was the worst time of my life.'

Melody couldn't help but laugh at his expression. 'Sorry, I really shouldn't laugh.'

Tumbles offered her a grin. 'Why not, Melds? It's a funny story.'

'And since that fateful day, Tumbles has lived up to his name with vigour,' Zai chuckled, shaking his head.

'Bloody oath he has,' Slim added, laughing. 'The number of times I've peeled your sorry arse off the ground, Tumbles, I've lost count.'

Tumbles grinned wider. 'At least I keep on keeping on.'

This sent everyone but Hasselhoof into chuckling mirth.

Melody enjoyed the cheerful repartee – it was so nice to have a good old belly laugh. She felt Zai looking at her, and her stomach fluttered when she met his eyes, his meaningful glance heating her cheeks and sparking her insides.

She squirmed with his unwavering attention. 'What are you staring at?' she asked quietly once the men started talking between themselves again.

'You should laugh more often,' he said, softly enough for only her to hear. 'It suits you.'

'Thanks.' She smiled self-consciously. 'You guys help me to smile. Quite a lot.'

'Glad to be of service.' He grinned and tipped his hat. 'I'll make sure to do it more often.'

Melody couldn't help basking in the warmth of this man – he was truly amazing.

CHAPTER 11

Halfway through her six-week stint at Rosalee Station, Melody couldn't quite put her finger on what exactly was wrong, but something didn't feel right. She'd woken at four am, edgy and overwhelmingly emotional. The silence she had sought comfort in over the past three weeks had become oppressive, so much so that she found herself smothered by it. Like a sailboat without a mast, she felt as if she were drifting aimlessly in a stormy sea of doubt and hurt and fear and confusion. She had been so sure in the days after she'd arrived at the station, optimistic that she was on the right path, hopeful she would have an 'aha!' moment, one that would instantly tip her topsy-turvy world the right way up.

But old habits die hard. Her deeply ingrained trait of second-guessing everything about herself was storming to the forefront, like soldiers going to battle. Was she running away from where she was meant to be in life? Was she overdramatising what Antonio had done? Was she, like he had roared at her the day she'd left, the root cause of their marital woes? Should she be back there, try to fix things?

Hot oil spat from the pan of sizzling bacon, landing on her arm, snapping her from her incessant thoughts. Cursing, she tried to ignore the sting of the searing fat while flashes of vivid clarity – of plates smashing, of demeaning comments, of him calling her terrible names, of him being caught, red-handed, with that other woman but then blaming it on her, telling her that it was because she wasn't doing her duty in the bedroom, forget the fact her mother was dying – permeated, stealing her breath and bringing rise to hot tears. Huffing, she fervently blinked them back. She'd cried enough over him. It was high time she faced the cold hard truth that he was all that the psychologist had warned her of. She needed to wean herself off the unrealistic fantasy of them ever being happily married, had to find a way to untangle herself from feeling like it was her job to fix him, to make him a better man, and to find a way to accept that she might also lose the café when she walked away.

Over the years of her stormy marriage, she had become a master of blotting things out, of finding consolation despite the seemingly forgotten wrongdoings of her husband. But the ghosts of her past were making themselves known – they'd been relentless in her sleep and even now, hours later, no matter how much she tried to ward them off, they were almost suffocating.

Bustling about the common kitchen, she was fighting to keep herself in the present. The wall she'd built over the years in her mind was one she didn't dare look behind too often, for the fear of the memories which lurked there, but now, here, within Mother Nature's embrace, without the distraction of the city and the innate need to just get though another day, she was finding herself peeking around the corners more and more, and the glimpses of what Antonio had done to her over the years were shockingly malicious, contrived and deliberate. Somewhere in her unconscious, she knew that, but it was a damn sight harder making herself truly believe it because when she did, it would mean she'd been living a lie, had been taken advantage of by a man she'd thought loved her, had been stupid enough to stay, to believe his apologies and half-hearted efforts to reel her in just enough to fool her again – day after day, year after year.

She'd been trained from very early on to push aside her gut feelings, to ignore her inner voice, to turn a blind eye to her bodily sensations, and over time had been moulded by him to believe his nasty untruths, all the while striving for his attention, starving for the occasional bursts of what she'd thought at the time to be love.

A broken man had gone and broken her. The bastard had made her his mirror.

Even though she'd accepted she had to leave the marriage, the reality of what she'd lived and survived came crashing down upon her, and she was suddenly desperate to get outside, to feel the heat of the sun, as if it would somehow scorch the hurt from her heart. Flicking the gas cooker off, she turned and, with one long stride after the other, rushed out the screen door.

Her rushed steps turned into a frenzied sprint and before she knew it, she was tearing across the house paddock, destination unknown. Reaching the far fence out of breath, she dropped to her knees, looked to the heavens and, with a deep inhalation, screamed louder than she ever had before. Her cries echoed all around her. She continued to do this until the wind had been taken from her, until she felt she had nothing left, until her throat was raw. Only then did she give in to whatever this was trying to erupt from deep inside of her – comprehension, consciousness, awakening, pure rage. Only then did she collapse forwards, spent, vulnerable, sobbing so hard it felt as if she were crying her tortured soul right out of her.

Time passed in a blur. She rose to her feet, feeling different, but how, she wasn't quite sure. Hands tucked into her pockets, she wandered back towards the common kitchen, her head clearer, and her heart less heavy. The ghosts still lingered but had lost their grip. Nearing the kitchen, she paused at the golden blanket of wattle trees and, closing her eyes, listened to the rustle of air moving through the long grass, coupled with the call of birds and the whinny of horses. Everything sounded clear, louder, and more beautiful. Eyes flickering open, she watched where a mob of kangaroos grazed, all five of them unperturbed by her presence. There was never a day that passed in the outback where she didn't bear witness to something that stirred her soul and touched her heart. The mob of Aussie icons reminded her of the many school holidays when she and her mother would go and stay in a little cabin in the Blue Mountains, for old time's sake. They would spend their days out riding through the bush tracks of the property where kangaroos would suddenly appear on the track, startling the horses, and her. They'd swim in the creeks and hunt down wild berries, and her mother would point out all the magical splendour of the bush. At night, her mum would help her to light the campfire, where they would cook their dinner over the hot coals and then roast marshmallows on long sticks they'd found in the scrub. That's when her love for cooking had really begun. Somewhere along the way, amidst the need to fit into the foodie society of urban life and make a go of it as a prominent chef, her yearning to prepare wholesome food had been overshadowed. But now, thanks to coming here, she was free to cook as she loved again. Just the acknowledgment of this had her racing back to the kitchen to finish preparing the men's lunches.

Half an hour later, eight sheets of tin foil had been torn off, and were lined up along the bench. Four pieces of buttered bread sat atop each one, a slice of cheese, three bits of bacon, and grilled onions on one side and her homemade garlic aioli on the other. Breaking eggs into the hot frypan, she marvelled at how orange the yolks were – free-range really meant free-range out here. Sprinkling some salt, she popped a lid on to help steam the tops to rich, gooey goodness. In her opinion, there was nothing more satisfying then biting into a bacon and egg sanga and seeing the yolk running down her fingers.

'Far out, brussels sprout. This kitchen smells like my kind of heaven.' Footfalls came up behind her. 'I know I keep telling you, but I'm going to say it again, you're spoiling us, Melody, big time.'

She turned to look up into Slim's smiling face. 'I don't mind, mate. I love seeing the grins on your mugs at mealtime. It makes every bit of effort worth it.'

'We're not going to want you to go, you know that, right?' Plucking a grape from the bowl, he tossed it into the air, balancing like a trapeze artist on one foot as he tried to catch it, which he did with a flourish.

'Aw, thanks, Slimbo.' A heartfelt smile filled her face – it was so refreshing to feel so wanted, so appreciated. She began packing the food into her usual basket. 'Are you going to take this out to the men today, mate?'

Slim shook his head. 'Oh, no, we knocked off early for lunch, and I've given the blokes a couple of hours rest before we head back out this arvo. So we decided to come to you for a change.'

'Oh, groovy, I'll set the table instead. Are the others far off?'

Plucking the orange juice from the fridge, he wandered over and grabbed a glass out of the overhead cupboard. 'Nah, they're just washing up. They'll be here in two shakes of a lamb's tail.'

Zai's deep laughter carried into the kitchen, enveloping her right before his presence did. Saying g'day to the men over her shoulder, she kept her gaze on the huge hunk of watermelon she was chopping.

The handsome tower of manly man saddled up beside her. 'Watch those fingers of yours, because the nearest hospital is hours away.'

'Don't you worry. I got this.' She offered a playful sideways glance, liking the shadow of hair over his strong jaw. Job done within half the time it would take a person without chef skills, she set the knife down and grinned at his expression of complete and utter awe. 'See, I still have all ten.' She held her fingers up, wiggling them.

'Holy heck, you're like the Houdini of slicing. Bloody impressive.'

Showbags was the last one to join them. Saying a quick hello to Melody, he skidded to a stop at Zai. 'You trying to grow a beard, mate?'

Zai chuckled and shrugged his big shoulders. 'Nope, just don't have anyone to impress out here.'

'Rolling out of bed and staying that way isn't going to be doing you any favours, even out here. You never know who you might happen to meet.' With utter banter in his eyes, Showbags looked to Melody. 'What do you think of a man who hasn't shaved, Melds? Yay, or nay?'

Talk about putting her on the spot. Personally, she liked the five o'clock shadow on Zai's angular jaw – it gave him a rough-around-the-edges air that she found very appealing. 'I dunno.' She shrugged. 'Eeether, either, makes no difference to me, it's not like I've got to kiss him, because then it might matter, because I don't like being sandpapered.' *Oh shit.* She was yabbering because this damn man rendered her senseless.

Zai's eyes crinkled at the corners.

She fidgeted beneath his red-hot stare. 'What?'

'So it would only matter if you had to kiss me?' He looked at her as if he could read her mind.

She rinsed her knife off at the sink. 'Yes, why is that so alarming?'

'It's not, but who said anything about kissing?'

'I did, because I was asked a question,' she shot back, looking from Zai to a very amused-looking Showbags. Oh crap, were her cheeks glowing red?

'Righto, don't stab me.' Zai held his hands up. 'I probably shouldn't be stirring you with a knife that size in your hand.'

She laughed, her unease disappearing – he always had the knack. 'Probs not.' Man oh man she had the hots for him – bad.

The ropey muscles in his neck stood out as he chuckled with her. 'Hey, when lunch is done, would you like to go for an arvo ride? I have to go and check a few of the fences out yonder and thought it might be nice for you to get out and about.'

'You know what, I reckon it might be just what the doctor ordered.' She wiped her hands on the tea towel, deciding not to mention she hadn't been in a saddle for more than five years.

'Sounds like fun, thanks Zai.' Her stomach sizzled as she imagined galloping alongside him, her hair flowing in the wind, a sunset on the horizon, sending shadows across his strong jaw, cue the romantic music …

'Good, great. I'll swing by around three to grab you.'

She snapped from her fantasy. A record scratching and the scene became realistic – her hanging on for dear life, hoping to god she didn't fall off and make a complete and utter fool of herself in front of this man.

'Earth to Melody …'

'Oh, sorry.' She drew in a breath. 'Three sounds good to me.'

All of them pulled a chair up at the table and tucked into their lunch. Once again, the men couldn't be grateful enough for her efforts, which were minimal compared to the café – just went to show how simple deeds were met with such gratitude in the outback. And there was a lot to be said about that. The thought that she only had three more weeks with these men, and especially Zai, made her heart squeeze awfully tight. Just how was she meant to say goodbye?

* * *

Unable to sit still, Melody found herself pacing the homestead in her bra and undies while waiting for the load of washing she'd hung out an hour ago to finish drying on the Hills hoist – the shirt she wanted to wear needed a few more minutes fluttering in the breeze. Counting down the minutes to Zai arriving – she had half an hour to go before she got to gaze at his handsome face again – she considered running down the hallway to grab a sarong to wrap around her so she could retrieve her clothes from the line a little more discreetly, but then couldn't be bothered traipsing all that way. The men were out yonder again, at one of the farthest paddocks, so she was safe. Nobody was about to catch her in her underwear. Just to make sure, she peered out the back door to where Zai usually left his boots by the back door of his cottage. None to be seen and not a movement in sight. The coast was clear. It was now or never.

Feeling a little risqué, she pitched herself out the flyscreen door before she changed her mind, dashed across the back verandah on her tippy toes – why, she hadn't a clue, but it just fitted with her little escapade – and down the steps. Albeit dust-filled, the gusty breeze alleviated some of the heat of the mid-afternoon sun as she made her mad dash to the clothesline. Just as she reached it, a sudden gush whipped the Hills hoist into a spin. Cursing beneath her breath, she chased after her T-shirt to put the brakes on the runaway line. From behind her, there was a resounding slam. Horrified, she turned to see the back timber door shut. She raced over only to find it jammed. *Crap.* What in the hell was she supposed to do now? It had been a good idea at the time; now she felt like a right idiot. Good lord, she didn't even have matching underwear on and to make matters worse, it was her fundi undies – her old cotton favourites with polka dots. She needed to get back inside, fast. Plucking the canvas floor mat from the back door, she tugged it around it herself as best she could. Then, in total stealth mode, she edged around the side of the homestead, praying she'd make it to the front door without anyone spotting her. With every man at work, surely she had good odds.

From beneath sleepy eyelids, Harold watched her sneaking sideways from where he lay sprawled out on the verandah. He tipped his head ever so slightly, as if trying to figure out what the heck she was up to. 'Oh, don't you start, mister,' she said to him in passing.

With only a gutsy sprint across the front lawn to go, a quickly approaching four-wheeler had her glancing down the dusty track while hiding behind a bougainvillea.

She swallowed down one cuss word, then another, as she watched Zai pull to a sliding stop, climb off, and stride down the garden path. What in the heck was she supposed to do now? To make matters worse, she inhaled a mouthful of dust hovering in wake from the motorbike and suddenly needed to cough. Covering her mouth, she tried to contain the urge, but she could only hold it back for a few seconds before spluttering, her eyes watering.

Spotting her as he climbed the front steps two at a time, Zai paused mid-step, met her horrified gaze, stifled a grin, and then tipped his hat. 'Should I even ask?'

'Probably not.' Embarrassed as hell, she tugged the floor mat in tighter, only succeeding in giving herself way more cleavage than should be naturally possible.

Clearing his throat, and with his smirk widening to his usual charismatic grin, Zai rested his forearms on the verandah railing. 'You know what, I have to say, I like your style.' Mirroring her gesture, he tipped his head to the side a little, as if rationalising the situation. 'Are floor mats a fashion trend in Sydney?'

'Ha, you're a funny bugger, Zai Wellstone,' she huffed.

'Are you going to stay there all day, Miss Melody?'

'No, of course not.' She sheepishly came out from behind the shrub and awkwardly manoeuvred up the stairs. 'I went to grab the clothes off the line, but the wind slammed the back door shut,' she said as he opened the flyscreen door for her.

'Happens to the best of us.' He stepped in behind her, his soft chuckle eliciting one from her too.

'The things I go and get myself into.' She rolled her eyes and turned to him, finding her gaze only inches from the soft rise and fall of his wide berth of a chest.

Wishing she could close the distance, Melody instead took a step backwards. Zai met her eyes, held her to the spot. She sucked in a breath, then another. The energy between was swiftly electrified. Clutching the top of the mat with one hand, she pointed down the hall with the other. 'I'm just going to pop some clothes on.'

'Yeah, that might be a good idea.' Zai's lips curled into an even more enticing smile. 'Because I don't reckon it'd be comfortable on the back of horse with that thing on.' He gestured back to the door with his thumb. 'I'm just going to pop back home and grab a couple of things. Will you be ready in twenty?'

'Yup, sure will be.'

'Right then, I'll be back in a mo with your chariot.'

'Okey-dokey, I'll be ready and waiting.'

They stared at each other for another few lengthy moments.

'I'll leave you to it, then.' He regarded her with a devilish grin, before disappearing out the door.

Dressing in record time, Melody was ready and waiting when Zai slowed to a stop at the front gate atop Sao. A gorgeous honey-coloured palomino trotted in alongside him, her reins held loosely in his big strong hands. Rising from the top step, she quickly made her way down to meet him beneath the shade of an old gum. She tingled from head to toe in his presence, insisting to herself that any woman standing in her Daisy Duke cowgirl boots would have had butterflies dancing in their belly too.

Shading her eyes, she looked up and into his smiling face, the dimples she so liked upon his cheeks veiled by the shadow of his wide-brimmed hat.

'Howdy partner, can I ride you?' Her attempt at honky-tonk twang was ridiculous, as was her ability to get dreadful foot-in-mouth – talk about her brain short-circuiting, and all because of what he did to her. 'With you, I meant. Wow, that wasn't how I meant it to come out.' Laughing at herself, she also like the way it drew a hearty chuckle from this charming hunk of man.

'Well, howdy there yourself, ma'am. And yes, you can ride with me.' Zai's twang was far better, and downright sexy. 'Anytime.' He even went and tipped his hat like they did in all the cowboy movies her mother had so loved to watch with a warm bowl of buttery popcorn between them.

Holy cow. This man knew how to work a woman's libido. 'Hi Sao.' She cast a glance at the muscular stockhorse between Zai's strong thighs, and then to the gelding's pretty sidekick. 'So who's this magnificent creature?'

Zai appeared chuffed that she'd noticed just how gorgeous the unfamiliar horse was. 'Melody, I'd like you to meet the newest recruit to Rosalee Station, Toffee.' He dismounted, touching down right beside her, then gently turned the horse towards Melody. 'And Toffee, this here is Melody. She's going to be your comrade today, so make sure you treat her real nice, okay.' He gave the horse a gentle caress on the muzzle.

In that moment, Melody wished it was her receiving such tenderness from him. Turning her attention from Zai's handsome face and back to the mare with the longest eyelashes she'd ever seen, she reached out and stroked the palomino's long, sleek neck. 'Well, aren't you the prettiest girl this side of Alice Springs?'

'Second prettiest,' Zai countered with his slow and sexy smile before leaning over to check Sao's back foot. 'You have number-one spot, Melody.'

Gobsmacked with the way he could pull off being so blatant so very causally, Melody's gaze unintentionally fell to the curves of his butt in his timeworn Wrangler jeans. Hot dang. The inner fire he kept kindling in her so effortlessly rose quickly and seared her cheeks – this man was a whole lotta temptation. She quivered a little with the thought of ever stepping over the friendship boundary – not that it was ever going to happen.

As she dragged her eyes away, they met with Toffee's, the horse's lashes fluttering as she gnawed a little on her bit. 'Don't listen to him,' she said gently. 'You truly are a stunner, Toffee.'

The mare's ears pricked forwards, listening intently. 'And you've got the kindest eyes too.' Reaching out, she ran her hands down the horse's silky mane. 'Where have you been hiding her all this time, Zai?' she asked as he sauntered back to her. 'I'd most certainly recall seeing her in one of the paddocks if I'd laid eyes on her before now.'

'I bought her for an absolute steal yesterday from the neighbour's daughter, Kelly. She's leaving home for uni in Melbourne and she didn't want him left out in the paddock all the time. He's used to daily attention.' He cleared his throat and took a few moments to continue. 'It broke my heart, watching Kelly say a teary goodbye, but at least she knows I'll love Toffee like no tomorrow.' He offered a slight shrug. 'Kelly has had Toffee since she was a foal, so they're bonded more than a blue sky and sunshine.'

'I could only imagine how hard that would have been for the poor girl.' Melody's heart squeezed as she recalled the day she'd had to say goodbye to her beautiful horse before moving from the Blue Mountains to Sydney as an eight-year-old. To her surprise, tears welled, but she quickly blinked them back.

Zai offered her a look of concern. 'You okay?'

'Yeah, sorry. Just remembering something.' She sniffed, hard. 'From a lifetime ago.'

'Memories can tug on the heartstrings, hey.' He turned and wrapped his arms around the horse's neck, his gaze still glued to Melody. 'FYI, Toffee loves hugs, so if you're feeling a bit down, pay her a visit. She'll help you to feel better quick smart.'

'Aw, how sweet.' She tried to smile, but the pain of the memories of riding through the Blue Mountains with her mother got in the way. Feeling the emotional quiver of her lips, she coughed to hide it.

Zai stepped in close to her. 'So, would you like a hand up?'

She looked up at the saddle. 'Yeah, I reckon I might need one.'

'Here you go.' He laced his fingers and held them down for her to step into.

'You sure I'm not too heavy?'

'You're an itty-bitty, Mel. Go on, climb aboard.'

'Okay, thank you.' She placed her boot into his hands and a hand on his shoulder.

Zai lifted her as though she were light as a feather. Sliding into the saddle, her stomach somersaulted. As she gathered the reins, Toffee stood still and calm, as if knowing her rider was a little nervous and in need of reassurance. Zai must have sensed it too, his hand lingering on Melody's leg a moment longer as he watched her get settled. She didn't like the feeling of him drawing it back to his pocket. Then, after another drawn-out instant, he began checking the length of her stirrups. Melody enjoyed watching him, his face a display of attentiveness to detail.

'All looks good to me.' He glanced up at her, his face shadowed by the brim of his hat. 'You feel comfortable?'

She hooked her heels in and wiggled into the timeworn seat of the saddle. 'Uh-huh. Hunky-dory.'

'Excellent. Let's head then.' He hoisted himself up a lot more easily than she just had. 'You good to go?'

'Yup, I think so.' She wasn't sure whether the quiver in her voice was from fear or excitement, or because of this man's charismatic yet gentle presence. Maybe it was all three.

'We'll take it nice and steady until you get the feel of her, okay?'

She let out a slow breath and nodded.

Heading towards the hazy ridges, they rode close together. The conversation quickly faded to captivated silence, the mesmerising landscape drawing most of their attention. And rightly so – it was stunning. The landscape's pulse was slow, deep, resounding, as if she was closer to Mother Nature's heart here, just like her father had told her it would be. Along with the outback's magnificence, the steady clip-clops on the dusty track filled her with delight. Swaying smoothly, it didn't take her long to fall into the rhythm of Toffee's steady gait. She couldn't wipe the grin from her face – it felt good to feel so … happy. Occasionally, she and Zai would glance at once another, and every time he caught her eyes, she quickly averted them, not wanting him to know just how attracted she was to him, with all that made him the admirable man he was.

That was, until he hooked her gaze with his and she was helpless to pull away. 'What is it?' The expression on his face was one she couldn't quite decipher.

'I'm just thinking how you look like you're right where you're meant to be.'

'I do?' She felt herself sit up straighter.

'Yup.' He asserted the fact with a confident nod and a gorgeous come-hither gaze.

All she could do for the racing of her heart was offer him an appreciative nod in return. She took a moment to catch her breath as she turned her attention back to the trail slowly rising upwards ahead. Faintly aware of the warm sunlight on her back and the gentle breeze stirring her hair, she was acutely conscious of this man's mesmeric presence, more so than she'd ever been. Spending time together was like heaven on earth. Or maybe it was very dangerous territory? Either way, she simply couldn't help feeling this way around him – and maybe she didn't want to.

'It can get a little tricky from here on in for a bit, so I'll take the lead until we reach the top.' As the track began to thin, Zai eased Sao in front.

Melody liked how he took charge and she was glad to follow him, especially for the fact of bearing witness to the muscles in his back and arms tautening as the track became a little harder to navigate. Carefully, steadily, she directed Toffee but also allowed her to take the path she was comfortable with when, out of nowhere, the mare tensed beneath her. As she glanced left to right, unease pricked the hairs on Melody's neck right before she spotted the brown snake coiling its way to standing.

Then it all happened so fast – too fast for her to gain a thigh-tightened grip to the saddle. With a fearful whinny, Toffee reared to avoid being struck. Panicking, Melody slipped then tumbled, time seeming to stand still as she fell through mid-air before she hit the dusty ground with a bone-rattling thump. Adrenaline hummed through her veins and she was unable to draw breath. Her senses whirled way too fast for her to comprehend her surroundings. Sky, clouds, rocks, sky again, all out of focus. But then they wavered, wobbled, began to steady … and that was right about when the pain kicked in, full force. And it was excruciating, so much so she couldn't move, nor did she want to try to. She fought to control the fear that wound tightly around her chest as she imagined having broken her back.

'Holy hell, Melody.' Galloping hooves neared her, quickly followed by the thud of boots hitting the ground. 'You tumbled a fair way. Are you okay, beautiful?'

Did he just call her … beautiful? Disoriented, she waited for the sky to stop spinning before she sucked in a hard-won breath and tried to turn towards Zai's rattled voice. He appeared at her side, his expression one of grave concern.

'Are you okay?' His voice was strong yet tender.

'I'm not sure. I'm too scared to move.' Every word was laced with searing pain.

His jaw muscles clenching, he gently brushed the tousled hair from her face. 'Shit, Mel, you're bleeding.' He ripped his shirt off, buttons popping, and carefully pressed the cloth to her forehead. 'Do you know what day it is?'

'Saturday?' she mumbled, unable to stop staring at his muscle-ripped chest.

'Spot on.' He looked her up and down. 'Can you move your fingers and toes for me.'

She tried and was relieved to be able to.

'That's good.' Zai looked to her. 'Where do you feel the most pain?'

Everywhere, she wanted to say, but then she slowed her breathing and did a scan through her body. Even though every bit of her ached liked buggery, she quickly came to the conclusion that it was her ribs that hurt the most. She placed a hand on her left side. 'Here.' She winced beneath her too-firm touch. 'Ouch, bloody hell. I think I might have broken something.'

Zai grabbed the hem of her shirt. 'Do you mind if I have a look?'

'Not at all.' Rolling a little to the right, she closed her eyes as he ran gentle fingers over her – she was oddly glad she wasn't wearing her favourite old cotton bra.

'I honestly don't think you've broken anything, but you're going to have a whopper of a bruise.' He helped her roll back to him. 'There's a doozy of one starting already.'

A flood of tears – from the adrenaline rush subsiding, the pain, and this amazing man taking such wonderful care of her – welled and rolled down her cheeks. 'So you think I'm going to live?' she finally asked, trying to make light of it all.

'I reckon you might, just.' He winked then took hold of her hands. 'Let me help you up. Slowly does it, okay? I daresay you're going to feel real light-headed.'

She gritted her teeth as, bit by bit, he finally got her to her feet. The world was a little wobbly and she had to take a few moments to try to steady herself. 'Holy moly, I feel like I've been hit by a truck.'

'Yeah, well, being thrown from a horse doesn't tickle.'

Hands going to her hips, she leant forward a little, the angle allowing her to breathe a little easier. 'You got that straight.' She loved the way Zai still helped balance her, his hands now resting on her arms.

'Everything's intact, Mel. You're going to be fine, I promise.'

She slowly straightened, her gaze travelling from his navel upwards, over his strong shoulders to his fetching eyes. 'That's good, but I'm not sure I want to ride ever again.' Just like someone waking up with a hangover after a night out and swearing off drinking, she didn't actually mean it. She'd come off a horse before, and probably would again.

'Well, all I can say to that is when you come off a horse, the only way to get over it is to dust yourself off and climb right back into the saddle again.' His gaze was soft and tender.

'Yeah well, you can take your saying and—' She stopped short, grinning at his cheeky smirk. 'What?'

He wiped at something on her cheek. 'The only thing sexier than a woman atop a horse, her hair flying in the wind, is one who falls off and wants to try again.'

'Is that your way of challenging me?'

'Might be.' Smirking sexily, he tugged his hat down a little. 'Either way, you're a true-blue jillaroo now.'

She felt her face warming, along with her heart. Why did he have to be so damn charming all the damn time? And so irrefutably gorgeous in his dusty jeans, boots and hat, with his tanned torso so gloriously exposed, along with a very sexy tattoo – she couldn't help but crave to kiss the place where his heart beat beneath.

'Come on then, let's get you back home so we can sort out these cuts and run you a nice hot bath.'

With the pain subsiding enough for her to think a little straighter, she suddenly remembered her horse. 'Oh my god, what about Toffee?' She looked left and right, her bottom lip clamped between her teeth.

'Oh, don't worry about her. She's probably back at the homestead by now.'

'I hope so,' she said, her voice drifting as another wave of light-headedness had her legs turning to jelly. She fell against Zai, her cheek settling right where she'd moments ago craved for her lips to be. 'Oops, sorry. I just feel a little woozy.'

'All good. That's pretty normal after the tumble you just had.' His arms circled her, holding her against him protectively. 'Just take a minute to breathe.'

Remaining there, she was glad for his encompassing embrace as the world gradually stopped spinning, and it was in these precious moments, she realised how she felt – as if she'd arrived home within his arms. It was an odd yet endearing sensation – one she didn't know what to make of.

'I'll double you back to the homestead when you're ready, Mel,' Zai said ever so gently as he untangled his arms from around her and tugged his shirt back on. Unable to be done up now for the lack of buttons, it framed the hard planes of his chest and stomach perfectly.

A faint moan rose from her throat – she didn't want him to let her go. Not ever. 'Oh, and here I was thinking I would walk,' she said playfully, giggling, but then wincing. 'Ouch, it even hurts to laugh.'

'Take it steady,' he said, holding her hand and slowly helping her over to Sao and eventually up into his saddle.

Sliding carefully in front of her, he glanced over his shoulder. 'Hang on nice and tight. We don't want round two.'

'You're a smartarse.' She grabbed a tentative hold of his hips. 'You know that, right?'

'Ha, I sure do, and you love it. And FYI, that's not tight, Miss Melody.' He took both of her wrists and carefully secured them around his waist. 'This is.'

'Gotcha,' she said, wishing she actually did have him, all of him, now and forever.

Zai carefully eased Sao into a smooth walk.

'You right back there?'

'Yes.' She centred herself, both in posture and internally. Being so close to him was doing crazy things to her. Once they reached the bottom of the ridges, she said, 'You can go a little faster, if you like.'

'You sure?'

'Positive.'

'Righto then but let me know if it gets uncomfortable for you.'

'Will do,' she replied, her cheek now resting upon his back.

It only took moments for Sao to fall into a smooth gallop. Giving in to the rhythm of the gelding's rhythmic gait, the three of them became one as Sao's long graceful strides ate up the terrain. Melody could feel the bunching of Zai's stomach muscles as they raced across the flats. She wondered if he could feel the brush of her breasts against his back, or the frenzied beating of her heart driven wild by being so close to him. She also wondered just how she was going to ignore the fire he'd ignited in her heart. And how things would change between them if he found out she was a married woman.

CHAPTER 12

Sitting on the floor beside the couch where Melody was sprawled out with a bag of frozen peas against her ribs, Zai tried to keep the conversation light as he stared at the hole allowing his little toe to poke out of his sock. He had spent the past hour wishing he could capture her mouth in an all-consuming kiss and was having a real hard time keeping his hands to himself. The way their bodies had melded together as they'd galloped back to the cottage was a sensation he'd never experienced before – it was as if she was his missing piece, the one that made him whole.

He'd now learnt that any skin-on-skin contact with her was like throwing a match to fuel, and the heat she'd left in her wake was lingering like a kindled fire within his soul. Nothing he did or thought doused it. Day by day, she was getting under his skin, more and more, and he couldn't help but find pleasure in the fact.

He was certain that this beautiful woman had changed him, had effortlessly made him want her in a way that only a man falling head over boots in love could. What in the hell was he meant to do with that? He wasn't even sure Melody liked him as more than a mate, and he wasn't about to go and ruin a friendship with her by giving in to his feelings. And with his reputation, Matt would almost certainly kill him if he went anywhere near his precious daughter.

'Earth to Zai.' Melody poked him with her foot. 'Why are you so quiet? Has the cat gone and got your tongue?'

'Ha, sorry, I'm just thinking about the fact that I don't really know much about you.' He watched her happiness quickly fade and couldn't help wondering what nerve he'd just brushed upon.

'Oh, okay. Well, I suppose we haven't really known each other for very long, so that's a given.' She half shrugged and turned her gaze from him and towards the curtains fluttering at the open lounge-room window.

'Well then, I reckon we should change that fact then.' He waited for her to agree and when she didn't, decided to prod a little further. 'Do you have any siblings?'

She remained staring out the window. 'Nope, and now that Mum's gone, I don't have any biological family, other than Matt.'

Zai's heart broke for her. 'Like, you mean, nobody at all?'

His question drew her face to his and she studied him through shadowed eyes. 'Nope.'

The question he was burning to ask her flew from his lips before he had time to stop himself. 'What about a partner? I bet a gorgeous woman like you has one back in the big smoke.'

'Like a partner in business, in crime, or something else entirely?' She stared at him with an increasingly defensive gaze.

'Wow, sorry.' He quickly retreated, not wanting to upset her – there was very clearly something she didn't want him to know, and it wasn't his place to pry it out of her. 'I was just trying to get to know you better, that's all. I thought a beautiful woman like you would most certainly be spoken for.'

One of her brows rose. 'Spoken for?'

He shrugged, as though it wasn't a big deal if she was, even though it would be a dagger through his heart. 'You know, engaged or married.'

'Nope.' It was short, direct, sharp even. 'Why are you so interested in my relationship status anyway?'

He shrugged her slightly frosty tone off and sighed away his frustration. 'I just am.'

She seemed to hold her breath as she considered this, then her lips pressed together as she regarded him for a few more uncomfortable moments. 'That's not a valid explanation.'

He huffed, rolling his eyes playfully in a bid to lighten the murky energy of the room. 'Okay, all right. I'll fess up.' He held his hands up as though a gun was pointed at him. 'It's just … the boys and I really like your cooking and I don't want to have to try and find another cook to step into your very capable shoes if you have to run back to the city for a boyfriend or husband.'

'So, essentially, all you care about is filling your stomach with my awesome cooking?' Her downturned lips twitched at the corners, but she held the smile back, just.

'Yeah.' He couldn't help the smile tugging the corners of his mouth either – thank god the brooding storm was passing. 'Pretty much.'

Frowning, she tossed a cushion at him and they both laughed.

Gathering himself, Zai brought his gaze to hers, hoping she could read between the lines of what he was about to say. 'All jokes aside, I really like your company, Melody, and I don't want you to leave.'

She went to say something, paused, and drew in a breath. 'I like your company too, Zai, but I can't stay here forever. My life is back in Sydney.'

Nodding slowly, he silently considered what she'd said, and everything she didn't say, her all-pervading gaze speaking volumes. The way she was looking at him told him she *did* like him, possibly as more than a mate … but he wasn't about to lay it all on the table without more, for fear of being firmly rejected. That would make things between them very uncomfortable. The bottom line was he had to work with her, and she was Matthew Walsh's daughter. As the seconds ticked on, the room fell awkwardly silent. Trying to find words to fill it, he came up short and instead watched her picking at the dirt beneath her fingernails.

'What aren't you telling me, Melody?' he finally found the nerve to ask.

She took her time answering, her lips parting then pressing together a couple of times.

'Why?' It was only now that she fleetingly brought her gaze to his.

Considering his reply, he sucked air through his teeth. 'Call it instinct.'

'Regardless of what anyone tells you, instincts aren't always right, Mister Wellstone.' Her lips were smirking, but it was clear to him it was to try and hide the secrets that were plain in her eyes.

'Hmm, interesting.' He nodded very slowly then shrugged. 'Each to their own opinions, hey.'

'Agreed,' she said, short and certainly not sweet.

As much as he ached to, he wasn't going to pursue this conversation any longer – now too afraid of what he might discover. For now, he wanted to live in the fantasy world where he and Melody had a fighting chance of becoming romantically involved one day. Until then, he was going to play it cool, calm and collected. He'd have to be content remaining her loyal mate. For now.

Melody yawned, overstatedly so.

Zai took it as his cue. Rising to his feet, he gathered the two empty coffee cups by the handles. 'Are you sure you don't want me to whip something up for dinner?' She hadn't eaten since breakfast and he was worried about her. 'Even some baked beans on toast? That'll be what the boys are having right now.'

'No, I don't really have an appetite, but thanks for offering.' She turned her full attention to him now. 'And thanks for taking such good care of me. I owe you.'

'No worries, and no you don't owe me anything.' *A kiss would be nice, though.* 'I'll head home and leave you in peace.'

'Okay.' She held a hand up, grinning. 'Could you just help me up to sitting before you go, please? Otherwise I might be stuck here all bloody night.'

'Of course.' Plonking the cups back down, he ignored her outstretched hand and instead wrapped an arm around her. 'Let me …'

And she did.

His heartbeat raced with being so close to her again. What did this woman have over him? It was like he was an addict and she was his drug – he simply couldn't get enough of her. As he positioned a cushion behind her back, their gazes met, and locked. There was but an inch between them. Could he close it? Should he? Did she want him to? Lord knew how much he wanted to.

A breathless second passed, followed by another. Helpless to stop himself, he closed the gap, his lips barely brushing hers just as he mentally slapped himself into line and pulled back.

'What the heck, Zai?' a very wide-eyed Melody said as he tried to get a grip on the situation, and his frenzied heartbeat.

It was jarring, seeing her so aghast, but he wasn't about to make a big deal of it. 'Fark, sorry. I don't know what came over me.' He ran his hands over his face before looking to her for a response.

'Insanity, maybe?' Her tiny lopsided smile lightened the mood a little.

'Ha, yeah, something like that, I suppose.' Zai shoved his hands into his pockets. 'I'm a bloody idiot. Please just pretend that never happened, okay.'

'Nothing happened.' She metaphorically zipped her lips.

'Thanks, Mel, appreciate it.' He took steps away, but then, turning, he rested his shoulder against the doorframe. 'I'm sorry I—'

She held her hand up, stopping him. 'It never happened, remember? So no need to apologise.'

He sighed, heavily. 'Right, yup, thanks.'

'No need to make a big deal out of nothing.' She waved a dismissive hand at him. 'Now be gone with you.'

'Righto. Well, I'll catch you tomorrow then.'

She nodded. 'Yeah, you will.'

Taking one arduous step after the other, Zai did as she asked and let himself out. Closing the door behind him, he tugged his boots on and descended the back steps. The darkness of night was a relief – he didn't want anyone to see how miserable he felt right now. Looking to the diamond-studded sky, he heaved a heavy-hearted sigh that for the second time in his life – the first being his high-school sweetheart – a woman was breaking his heart.

* * *

Mid-morning sunshine stretched across the hardwood floors of the lounge room and reflected off the television as Melody hung the phone up after reassuring her dad, for almost half an hour, that she was going to be okay. Easing back into the couch, she felt a fresh wave of pain ride over her as she rested the ice pack up against her aching ribs, left black and blue from her fall to hard-packed earth. Having been given the day off to recuperate, she was glad for the rest, although she was finding it incredibly hard to distract her thoughts from her near-kiss with Zai. Even thinking about it now had her feathering her fingertips over her lips as she imagined what it would feel like to have his mouth, and his body, pressed up against hers. She knew, without a shadow of a doubt, it would be mind-blowing.

Allowing her mind to wander, she imagined what would have ensued if she'd tumbled into the ensnaring moment that had stolen her breath and leant into his kiss, into all that was him. They wouldn't have been able to put on the brakes – it would have been the spark that incited a wildfire. With a quiver, she envisaged unbuckling his belt and helping him slide his jeans from his hips before he did the very same to her, the pair of them then stumbling down the hallway, unable to keep their mouths and hands from one another. When they reached her bedroom door, he would lift her and carry her to the bed. Everything else that would follow she imagined in slow motion – every touch, every kiss, every stroke, every breath, and how she would quiver beneath him while he whispered in her ear how deeply he felt for her, and she for him, while he slid inside of her and the two of them became one. And then, over and over again, all night long, until the sun came up and they finally succumbed to sleep in each other's arms, her head resting upon his divine chest.

What in the hell am I doing?

Mentally slapping herself, she brought her attention back to the present. She had to stop being so lustful, especially for a man she considered her closest friend here. It would do her no favours with the mess she was already in back in Sydney. Giving in to her desires for Zai, as intense as they were, would be dangerous territory, because she damn well knew once she had a taste of Zai, she wouldn't be able to stop wanting more. Every bit of her had wanted to lean in and meet him, but she'd fought tooth and nail to stop herself in that breath of a second. Zai didn't know her situation, and after avoiding the truth when he'd asked point-blank, it would have been so very wrong to give in to her cravings for him. She didn't come here to fall for a man. She'd come here to find her father, and herself.

Then again, Zai Wellstone wasn't just any man – he was so much more than that. He was all she'd ever lacked in Antonio and more, much more, in fact. And the better she got to know him, the farther she tumbled into liking him. She really needed to get a grip before she did something stupid. She didn't want to hurt Zai, nor did she want to be hurt. She had to remember he had a reputation of being a womaniser, and she was also still legally married. Their timing just wasn't right, nor would it probably ever be.

Dragging her gaze from where Patrick Swayze was twirling Jennifer Grey across the dance floor – *Dirty Dancing*, her all-time favourite film – she stared at where she'd watched the man who'd climbed inside of her heart as effortlessly as he mounted a horse stride away from her last night. It had torn her heart to shreds, having to be so cold and aloof with him, but what else was she meant to do? Anything else would have been leading him on. He didn't deserve that. She had to draw the line somewhere. But far out, she really didn't want to … why did life have to be so complex?

Chewing on a corner of her fingernail, she jumped when a rap at the front door snapped her from her train wreck of thoughts. 'Coming.' Easing up from the couch, she hobbled to the front door like an eighty-year-old woman – she'd gone and forgotten just how much being thrown from a horse hurt like buggery, especially the next day.

Tugging the timber door open, she met with the very eyes that always had a way of stirring her soul. 'Oh, hey, you.' She drew in a quiet, calming breath. 'I thought Slim was coming to my rescue.'

'Hey there yourself.' Zai cleared his throat. 'And sorry to disappoint, but Slim has been waylaid with a broken pump at the far paddock. So I'm next in line to come to your rescue, I'm afraid.'

'Sorry, that sounded really rude.' Shaking her head, she rolled her eyes at her foot-in-mouth. 'I honestly didn't mean how it came out.'

'All good.' He shrugged, tipping his head a little to the side. 'You know you don't need to keep the place locked up like Fort Knox out here?' His lips widened into a grin.

'Ha, yeah. Habit, I suppose.' She liked the way his smile was always as real as he was.

'So.' He tapped a shifter against his palm. 'You have a leak?'

'Oh, yeah, I do.' The flyscreen door between them felt like a brick wall.

'Well, aren't you going to invite me in so I can fix it?'

'Oh, yeah, sorry.' She moved back and, after kicking off his boots, he stepped inside.

Zai strolled past her with a loose-hipped swagger, and she couldn't help the fact that her eyes went straight to the perfection of his butt in his Wrangler jeans. She could only imagine him in a bar back in Sydney – he'd only have to pull up a stool and before he'd even ordered a drink, women would be swarming him like bees to honey. A burly manly man like him could have his pick of the litter.

'So how are you feeling today?' He glanced over his shoulder. 'A bit how-ya-doin', I bet.'

'Very sore, but I'll survive.' She followed him into the kitchen, trying to look anywhere else but at his chest as he stripped off his T-shirt. 'I've already got everything out from underneath the sink.'

'Great, thanks.' Totally at ease in her company, as if last night had never happened, he tossed his shirt over the back of the dining chair. 'I'll get to it then.'

'Mm-hmm,' was all she could get past the beating of her heart in her throat. Was he taking his shirt off for good reason or just to tease her, show her what she was missing out on? She had to silently admit it was one hell of a lot – he was a whole lotta man.

She watched him lie on his back and squirm into the cupboard beneath the sink to get to the blocked U-bend – with his broad-shouldered build, it was a tight fit, but he got there, after a bit of grunting and groaning. She felt like a complete idiot for accidentally tipping the tea leaves down the sink at some ungodly hour this morning. Although, she had been sleep deprived and a little high on painkillers.

'Can you pass me that shifter, please, Mel?' Zai's hand shot out and he gestured to the vicinity of the dining table. 'I went and left it over yonder.'

'Oh, yup.' Reaching out, she grabbed it and quickly passed it to him. 'Here you go.'

Melody found herself glued to the spot, her gaze stuck to him. With his attention elsewhere and unable to see her, she had free rein to perv to her heart's content. What she'd give to trail kisses over his tattooed chest, then slowly downward over his six-pack abs to the place that disappeared beneath the timeworn leather belt. She imagined the scene that could transpire if she gave in to her yearnings. There was no doubt the sexual tension between them would explode the minute her lips touched his. She envisaged him swiping everything to the side and hungrily lifting her up onto the kitchen bench. His breath would be hot and heavy as he tore at her clothes, his deep voice teasing her while she stripped him of every inch separating them from being skin to skin. Then, with both of them gloriously bare, he would pause, his hand cupping her face as he kissed her assertively, bringing her to a toe-curling point, begging for him to be at one with her. Needing her too, he'd succumb to her pleading and, grabbing her hips, he'd thrust deep inside her, claiming her, making her his as she clung to his shoulders, gasping. Her face buried in his neck, she would moan at her tingling ascent to ecstasy and he would join her as they jumped over the edge together, sweaty and breathless and shuddering, mind-blown and completely satisfied …

It was at this point that Melody realised her eyes had closed and she was leaning against the kitchen bench for support, her legs trembling, her hands gripping the hem of her shirt. Heat travelled from her head to toes, filling all the gaps in between in the most dizzying of ways. Her breath was hitched, her bottom lip caught between her teeth. Her wakened libido growled from deep inside and before she had time to stifle the flurry of emotions, a moan surfaced. Her hand instantly went to her mouth to stop another, and it was only then that she realised just how fast her heart was beating.

'Did you say something, Mel?' Zai's voice travelled from beneath the sink, as did the clink of the shifter.

'N-no. Nope.' Not thinking straight and needing to do something, anything, with her hands, she went and dumped the glass of water she'd left there this morning into the sink, subsequently dumping it all over Zai. 'Oh shi—' She stopped short, grimacing.

'Hey!' Shooting up to sitting, Zai smacked his head on the ledge of the cupboard on the way out. 'Ouch, shit.' His hair and face were drenched. 'Good on ya,' he said, with a goofy grin.

Melody basically watched the egg on his forehead form before her very eyes. 'Oh my god, Zai, I'm so sorry.'

'Is it a doozy?' He brought his fingertips to it. 'Dang tootin' straight it is.' He grinned again. 'Far out, talk about making a man work for his supper.'

'You did a job of it.' She dashed and grabbed the same bag of peas she been defrosting against her ribs last night. Returning to his side, she knelt down and pressed it to his head. 'And who said anything about supper?'

Zai rested his hand over hers, both of them now holding the peas in place. 'You did, just then.'

'Ha, you're good, Zai Wellstone.' She was unable to stop the grin spreading across her face. 'I suppose I should make you some dinner, seeing as you've sustained a head injury from helping me out.'

'Oh, you might have twisted my arm.'

Melody enjoyed their familiar banter – it helped make everything feel natural between them again. 'You reckon you could handle lamb chops with a potato bake and …' grabbing the bag of peas from where Zai had just plonked them to the floor, she held them up '… peas?'

'Oh, it'll be a tough gig, but I reckon I could.' With his knee-buckling smile, he ducked back out of sight. 'Although, to be honest, I think I can do one better.'

'How so?' Her curiosity piqued, Melody bent to try to see his face.

'I'm going to cook for you.'

'You are, are you?' Bam. Another jolt of whatever he seemed to do to her hit her fair and square in the belly. 'Is it safe?'

'What, in here?' His deep voice carried from the cupboard.

'No.' She crouched down and was finally able to meet his eyes. 'I meant, is it safe letting you cook for me?' A smirk itched to surface on her lips.

His eyes turned rousingly playful. 'You saying I can't cook?'

'No.' She shook her head. 'Just didn't think you'd be the type to.'

'Well, you got me all wrong, Miss Harrison slash Walsh.' He shook the shifter at her. 'I love cooking, and eating. And watching cooking shows.'

'You do?'

'No word of a lie.' He cast her a sidelong glance. 'Can you pass me something to tip whatever is clogging this bugger up into.' He wiggled the piece of pipe.

'That'll most likely be tea leaves.' She grimaced as she passed him an empty ice-cream container.

He took it from her. 'Tea leaves, huh? Righto. You do know you're meant to brew your tea in a teapot, not down the sink?' His smirk was endearing.

'Smartarse.' Just as she suspected, he banged the piece of pipe and a clump of earl grey leaves plopped out and into the bucket, along with gloop and god only knew what. 'Ew.'

'Uh-huh.' He passed her the bucket of gunk and got back to it. 'You still keen for a cuppa?'

She looked into the container. 'I think I'll pass.'

A couple of minutes later, all was well under her kitchen sink again.

'Thanks so much, Zai.' She watched him wipe his clean hands onto the towel then tug his shirt back on. 'You want a beer before you head off?' She really didn't want him to leave.

He checked his watch 'Thanks, but better not. Got a bit to get done before knock-off.'

She followed him down the hallway. 'Okay, what time would you like me to head over for dinner then?'

He stopped at the door and tugged his boots back on. 'About five-thirty sound good for you?'

'Of course, it's not like I have any other plans.' She leant against the frame and shoved her hands into her pockets.

'Geez, talk about making a man feel special.'

She went to respond but he reached out and gave her arm a quick squeeze. 'Just kidding.' Grabbing his hat from the banister, he tugged it on. 'FYI, I've had my infamous chilli con carne going at it in the slow cooker since sunrise.'

'Oh, yum, I love a good chilli.' Melody couldn't recall the last time she'd had it.

'Well, prepare to be wowed because mine trumps everybody else's.' He wiggled his brows self-assuredly. 'We'll have that beer when you head over too.'

'Okay, sounds like a plan.' She watched him stride away, his long-legged gait and the confident way he carried himself sexy as hell.

Three hours later, with her mouth watering from the scrumptious aroma wafting from the slow cooker, a freshly showered, delicious-smelling tower of manly man reached into his fridge and grabbed them both a longneck. Twisting the lids off, Zai passed one to her.

'Cheers,' she said, chinking her bottle against his.

They took a long swig, saying, 'ahh' in unison.

Zai held his up. 'Want to knock the rest of this back outside?'

Melody loved the idea. 'Yeah, why not.'

Side by side, they wandered out to the golden glow of the setting sun. Settling themselves into the day bed on the back verandah of the cottage, they watched the lustrous orb begin to fade into the horizon, as if sinking over the curve of the earth. As usual, Melody found herself in complete and utter awe. Never had she seen such beautiful sunsets, or sunrises, as the outback of Australia provided. A sneaky sideways glance told her Zai still found them as captivating as she did, even after all his time here. She totally understood the magic of Rosalee Station never getting old – it was a place unto itself, a living, breathing landscape with so much to appreciate.

Taking a thoughtful gulp from her beer, she wholeheartedly wished she could fit into this world that Zai slotted so perfectly into. There was something to be said about the healing qualities of the solitude here, far away from technology and the hustle and bustle of city life. Rosalee Station had been exactly what the doctor had ordered – it was going to feel strange arriving back to the bright lights of the city. A part of her, a really big part, wanted to stay here forever, living in this bubble she always seemed to find herself in when she was in the company of Zai. But life didn't work like that. The reality was, she had to go back and sort out her life, and where she wanted it to go from there.

Zai turned to her. 'Ready for some fodder?'

'Sure am. Would you like a hand dishing it up?'

'No, I got it. You stay here and rest those ribs of yours and I'll bring us a bowl each out here.' He smiled gently. 'It's going to be too much of a nice night for eating inside.'

Melody looked to the peach-coloured sky then back to him. 'Yeah, I agree.'

Collecting them another beer and their bowls of chilli con carne topped off with generous dollops of yoghurt, Zai returned. He sat, this time a little closer, so much so that his legs brushed up against Melody's, sending skitters of butterflies through her. Although it was dangerous territory, Melody didn't flinch – she liked the fact that he wanted to sit so near to her.

The mouth-watering scent tempting her tastebuds almost as much as this delightful man, Melody eagerly dug in. Her first mouthful was absolutely divine. 'Oh my gosh, Zai,' she garbled. 'This is seriously the best chilli I've ever tasted.'

'See, I told you.' He nodded slowly, his face a picture of satisfaction.

Over casual conversation and mouthfuls of rich, spicy food, the sun finally bowed out and gave way to the glimmer of the first star. It wasn't long before the sky was a blanket of diamonds, the full moon a shining beacon amidst it all. She recalled some of her mother's last words about looking to the stars when she was missing her. Smiling softly, she took great comfort in the fact that her mother would be looking down upon her from such a stunning, radiant sky. With her bowl basically licked clean, she secretly watched Zai's moonlit face as she continued to slowly sip her second icy beer. He looked as if he were up among the brilliance of it all, catching the stars in his hands. She longed to go to that place with him, where nothing else mattered, where they could just be. Even so, back here on earth, it was so nice to feel so peaceful in his company. He was her mate, her confidant, her shining light in what had been a very dark world. She had to count her blessings at having met a man as genuine and caring as he was.

Even so, deep down, beneath the turmoil of her life, she knew she wanted way more than what they had right now. It was a pipe dream, something that would never become her reality, but it didn't stop her heart longing to be matched with his.

CHAPTER 13

Zai kept catching Melody's sneaky glances, not that he let on. He liked the way she was looking at him, with a deep curiosity and that slow easy smile on her kissable lips – it gave him a glimmer of hope that they might, possibly, maybe, still have a chance at something more than only friendship. He'd learnt that, when it came to Melody, easy does it – he needed to take it nice and steady. Akin to working with horses, he had to let her gravitate to him, but first and foremost, she needed to trust him and to know without a shadow of a doubt that his intentions were pure and from the heart. With that contemplation, while staring into the darkness that seemed to go on forever, he had an idea

Leaping to his feet, and startling her in the process, he took his chance and grabbed her by the hand. 'Come on, I have something I want to show you.' He tugged her from the seat.

'Do you now?' She dug her heels in, eyeing him cautiously. 'What is it?'

He wasn't about to reveal his little adventure until she was belted into his LandCruiser. He wanted to make this a night for her to remember, in all the right ways. 'I can't tell you or I'd have to kill you and bury you in the backyard.' He wiggled his brows, trying to look sinister and failing miserably, bursting into laughter when she did.

'Well, in that case, Mister Axe Murderer,' she said finally after gathering herself. 'I'd best let you reveal the secret when you're ready to.'

Grabbing a bottle of tawny port from the top of the beer fridge on the way past, Zai was chuffed when she allowed him to lead her down the steps, across the lawn, damp against their feet from the sprinkler, and to his four-wheel drive. He went to the passenger side and opened her door. 'Your chariot awaits, so in you hop.' He waved an arm flamboyantly, eliciting more giggles from her.

'This better be good, Mr Wellstone.' She slipped on her seatbelt and flashed him a knee-buckling smile. 'Or else,' she added with a wink.

He shut her door, leaning on the open window frame. 'Or else what?'

'That's for me to know and you to find out.'

'Ha, you got nothing. I can see it in your eyes.' He tapped the bonnet as he wandered around to the driver's side, smirking at her through the windscreen.

Sliding behind the wheel, he tugged his door shut, revved the old girl to life, turned the stereo up enough to enjoy the honky-tonk drawl of Garth Brooks, and hit the accelerator. They fishtailed a little down the dirt drive before he regained traction. Flicking the headlights to high beam and switching on his bright spotlights, he turned her eyes as wide as her smile. Circling the stables, he slowed, then turned off the usual track, pulling to a stop at a gate they barely used. Jumping out, he swung it open, rolled in, then alighted to shut it behind them. Then they were off again, bouncing across an unused paddock towards the place he found to be the most magical in all of Rosalee Station at night. It was the only place on earth which had the power to rekindle his sense of childlike wonder – he hoped it did the same for Melody.

'So, where are we going?' she asked, bouncing in her seat, her grip deathlike on the handrail above her head.

Tapping his thumb in tune to the famous country song, 'Ain't Going Down ('Til The Sun Comes Up)', Zai grinned. 'You'll find out soon enough.'

It took a good ten minutes for them to reach the rickety old lean-to, and he pulled into his usual parking spot, hurriedly switching off the engine and all of his lights. It was only then, with the velvet black of night enveloping them, that the ordinary landscape turned ethereal and otherworldly – a cascade of flittering light, the enchanting show became visible above the glimmer of the water's surface, transcending time and space.

'Oh my god, Zai.' Her voice gushed out. 'I've never seen anything so beautiful in all of my life.' In a dreamy daze, she pushed her door open and stepped out and into the bewitching landscape, aglitter and aglow with hundreds, if not thousands, of fireflies.

In awe of the living fireworks spectacle, powerful yet so peacefully silent, Zai joined her, leaving a little distance between them. Drawing in a deep breath, he allowed her all the time she needed to stare in wonder at the magical scene before them. He observed the fireflies' luminous dancing with absolute delight in his heart, just like he always did when he came here. Melody blinked slowly, enraptured, her reaction sparking happiness deep within his soul. It took his breath away, almost as much as her beauty.

'It's like a portal to another time and place,' she said softly, her hands resting over her heart.

'It sure is.' He turned to catch the reflection of the fireflies' light in her eyes. 'I take it, from the dreamy look on your face, you think my surprise is worth it?'

She nodded. 'Oh my god, yes. So very worth the bumpy ride out here.'

'Believe it or not …' He looked back at the flittering specks of light. '… the males are the biggest flashers.'

She skimmed her wistful gaze to him, the tiniest of grins emerging. 'You're pulling my leg?'

'Nope, true fact. And when a female firefly fancies one of the males, she blinks faster.'

'Wow, that is super cool.'

'And another titbit – they aren't actually flies, they're beetles.'

'Geez, look at you go, Wellstone.' She was very clearly impressed. 'You're a wealth of information, aren't you?'

'I'm not just a pretty face.' He chuckled and so did she. 'I know something else too.'

'Oh yeah, what's that?' She said it just as she rested her head against his arm, her gaze now glued to the natural spectacular.

He took a moment to consider his next sentence, one that could go either way, but caught up in the moment, he just had to say it. 'They're delicate and beautiful, just like you.'

She looked up beneath her long lashes. 'Aw, Zai, you really are such a sweetheart.'

'Shh.' His heart exploded in his chest as he held a finger to his lips. 'Don't tell anyone, okay? It's only for you to know.'

She mimed zipping her lips, then said, 'It'll be our little secret.'

He liked sharing secrets with her. One hell of a lot. It made him feel a special part of her life. 'Would you like to kick back in the tray of the cruiser and watch all this a little longer before we head back?'

She didn't miss a beat with her reply. 'Actually, yes, I'd really love that.'

Zai almost floated back to his hard-as-nails four-wheel drive – talk about acting like a lovesick schoolboy. He'd never felt like this in all his life. Leaning over the side, he unrolled his swag so they had somewhere soft to lie. 'Ladies first.' He held his hand out and helped her up.

Climbing in beside her, he left a tiny space between them so as not to make her uncomfortable, then clasped his hands behind his head. 'It's like heaven on earth, here, isn't it?' He almost whispered every word while staring at the blanket of stars above them, and then back to the dancing, radiant fireflies.

'Damn straight.' A tiny sigh escaped her. 'City people don't understand what they're missing out on by never making their way out here.'

'So you're glad you ventured beyond the bright lights?'

'Oh god yes. It's nice to run away from it all, to be honest.'

Zai considered this, weighing his response. 'You have to ask yourself, though, are you running from something, or to something?'

She nodded, returning his thoughtful contemplation. 'Hmm, very good question.' She took a few moments before she answered. 'Can I be annoying and choose both?'

'We live in a free country, so you're allowed to do whatever you want.' He grinned. 'Even being annoying by choosing both.'

She gave him a playful slap. 'You shit-stirrer.' Her brows rose. 'So I'm allowed to do whatever I want, hey?'

He met her perplexed gaze, considered, then shrugged. 'Of course you are. Life isn't worth living if you don't do what you want, and that sometimes means taking risks.' His double-meaning comment planted, he grabbed the bottle of port from beside him and removed the lid. He offered it to her. 'Sorry, we'll have to rough it and drink straight from the bottle because I forgot the glasses.'

'Fine by me.' She grasped the bottle and took a swig. 'I'm a risk-taker from way back.'

'Ha, look at you go, you rebel you.' Zai adored her feisty spirit, along with everything else that made her the mesmerising woman she was.

Pulling her knees to her chest, Melody went silent for a few long moments, while taking little sips. 'You know what, come to think of it, I guess you're right in saying life is all about risks. Because if we don't take them, we just stay stagnant.' She pouted a little, as if really pondering this. 'I mean, if I hadn't taken the risk of finding my dad, I wouldn't know how wonderful he is, and I wouldn't be sitting here with you in the middle of the Australian outback, drinking from a bottle of port while watching the most amazing show I've ever seen.'

'That's it. Life is all about living it to the full, Mel.' Zai rested up on one elbow, so he was more or less facing her. 'So, seeing as we both agree on the risk-taking, are you ready to take a risk with me?' He wasn't sure exactly where he was going with this, but hell, he was going to go with the flow of the relaxed yet electrified vibe.

'Hmm. That all depends on what sort of risk you're on about, Zai.' She studied him over the bottle as she took another swig.

In that breath-held moment, he came dangerously near to closing the last little bit of distance between them and kissing her. 'Do you trust me?'

She didn't flinch. 'That depends.' But her breath quickened.

Zai could smell the sweet scent of port on her breath. He gave her a lingering smile. 'On what?'

'What you're on about.' She gripped his gaze with hers.

Oh man, he so wanted to kiss her, but he wasn't going to give in to his impulses.

'Follow me.' He sat up and jumped off the back of the ute. 'Come on.' Grabbing her hand, he urged her to follow.

She resisted and planted her butt firmly, the look in her eyes full of cheeky competition. 'You have to tell me what you're doing first.'

'Nope. Like I said, you just have to trust me.' He shrugged lightheartedly. 'I mean, come on, have a look at what I just surprised you with. And this is only going to top the night off.'

'Promise?'

'Scout's honour.' He gave her hand another tug. 'Who knows, you might actually enjoy yourself even more than you already are.'

* * *

Feeling a little tipsy from the beer and port, Melody took great delight in the playful banter and the easygoing company of this captivating man. And as she allowed him to lead her towards the glimmer of the dam, lit up beneath the flickering of courting fireflies and the blanket of twinkling stars, she realised it had been forever since she'd let her hair down and had silly fun – boy oh boy it felt good. There was something so very special about Rosalee Station, and Zai, that made her feel weightless, worriless and free.

They reached the water's edge and she spun left to right, looking for whatever he was going to do to outdo what was already an amazing night. 'What are you up to, Wellstone?' she asked, meeting his mischievous gaze.

'I'm going to turn around while you strip off and make a run for the water, and I won't turn back until you're all covered up by it.'

She spluttered a choked laugh. 'You're kidding, right?'

'No way, Jose. I'm deadly serious.' He wiggled his brows, grinning. 'And before you refuse my chivalrous offer of giving you upmost privacy for your very first starkers run, I recall you saying only half an hour ago that you're a rebellious risk-taker. So prove it, Sweet Melody.'

Melody's breath hitched – the only other person who had ever called her that was her mother. It felt like a sign from the starry heavens to lay her trust in this beautiful man. So she did.

Stripping off, she covered her breasts as she ran for the water, squealing as she splashed into the coolness. The fireflies flittered out of harm's way, hovering above.

'Okay, you can turn around now,' she called, dogpaddling to stay afloat.

Zai turned to face her. 'Now you have to turn around, Melody, so I can get nekkid.'

'Nekkid, hey? Righto.' She spun around just as something brushed across her foot. Screaming in fright, she almost walked on water.

'You right in there?' Zai's voice travelled to her, as did the thump of his feet running towards the dam.

A loud splash had her turning back to face him. 'Yeah, all good. I just felt something touch my foot.'

'That might be the swamp monster that lives in here.'

'Stop it.' She splashed water towards him and he ducked beneath, avoiding it.

Seconds later, he rose, closer to her. 'No way, you love it.'

She grinned. 'Who says?'

He grinned back at her. 'I do.'

All Melody could do was laugh, and it was the loudest, most liberating laugh she could recall in what felt like forever. To top it all off, this was one of the rarest moments she'd ever had – as naked as the day she was born, swimming in a dam with a kind, arrestingly handsome man beneath an effervescent canopy of animated stars of both the living and celestial kind. There could be no place on earth closer to heaven. She could feel her mother here with her and it warmed her heart. It felt as if she'd fallen out of time and into a blissful world where nothing and nobody could hurt her.

Floating aimlessly with Zai close beside her, she marvelled at this hidden wonder, one she felt so privileged to see. Surrounded by the silent sparks, she felt a profound connection to this land, a land her father and his forefathers had called home. And suddenly, she felt she was home, in every sense of the word. It was an overwhelming yet peace-filled sensation, one that brought tears to her eyes. Call it serendipity or an epiphany – Zai had just given her the answer she'd been searching for. The country was where she belonged. She just hoped she could make it so.

Spinning to Zai, she kissed him on the cheek.

Eyes wide, his hand went to where her lips had touched. 'Wow, okay. What was that for?'

She shrugged, as though it was no big deal even though she knew that it was. 'Just for being the amazing man that you are.'

Considering this, and her, in the most intense of way, he ran fingers through his wet hair. 'I'm not that amazing, but if you say so, I'll take it.'

'Seriously, you can take my word for it. You truly are.'

'Thanks, Mel. And just for the record, you're pretty amazing yourself.'

'Stop it, Wellstone, before you make me blush.' She shoved him playfully when all she really wanted to do right now was wrap her arms and legs around his body and kiss him.

'Should we head home?' he asked finally, breaking the lingering silence.

'I don't really want to, but yeah, I suppose we'd better. It's getting late.'

It was long past midnight when they finally extracted themselves from the water. Zai stuck to his promise and made sure to keep his back to her as they got dressed. On the flip side, she hadn't promised a thing, and took great gratification at watching his butt glowing in the silvery starlight, and also the way his muscles stretched and bunched as he tugged his clothes back on.

'You decent?' he called.

'One sec.' She tugged her dress over her head. 'Yup, all good.'

He swivelled and strode towards her. 'Come on, then. Let's get you home, beautiful.'

And there it was again, that glorious tingle that spread from her head to her toes every time he called her something other than her name. Climbing into the four-wheel drive, they bumped their way back to the homestead to the tunes of what Zai told her were Chris Stapleton. Melody loved the singer's husky voice, and the lyrics were beautifully heartfelt – fitting for the night they were having.

Pulling up beneath the towering paperbark, Zai killed the engine and gently stopped her from opening her door by grabbing her hand. 'Wait, I'll come round and let you out.' A little squeeze and he let her fingers go.

Melody's already swooning heart melted even more. 'You know I can do that myself, right?' Where on earth had this chivalrous, kind, sexy, thoughtful man come from?

'I know, Little Miss Independent, but I like to do it for you because a lady should be treated like one, always.'

Her heart pitter-pattering, she watched him scoot around the front of the LandCruiser and to her door. There was a split second, as her door swung open and he took her hand into his, that their eyes met and in that poignant abyss between her exhalation and inhalation, she felt a mind-blowing rush of something she'd never experience before. And she knew, without a doubt, what it was. Deep, unconditional, love. Finally, she'd gone and found it, at the most unfavourable of times, when she was helpless to do anything about it.

What in the heck is the universe playing at?

'Earth to Melody.' Zai's deep voice lured her back. 'You can get out whenever you're ready.'

'Oh, sorry. I must be tired from all the gallivanting.'

She thanked the billions of stars above that he was there to guide her from the passenger seat because she was sure as anything that she wouldn't have been able to stand on her own two feet without his body to stumble against when they hit the ground. He steadied her when she did, chuckling. Literally, and metaphorically, he was turning everything she'd believed to be true in her life upside down, and to be honest, she liked the view from where she was dangling – all she wanted to do now was let go and fall completely and utterly into all that was him.

But she couldn't. She was lawfully married. And he didn't know a damn thing about it. And she'd gone beyond the point of making it known to him. Now it would seem like a blatant lie, one that would be very hard to explain her way out of, and she hated the fact. What had she been thinking, keeping it from him? Her heart sank to her feet. Hindsight was an absolute bitch.

He walked her up the front steps and across the verandah, stopping short of the welcome mat at the front door. 'I hope you've enjoyed tonight as much as I have?'

'I most definitely have, thank you, Zai.' He'd given her a memory she'd treasure for a lifetime.

'It was my absolute pleasure.' His killer dimples froze her to the spot.

The increasing sexual tension made it hard to breathe, as did the irrefutable love swirling in her heart, begging to be let free. But, pushing it down, she squeezed some oxygen through her slightly parted lips. If she were reckless, a thousand scenarios could happen right now, but one outdid them all – him, in her bed, gloriously skin-on-skin with her so they could be at one, making sweet love all night long.

'Right, well.' Zai sucked in a deep breath. 'I'd better let you get inside.' He checked his watch. 'We have to be up in less than five hours to start the day.'

'Wow, yes, okay. I'd better let you get some sleep too.' Thankful for his resolve, she broke the stare and turned away before she went and did something really stupid, like kissing him, walking straight into the closed door in her haste. 'Oops, far out. Silly me.'

'You're meant to open it first, Mel.' Zai's hand came to rest on her back, his chuckles as light and gentle as his touch. 'You okay?'

'Yup.' Wishing the ground would swallow her whole, she laughed and spun back to face him, hoping to god her face wasn't the colour of beetroot. 'Night, Zai. Catch you tomorrow.' She half grimaced. 'Actually, make that catch you today, in a few hours.'

'Ha, yeah. We can be tired buggers together.' He leant in and, just missing her mouth, brushed a kiss on her cheek. 'Night, Sweet Melody. Have the sweetest of dreams, won't you.'

The way 'Sweet Melody' rolled off his tongue for the second time tonight … *Bam*. There was that shock of electricity again. All she could do was smile through the zap, the budding emotions inside her robbing her of any appropriate words. Pausing for a brief second longer, she finally tugged her gaze from his, turned, opened the door and stepped inside.

Zai's footfalls fell across the verandah then down the front steps. She'd usually wait and wave him off, but she closed the door and rested her back up against it, both her hands resting over her heart. Her mind flew back over the dreamlike evening, and she couldn't help the sigh on her lips or the racing of her pulse – she was a woman, falling, precariously fast. Zai Wellstone had won her over but, regardless of the fact, she needed to tread extremely carefully. There were feelings involved on both sides, and she wasn't about to go playing with the fire that had ignited between them. She wasn't going to risk burning him, or herself, which was inevitable when she went back to the city. And with that depressing thought, her buoyant mood sank. She needed to get off the damn cloud she was floating on and plant her feet firmly back on the ground, and bloody well stay there. Fairytale endings were for the books and movies she so loved to read and watch, not for real life. It was time to draw the line between mateship and relationship, and not dare step over it.

CHAPTER 14

At the end of the following week, Melody had done exactly as she'd promised herself – for nine long, gruelling days. As hard as it was to resist the magnetic attraction that had the power to drag her heart towards Zai's the second he was anywhere near her, she was succeeding, if only just, in staying over her side of the boundary she'd silently created. She could tell it was baffling, and possibly even frustrating, for Zai, with her being a lot more detached than he was used to, and a lot more platonic, but she didn't owe him an explanation, especially when nothing amorous had happened between them, other than intense feelings of wanting to ravish each other. Her feelings ran deep for him, of that she was certain, but he didn't need to know that – it would only complicate things more. And whether her choice to draw the line so definitively yet so silently was right or wrong, she reminded herself not to make a mountain out of a molehill each and every time she found herself wanting to explain the hurt look in his eyes away. Nobody here, not Zai, nor her father or Sarah, needed to know of her broken marriage – that was her mess to sort out when she went back to Sydney. And sort it out she would.

Flicking the fluorescent lights off in the common kitchen, she undid her messy bun and ran her fingers through the ends before pulling the sweaty hair up into a high ponytail. With the brimming dinner basket in her hands and the old homestead dog in tow, she strode across the shimmering red dirt and climbed behind the wheel of the dusty old four-wheel drive used for errands around the station. Old Harold did his usual trick and jumped through the open window, landing himself on the passenger seat. Kicking a couple of empty Coke cans out of the way, she revved the old girl to life, the almost empty bag of Minties in the centre console urging her to have one. And so she did – just like that. If only the same could have been said for her urges regarding Mister Knock-Her-Socks-Off Wellstone. She half laughed, half groaned with the predicament she was in, the Mintie almost sticking her jaw together in the process – there was a knack to eating the Aussie legends unless one wanted their teeth clamped together by the sweet morsel.

Pressing the button to spray some water onto the windscreen, she momentarily flicked the wipers on, the two coppery arches made clearer as the film of red dust shifted. Then, tugging her seatbelt on, she turned the ABC radio up – tuned in by the strategically placed wire coathanger on the bonnet – then ground the old gearbox into first gear and lunged forwards towards where the men were branding and sorting for the day. Bouncing along the earthen track, she drew comfort and strength from the countryside surrounding her – there was something to be said for the solitude and sheer grit of it all. And there was also a hell of a lot to be said for the men and women who called a place so isolated, sometimes brutal and quite often unforgiving, home. She was proud her heritage made her part of it all.

Singing the lyrics of 'Mammas Don't Let Your Babies Grow Up to Be Cowboys', she crossed the second of three cattle grids – the Waylon Jennings classic had been one of her mother's favourites. Her heart warmed and sweetened as she recalled singing it with her mum, in the car, while washing up, whenever the opportunity arose. It was a beautiful reminiscence. And for the very first time since losing her, she embraced the memory without tears rising. It felt so good to recall her mum with fondness instead of grief. Although the sadness still lingered, and always would, her gratitude of having the years she did with her amazing mum finally outshone the gloominess, like the sun pressing through clouds. Being at Rosalee Station, where the landscape was as raw and real and rich as the people who lived here, it felt like a huge step in the grieving process had been accelerated. God really did work in mysterious ways.

A pesky fly buzzed around her face and she hopelessly tried to shoo it away, but it was hell-bent on trying to cling to her lashes. Doing the Aussie salute, she finally swatted it out her open window, only for another to buzz through Harold's window and land on his snout. He nipped at the air, trying to catch it, his teeth snapping. She couldn't help but chuckle at his antics before gasping when he succeeded in swallowing it. Even the bloody flies were determined to be hard-as-nails out here, but Harold knew how to beat them at their game – not that she was about to start swallowing flies.

Bouncing over the final cattle grid, she did her best to ignore the beads of sweat rolling down her back and between her breasts. The air-conditioner was still on the blink and the dust-laden wind floating through the open window was searing. She'd tried rolling it up, once, and had felt like she was being roasted in an oven. If it were at all possible, the weather pressed in upon her more than ever. It had been relentless over the last couple of days, making them all a little less patient with one another, especially Hasselhoof. He seemed to be getting broodier as the days zoomed past.

Humming to the next country tune, one by the brilliant Adam Brand, and without another soul in sight – not something common in the place she usually called home – a bubble of rashness rose. Having broken from the ranks of the kitchen, and with nothing but open countryside rolling out around her, she felt free, and a little reckless. Should she have a little harmless fun? she thought with a little smirk. *Why the heck not …*

Cranking the steering wheel to the left, she squealed with delight as the back-end fishtailed and an even bigger plume of dust was left in her wake. She righted her forward track then, spurred on by the rush, did it again, the opposite way, feeling like a wild rebel out of something like *The Dukes of Hazzard*. But then, just as she tightened out, without warning, the four-wheel drive jerked to a teeth-shattering halt. Harold gave her a sideways what-did-you-do-that-for look from beneath his brow-wrinkled eyes. She couldn't blame him, as she was asking herself the same question. Her knuckles white from gripping the steering wheel, she sucked in another sharp breath as she stared apprehensively out the windscreen. What in the hell had she hit? Putting the four-wheel drive into neutral then yanking on the handbrake, she flung the door open and jumped out. Her heart stopped, and she grimaced. The front tyre was as flat as a tack.

Panic rose. In a couple of hours, it was going to be pitch-black out here. What in the heck was she going to do now? Tears threatening, she pressed the heels of her hands into her eyes, reprimanding herself for allowing such recklessness to rise – it always ended badly when she did. She'd have to swallow her pride and contact the guys. She needed to ask for help.

Leaning back into the four-wheel drive, she grabbed the two-way. 'Hey boys, it's Melody, can any of you hear me?'

She was met with crackle and an unnerving silence. *Oh, crap.*

Straightening her shoulders, she drew in a calming breath – not that it did much good – and tried again. 'Zai, Slim, Hasselhoof, anyone?'

Again, nothing but radio silence met her.

Right, what in the hell was she meant to do now? Surely when she didn't arrive with the smoko, they would come looking for her. Wouldn't they?

Maybe ...

With a deep exhalation and a few expletives, she slipped the handset back into the harness on the dash then, hand on hips and with her lips caught between her teeth, experienced another lengthy moment of absolute panic. She'd never changed a tyre in her life. Didn't even have a clue where to start. That's what her roadside assistance was for. Fat chance of that out here. The thought actually made her chuckle – living in the city had allowed her the luxury of being inept in so many things that country souls essentially had to know simply to survive. Far out, talk about stretching a person past their comfort zone – this place certainly had the knack for it.

Deciding there was no time like now to learn the art of changing a tyre, she drew in another deep breath. Then, mentally regathering herself, she firmly told herself that she had this. Hopefully. Possibly. If not, she'd just have to fake it until she made it because by the sounds of the static on the two-way, there'd be nobody to come to her rescue anytime soon. So much for her knight in shining armour. Then again, she'd never needed one before, so why start now?

Folding the driver's seat forward, she spotted the dust-covered jack, jack handle and wheel brace buried beneath empty chip packets and a roll of fencing wire. Heaving it all out, she placed it on the ground and went in search of the spare tyre. Trailing her gaze from top to bottom, she finally discovered the spare secured behind the drums of fuel and water strapped to the back. Almost ten minutes later, after much grunting and groaning and hitting her funny bone hard enough to bring tears to her eyes, she succeeded in rolling the tyre off the tray, strategically landing it beside her gathering toolkit. Dusting her hands off, she felt a bubble of accomplishment.

Hightailing it over the side, she felt her boots hit the ground with a thud. Wiping beads of sweat from her brow, she crouched down to evaluate her next move. It didn't look too complicated, and that helped to buoy her fleeing confidence. Positioning herself beside the offending tyre, she knelt down and slid the jack beneath the chassis. It took a few goes for it to do what she wanted. Then, cranking it as hard as she could, she ignored the burn between her shoulder blades as she gritted her teeth and dug her heels in for traction. It was tough going but she persisted, and the four-wheel drive rose, then rose some more. She squealed in delight when it got to where it needed to be for her to begin her next test – taking the flat tyre off.

Before rising to the challenge, she grabbed her water bottle from the cab and took a decent glug – the relentless heat was making her feel a little dizzy. Harold had the idea – the old cattle dog was lazing beneath the only shade for miles, provided by a lone cluster of mulga trees. As she grabbed the wheel brace and hooked it onto the first of the nuts, the distant beat of horse hooves brought her to her feet. Raising a hand to shade her eyes, she squinted into the blinding sunshine. An Akubra-topped silhouette appeared through the heat-haze – it was a scene right out of an old Western movie. And when she spotted who it was, just like the horse's thundering hooves, so too did her heart beat just as fast, and just as passionately.

One hand resting on her hip and the other still gripping the wheel brace, she watched the horse and its rider skid to a stop just shy of her.

'Howdy, Miss Melody.' The two-day stubble surrounding Zai's kissable mouth was all she could see, the rest of his face shaded by his hat. 'You were running a little late, so thought I'd come check on you. Bit of car trouble?'

'Hmm.' She glanced at the sorry state of affairs she'd found herself in, and back up at Zai's gorgeous face. 'You could say that.'

'So, tell me, with nothing much for miles and a track as flat as a tack, how'd you manage to flatten a tyre?' His lips seductively curled into that knee-buckling smile.

'I, um, well …' She tried to keep the embarrassment out of her voice, but it just crept in. 'I kinda tried to fishtail, and before I knew it, this happened.'

'Fishtail, hey?' His chuckle was deep and throaty. 'I never imagined you to be the kind to like that sort of thing.'

'I have a rebellious side, I just don't show it much.' She was gushing beneath his stare, and hated the fact, but with him looking so rough and ready atop his horse, his get-up the epitome of a true-blue countryman, she just couldn't help herself.

'I like your rebellious side. You should let it out more often.' Sao shifted a little impatiently. 'Whoa, buddy, ease up, now.' Flaring his nostrils, Sao danced on the spot, blowing out an almighty sigh. Shifting his weight in the saddle, Zai leant in and gave the gelding a rub on the neck. 'We'll get back to it all soon, buddy.' He looked back to Melody. 'So, do you need a hand or have you got it covered?' There was a playful lilt in his voice.

'I have it covered, but seeing as you're here, I'll let you take over.' She was so grateful for his arrival.

'Righto then.' Anchoring one boot in the stirrup, he swung his leg over in one fluid movement and, with a thud, was at her side, his tall frame providing her some much-needed shade. 'Hand me that wheel brace, cowgirl, and let's get this show on the road.' He took it from her and got to work. 'The men are going to be chewing their arms off if they don't get their dinner soon, and don't even get me started on Hasselhoof's mood today. Lord bloody well help us if he goes hungry.'

Standing back while affording a chuckle at an image of Hasselhoof with smoke coming out of his ears and nose, Melody watched Zai change a tyre as if he were manning the pit stop of a famous Formula One driver. Why did he always have to make everything he did so effortlessly sexy?

He straightened, put the tools away and tossed the flat tyre into the tray, then brushed his hands off on his jeans. 'Right, you're good to go.'

'Thank you, Zai, you're a lifesaver.'

'Ha, I wouldn't go that far, but you're welcome.' He mounted Sao in his usual easy style and gathered the reins in his hands. Behind him, the sun was beginning to drop from the sky, sending a scattering of golden hues splashing across the blue and a shadow across his strong-angled jaw. 'I'll meet you there then.'

'Roger that,' she responded, feeling countrified with her lingo. 'I'll be right behind you.'

He gave Harold a whistle and the dog straightened, stretched, then languidly made his way back, jumping through the window and sitting on the passenger seat, panting like billyo. With a tip of his hat, Zai turned Sao around on a threepenny bit and galloped away. Melody saddled in beside her doggy mate, giving him a quick ruffle behind the ears before she took another glug from her water bottle and revved the old girl back to life just as Zai disappeared into the hazy horizon. She quivered in his wake; he was just so much of an alpha male, and it was intoxicating.

Ten minutes later, she was at the camp and got to work setting up for dinner – not long and the sun would be bowing out for another day. She was really looking forward to spending the night out here – her first one since starting the job. Grabbing the chicken-wire frame she'd whipped up and laced with fairy lights, she propped it behind the fold-out table, covered with a tablecloth, and placed the tin plates, cups and cutlery off to the side, leaving space for the feast she'd prepared. It was going to be fun welcoming the men back to her pimped-out camp – such a contrast to the stunning wild landscape. Setting up the single gas burner, she popped the pot of lamb rogan josh on a low flame, unpacked the container of jasmine rice and placed it alongside the bowls of pappadums and garlic naan. Then, with everything ready on the dinner table, she busied herself starting the campfire – a skill her mother had taught her as a teenage girl, and one she was very thankful for now. It took a few goes, but it wasn't long before the kindling caught with the logs she'd strategically placed. Satisfied with her effort, she pulled up a camp chair and propped her feet up on a stump one of the blokes would have been using as a stool. The setting sun ignited the cloud of dust hovering above the men on horseback, making it appear as if a trail of golden glitter had been poured from the heavens. It was a sight to behold. She watched in awe as they rounded up the last of the cattle and tucked them away for the night in the holding yard – the five of them certainly worked like a well-oiled machine.

The last of the light had faded from the sky by the time they all lumbered into camp with wider-than-normal gaits – a telltale sign of their extra-long day in the saddle.

'Hey there, Melody. Wowser, this place looks schmicko with those lights.' Offering her a nod, true to form, Tumbles tripped over his own feet and almost hit the dirt, only saving himself by stumbling into Showbags.

'Hey, Tumbles. Cheers, mate.' Melody couldn't help but laugh – the bloke was a walking disaster if ever she'd seen one. 'And careful, before you go breaking something, or yourself.'

Showbags gave his mate a playful shove. 'Careful, shithead, you almost knocked me over.'

Tumbles stumbled again then entertainingly righted himself. 'Yeah, but I didn't, so I should have tried harder, hey Showbags.'

'It does look schmick.' Eyeing the fairy-light-lit table, Zai stopped short of Melody and tossed the whip he had slung over his arm onto the tack table. 'It takes skill to trip over thin air, hey Tumbles.'

Tumbles pulled a hilarious sad face. 'I don't know why I stay working here when you lot are always picking on me.'

'That's because you're an easy target, bud.' With a shake of his head and a deep chuckle, Slim wandered towards the simmering pot and drew in a huge sniff. 'Cor, bloody hell Mel, that right there smells amazeballs. What is it?'

'Cheers, Slim. It's an Indian curry. I hope you guys like it.'

'Oh bloody hell, why do we have to have Indian food when we're in the middle of the outback? It makes no bloody sense,' Hasselhoof grumbled, shrugging when all the men shot him a don't-start look. 'What? It makes me fart like buggery all the next day.'

'I'm sure we will all love it. You've gone to a lot of trouble again, Mel, and these lights are bloody tops.' Slim ran his wide-eyed gaze over the impressive spread. 'Gee whizz, we even have pappadingys. Talk about spoiling us rotten.' He turned back to Melody, his face a picture of glee.

'You mean pappadums,' Melody said with a chuckle.

'Yeah, those thingamajigs.' Slim grinned. 'I love me some pappadingys.'

'That's good to know.' Still chuckling, Melody busied herself dishing up generous bowls of curry while the men washed their hands in a bucket of soapy water.

The hum of conversation and the crackle of the campfire blended in with the sounds of the Australian outback at night – the chorus of the insects, the distant howl of the dingoes, bellows of the cattle and the whinnying of the horses. Plates gathered, the men parked themselves around the centre of gravity – the fire. Melody pulled up a chair between Zai and Slim. The flames crackled and popped, and glowing red sparks danced and twirled up into the rising smoke. The firelight cast shadows over the men's weather-beaten faces as they tucked into their dinner. Other than the crunch of a pappadum and the moan of foodie pleasure, nobody said a word. Melody took the silence as the greatest of compliments.

'That was bloody delicious, Mel, thank you.' As usual, Slim was the first to finish.

'Cheers, mate.' She pointed towards the table with her fork. 'There's plenty more there, so help yourself.'

'You know what, now you're twisting my arm, I reckon I will.' He stood but didn't completely straighten. 'Cor, my bloody back feels like it's about to snap in two.' He took measured steps towards the table, looking double his age.

'Ha, you look like you might need a walking stick soon, Slimbo,' Tumbles garbled through a mouthful of food.

Slim gave him the finger over his shoulder and all the men, other than Hasselhoof, cracked up. Melody loved the sound of Zai's deep throaty laughter – it always found a way into her heart.

Hasselhoof got up so slowly it was almost as if Melody could hear his bones clicking into place, and she grinned to herself as she watched him join Slim at the table, helping himself to another bowlful.

Zai offered her a knowing glance. 'So it appears you do like Indian curry, Hasselhoof?'

Hasselhoof's shoulders lifted. 'Fills the gap, I s'pose.' He took bigger than usual sidewinder steps back to his chair.

'Have you gone and put a bigger than normal stick up ya butt, Mister Grumbles?' Showbags dared to ask, his face the picture of mischief.

'Lay off, would ya?' Hasselhoof groused, glaring in Showbags's direction. 'If you'd spent the best part of your childhood with your legs wrapped around a milk bucket, and the rest of your days glued to a saddle, you'd probably walk a little different too, buckaroo.'

'I'm no American cowboy, Hasselhoof. It's jackaroo to you, thanks.' Trying to appear serious, Showbags couldn't hide the tilt of a smirk forming on his lips.

Hasselhoof made the growling sound he always did when he was about to blow his stack.

Melody and Zai briefly locked amused gazes.

'So who here knows where the term jackaroo came from?' Slim asked quickly, as if trying to sway the conversation to a lighter one. 'Anyone?' Folding his hands, he rested his elbows on his knees, eyeing everyone with keen interest.

'It was originally a white settler that chose to live outside the boundaries of a settlement,' Hasselhoof said nonchalantly before shoving a pappadum in his mouth.

'Nah way, I've been told that jackaroo was made up from a combination of the common name back then, Jack, and the Aussie icon, the kangaroo,' Showbags added enthusiastically.

Tumbles chuckled. 'Aw, come on, Showbags, that's bullshit and you know it.'

'Excuse me, mister, but …' Showbags's brows shot up and he shook his head as if about to scold a child. 'It says it in the Oxford dictionary.'

'Pfft, pull the other one, it does not,' Hasselhoof bellyached.

Showbags turned his attention to the grumbling old coot. 'Does too.'

Hasselhoof gritted his teeth as his gaze turned to slits. 'Does. Bloody. Not.' Every word was fired like bullets. 'Do us a favour and grow up, would ya?'

'Far out, righto.' Showbags held his hands up. 'Stop being a grouch all the bloody time. I was just stirring Tumbles is all.'

Scraping the last of his dinner from his tin bowl, Hasselhoof eyed Showbags like he was about to reach out and wallop him. 'Stop calling me a grouch, 'cause I promise you, this ain't anywhere near grouchy.' He stood, dumped his bowl into the washing-up container, yanked his bag from the shadows, and stomped away, grumbling to himself.

'We love you too, Hasselhoof,' Showbags called after him.

'Eff you, smartarse,' was the short, sharp response from the darkness.

Zai tossed his screwed-up napkin in Showbags's direction. 'Stop stirring the old bugger, would you?'

'Ha, I can't help myself, he's just so much fun to bait.' Showbags rose from his heels and gathered the plates from everyone. 'I'll do the washing up tonight, you lot just kick back, or whatever you want to do.'

'Oh, cheers, big ears.' Slim stood too and gathered his bathroom bag. 'I'm off in the opposite direction to Hasselhoof for a freshen up.'

'I'll head into yonder thata way, then,' Tumbles added, pointing off to the right, well out of the way of his two fellow stockmen.

That left Melody alone with Zai, and she liked it, possibly a little too much. Full to the brim and feeling cosy by the fire, and in his company, she stretched her legs out, half stifling a yawn. 'I suppose a hot shower is out of the question?'

'Ha, you suppose right.' He offered her an amused sideways glance. 'Afraid out here, it's a bucket of cold bore water and a washcloth, if you're lucky.'

She shivered at the thought. 'I can't believe how cold it gets as soon as the sun is gone.'

'Damn straight it does. It goes from one extreme to the other.'

'Hmm, yeah, this place seems to have the capacity for extremes.' Resting her head back, she found herself lost in the vastness of the star-studded universe circling around them, as if she were seeing so far, she could make out the curves of the earth. 'It's so peaceful out here. Almost ear-ringing, if that makes any sense.'

'It makes perfect sense.' The crackling campfire was now glowing red embers, and smoke coiled up and into the velvet black sky. 'It's a whole other world, isn't it?' Zai took his gaze from the beauty of it to her. 'Stunning, in fact.'

'It sure is.' She couldn't help but wonder if he was referring to her.

'If you grab your swag,' he said matter-of-factly, 'I can help you set it up in the tray of the LandCruiser, if you like. You'll probably feel safer up there, away from all the creepy crawlies.'

She went to say that'd be great when an image shimmied into her mind of her swag leaning up against the tree the LandCruiser had been parked beneath. A sucker punch of realisation had her sitting up straight. 'Oh crap. With all my rushing about to get here, I forgot to chuck it in the back.' She shook her head. 'I feel like a bloody idiot.'

'Hmm, no wuckers. We'll just have to ad lib.' A cheeky smile hinted on his shadowed face.

She tipped her head to the side, regarding him. 'How so?'

'You'll have to crawl in with me, or risk dying of frostbite. Or snake bite.'

She shuddered at the thought. 'All good. I'll just crash in the LandCruiser.' The butterflies he always roused inside of her had gone absolutely crazy.

'Trust me, it gets real cold out here in the middle of the night. You're going to want to snuggle up to keep yourself warm, seeing as you don't have a swag to wrap around yourself.' He gripped her gaze with his. 'I promise I won't bite.' The sexy glint in his eyes spoke otherwise.

She bit her bottom lip to curb a quiver as she imagined him doing just that, on the very place she so liked to be nibbled at the back of her neck – not that he knew that. Or ever would. God help her if he ever found out – she'd be absolute putty in his big, strong hands. They remained silent, staring at one another. She frantically tried to find something, anything, to say, but they were saying so much without uttering a single word. Something flared in his gaze, and it had nothing to do with the fire reflecting within them. It had everything to do with the inferno of carnal tension gaining momentum between them. She inhaled sharply. Dragging her gaze from his and to the starry night sky once more, she silently asked her mum for a shot of fortitude because this boundary fence she'd mentally created was proving damn near impossible to stay on the right side of.

'So, that's a yes, I'm gathering,' he finally said softly, now the men were back in camp and wandering about, getting their swags rolled out.

'Mm-hmm,' was all she could manage.

'Nice,' was all he said as he rose from his chair. 'I'm going to go and freshen up. You should take the opportunity to as well. I'll catch you back here for sleep time.'

'Uh-huh.' She allowed him to help her from the chair. 'Sounds like a plan.'

She watched him wander one way, bathroom bag in hand, and then she went the other, making sure to stick close to camp in case she needed saving from some night creature, but far enough away to be hidden by the shadows as she stripped down, teeth chattering. Using her packet of wet wipes, she wiped herself down, pulled on her trackpants and matching long-sleeved top, glad for the warmth, then quickly brushed her teeth. Never again would she take a hot shower for granted. It took her all of ten minutes, but once she got back to the camp, now barely lit by the dwindling campfire, she found every man in his swag, including Zai. Hasselhoof and Tumbles were already waging a snoring war, Slim was out cold and Showbags was way too quiet to be awake.

'Far out, talk about lights out,' she whispered.

'Yeah, they don't take long. Everyone's buggered by this time of the night.' Propping himself up on his elbow, Zai flicked the blankets back, shifted over in his swag and patted beside him. 'Now, come on, you. In you hop.'

She slid in beside him and he snuggled in behind her. 'You'll be surprised by just how well you sleep out here.'

Feeling cocooned within the all-in-one mattress and sleeping bag, she allowed herself to settle into him. And instead of racing, like it usually did, her heart took a long slow beat, followed by another – she felt so safe wrapped up against him. 'I'll take your word for it. And tell you if you're right in the morning.' She knew she was going to sleep like a log, wrapped up in this remarkable man's arms.

'Night, Sweet Melody.'

Her heart swelled. 'Night, Zai.'

He rested his head down and she could feel his slow, warm breathing on the back of her neck, right where she loved to be nibbled and kissed. It sent a skittering of goosebumps all over her – she was glad for the clothes separating them, otherwise he would have felt the effect her was having on her right now. Feeling super sleepy, she closed her eyes and slipped into a trance where she and he floated amidst the stars above. And for the very first time since laying her eyes on this gorgeous man, she felt a piece of her heart slip and tumble into his before she even had a chance to stop it. And to top it all, for the very first time in all of her life, she finally had a glimpse of what true, soul-deep adoration should feel like, with a man who cherished her simply for being herself. Who was she kidding? She'd gone and fallen in love with him weeks ago. She just wished things were different, so she could tell him so. And then, allowing the feeling of this to sink deeper into her heart, she drifted and slipped into the deepest, most contented sleep she'd ever had, dreaming of a life where there were no barriers, no reasons not to let him see just how much she loved him. If only it was a place she could forever stay.

CHAPTER 15

Harsh beeping dragged Melody from her sound sleep. It took her a few moments to grasp where she was, and who she was snuggled up against. The realisation it was Zai buoyed her heart into the twinkling blanket of stars above – she wanted to stay in his arms forever. But duties, and reality, were calling. Groaning, she snaked a hand out from the warmth of the swag and turned her alarm off. It felt as if she'd just stuck her hand in a fridge. It was freezing – Zai wasn't pulling her leg when he told her it got icy cold. The men were stirring from their slumbers too, grunts and groans coming from every direction, as did the sound of swags being yanked up and pulled in tight.

'Bloody hell, it's so cold, my nipples are going to roll off.' Tumbles's unmistakable voice travelled and was met with chuckles. Amidst the mirth, of course, there was a single grunt from Hasselhoof.

'Your turn to get the campfire started, Tumbles.' Slim's baritone voice echoed through the pre-dawn silence.

'Yeah, righto, you slave driver.' Tumbles's chattering teeth were followed by a loud yawn. 'Then again, I reckon Showbags should step up and show us what he's made of in the fire-starting department, the slackarse.'

'Oi, buddy, I did it yesterday, remember?' Showbags chimed back.

'Would you lot shut up and let a man wake up in some peace and quiet for bloody once,' Hasselhoof groused. 'Anyone would think we're at summer camp.'

'It's always lovely hearing your happy singsong voice in the morning, Hasselhoof,' Showbags said, stirring again.

'Get buggered, fart features,' Hasselhoof retorted.

'I beg your pardon. I don't fart, I poof glitter and stardust.' Showbags's attempt at a posh English accent was horrendous. 'And every time I do, it smells like roses.'

Melody chuckled, as did the rest of the men, including Zai.

'And there you have it, bright and early, another day of bantering has begun.' Zai's gravelly voice brought a smile to Melody's lips. 'Good morning, cook,' he added, way sexier than any other person on the planet could possibly be while saying such a simple statement.

'Good morning, you. I better get up and start feeding you hungry lot.' She went to unravel herself from the most protective embrace she'd ever had the pleasure of lying within.

But he trapped her within his arms, pulling her closer. 'Before you go, tell me. Did you have the best sleep ever?'

His strong, hard body pressed into her, from head to toe. 'Yes, I actually did.' She seriously wanted to stay here all day and make sweet, wild, hot love to him.

'See, I told you so.'

The camp lit up as Slim fired up a gas lantern.

'Mm-hmm, you sure did.' She purred from the depths of her contented soul.

'You might have to try it again, this sleeping out under the stars in a swag, with me, of course.' He murmured into her hair. 'It wouldn't be as much fun otherwise.'

Melody quivered. Zai's husky whispers so close to her ear were driving her wild, making her ache for him in places she shouldn't. She had to get up. Now. Before she rolled over and did something really stupid, like kiss him, hot and hungry, or ripped every shred of clothing from his delectable body.

And so she got up, almost bounding from the swag in her haste to curb her insatiable appetite for him. 'Come on, Tumbles, get this fire going, would you, or I'm not making you any brekkie,' she said jovially as she passed.

'Righto boss, on it.' He jumped up, hitting his head on an overhanging branch. 'Ouch. Bloody hell, who put that tree there?'

Melody chuckled, shaking her head. 'Whatever would we do without you around for laughs, Tumbles?'

'Hey, you got me for that too, Melds,' Showbags chimed in.

'That we most certainly do. You pair are as hilarious as each other,' she called back.

'Nope, hands down, I'm way funnier,' Tumbled hollered.

'Whatever, Tumbles, more like way clumsier.' Showbags rose from his swag and stretched.

The two men gave each other the bird and laughed.

Walking over to the drum of bore water up on the back of the LandCruiser, Melody opened the tap and filled the wash bucket. Plonking it on the tray, she splashed some of the cold water onto her face, trying to jolt some life, and sense, into her. Her usually bouncy hair was frizzed by the bore water and lack of a good brushing, so she resigned to pulling it into a messy bun – she'd deal with the knots later, when she had some conditioner and a wide-toothed comb.

Feeling somewhat refreshed and awake, she got to work making the men a full Aussie breakfast in the two cast-iron pans Tumbles had thoughtfully set up over the campfire. By the light of a lantern and the flicker of the fire, she stealthily avoided spits from the bacon and sausages as she manned it, tongs at the ready. In place of the billycan Showbags had just boiled and was now twirling like a pro in circles with a wide spin of his arm overhead – she prayed to god the lid didn't somehow come off and scald him – she hung a pot of eggs in water over the fire. Boiled eggs it would be. Zai got to work beside her, toasting a heap of bread in the wire contraption Slim had apparently built when he'd first started here – it worked an absolute treat. An hour later, they were sitting round the fire, bellies full, pannikins in hand, almost ready to start another day in the saddle.

And that was when Hasselhoof decided to hit her with an absolute sucker punch. 'So, tell me, Melody, how do you know for sure that your mum wasn't wrong about Walshee being your old man?' Arms folded, he twirled a toothpick in his mouth, his beady eyes drilling into her, his bushy brows deeply furrowed. 'I mean, he's a wealthy bloke, including being an heir to this place, so you have a lot to gain by being his daughter.'

The atmosphere of the camp went from jovial to serious in an instant.

'I, um, uhh ...' The shameless question had come out of nowhere, and she found herself momentarily lost for the right words.

'Because she just does, Hasselhoof.' Zai's tone was sharp, direct – as was the cautionary look he was now giving his fellow stockman. 'Don't ask questions about things that ain't any of your goddamn business.'

'Yeah, righto, Wellstone. Just asking, bloody hell.' Hasselhoof shrugged as though it wasn't a big deal. 'I would have asked for a DNA test if some stranger turned up at my door, telling me she was my daughter. I ain't as trusting as Walshee. But that's just me.'

'Geez, Hasselhoof. This isn't something you should be asking, so lay off, would ya,' Slim growled.

Showbags and Tumbles looked more sombre than Melody had ever seen them.

Hasselhoof went to retort, but Zai held his hand up. 'I wouldn't say another word if I were you.'

Melody hadn't even stopped to think of such a thing – her mother's word was one she took wholeheartedly and without a shadow of a doubt. To get a DNA test would be her disrespecting her mother's word and memory. Anger rose in her chest and tightened her throat. She bit back expletives, instead glaring at Hasselhoof. He actually had the audacity to glare back at her. He may have been the camp grump, but this was personal. Very personal. Choked up by a rush of intense emotions, the sting of tears threatened. She turned her back to them and caught her breath – no way was she crying because of some cold-hearted bushie. Zai's hand came protectively to her back and stayed there.

She didn't need a damn test to know Matthew Walsh was her father, and the fact that he hadn't even suggested such a thing to her when she'd told him he was her father spoke volumes about the man Matt was. Besides, put the two of them side by side and anyone could see the father–daughter resemblance from a mile away.

'Cat got your tongue, Melody?' Hasselhoof had the nerve to ask.

'What in the bloody hell, arsehole, haven't you got better things to do than pick on a harmless woman.' Zai's fury was unmistakable. He rose and closed the distance with determined strides, stopping short to tower over where Hasselhoof was sitting on a stump. 'Leave her the hell alone.'

'Shut your trap, Wellstone, before I—'

Zai's body tensed and his free hand clenched. 'Before you what?' It was snarled through gritted teeth.

Hasselhoof unravelled from his stump and put his fists up. 'Come on then, big gun. Let's see what you got.'

Melody finally found her voice. 'Both of you, stop it. This isn't worth fighting over.'

'Yeah, you two, enough of that.' Slim stepped into the makeshift boxing ring beside the campfire and made a barricade between the two men. 'No need for fists to fly. Let's be honest, we all know what's going to happen if they do.'

'Oh yeah?' Hasselhoof dropped his fists to his side and turned his glare to Slim. 'What's that?'

'Come on, Hasselhoof.' Slim was stifling a grin now. 'You'll be flat on your back with a broken nose, if you're lucky. Zai might hurt his pinkie.'

If looks could kill, Hasselhoof would have murdered Slim in that very second. Turning on his heel, he stomped off towards the horses. 'Bugger the lot of you,' he bellowed once he was at a safe distance. 'You can all go to bloody hell.'

After sharing a couple of disgusted looks, the men looked to Melody, asking if she was okay. Although still hurt by Hasselhoof's lack of tact, and suggestion her mum could have been lying, she nodded and tried to brush it off. She didn't want to make matters worse. She'd known Zai would have had a fiercely protective side but seeing it in person was impressive. And to know it was all because he was defending her and her mum … She'd never had any man do that for her before, not ever. How in the hell was she meant continue to resist a man who made her feel more loved than anyone, other than her mum, ever had? Taking a deep breath, she tried to rein in her myriad emotions – anger, shock, hurt – all overpowered by deep undeniable love.

Zai came to her side and gently tipped her face to his. 'Are you okay, beautiful?'

He just called me beautiful …

'Yeah, I'm fine.' She gave him her best smile but could feel it trembling at the edges. 'I've dealt with way worse than the likes of him. It just shocked me, and kinda put me on the spot.'

'Of course it bloody well did, the heartless bastard.' Zai's jaw clenched again as he shook his head. 'He's lucky I didn't biff him one.'

'I'm glad you didn't. It wasn't worth coming to blows over.'

'You're worth protecting.' His eyes filled with stormy intensity. 'I'll always have your back, no matter what.'

All Melody could do was stare at him, her admiration for him growing by the second.

His hand came to her arm and rested there, protectively, reassuring. 'I'll catch you back at home, okay?'

She gave him a swift nod, feigning a resilience she was far from feeling. 'Okay. Have a good day. And thank you for looking out for me.'

'Always.'

Melody cleared what she wanted to say from her throat. If only she could fall into his arms and tell him how much she wanted to stay within his embrace because she felt so safe, so home, so loved when he held her close.

'Drive safely back to the homestead. No fishtailing, Miss Daisy Duke.' His baby blues lingered. They both took a breath before he turned and strode away from her, taking one last look over his shoulder while he adjusted the brim of his hat.

Packing the camp up just as the sun began to rise from the thin red horizon, spilling a painter's pot of blue, pink, purple, gold and red, she watched the guys huddle around the map Slim had spread out on the bonnet of the LandCruiser. Hasselhoof wasn't part of the team meeting, instead sulking over at the holding yards, a cigarette hanging from his lips. She half listened to the stockmen discussing the paddocks and plan for the day's muster – it was way more intricate than she'd imagined and made her admire Zai even more. Twenty minutes later, and they were all mounting their horses. Zai gave her one last arresting nod before galloping out of sight.

Melody hollered to Harold and he hobbled over from the shade of the trees. Without needing an invitation, he got himself settled in the passenger seat. With her travel companion safe and sound in his usual spot, Melody jumped behind the wheel. As much as she'd enjoyed the night spent beneath the canopy of stars, wrapped up in the arms of a very handsome man, Hasselhoof had soured the experience with his thoughtless interrogation. She was hoping, after a long hot shower, she could shake his negative comments off. She had planned to talk to her dad sometime today and was undecided as to whether she would tell him about what the old grump had said.

Gripping the steering wheel, she turned in the direction of the homestead, glancing in her rear-vision mirror to watch the trail of dust spiralling behind her.

* * *

Three days passed before Hasselhoof even had the decency to speak a word to her again, and even then, it was only three: 'Dinner was okay.'

No appreciation for her going above and beyond with her meal choices, no apology for being a dick. It irked her that he treated her like it was she who had caused the rift in the first place. Some people were honestly so ignorant to the feelings of others. The vibe of the men was far from light when Hasselhoof was around – the whole equilibrium thrown off centre because Slim, Showbags, Tumbles and Zai all agreed what the man had done was unacceptable. It had been the final straw to them putting up with his constant bellyaching. She'd chosen not to tell her dad, not wanting to stir up any more dust – she'd rather it settled.

Heading towards the kitchen to begin her dinner duties, she looked down at her loyal companion, thankful for Harold's constant company. Reaching the back door, the old cattle dog collapsed in his usual spot and rested his chin against the hard-baked earth, sighing, as if resigned to spending the rest of the day here.

'It's a dog's life, hey boy.' Melody crouched down and gave him a scruff behind his greying ears. 'I reckon you would have earned your keep, in your younger years, so I'd lay around all day too, if I were you.'

Harold replied by giving her a quick lick to her hand.

Stepping into the coolness of the common kitchen, she flicked the radio on, washed her hands, and got to work. Shepherd's pie was on the menu, along with a garden salad and garlic bread, followed up with baked cheesecake for dessert. Strapping on her apron, she allowed herself to get lost in slicing, stirring, tasting and manning the oven while humming and singing to one familiar tune after the other. Before she knew it, the men were wandering in, freshly showered, weary and famished.

With the flywire door thumping closed behind him, Hasselhoof pulled up a chair at the farthest end of the twelve-seater table and buried his nose in a magazine. Tumbles and Showbags did their usual routine of stirring each other up while setting the table. Slim helped himself to a couple of homemade chocolate chip biscuits from the tin while he got himself a cup of tea. And Zai, much to her pleasure, focused all his attention on her, and the food she'd lovingly prepared.

'It smells absolutely bloody amazing in here, as usual,' Slim muttered between bites.

'Damn straight it does.' Zai nodded in agreement. Eyes wide, he checked out her pièce de résistance – the white and dark chocolate swirled orange cheesecake. 'Holy moly, I can't wait to tuck into this beauty.'

'Thanks, guys. Hopefully it tastes as good as it looks, hey.' Grabbing a serving spoon, she started dishing up generous servings of the shepherd's pie. 'Make yourself useful, would you, Wellstone, and put the salad and garlic bread on the table for me.' She flashed him a sassy smile.

'I can make myself more useful by taste-testing this first, if you like.' Grabbing a fork, he hovered it above, teasing her as if he were about to dig right on in. 'Mind if I help myself?'

'You know the rules of my kitchen, mister. No sneaky sampling.'

'Oh, come on, just this once.' He dropped the fork a little lower, so it was just touching the top. 'Please?'

Melody snatched the fork from him. 'Behave, Zai Wellstone, before I ban you from my kitchen forever.'

Hands shooting up, he grinned. 'That'd be like a life sentence.' Collecting the salad and garlic bread, he paused beside her. 'Actually no, I take that back. It would be two life sentences without any chance of parole.'

She clouted him with her tea towel. 'Oh, stop it.'

'I'm being deadly serious.' He leant in a little closer, dropping his voice. 'Your cooking is the only thing I look forward to every day. Oh, and your ability to have an adult conversation.' He tipped his head a little to the side, gesturing to where Showbags had Tumbles in a headlock. 'Putting up with this immature pair all day long can send a man batty.'

'Oi, Wellstone, we can hear you, you know,' Showbags chuckled, ruffling Tumbles's already chaotic head of hair, then finally let his mate go. 'Anyone would think you're trying to impress the cook for brownie points,' he added brazenly, his stride as cocky and proud as a rooster. 'I'm onto you.' He waggled a finger in Zai's face. 'Mister Smooth.'

'Shh, don't give away all my secrets, buddy.' Laughing, he slapped his mate's finger away then unloaded the plates of food into the middle of the table.

'Yes, always the charmer, aren't you?' Melody said in passing as she plonked two plates down and went back for the others. She loved how Zai made her laugh more genuinely than she had in what felt like forever – it always helped to lighten the load of hurt in her heart.

Zai scooted in and helped her with the last of the dishes. 'Only when there's a pretty lady worth charming.'

Warm fuzzies filled her soul, but she wasn't about to give too much credit to them. 'Is that so, Casanova?'

There was a fleeting shadow of hurt in Zai's eyes. 'I'm more like Romeo than Casanova, thank you very much.' It was said jokingly, but the intonation of defence was evident. 'And one day, I hope to find my Juliet.'

Tumbled looked at his mate as if Zai had lost his marbles. 'Pfft, whatever Wellstone.'

Showbags dropped to his knees, his hand on his heart. 'Oh Romeo, Romeo, wherefore art thou Romeo.' He'd tried to alter his voice to resemble a woman's but had hilariously failed.

Zai chuckled and shook his head. 'Bugger off, you pair of shitheads.'

After eight days straight in the saddle, and with the hot weather wearing all of them thin, dinner was quick and the clean-up was even quicker. Zai was the last man standing, refusing to go until he'd walked Melody back to the homestead, as he always did. Reaching up on her tippy toes, she tucked the bottles of sauces back into the pantry, sighing wearily when she closed the door. After a nice hot shower, she was looking forward to hitting the sack.

'I think that's everything.' Zai straightened the chairs into place at the table. 'You good to go now, Sweet Melody?'

Her heart pitter-pattering with his chosen nickname for her, she took one last look around and, happy the place was spick-and-span, nodded. 'Yup, sure am.'

Just as they went to step outside, with Harold hot on their heels, a resounding boom of thunder had both of them almost jumping out of their skins. The usually tough-as-nails Harold ducked, cowering at Zai's feet. His terrified eyes darted from Zai to Melody, and his tail all but disappeared between his legs. Melody gave him a reassuring pat on the head. Then the sound of the generator ceased and the power cut out, leaving them in a world so dark, she could barely see an inch in front of her until her eyes adjusted.

A pocket torch flicked to life, illuminating their path home. 'Talk about timing, hey.'

'Where'd you pluck that from?' she asked.

'I always carry this little beauty with me when I head out at night. You never know when the power will cut.' He held it beneath his chin, lighting his face in an eerie kind of way. 'Or when you need to scare the pants off someone in the black of night.'

'You tripper.' Melody laughed at his antics. She seriously wished he could get her pants off, even if it meant scaring her. Falling into step with him, she was relieved for the sense of safety his company brought. 'Thank goodness we didn't lose power when I was cooking, otherwise you lot would have gotten a can of beans each for dinner.'

'A few months back, none of us would have cared much, but now you've spoilt us all.' Halting his steps, Zai looked to the menacing dark clouds rolling across the moonlit sky, quickly swallowing the glittering stars, as if ravenous. 'I reckon this is going to be one cracker of a storm.'

'Looks like it.' Melody stood close to him as she followed his gaze. 'It certainly explains why it's been so damn hot the past couple of days.'

Zai placed his hand on the small of her back and gently pressed her onwards. 'Come on, we better get you back before it hits.'

Heads down, they walked quickly, Harold sticking close behind. Time barely passed between each flash and rumble, and the earth felt as if it were trembling beneath her feet. In a matter of seconds, the humidity of the day was gone. The inky darkness closed in on them, and the fast moving clouds cast creeping shadows across their path. Just as they were heading up the homestead steps, forks of lightning split the sky once again. A deep rumbling echoed before a rifle-crack of thunder detonated, followed by another. Whining, Harold scurried to the front door and pressed himself flush up against it, his fearful gaze begging Melody to let him inside – a place he quite often didn't care to be. Melody crouched down at her doggie mate's side, soothing Harold as much as she could with nervous fingers. She shivered, both from the abrupt change of temperature and the ferocity of the storm rolling in at alarming speed.

Zai didn't appear fazed in the slightest. 'I'm gathering you've never seen an outback storm in full swing?'

'No, never.' She straightened, kicking off her thongs.

'You're in for a real treat then.' He pointed to the swing chair, squeaking as it swayed in the gusty breeze. 'You need to grab yourself a drink then plant yourself there so you can watch it all unfold.'

'I'm not sure I want to stay out here to watch.' Shoving the door open, Harold launched inside the house, his scuttling feet disappearing into the darkness.

'Really? Well, I can stay here with you, if it makes you feel better?'

She almost knocked his offer back, but the thought of sitting in the dark house on her own, with the storm lashing outside, stopped her from being so silly. 'That would actually be nice, thanks Zai.'

He clearly didn't need any more of an invitation as he kicked his boots off. 'Great, let's go and grab a beer and get back out here before we miss the show.'

'Sounds like a plan, but I think this weather calls for a bottle of red.' She stepped past him. 'What do you think?'

He shone the torch down the hallway, now shadowy and a little spooky. 'Even better.'

While Zai got Harold settled on a blanket beneath the dining table, Melody's heart swooning with his reassuring pats and gentle words, she gathered wine and a packet of peanut M&Ms – her guilty pleasure. The rumbles and cracks grew increasingly closer and echoed around the dark house. Just as they stepped back out onto the verandah, with two glasses, a bottle of cab sav, sweet treats, and a blanket, the heart of the storm opened up upon them. The scent of impending rain was refreshing. Sinking into the swing chair, nice and close, Zai flicked the blanket over their legs. With him holding the glasses, Melody poured them both some wine. An earth-shuddering thunderclap boomed directly overhead, rattling the glass of the windows and reverberating deep within her bones. Then the biggest strike of silvery-blue lightning she'd ever seen split the graphite sky in two, the electromagnetic force somehow kick-starting her heart and sending her caged spirit soaring. The sheer energy swirling around them was mind-blowing.

Like a heaving breath by the mouth of the heavens, the wind picked up and tossed a scattering of leaves across the verandah just as the first drops of water struck the iron roof so heavily, it was impossible to hear anything else. Curtains of rain stabbed upon the dry, dusty earth and quickly formed puddles of rusty water. Transfixed and overwhelmed by the spectacle unfolding before her, Melody breathed in deep – it smelt so wonderful and so different to the storms in the city. Clean. Invigorating. Pure. The gutters quickly filled with the deluge, and water poured out of the downpipes. Frogs croaked noisily, as if rejoicing. She could almost sense the earth quenching its thirst. The fragrance of what she could only describe as renewed hope clung to the air, making her feel the same. Further bits of her broken heart slipped back into place, making her feel more whole, more centred, more sure of what she wanted – and also of what she didn't want. Never would she have believed that a storm could be so therapeutic, so soul-opening.

Zai was quiet for a while, looking up at the sky as if he too was searching for the answers she was stumbling upon. She ached to know what he was contemplating.

'What are you thinking about?' she asked, gently.

He turned to her, his eyes a little sad. 'I'm not sure you'd want to know.' He quickly looked away, clearing his throat.

'Trust me, I really do.' She held her breath, hoping he was going to let her in – he deserved the same sort of comfort that he gave to her.

He heaved a sigh and looked to his clasped hands. 'Do you sometimes wish things were less … I dunno, complicated?' He lifted his gaze back to her, and it was filled was so much tenderness, it stole her breath.

She resisted the urge to interpret it. 'Of course I do.'

He went to respond, but his mouth closed tight and he shook his head. It took him a few lengthy moments to try again. 'I struggle with feeling like the black sheep of my family.'

She tipped her head and placed a hand on his bouncing knee. 'How so?'

Zai explained why and she listened intently to his words, her heart breaking for him. She may have lost her mother and only just found her father, but at least she felt loved by both of them. He, on the other hand, felt like a failure in his parents' eyes, and that would be a very heavy cross to carry.

She touched his arm. 'You're a good man, Zai, and a damn hard worker. They should be proud of you, not reminding you every chance they get that you're not living up to their idea of success.'

He turned, took her hand in his, and brought it to his lips, kissing it. 'Thank you, Melody, for making me feel like you have my back. You don't know how much that means to me.'

'Of course I do, just like you have mine.' She offered him a gentle smile, wishing she could do more than that to let him know just how much she cared for him.

'You really are a special woman, Sweet Melody.'

'Thank you,' she said, blinking back tears.

A lengthy silence followed, the lingering of words unspoken weighing heavily on the rain-scented air. If only the time could stop ticking, and the world stop spinning, for just a little while, so they could be in a biosphere of their own where nothing and nobody else mattered.

'The water tanks and dams are going to be overflowing before we know it.' Zai leapt to his feet and grabbed her by the hand. 'Come on, let's have ourselves some fun.'

'What are you doing?' she asked as she was tugged to her feet.

He hauled her towards the steps. 'What does it look like?'

Planting her feet squarely, Melody put the brakes on just before they descended the steps. 'From where I am, it looks like you've lost your mind, Mister Wellstone.'

'Oh, come on.' He sighed lightheartedly, rolling his dreamy eyes. 'Haven't you ever run around in the rain?'

She couldn't help but laugh at the childlike wonder on his oh-so-manly face. 'No.'

'Well, now's your chance.' He held out his hand. 'May I have this dance?'

She almost stopped herself, but then thought, what the hell. In the city, rain was something she, and everyone else, absconded from. And she was tired of turning her back on the simple pleasures of life. She only lived once, as Zai often reminded her, so to hell with it. She was going to dance like nobody was watching and get drenched through to the skin while doing so.

'Okay then, you've twisted my arm.' Once again, Zai was flipping everything she'd ever known on its head, and she loved every single second of it.

If she was being honest with herself, she also loved every single inch of him, inside and out. Because for the very first time in her life, she felt as if a man truly saw her, and adored all that made her, her. That was authentic love. A love worth risking all for.

CHAPTER 16

Spinning Melody around in the rain, seeing her face aglow and hearing her unadulterated laughter was music to Zai's ears, and a sweet symphony to his stormy soul. All of her calmed all of him. There was so much light in her, overflowing and filling the darkest parts of him, parts he'd believed would never see the light of day. Up until crossing paths with her, he'd truly believed he wasn't relationship material, had told himself he didn't need love, that it was too much of a complication, and all because he assumed he wasn't worthy of being unconditionally loved. Year after year, he'd owned his Casanova reputation, but now he wanted it gone. Forever. He wanted Melody to trust him when he finally found the courage to tell her exactly how he felt about her, and about the possibility of a beautiful future together. Just thinking about it now made his stomach somersault, then backflip. What if she didn't feel the same? What if she knocked him back, and it ruined the wonderful friendship they had? What if … no, he had to stop this. For once, he had to believe in himself, and his self-worth.

He had enough friends, and when it came to her, he wanted, needed, more than friendship. But how was he meant to tell her?

He knew it had been his choice to armour up his heart, and build a fort for good measure, but it was also conditioning from his hard-hearted, hard-headed father. Just being around Melody had helped him to see this clearly. He'd never wanted to be the same as his dad, had actually believed he was nothing like him, but unwillingly, he'd become a little hard-hearted and a little hard-headed too – until the mesmerising Miss Melody Harrison-Walsh had pirouetted into his life and shown him what real adoration and companionship felt like. Somehow, someway, he had to make her his. He wanted to love her like no other. He wanted to see her smiling face each and every day for the rest of his life. He wanted to have a family with her. The certainty of this both terrified and electrified him beyond comprehension. So, for now, all he could do was run with it, allowing each and every passing second with her to haul him towards where they were meant to go. He had to just be, with her.

And in this very moment, he was having the time of his life, swept up by this majestic woman. Whirling her into his arms, he continued to sway her around the yard to a silent tune of their own, their feet squelching and their clothes wet through to the skin – sweet, soft skin he was dying to kiss from head to toe. Their harmless, playful flirting quickly turned into something deeper, and more meaningful … she was everything he hadn't been aware he was searching for, and more, so much more. As she rested her head against the place his heart raced, he felt a very big part of himself slip into perfect position. He'd been trying to find his niche in this world for as long as he could remember, had ached to discover his home – never had he believed it would be found in a woman. Yet, here he was, certain of exactly that.

He ran his hand up her back, and down her arm. Goosebumps rose beneath his touch as she lifted her face from his chest. Dark lashes swept her cheekbones before her heavy-lidded gaze met his, the depth within telling him everything he needed to know. He'd never found himself as lost for words as he was right now. Her slightly parted lips tempted him to savour the sweetness of them. He wanted her more than he'd ever wanted anything in his life. What if he never got another poignant moment like this to make his feelings known?

Desire exploded in his chest. Restraint was instantly beyond him. They'd stopped moving, yet so much moved between them. He needed her. Now. Reaching out, he slipped strands of wet hair behind her ears, then trailed his fingers down her cheeks. So much was said in that silent, breathless moment. He was close enough to kiss her. She clasped her bottom lip between her teeth, driving the last of his breath out of his lungs. A blush broke out along her cheeks when the curves of her body met with the hard planes of his, in every sense – he couldn't hide his attraction to her any longer. It was completely out of his control.

They remained like this for a heartbeat, and then another, their inhalations and exhalations mingling, their eyes locked to one another's, their hearts beating against each other's. Then time stood still, and the entirety of the world faded away, leaving just her, and him, here, now – there was never a better moment to grab hold of. So he jumped off the proverbial cliff he'd been balancing on. Leaning in, he tenderly kissed the droplets of rain from her lips, slowly, softly, carefully, savouring her, and also allowing her the time to pull away, to stop him, before he gave in to her, wholly and solely.

But she didn't.

Instead, she urged him to kiss her harder, deeper, tugging his belt loops and drawing his waist even closer to her. But he still held back, just that little bit. He wanted her to really want him. He needed her to be sure. Because once they crossed this line, there'd be no going back for him and, hopefully, for her. Then, when she laced her fingers around the back of his neck, and whispered how much she wanted him, that was the exact moment he irrevocably, for the very first time in his life, let go of any inhibitions. When he felt her smile against his lips, he finally threw caution to the wind and pulled her closer, making sure as hell she knew he was about to tear his armour off, lay her down, and make love to her.

And it was then that she pulled back, just a little, to look up at him. Her gaze was uncertain, and a little wary. 'What are you doing to me, Zai?' she whispered between panting breaths.

Panic fuelled his already racing pulse into a wild gallop. Hell. What was he doing? He almost went to retreat – his usual defence mechanism – but he wasn't about to make her feel discarded in a moment as intense at this. But he couldn't find the words he'd rehearsed, over and over, for this very moment. His head spun. His mouth went dry.

'Just hanging out with a really awesome chick who's also taking my breath away.' He instantly wanted to slap himself for saying something so blasé when he sought to state the polar opposite.

'Really?' She tipped her head just a little but enough to make it known she was contemplating this. 'Because in my experience, when guys hang out, they're usually only chasing one thing.' She inched away from him.

Zai pulled her back, tight. 'Melody, please believe me, I'm not chasing anything.' His words were desperate and he didn't care. He had to make this right. 'I'm just going with what feels natural, and right, and real … and that's all of you.'

She went to say something, but then her words seemed to jam in her throat. She looked at him intently, like she was searching for something more specific. But right now, as much as he ached to, he just couldn't give any more to her – this was all new to him, this sensation of falling in love, and he was terrified of being rejected, of ruining what could be so magical between them, of his heart being shattered if he couldn't love her like he burned to because she didn't want to let him into her big, beautiful heart.

God help him if that were to be the case.

A sigh slipped from her lips, her eyes closing softly. Then, without a word, her arms went back around him and she rested her cheek upon his chest. Breathing a sigh of silent relief, he laced his hands around her waist. The closeness between them right now was unfathomable, the intensity of the all-consuming passion limitless. The rain had eased to a soft sprinkle, the thunder and lightning was now off in the far-flung distance. Resting his head against her wet hair, he swayed her around the backyard – it was as if the universe was conspiring to make this the most romantic night ever. And he thanked the powers that be for such a beautiful blessing. Heat swirled deep inside him. His heart raced with quick, hard beats, and he hoped she could feel it. He wanted her to know just how deeply he felt for her without having to utter a single word. By god, he so desperately wanted to make love to her. But he wasn't going to go that far. This, right here, was everything they needed, for now.

They swayed like that for a while, until he felt her shiver within his arms. 'Are you getting cold, beautiful?' he asked, gently.

She nodded against him. 'I am, but I don't want this night to end.' She brought her eyes to his and blinked faster, as if she were warding off tears. 'I've never felt so …' She cleared her throat and shook her head, then buried her head against him once more.

'So what?' he dared to ask.

'So … everything,' was her muffled reply.

His heart reached deeper into hers and tightened around it. 'I'll take that,' he said, smiling. 'I should let you get some sleep, gorgeous lady.' He stopped swaying and untangled them enough to be able to look into her eyes. 'We have to be up in less than …' He took a moment to see the time on his watch, '… five hours.'

'Oh, wow, is it that late already?' She sniffed, hard, and then slowly stepped out of his embrace. 'Time flies, hey.' Her hands went into the pockets of her cute denim shorts.

'Whenever I'm with you, damn straight it does.'

The way she looked at him made his heart skip a beat. 'Thank you, Zai, for another amazing night beneath the stars, and the rain.' She sucked in a breath and then slowly exhaled it away.

'Yeah, we seem to be making it a habit.' His hands went into his pockets now. 'A habit I'm really liking, by the way.'

'Me too.' Rocking back and forth on her heels, she did that thing that drove him nuts and bit her bottom lip ever so coyly.

'Come on, then.' He gestured to the homestead with a tip of his head. 'I'll walk you to the door.'

She laughed softly, pointing towards it. 'It's just there. I'm sure I can make it safely.'

'That's not the point.' He reached out and tugged a hand from her pocket.

She allowed him to lead her across the back lawn and up the steps, the distance between where they'd danced and the door too short – every second with her counted so very much. Facing him, she rested against the screen door and held his gaze. He almost took her back into his arms and told her how deeply he was falling in love with her, but fear and a shot of willpower stopped him. It was an unfamiliar sensation – he'd never been afraid of anything.

He rubbed a hand over his stubble. 'Well, night, lovely.'

She licked her lips. 'Night then. Have a good sleep, won't you.'

'I will. You too.' Forcing himself to turn and walk away, he took one last look over his shoulder and then disappeared into the blackness of night, taking a piece of her with him – it was a lot more than he'd expected to leave with.

Twenty minutes later, after pacing his back verandah while staring at the homestead, Zai found himself back at her front door, standing before her. She looked at him with wild passion in her eyes. Something fierce and possessive rose within him. He was helpless and there was nothing he could do to stop himself from grabbing hold of this moment, no matter the consequences. So he took her in his arms and kissed her, hot and hungry, his desire building like a wildfire. To his relief, she gave in to the moment too, begging him to follow her inside so he could make love to her, all night long. He didn't need any further invitation. Picking her up while kissing her, he carried her into the house, and to her bedroom. Finally, they were going to jump over the edge and freefall into one another – she was going to be his, now and forever. He would make it so.

Placing her on the bed, he undressed, as did she, each of them watching the other the entire time. Revealing his body, heart and soul to her with absolute abandonment, he climbed on top of her and, taking her wrists, held them to the bed as he kissed her long, slow and deep. Her breathing quickened, became raspy. She pleaded with him to be at one with her. Wanting to make their very first time last, he held off surrendering until he couldn't take it any longer. Then, he slowly slid inside her, taking great pleasure in her sharp inhalations and her pleasure-filled exhales as her nails dug into his back. Arching into him, she hooked her legs around him, begging him to go deeper, and he gave her what she hungered for, making sure to slow it down so she felt every skin-tingling stroke. She rolled her hips in unison with his, and they moved with one heartbeat, one soul. Climbing to dizzying heights he'd never been to before, he teetered there until he didn't know how much longer he could last. His fingers dug into her hips as he thrust faster, harder, and it was only when he felt her tighten, when he heard her shuddering gasps, that he too let go, tumbling into the euphoric abyss with her, swirling in each other's arms until they were breathless.

And that's when Zai woke, hot and heavy, to the dawn sunlight creeping between his curtains, with a hunger fiercer than he'd ever felt before. His erotic dream was going to leave him feeling ravenous for her. He sat up, growling beneath his weighty breath – if he could get his hands on Melody right now, she'd be in trouble. Running his hands through his short-cropped hair, he tried to shake the yearning from his heart, and other places that didn't need any more temptation. Tossing the sheet back, he climbed from the bed. He needed a cold shower. Now. Before he drove himself totally insane with need for her. Miranda Lambert's song 'I Feel a Sin Comin' On' came to mind as he plucked his towel from behind the door and sauntered down the hallway absolutely butt-naked.

An hour later, after he'd eaten satisfying breakfast of baked beans and fried eggs, the cattle lifted their heads as he and Melody tore alongside the rustic picketed barbed-wire fence on the quad bike, her arms wrapped around his waist to secure her seat, her hair blowing wild in the wind. He was enjoying his sneaky glimpses of her in the rear-view mirror, her face a picture of utter contentment. Her spirit was alive here – he just needed to get her to see it for herself, if she didn't already, so he could persuade her to stay longer. The city didn't suit her. He – they – needed more time here, where their hearts were at home and free.

Spotting where two wires were broken, he pulled to a stop, grabbed his tools from the crate roped to the front of the four-wheeler then, after Melody had leant back, jumped off. Once the wires were taut, he used pliers to join the ends, loving the way he could sense her eyes burning into his back. The attraction between them was unmistakable, although neither of them had mentioned a word about last night. He wasn't sure if that was a good, or bad, thing.

'Good job, cowboy,' she said. Her smile was different since last night's kiss. Instead of companionship, it was filled with tantalising sensuality.

'Why, thankya, cowgirl.'

Climbing back aboard, he revved the bike to life and cut across an open paddock, towards the homestead. Next on the agenda was a flutter in the chopper, to check on the far-reaching paddocks.

They pulled up beneath the shade of the shed. 'You want to grab a drink before we head off again?'

'Sounds like a plan.' She hitched her leg over the bike and hopped off. 'You keen for a can of cola?'

'Is the pope Catholic?' Falling in step beside her, he shoved his hands into his pockets. He was doing everything he could to keep his hands to himself, but if she flashed him that come-hither gaze one more time, he was seriously a goner.

Just as they were nearing the homestead steps, she turned to him. 'I've been meaning to tell you, I really enjoyed last night, Zai.' Her eyes fluttered. 'Thanks again for asking me to dance in the rain with you. It was something I'll never, ever forget.'

His heart catapulted from his chest.

Oh shit.

His hands itched to reach out and pull her to him, but he fought the sensation. 'I'm glad I'm getting you to release that wild country-girl side of you.' Clearing the longing from his throat, he tugged the brim of his hat, a nervous twitch. 'Because hot damn, it suits you, one hell of a lot.'

She blushed just a little. 'I must admit, I'm loving it here.' Opening her arms wide, her mouth matched them. 'I feel so free, and so … me, as if I've finally found a piece of myself that I never knew existed, and I don't mean my father, but … more about my core, if that makes any sense.'

'It makes perfect sense.' He watched her lean into the drinks fridge at the corner of the verandah, unable to drag his eyes from the perfect curves of her butt in her diamanté-studded jeans until she turned around and her beautiful coffee-coloured eyes drew his like magnets.

'Here you go.' She handed him an icy can and a Snickers chocolate bar. 'I thought we needed a bit of sustenance too – the sugary kind.'

'Blimey, Miss Mel, you're spoiling me.' Snapping the can open, he took a big glug, stifling a burp. 'Oops, 'scuse me.'

She looked to him with absolute mischief, and then, to his surprise and amusement, outdid his burp tenfold. 'Pardon me,' she said, laughing, before chomping down on her Snickers, groaning in pleasure.

He chuckled at her contented eye-roll of chocolatey pleasure as they sat on the top step, yacking about this and that while they finished their drinks and devoured their chocolates. Then, with time ticking, they got back to it.

Melody slid into the chopper and pulled on her seatbelt, triple-checking to make sure she was buckled in nice and tight out of habit. She didn't think she would have dared to go up with anyone but Zai at the helm. 'It feels so strange, knowing the door will be open the entire time.'

'You'll love it, it makes you feel so free up there in yonder.'

'Ha, I'll soon find out, won't I?'

'You sure will.' He passed her the headset. 'Pop this on so we can chat while we hover.'

She slipped it on and adjusted the microphone so it was near her mouth. He checked everything twice then, with the flick of a switch, the Robinson whirred to noisy life. The blades sliced the air, whop-whopping rhythmically.

He looked to her. 'You good to go?'

She nodded. 'Sure am.'

The powerful engine hefted them to the sky in seconds. As always, Zai felt as if he'd left his stomach on the ground for the first few seconds. It was a sensation he never grew tired of, and from the look on Melody's face, and the fact that her hands had gone to rest on her stomach, she felt the same.

From the ever-changing office window in the bright blue sky, they watched mammoth grey kangaroos bound away with mind-blowing power and idle cattle raise their heads. Bulls with horns that could kill in a lethal instant pawed the flat copper-red ground, defending their territory, their beady eyes burning into the bottom of the chopper as it sped over them. Scribbly gums gathered in clumps, as if it were safer in numbers. Barbed-wire fencing stretched out as far the eye could see, dividing the million acres and twenty thousand head of cattle calling Rosalee Station home from the neighbouring property. Zai couldn't even begin to imagine the manpower it would have taken to erect what appeared to be a perpetual boundary – another reminder of the sheer grit and determination of the country souls that had worked this land before him. He was so proud to be a part of it all. As they flew over rocky ridges and open paddocks, the occasional glimmer of dams caught his eye, making him squint into the brilliance.

'Rosalee Station is such an amazing place,' Melody finally said, her gaze glued to the wonder outside.

Zai couldn't help the broad smile that planted on his face. 'I told you that you'd end up loving it here.'

She nodded, eyes wide. 'Yes, you sure did. And so did my dad'

'Could you imagine yourself living out here, long-term?' It had been a question burning inside him, and it felt the perfect time to ask.

After a short moment of silence, she shook her head. 'I can't believe I'm about to say this, but I reckon, if my situation was different, I could.'

'What situation is that?' He couldn't help it. He had to know.

She wavered as she fumbled with the hem of her T-shirt, then shrugged. 'My entire life is back in the city, so it's not as simple as just pulling up stumps.'

Zai could tell from the tense expression on her face that she was keeping something from him, and he hated the fact. He wanted her to believe she could tell him absolutely anything. With his heart beating in his throat, he turned away from her, focused on the striking landscape beneath them, and took a calming breath. 'Life is only as complicated as you make it, you know that, right?'

She avoided his gaze. 'I wish I could say yes, but some things are out of my hands, I'm afraid,' she sighed, sinking in her seat. 'Like I said, sometimes things are not that cut and dried.'

'We all have the power to change our lives, Melody, no matter what.' He fleetingly met her gaze to hit the point home. 'We only get one shot at life, and we have to make the most if it.'

'Yes, you're right, we do.' Something passed across her face, but she looked away too fast for him to decipher what it was.

'Hold on tight to that thought, Mel, won't you?'

She nodded but remained silent. Zai knew in his gut that there was something very significant she wasn't telling him. If only she knew he would never judge her for anything. But he didn't want to force her to open up so he let it be, for now. He wanted her to take this experience away as fondly as she had all the others they'd shared. If only she knew just how much he loved her, maybe the situation she was referring to would change. In a heartbeat.

CHAPTER 17

It was Melody's first day off in what felt like forever. After a solid nine-hour sleep, not even waking up in the middle of the night for her usual trip to the loo, she awoke a renewed woman with a profound internal peace she had never experienced before. Even her footsteps felt lighter as she padded out of the kitchen and down the hallway, as if she were walking on air. Zai had a lot to do with her floating on cloud nine, as did being here, where her heart beat in sync with the commanding pulse of the heart of the outback. The gorgeous hunk of man was on her mind, in sleep and when awake – she'd dreamt about him all night long. She couldn't stop thinking about him, or how he made her feel, and she didn't want to try to anymore. He was right. She only had one shot at this life, and she needed to take the reins of it back and ride it like she stole it. Her mother would want her to be happy, even if it meant abandoning her beloved café to Antonio. And Zai Wellstone made her very happy. Never would she have believed a connection like this was possible, but here it was, hitting her fair and square in the heart – she needed to take heed because if she didn't, she knew she would regret it for the rest of her life. And she was so sick of regrets.

Her daybreak cuppa had become her norm over the past month, and the aroma of the coffee invigorated her as she traipsed across the coolness of the timber floorboards. She sank down and cradled it in her hands as she watched the sun peeking over the distant copper ridges, the scent of the lemon myrtle shrubs planted beside the back steps drifting on the gentle wisp of a breeze. Not long now and the sky would be cast in crimson and gold, then merge to the warmth of tangerine before sapphire blue stole the show. It was a beautiful way of Mother Nature delivering on her promise, day after day after day.

Her eyes smiling at the view, she felt a familiar cosiness settle into her core – she was going to treat this sunrise as her curtain call. There was something so comforting, and healing, about witnessing the birth of a brand new day in this vast, rugged landscape that was millions of years old. And the fact that it was her birthright to call it home made her heart sing with joy and pride. If only there was a way for her to open a café out here; now, wouldn't that be a wonderful challenge? She could make use of native Australian produce and the local beef, making it a place to be included on every grey nomad's trip along the red dirt roads of central Australia. It was a fleeting contemplation. A girl could dream, she thought, watching the cottony clouds floating across the ever-lightening sky.

With the sun quickly rising, silken cobwebs studded with diamanté dew tangled between the swaying grasses of the homestead paddock. The sun's warming rays caressing her face, she squinted into the brilliance of it all. Backdropped by the stables, Sao and Toffee lifted their heads, the two horse's coats aglow, their tails swishing. It was a scene one had to immerse oneself in to truly appreciate – not even a camera's lens could catch the magnificence that was all of Rosalee Station at daybreak.

Turning her attention to the cottage Zai called home, Melody felt the flutter of the butterflies only he gave rise to. And in that moment, she thanked the god that had taken her mother way too early for bringing her an angel to help heal her broken heart, and to show her what true, unconditional love felt like. And if she was being completely honest with herself, she wasn't just falling in love with Zai – she was already deeply in love with him. How could she walk away from that, from him?

With a deep, restorative inhalation, she knew, without a doubt, that she needed to turn her back on her past, turn over a new leaf. As scary as it was to consider losing her beloved café and having to file for a divorce, as well as packing up her life, along with Magic, and moving to the country to start all over again, it was nothing compared to the thought of losing Zai. It was time she lived in the present and treated every moment as a gift to be savoured. Her gut kept telling her what to do – and it was about time she bloody well listened.

As if right on cue, Zai emerged from the cottage, a picture of absolute masculinity in his jeans, shirtless, barefooted, hair damp and a cuppa in hand. 'Good morning, Melody.' His smile outshone the sun as he strode towards her, closing the distance between them.

'Morning, Zai.' Standing, she left her empty cup and padded down the steps, meeting him in the garden. 'How'd you sleep?'

'Like a baby. You?' He raked his fingers through his short-cropped hair and in that moment, Melody caught a glimpse of an idyllic future, one where she was his wife. It wasn't hard to imagine. It would be a dream come true, waking up to him day after glorious day.

'Yeah, really good.' Needing to do something with her hands, she leant and gave Harold, who had just arrived at their feet, a rub behind the ears. 'Oh, good lord, you smell like death, and then some.'

'Bloody hell, boy, what have you gone and rolled in?' Sniffing the air, Zai screwed his face up. 'How about we give him a bath?'

'I reckon that's a great idea because there's no way he's coming anywhere near me smelling like that.' Gazing into the depth of Zai's beautiful blue eyes, she wished she could kiss those tempting lips. 'I'll go and get some shampoo while you grab the hose from around the side of the house, if you like?'

'Plan, Stan.' His gaze travelled over her with a sensuality so raw, it stole her next breath. 'And after we de-stink old Harold, how about I cook us some brekkie?'

'That sounds lovely. What's on the menu?'

'I reckon some of my famous cheesy French toast might hit the spot nicely. You dig?'

'Ha, yeah, I dig.' She knew what else would hit her spot nicely. Her body flushed just thinking about it. 'I've never had savoury French toast.' They certainly weren't just friends; a friend didn't have the capacity to do what he did to her, especially without a single touch of his hardworking hand.

'Well, there's a first for everything. I reckon you'll be hooked once you take your first bite.' He wiggled his brows, his dimples deepening. 'You'll never look at French toast the same again.'

There was a smoky edge to his voice, one that made her want to touch him all over. 'We'll soon see if you walk the talk, Chef Wellstone.' With a challenging grin, she managed to pull her gaze away from his – but it wasn't easy.

'Ha, righto. Challenge accepted, missus.'

The way he called her missus melted her. 'I'm going to get the shampoo.' She willed the mushy pile of her heart to stop beating so fast as she spun and took quick steps away from the temptation of him. 'Back in a sec.'

Zai's harmonic whistling trailed off as he disappeared round the side of the house.

Melody hightailed it down the hallway, grabbing the shampoo from the bathroom and an old towel out of the linen cupboard. Pretending Zai didn't affect her libido, or her heart, was beginning to prove extremely difficult, but she didn't want to cross the final line before sorting out the mess of her life back in Sydney.

A couple of hours later, with Harold smelling like roses, and her and Zai's bellies filled with what Melody had had to agree was the best French toast she'd ever sunk her teeth into, she and Zai were kicking back on the settee on the patio of the cottage, feet up on the wagon-wheel coffee table with freshly made Bloody Marys in hand, staring out at the endless view.

'I feel a bit naughty, drinking at eleven in the morning.'

'It's five o'clock somewhere.' With a sexy, casual shrug of his broad shoulders, Zai took a bite from his stick of celery. 'And it's our day off, so let's live it up and make the most of it.'

'True that.' She took another sip of the perfectly spiced cocktail that left her tongue tingling in its wake. 'This is divine. What did you put in it?'

'Ahh.' He looked to the roof as if trying to recall. 'Tomato juice, a squeeze of lemon, a splash each of Worcestershire and Tabasco, some pepper, a teaspoon of horseradish, and a double nip of my homemade jalapeno vodka.'

'Wow, a total concoction of yumminess.'

'Only the best for you.' He grinned, then added, 'Oh, and I forgot that I also chucked in a little bit of love. For added flavour.' His eyes twinkled over the rim of his glass.

Melody couldn't help the dreamy smile that touched upon her lips, or the warmth that filled her heart to bursting. 'Ah, that's why it tastes so good.'

'Mm-hmm.'

All of a sudden, the loud growl of an engine at its peak approached, then an old Holden Kingswood sped past like a lost rally car, the chassis almost dragging along the ground, the passengers crammed within it hooting and hollering.

Eyes wide, she turned to Zai, who was already chuckling. 'Did I seriously just see that?'

He nodded, slowly. 'You sure did.'

'Where in the hell would they be going in the middle of nowhere?'

'Looks to me like thata way.' He jutted his thumb to the left of them. 'Apparently it's a short cut to Alice Springs, or so the mob over yonder likes to think. God love 'em.'

She cracked up with laughter, as did he. The vodka was going straight to her head, and legs, and …

As their laughter subsided, another sensation settled into place, one filled with hunger and need. This was dangerous. They were way closer than they should be. She stared down at her toes. Then, desperate to move before she made a move on this tower of manly man, she stood and wandered over to the banister, pretending to gaze out at the scenery as she caught her breath.

Oh crap.

With a start, she spun to find he'd come up behind her. He rested his hands on either side of the railings, trapping her to the spot. She went to tell him to stop because she was still a married woman – he needed to know, now, before anything happened. She wanted to do this right from the get-go so there wasn't anything that had the power to tear them apart … but he brought a finger to her lips and traced them with such tenderness. It was the most intimate of touches, one that stole any bit of restraint she had left. She quivered, then inhaled sharply when he dropped his hand back to his side.

'Do you want me to stop?'

Too breathless to say it out loud, she slowly shook her head.

'Good. Because I don't want to.' He grabbed her hips and pulled her close. 'Because you, Sweet Melody, are the sexiest woman I've ever met.' His voice was low, husky and rasping. 'And I don't think I can get through another day without making love to you.'

She found her voice, but it was trembling. 'Are you sure this isn't just lust, or vodka, or both, talking?'

'Hell no. I want to taste you, breathe you in, drink in your secrets, learn every inch of you. What makes you quiver, what makes you gasp, so I can do it over and over again, all day long, and well into the night.' His smile was slow and sexy. 'We have almost twenty-four hours before we have to be back at work, and I want to make the most of it, with you.'

He was so damn convincing, and so damn arresting, that she had no other choice but to succumb – there was no way her legs would carry her away from him, no matter how hard she tried to take steps. This was the moment she'd been fantasising about since she'd first laid eyes on him.

Dipping his head, he brought his lips to hers, demanding her tongue with his, while confidently directing her towards the back door of the cottage. She walked backwards and he came with her. They bumped into the wall. Then she rose up onto her toes and he drew her closer still as he opened the door, spun her inside and then closed it behind them, making sure to lock it – he clearly didn't want them to be interrupted.

'You're driving me crazy, beautiful.' He pinned her to the door, his hands holding her wrists high above her head, his gaze gripping hers. 'I want you so bad it hurts.'

'I want you too.' His touch sent fire rippling through every cell in her body. Nerves danced in her belly, as did this addictive warmth. 'But we … I …' She stammered and stumbled over her words. She didn't want to stop him, or this.

He brought his mouth to hers again, the intensity of his caress surging her body to life. His heated kisses continued over her collarbone, feathery, silk-like, and then he brought his mouth to where her pulse beat desperately in her neck, pressing kisses there. Sliding his hands around her waist, he pulled her to him hungrily. She entwined her arms around his neck, wrapping her legs around his waist. He carried her to his bedside before she brought her feet back to the floor. Holding his desire-fuelled gaze, she helped him tug his shirt over his head then slid her hands up and over his chest, exploring each and every muscle ridge, then tracing the tribal tattoo that fanned over his right shoulder. He went still, closing his eyes for a few breathless moments, and when he brought his gaze back to hers again, the craving within them awakened a feminine roar from deep inside her.

She needed him, all of him, now.

He gently pushed her backwards onto his bed then, after ridding himself of his jeans and underpants, climbed on top of her, carefully bearing his weight. His long, thick hardness pressed into her as he slowly stripped her of her clothes, taking his time to drink all of her in. Then, with both of them stripped bare, his hands and mouth explored her every inch, his gentle caresses mixing with firmer touches, sending her to places she'd never been before. When he finally brought his skilful mouth between her legs, waves of pleasure washed over her, giving rise to endless goosebumps and moans of absolute bliss. He quickly brought her to the brink and once she was there, stopped, teasing her by kissing the insides of her thighs.

'Please, Zai. I need you inside me.' The growling voice didn't resemble her own as she drew him up and to her. 'Now.'

He did as she asked. Her fingernails dug into his back, marking him, as he pressed into her. Her breath hitched, vision blurring, as he filled every piece of her perfectly. He found a tingling rhythm and she rode it with him, bringing her hips to his, harder and faster. Soon she was on the edge, as was he. She wrapped herself around him and they breathed into one another. With a few more thrusts, he met her at the pinnacle and they balanced there, together, both of them shuddering, breathless, groaning. And then, when she couldn't hold on any longer, she released and tumbled into him, faster and deeper than she'd even fallen before. And the most beautiful thing was he was right there to catch her, holding her so tightly as they fought to catch their breaths, yet so tenderly, allowing her for the very first time in her life to feel real love and respect.

As day turned to night, Melody found herself wandering in and out of sleep. It was as if the outside world didn't exist anymore. And if only that were really so – she'd be more than happy to stay here, with Zai, forever. She had never felt so satisfied in all of her life – mind, body and soul.

After making love for the third time, they'd lain together for a long time, a tangle of legs and arms, neither of them feeling a need to fill the beautiful silence. Her head now resting on his chest, her tender thoughts harpooned her to him in the most intense of ways. Forget about falling – she'd totally plummeted, hard and fast, and was deeply in love with this amazing man. She took great enjoyment in the sound of his heart beating against her cheek, as well as the feeling of his fingers sliding featherlike up and down her back. Tingles shot all over her, invigorating her very core, making her want so much more of him. His kisses had held all the promises she'd always longed for in a partner, tenfold. She was totally lost to this man, and she loved it. No longer did she feel like she was aimlessly wandering the earth, trying to find her place, her purpose. He was her landing place, her home.

But as dreamy as it all was, the reality of the situation was that she had to tell him about everything, now. He deserved to know her truth.

'Are you okay?' His voice was tender and husky. 'You seem a million miles away, my beautiful lady.'

She glanced up at him from beneath her lashes. 'Yes.' She brought her chin to his chest. 'How about you?'

He gently touched her face, studying her with a deeply passionate gaze. 'Couldn't be better.'

'Good.' She brushed her fingers over his collarbone, admiring the intricate curves of his tribal tattoo that skated over his shoulder and out of sight.

'Your fingers feel like flames.' Exhaling with her gentle touch, he kissed her on the nose. 'You're a very special woman, Sweet Melody. I hope you know that.'

'If you say so.'

'Oh, trust me.' He arched his eyebrows. 'I know so.'

'Well, you, Zai Wellstone, are a very special man.' The need to tell him everything about the life he knew nothing of was becoming overwhelming.

'I'm glad you think so.'

'I know so,' she added with a slightly wobbly smile.

Her voice of reason stormed to the front of her mind. *Just say it, Melody. Tell him …*

'So what now?'

Zai's voice brought her back. 'What do you mean?'

'Are we official?' He grinned a little self-consciously. 'I really want the world to know how lucky I am to have you as my gorgeous girlfriend.'

Her stomach clenched into a tight fist. 'I'm not sure I'm comfortable with that just yet.' She needed to make things completely final with Antonio before revealing what she and Zai had together.

Hurt flashed across his face. 'Why? What are you so afraid of?'

It was a valid question, one he deserved an answer to. She tried to form the right words, looking everywhere but at him.

His body tensed and his eyes were intent as he formed his next question. 'Melody, what haven't you told me?'

She wilted a little under his interrogative look. 'There are some things you don't know about me yet, things I need to do before we can tell the world we've fallen in love.'

He slid out from beneath her cheek and sat up. 'What kind of response is that?'

Her mind raced, her breathing quickening – how in the hell was she meant to say this to him? 'I'm … kind of married. But not in the usual sense,' she added quickly.

'Married?' Inching away from her, he scanned her face, his eyes turning cold and hard. 'What in the hell are you on about?'

Feeling downright dirty, she knew it was time to come completely clean. 'He cheated on me and I moved out to my Aunt Sally's place. But my mother was sick and all my attention and time was on her, and now we're kind of having a trial separation of sorts so I can figure out what I want.'

'What in the hell, Melody.' He shot from the bed as if she were venomous, taking the sheet with him. 'Don't you think this should've been something you told me about ages ago?'

'Yes, of course I should have.' As she pulled the doona up to her chin, she did her best to hold his increasingly stormy gaze. 'I just didn't know how to.'

'You didn't know how to?' He stared as though she were out of her mind. 'How about just saying, "I'm married" before sleeping with me? Because that would have been a damn good start to a conversation we should've had before doing this.'

Her mind scrambled for all the excuses she'd given herself, and even though they'd sounded reasonable in her head, saying them out loud was another thing. 'I suppose, deep down … I didn't want to lose the possibility of there ever being an us.'

'Well, for the record, you've gone and done that by doing this.'

She fought to not burst into tears. 'I don't know what you want me to say.' Her stomach clenching, she watched feelings chase over his face – anger, resentment, disappointment, and hurt. And she'd caused all of it.

He breathed in deeply before huffing it away. 'I thought I was more important to you.' The muscles in his jaw clenched. 'But I was a fool for believing that.'

'No, you're wrong. You mean the absolute world to me, Zai.'

He fired a tempestuous look her way. 'You have a real funny way of showing it, Melody.' His heated gaze burnt her like a branding iron.

'I showed you this afternoon just how deeply I feel about you.' It was a desperate, last-ditch effort to get him to believe her.

'Anyone can jump in the sack. It takes a decent person to do the right thing from the start if you expect it to go anywhere.' His voice was wavering, torn.

She knew he was speaking out of anger, and she couldn't blame him. She'd broken her promise to always be honest with him – she had no right to defend herself. Not wanting to say anything she'd regret, she tightened her lips and shook her head, blinking faster.

He regarded her, tears shimmering in his baby blues as understanding dawned between them. 'This was a mistake. I never would have slept with you if I'd known you were married.'

He was dead-on. She blew a breath, wishing her guilt would go with it. 'I know.' She felt like the worst person in the world right now, times a million.

'I'm not sure how I feel about you anymore.' He wouldn't meet her eyes, then he turned his back.

'I think it's best I go,' she said in a whisper, all the butterflies he'd created within her dropping, dying.

'Yeah, maybe it is,' he replied, staring out the window into the darkness of night.

CHAPTER 18

After a sleepless night – spent tossing and turning for the first half, then wandering the hallways of the homestead until dawn crept over the horizon – Melody felt like absolute crap. It felt as though a lifetime had passed since she'd arrived here. Tomorrow, her dad, Sarah and Beau would be arriving, and a few days after that, her grandparents, who she was still to meet. And Georgia – Matt's sister – and Patrick and their boy, Danny, would be rolling back here for Slim and Sherrie's wedding too. Talk about terrible timing. Just when she'd thought she'd reached a point of knowing where her life needed to be, her possibilities with Zai were done and dusted, gone forever, all because of her stupidity. She didn't hold a glimmer of a chance that the fire they'd ignited so naturally could ever be rebuilt from the ash that remained. And she couldn't blame him in the slightest. This was all her fault. She'd done the wrong thing. Part of her wanted to run to him, to tell him just how much she loved him and how utterly sorry she was, that she would do absolutely anything to make it up to him. But the other part of her knew that would do no good. Zai was a man of high morals and, however unintentionally, she'd gone and played him for a fool.

She suddenly, desperately, needed to talk to Sarah. She grabbed the homestead phone and dialled her mobile number, rapping the desk with her fingers as she waited.

'Hello Melody.' Sarah's voice was singsong sweet.

'Hi Sarah, how's the drive going?' Melody couldn't help the melancholy in her voice.

'Yeah, really good. On track to arrive tomorrow.'

'Wonderful.' Melody wished she could sound as pleased as she was – she couldn't wait to see the three of them.

'Is everything okay? You sound a little upset, love.'

'I'm okay, sort of … do you have time to chat?' Her voice sounded ridiculously high, but she resisted the urge to clear it. 'I need a wise woman's advice.'

'I'm not too sure about the wise part, love, but yes, of course.'

'Have you got somewhere private we can talk?' She didn't want her father hearing any of this.

'We've just parked and your dad is grabbing some fish and chips from the roadhouse, so we have about ten minutes of privacy.'

Having collected herself enough to dive into an explanation that seemed to veer from one situation to the other, Melody finally paused and swallowed down the ball of emotion gathering in her throat. She had chosen to leave out the fact she and Zai had slept together – that was just too much for her to confess.

'Okay, so let me put this into perspective.' Sarah's tone was thoughtful. 'You and Antonio agreed to take time out and that's when you came to find your dad, and then you went out to the station and Zai has won your heart.'

'Yes, that pretty much sums most of it up.'

'Right, well, it's not something that can't be rectified, given some time.' She sighed, and then drew in a breath. 'I'm not sure how your dad is going to feel about you and Zai hitting it off. Zai's got a rep as a bit of a heartbreaker. I mean, as much as I adore him, I'm not sure if he's relationship material, Melody.'

'I know, and I understand what you are saying, but he's told me he's in love with me. And I believe him.' She choked back a sob. 'Then again, he may not be any longer, after …'

'After what, Melody?'

Melody couldn't hold back her tears any longer. 'I've gone and ruined everything,' she said between sobs.

'Oh, love, how so?'

'I slept with him.' She felt her cheeks redden and her insides squeeze with shame. 'Before I told him I was still married.'

'Oh, okay. Right. Well, that does change things.' Sarah didn't sound judgemental in the slightest, but very concerned. 'I know Zai, and he wouldn't have taken the news well.'

'No, he didn't. Not at all.' Plucking a tissue, Melody blew her nose and wiped at her cheeks.

'You can't help who you fall in love with, Melody, and you also can't help falling out of love with someone who has treated you like Antonio has. I do think you need to call it quits with him sooner rather than later. Before you try to sort out this mess with Zai.'

Melody sat up straighter, squaring her slumped shoulders. 'You're right. I need to call him today.'

'Yes, I think that's a good idea. And honestly, if Zai was being honest when he said he's in love with you, give it some time. True love doesn't go away easily, Melody, so don't give up on him yet, okay?'

'Okay. Thank you.' She heaved in a breath. 'Can you please keep this between us for now?'

'Of course. You want to tell your father yourself?'

'Yes, and I'd like to do that to his face, when you get here.'

'Of course. Girl code it is. My lips are sealed.'

'Thank you, Sarah, for everything.'

'Don't mention it, love. You're family, and I'll always be here for you, anytime, day or night, always. I don't ever want you to feel alone.'

'You're an amazing woman, Sarah.' Raw emotion squeezed Melody's heart and brought fresh tears to her eyes, but these ones were born of feeling valued as part of the Walsh family. 'Hearing you say that truly means the world to me.'

'Stop it, you're making me cry now.' Sarah sniffled. 'Now, off you go. Pull on those big girl boots and sort this out so you and Zai can live happily ever after and give me and your father our very first grandchild.'

The very thought of getting to a place like that with Zai buoyed Melody's heart – what a dream life that would be, in a prefect world. 'Onto it. Bye, Sarah.'

'Bye lovely. We will see you tomorrow, and please call me if you need me in the meantime, okay?'

'Okay, I promise I will. Bye for now.' Hanging up, Melody felt the strength she needed to make things as right as she possibly could – even if that meant she and Zai would only be friends. If that were the case, she'd just have to find a way to deal with it.

Her heart pounding, she dialled Antonio's mobile number. It rang … and rang … and rang. Just as she was about to hang up, a woman's voice answered. 'Hello.'

Melody blinked. 'I'm sorry, I must have dialled the wrong number.'

'Oh, who were you after?' The woman's voice was unfamiliar.

'Antonio.' Melody's eyes narrowed.

'Oh, okay, and who are you?'

'I'm Melody. And who, may I ask, are you?' She sucked in a strident breath with a sudden realisation that she was talking to the buxom blonde she'd briefly met behind the gym. 'Is that you, Kelly?'

'Uh-huh …' There was a pause, and then a gasp. 'Oh my god, Melody! He told me you guys broke up when you left town.'

Melody's voice hitched. 'He did, did he?'

There were muffled angry voices before Antonio's came down the line. 'Hey, I wasn't expecting a call from you.'

'Clearly.' She cringed, more for Kelly's sake than his. 'Do you have something you'd like to tell me, Antonio?'

Antonio cleared his throat. 'Oh, yeah, well—'

'You don't have to lie or try to explain yourself. We've grown apart, Antonio, and we're holding on to a shadow of ourselves, and for the sake of what?'

'Yeah … I hate to admit it but you're right,' he sighed weightily. 'I'm sorry it's ended like this.'

'Me too.' She breathed in deeply, using her exhalation to force out the rest of what she had to say. 'I called to say I'd like a divorce. Hopefully, we can work out my share of the café and our apartment fairly and amicably.' There was a long pause and Melody fought to control her shallow breath. 'Please, Antonio. Don't make this any harder than it has to be.'

'I'm sure we can sort it out.' His words were curt.

'Good, great.' Melody almost punched the air. 'I'll be back in town in ten days and we can sort it all out then, if that's okay with you.'

'Yes, that suits me. You take care now.'

'I will. You too.'

And with that, she ended the call and sat for a few long moments – a four-and-a-half-year relationship ended, just like that. She knew without a doubt that because he had Kelly there to fill the void she'd left – if the poor, unsuspecting woman could forgive him for lying to her, god help her – Antonio would be a lot more cordial. He didn't need her to give him what he wanted anymore. The universe couldn't have aligned things any more perfectly.

Now it was time to find the love of her life and tell him she was deeply sorry, and that she was head-over-boots in love with him, and hope to god he forgave her. She wanted to explain to Zai that even though she didn't have all the answers right now, for the first time in her life, she didn't need them – because she knew with absolute certainty that she couldn't bear the thought of life without him.

Heading outside to the glowing warmth of the midday sunshine, she stifled a surprised bubble of laughter. Slim, Showbags and Tumbles were out on the back lawn of the workers' quarters, beers at the ready – the pre-wedding celebrations had clearly begun a few days early. Showbags had a towel around his shoulders and Slim had a pair of clippers in hand. Tumbles was watching it all with a goofy look on his face. Melody almost didn't want to look.

Crossing with long strides, she stopped short of them. 'Hey, you lot.'

'Howdy, Melody. You're just in time for the show.' With a cheeky grin, Slim lined the buzzing clippers up and went in for the kill. Scooting it up the centre, he was clearly having a hard time holding himself together. 'I've made you a landing strip, Showbags.'

'Ha, he sure did.' Tumbles pointed then fell back on the grass, laughing.

'You better not leave one of your groomsmen looking like a baldy, Slimbo.' Showbags peered up. 'Or I might just have to shave one of your eyebrows off while you're sleeping.'

'Ha, Sherrie would whip your arse if you did that,' Tumbles said, following it up with a grimace.

Showbags grinned. 'I'll just tell her you did it, Tumbles.'

Slim laughed and continued on clipping.

Chuckling at their antics, Melody looked to the cottage, praying to god Zai had popped home for lunch today – she desperately needed to talk to him. 'I'll leave you boys to it, then.'

'Yeah, righto. Catch ya, Melds.' Tumbles gave her a wave.

Showbags pulled an oh-lord-help-me face that only she could see as she walked away.

She shook her head, still chuckling – the three guys were the brothers she'd never had. But her smile quickly faded as she reached the front door of Zai's place – she couldn't be more nervous if she tried.

His boots were by the welcome mat, so she had no doubt he was home. Taking a deep breath, she gave three hard raps to the front door then waited. Almost a minute passed. She knocked again, this time a little louder. Again, she was met with silence. Her heart sank even lower. Zai obviously needed time, and she wasn't about to break the door down to get to him. But being ignored by him still hurt. So, willing herself not to burst into tears, she turned around and took one foot after the other away from where she knew Zai was, back towards the homestead, giving the chuckling group of guys a wide berth – she wouldn't be able to hold herself together if she had to stop and talk.

Would Zai ever give her the time of day again, at least enough to be able to explain everything and to offer her heartfelt apology? Oh god, she hoped so.

* * *

Three days later, with the unconditional love of her new family and friends surrounding her – a time when she should have been on top of the world – Melody found it almost impossible not to burst into tears at the rowdy homestead dinner table. Seated as far away from her as he could possibly be, between her father and her grandad, Steve, Zai avoided looking in her direction. And he wasn't answering her knocks at the cottage door either, even though she knew he was inside at least some of the times. She'd even tried to corner him alone in the kitchen, but he'd quickly made an escape, muttering something about needing to check in with Slim on some wedding plans. Despite Sarah telling her otherwise, Zai very clearly loathed the sight of her. She was starting to believe her chance with him was well and truly gone.

Needing to do anything but sit here with her heart in her throat, Melody quickly rose and gathered some of the empty plates. Then, disregarding her dad's worried glance in her direction, she made a beeline for the kitchen and started to rinse the plates and cutlery off before piling them all into the dishwasher.

Following the pitter-patter of footsteps, Judy's hand came to rest on her arm. 'Are you okay, love?' she said ever-so-quietly. 'You seem a million miles away.'

Turning to look into the kindest blue-grey eyes, crinkled at the edges from years of sun and laughter, Melody blinked faster as she tried to smile. 'I'm okay, thanks Grandma. Just really tired.'

'Are you sleeping, love?' Judy asked, her gentle tone concerned.

Leaning against the kitchen bench, Melody shrugged a little. 'Not really.'

'I see.' Offering a look of sympathy, Judy seemed to consider what she was about to say next. 'Does it have something to do with what's happened between you and Zai?' There was a deep knowingness in her gaze. 'I hope you don't mind, but Sarah and Georgia filled me in over a cuppa this morning when I mentioned you seemed unhappy and I was worried about you.'

Melody took a moment to catch her stolen breath. She wasn't used to having a family knowing her deepest feelings, but it was comforting to have their unconditional support. She cleared her throat, once, twice, but found it impossible to find the right words.

Judy took her hand and gave it a squeeze. 'He'll come around. Just give him some time.'

After a lengthy pause, Melody finally found her voice. 'That's what Sarah keeps saying, but I'm not so sure.' She choked back a sob. 'I'm so desperate to try to explain things to Zai, but he won't give me the time of day.'

'Oh, my love, you're both standing in the fire right now, and you can't see for the flames.' Judy sighed softly. 'Trust me. If you take a few steps back, you'll both get the breathing space you need without burning each other more.'

Considering this, Melody nodded. 'Yes, you're right. I know I just need to let him come to me when he's ready to, but I'm so scared he might never talk to me again. And to be honest, I wouldn't blame him.'

'Hmm.' Judy drew in a breath. 'I've known Zai for many years, and he's not one to leave things up in the air. And he hates seeing the people he cares for hurting. I truly believe he will talk when he's ready to.'

'I hope so,' Melody replied.

Georgia and Sarah moseyed into the kitchen with Danny and Beau in noisy tow, the hullaballoo of the two boys giving Melody a moment to gather herself.

Plonking a pile of serving dishes onto the sink, Georgia took her by surprise as she wrapped her in a hug. Sarah joined in, as did Judy, until the four of them were all squished together. No words were spoken, but the unity Melody felt amidst the three strong, country-hearted women gave her the strength she knew she would need to get through another sleepless night of heartache. Hopefully, before she headed back to the bright lights of the city to sort out her life next week, Zai would come around.

CHAPTER 19

Not overly familiar with this part of the station, Zai gazed from the rocky ridgeline off to the side to the uneven earthen track in front. He should slow down, but he was eager to get home so he could stand beneath a hot shower and hopefully wash away some of his weariness. Hurtling along in top gear, the four-wheeler's front tyres hit a crevice, man and quad momentarily flying through the air as if defying gravity, landing seconds later with a back-breaking thump. Groaning, Zai gripped the handlebars as he regained control – out here wasn't the place to be reckless, given the notorious stability issues of quad bikes, but today his care factor was close to nil. With the sun in his eyes, he tipped his hat to ward off the glare of the setting sun. He only had one more job before he could call it a day, checking the rear fence line. Not an easy feat, given the gruelling countryside – he was thankful for Slim, coming in from the opposite direction. He didn't have eyes on his mate just yet, but could hear the revs of his inbound quad bike. The plan was to meet in the middle and then head home for some well-deserved beers.

Chasing the last of the day's light, he flew along the bumpy ground at a speed he'd usually consider hazardous, but his mind was somewhere else, on someone else. It had been hard ignoring Melody's knocks on the cottage door the past couple of days, as well as sitting as far away from her as he could at every meal. He was avoiding her like the plague, which was hard given that Matt and Sarah had arrived, as had the rest of the crew in preparation for the wedding tomorrow. But he wasn't ready to talk to her. Even after four days, it felt as though the axe she had proverbially struck him with was still lodged in his back. Why did she have to rule his every thought, take his every breath, control his every heartbeat? With blinding intensity, he recalled the softness of her skin beneath his fingertips, his mouth, and the depth in her eyes as he'd made the sweetest and hungriest of loves to her. In the throes of passion, he'd graduated from dreams to reality, and by nightfall, had already imagined them together, engaged, married, with kids. But then she'd burst his bubble in the most gigantic of ways.

She was a married woman. And she'd lied about it.

How had she thought he was going to feel when he found out? Then again, maybe he needed to put himself into her shoes …

Abruptly, his thoughts changed direction, dragging his heart along for the ride. She'd looked so wounded when she'd left and with his anger subsiding, little by little, something inside him softened. She had been through a lot, had lost a lot. He couldn't blame her for being so messed up and, in turn, messing everything up between them. Damn, he wanted to be the one who showed her what she needed. If he were being completely honest with himself, he'd officially reached the point of not being able to walk away – there was no way in hell he'd be able to switch off his feelings for her. They ran too deep, too strong. So what was he playing at? This was achieving the opposite of what he wanted so badly. And that was her. The sudden desperation to tell her had him spinning the quad bike around. He wanted to take her into his arms, to feel her heart-stopping, smouldering kiss again. He wanted to tell her he forgave her, and that he wanted them to be together forever, because they'd get through this together, no matter what it took.

And that's when the front tyres clipped something unseen again … but this time, as if in slow motion, the four-wheeler motorbike flew through the air, tumbled, and then, tipping down a steep ravine, landed with him pinned beneath it. Searing pain sliced into the back of his head and reverberated through the rest of his body. The pain so excruciatingly intense, he almost vomited. Twice. He tried to lift the motorbike, but it was impossible. He tried to calm himself, took a few tiny breaths – the weight of the bike was crushing the air out of him. Was this how he was going to die? No, he couldn't. He had to get to Melody and tell her everything.

Using every bit of strength he could muster, he tried to push it off him again, but it wouldn't budge. He quickly scanned his body from head to toe. He couldn't feel his right leg … had it been cut clean off?

'Holy shit, Zai! Hold on, I'm coming buddy.' Slim's bellowing voice echoed as he half ran, half slipped down the side of the steep ravine.

Zai tried to answer but before he could, he started choking on something.

Is that blood?

With a force that would usually be beyond any mortal man, Slim shoved the bike from him. The look on his face spoke of everything Zai feared. With terror gripping him, he tried to move his toes, but couldn't even feel his legs.

Slim dropped to his knees, pulling a handkerchief from his pocket and dabbing Zai's head and mouth. 'Shit, Wellstone, you've gone and done a damn good job of it, haven't ya mate?' He pointed back up the ravine. 'You're gonna have to stay here while I go back up and two-way for help.'

Unable to form words, and finding it hard to draw a breath, Zai watched his mate clamber back up the ravine and disappear out of sight. He hovered between darkness and blinding light, in a world where he started to wonder if he were even still alive. The pain dissolved into a bizarre kind of peace and he drifted there for a little while. Ebbed and flowed with it, as if riding on a wave. Then the world faded further from him still, until he could hear nothing but silence. A blurry haze had him blinking faster, but with everything out of his control, the sweet blackness took his fear, his agony, and him.

* * *

With her adoring newfound family surrounding her, Melody was trying really hard to get into the happy pre-wedding spirit, but couldn't find an ounce of joy within her broken heart. Standing at the Aga cooker in the homestead, she manned a huge pot of beef stroganoff while Sarah, Aunt Georgia and Grandma huddled around the big oak table that dominated the centre of the kitchen, plates of food strewn from one end to the other. She found immense comfort in their company, the atmosphere in the room one of family and union and love. Never had she felt so welcomed anywhere in all of her life. It almost brought her to tears to know she'd had this family all along, and had missed out on so many years with them. But she had to look to the future and be grateful she had that to share with them all.

The radio announcer introduced the next song. 'Well, folks, let's have ourselves a little bit of good old-fashioned fun now with Rednex's hit song, "Cotton Eye Joe".'

'Oh my gosh, I love this song.' Sarah took Georgia by the hands and dragged her away from the table. 'Come on, sis-in-law, dance with me.'

Georgia laughed, tossing the potato peeler onto the bench. 'Righto, let's get down and dosido like nobody's watching.' She looked to Melody. 'Come on, my gorgeous niece. Come and dance with us.'

Melody was saved from doing so when the back door burst open and Showbags rushed in, his usual sunshiny face grave.

Judy turned from where she was icing cupcakes for the wedding tower, spatula in hand. 'What is it, Showbags? Is our Slim getting cold feet?'

'No, it's Zai.' His words were rushed and breathless. 'He's rolled the four-wheeler up at the ridge and he's hurt, real bad. Slim just radioed it in.' There were resounding gasps from the women as he sucked in a quick breath. 'He's called the medic chopper and it's almost here. Matt is on his way back from the neighbours' place in his chopper too.'

The walls almost swallowed Melody up. Dread filled her as sheer panic rose in her chest. *No.* She couldn't lose Zai. The ground shifted beneath her feet. She grabbed hold of the bench in a bid to remain upright. Her head spinning, she only caught snippets of what everyone was saying.

Unconscious.

Shallow breathing.

Blood.

Lots of it.

Oh god no.

Judy's voice snapped her back to it, and the tug of Sarah's hand on hers had her running alongside the women and towards the waiting LandCruiser, her grandad Steve at the wheel. They all piled into the back. The drive to Zai seemed to take forever, and when they finally got there, the sight before her was earth-shattering. Zai was on the ground, his body lifeless, a group of medics surrounded him. She tried to get to him, but a medic told them to keep back. Her heart beating rapidly, as if trying to punch through her chest, an ominous cloud hung over her head as she tried to convince herself that he was going to pull through this.

The deep whop-whop of another set of chopper blades sliced through the air as her father brought the chopper down. She squeezed her red eyes shut against the dust and grit as she said another silent prayer. She watched her father leap from the Robinson, the blades still rotating, and sprint across the cracked red earth. His face the epitome of urgency, he met with Slim, Patrick and Steve as Zai was lifted from the ground on a stretcher and loaded into the waiting emergency helicopter. Judy and Georgia ran over to the boys, but Sarah stayed by her side, an arm linked into hers. Melody was thankful for the support because her wobbly legs simply wouldn't move, nor did they have the strength to hold her up on their own.

Next thing, she was loaded into the chopper with Sarah, her father at the helm. Time passed in a blur of tears and her silent begging to god to save Zai. She couldn't bear the thought of losing him, of not getting the chance to tell him how much she loved him and how sorry she was for all the heartache she'd caused him. After what felt like a lifetime, they landed near the Mount Isa hospital. Melody couldn't get out of the helicopter fast enough. Heading towards the front doors, she almost slammed into them when they took a split second to open. Desperate to get to the man who owned her heart, her long strides turned into a sprint as she willed the stark white walls not to close in on her.

She skidded to a stop at a desk where a middle-aged nurse lifted her eyes from a folder. 'Can I help you?'

'Yes, I'm looking for my boyfriend, Zai Wellstone. He was airlifted here after a motorbike accident.'

'He's still in surgery, but you can wait in the visitors' lounge.' The nurse came around the counter and gestured to a room to the side. 'There is coffee and tea and UHT milk, if you'd like a cuppa.'

'Thank you.' The emotional lump in her throat was making it terribly hard to breathe. 'How long do you think it'll be before we hear something?'

'I'm honestly not sure, but I will let you know as soon as he's in recovery, okay?'

'Okay, thank you.'

After filling out some paperwork and calling Zai's parents, her father and Sarah joined her in the waiting room. Meeting her worried gaze, Matthew Walsh remained silent and pulled her into his arms. 'He's going to pull through this, sweetheart.'

'I hope so, Dad.' It was the very first time she'd called him what she'd longed to since meeting him for the very first time, and his hug tightened that little bit, showing he was pleased to hear it. 'Because I love Zai so much.' She hadn't told him about their love affair yet, hadn't found the right time to do so, but now seemed as fitting a time as any.

'I know you do, Melody. I can tell by the way you look at him. It's just like Sarah looks at me.' He stroked the back of her head. 'And you make sure you tell him how much you love him when he wakes up, okay?'

She nodded against her father's chest. 'I will.'

Unravelling from his arms, she shared a sad smile with Sarah before slumping down in the timeworn lounge chair. Sarah placed an arm around her shoulder, and the two of them huddled against each other. Rubbing her gritty eyes, she exhaled loudly. Now all they could do was wait. So she prayed like she'd never prayed before, going as far as to promise she would do anything god wanted of her if only he would bring Zai back to her.

And as the minutes ticked by and became an hour, then another, she replayed every magnificent moment with him. Every interaction. Every kiss. Every touch. She tried to grasp it all, for if she lost him, so help her god – she wanted to hold all these memories dear forever.

'Melody.' Sarah's voice was a whisper. 'Can I get you something to drink or eat, love?'

'No, thank you.' Her right leg was bouncing and she made a conscious effort to calm it.

'He's going to be okay. You've got to believe this.' Sarah's tone was soft but profoundly reassuring. 'Zai needs you to have faith in his strength, now more than ever.'

Overcome with emotions, all Melody could do was nod. She, her dad and Sarah had each other's backs and right now, more than ever, that meant the world to her. Tears glossed her vision again. She clamped her quivering lip between her teeth. The shiny floor and the strong scent of disinfectant made her more nauseated. The clock on the wall ticked loudly, to the point she thought it was going to drive her insane. It had been over two hours and still no news. Her sense of dread increased – she had to move. Now.

Striding out of the confines of the waiting room, she dragged in deep breaths while pacing the length of the corridors, unable to settle the nerves running riot in her belly. She soon returned and sat herself between her dad and Sarah, feeling a much-needed boost of strength. Time seemed to slow to a painful pace, every second another one where she could lose the love of her life. Tears continued to fill her eyes and she repeatedly brushed them away. Like her father and Sarah said, she had to hold on to the belief that Zai was going to pull through. There was nothing she could do or say to ease her pain, or anybody else's. Right now, all they had was hope.

Ten minutes later, a weary doctor in blood-spattered scrubs with a mask pulled to the top of his head stepped into the room, his face grave. The three of them jumped to their feet. The doctor's gaze momentarily slipped to the floor. Dread crept deeper beneath her skin and squeezed her soul excruciatingly tight. Her knees gave way, but Sarah grabbed hold of her, preventing her from hitting the floor. Her dad stepped forwards, as if shielding her and Sarah from what was about to be said. The doctor fastened his weary gaze upon him. Her breath hitched as she held it. Bile inched up her tight throat as a familiar emptiness crowded her chest. It was going to be devastating news.

Losing all hope, she closed her eyes, not wanting to hear what he was about to say – her heart wouldn't survive the anguish of losing him.

* * *

Zai felt himself rise from the fog, but only halfway, to a place where he was acutely aware of how cold, confused and terrified he felt. As he battled his way through the claws that wanted to drag him back to the darkness, images flashed before him like a kaleidoscope – a speeding blur he couldn't stop. They were of days gone by, happier times as a child, then as a teenager and swiftly into his twenties. Then, lastly, Melody's face swam into his apparitions, as did the soothing sound of her voice.

Awareness slowly slid into his consciousness. Pain began to register in varying degrees, hazed by the wooziness of strong painkillers. There was a softness beneath him that hadn't been there when he'd fallen from the bike, but whatever it was, it felt like it was spinning. And someone was asking him if he could feel something, anything. He tried to open his eyes to tell whoever it was he couldn't feel a damn thing. But even his eyes wouldn't move. He tried to turn his head to the kind voice, but he couldn't even do that. His heart practically stopped as he deliberated whether he was alive. Was he dead? Was this heaven? A sudden pounding in his head had him sucking in a desperate breath. A voice so familiar to him made him storm to the forefront, giving him the push he needed to finally open his eyes. And when he did, the world he found himself in was unbearably light.

Blinking, he urgently tried to focus.

White walls.

Beeping machines. A steady drone pounding out every beat of his heart.

Unable to stand the light, he squeezed his eyes closed again.

He was alive.

He was going to be able to tell Melody just how much she meant to him.

'Zai, can you hear me? It's me, Melody. Please, wake up, baby.'

His Sweet Melody. She was here, right beside him. With an almighty effort he flickered his eyes open and he fought to keep them that way. 'Mel.' He squinted against the intensity of light, desperate to see her face.

'I'm right here, Zai.'

Her voice was soothing, angelic, as was her touch on his hand. He wanted to get up, to take her into his arms, but he couldn't move. It felt as if a great weight was pressing down upon him, pinning him in place, making it hard to take a decent breath. Then another thought struck him, full force ...

Holy shit, I am paralysed?

Terror gathered inside him, condensing and rolling like crashing waves against his chest. He darted his gaze left to right then finally found a point of focus – a picture of a beach on the far wall. Running footsteps clapped into the room and a nurse appeared. With her on one side of the bed, he turned his head to see his beautiful angel's face come into his line of vision. He fought to find his voice. His mouth felt as if it was filled with cottonwool.

He tried to smile but wasn't sure if he was achieving it. 'Hey, you,' was all he could mutter.

'Hey, yourself.' Melody clasped his hand between both of hers. 'I thought I'd lost you, Zai.' She blinked faster and tears fell.

Seeing her break broke him. 'I'm not going anywhere.' He tried to smile again, and this time he felt it, all the way in his soul. 'You can't get rid of me that easily.'

'I love you, Zai Wellstone, so much.' She leant in and lingered a kiss on his cheek.

He gave her hand a tender squeeze. 'I love you too, beautiful.'

Two heads popped in beside her, Matt and Sarah's smiling faces lifting his heart even higher.

'About time you woke up, bud,' Matt said with his trademark grin.

'Yeah, mister. You scared the bejesus out of us all,' Sarah added warmly.

He smiled into each of their faces, feeling utterly whole and complete – this right here was the kind of family he'd never had. The ones who loved him unconditionally, who had his back and would move mountains to make sure he was cared for and happy. And that now included Melody who, one day, he hoped to make his wife.

CHAPTER 20

It had been almost six months since the accident that almost took Zai's life, and the months had floated by in a blur of happiness for Melody. So much had changed, for the better. And now here they all were, back where they had been, sitting on bales of hay, watching Slim marry the love of his life. The only difference was that instead of being at her forever home, Rosalee Station, the wedding was being held on the beach at Palm Cove, where Slim and Sherrie had relocated. And it was the perfect day for it too – the sky was a sea of blue with only a few cottony clouds floating listlessly upon the gentle sea breeze.

Seated in the front row between her dad and a very pregnant Sarah – two weeks and she'd be due – and her wonderful grandparents, Judy and Steve, and the motley crew behind her (minus Hasselhoof, who'd been fired on the spot for losing his cool with her grandad), she had a perfect view of the two lovebirds. Though she was meant to be watching the bride and groom, she was having a hard time keeping her eyes off the best man – her man. As the ceremony progressed and the celebrant spoke of commitment and love and becoming one, she and Zai kept catching each other's gazes, the hint of a smile on the lips she so loved to kiss telling her of everything he felt, and everything he wanted to do to her later. He still had the power to make her blush beneath his stare. She thought she'd loved him back then but boy oh boy, she loved him so much more now. Each and every night, she fell asleep in his arms to then wake to his smiling face, her heart slipping more into his as she fell deeper, harder, and more passionately. There seemed to be no limit to their beautiful love story – they continued to write it, together, every single day they lived and worked together in the heart of the country. Walking towards their future, hand in hand, one step at a time, was all she could wish for, and more. She was so proud of Zai, landing his dream position after Slim retired from his job as manager of the station to open a stockfeed place in Cairns. And she was so happy Zai's parents had finally given him their blessing to follow his heart and do what made him happy. The shock of his accident and how close Zai had come to death, coupled with a long deep and meaningful with Steve about accepting Zai for the countryman he was, had made them take a real hard look at themselves and how unfair they'd been with their only son. It had been a very teary apology, one she'd felt honoured and blessed to bear witness to, at Zai's hospital bedside.

'Gregory Mark, do you take Sherrie Fay to be your lawfully wedded wife, to have and to hold, in sickness and in health, for as long as you both shall live?' The celebrant's voice was strong and sweet as it echoed over the microphone.

Melody found it so strange to hear Slim's real name.

'My bloody oath I do,' was Slim's strident reply.

The crowd chuckled and calmed again as they listened to Sherrie echo the same. Almost half Slim's size, Sherrie held on tight, as if she would fall over if she didn't. Her brunette hair was in spirals and hung to her waist, and her princess-style dress looked exquisite on her petite frame. Minutes later, with rings on their fingers and grins on their faces, the celebrant pronounced them husband and wife.

'You may now kiss your bride, Slimbo,' the celebrant added.

Slim didn't need any more of an invitation and, gently bending Sherrie back, kissed her like he damn well meant it.

'Get a room, you two,' Showbags called out as they straightened.

'We already have, Showbags,' Slim hollered back to his mate with a wink.

Family and friends cheered and hollered and a few hats were thrown in the air as Slim proudly walked his wife through the arch of arms while being showered with rose petals and confetti.

Sidestepping her aunty Georgia and uncle Patrick, the two of them busy reprimanding Danny for throwing a handful of sand at Beau, Melody rushed over to Zai and wrapped her arms around his shoulders. 'You look so handsome in your suit and snazzy black hat, Mister Wellstone.'

'Why, thankya, my beautiful lady.' Zai smouldered sexily as he looked her up and down. 'And you, Sweet Melody, look absolutely stunning in that dress.'

'I'm glad you think so.' She smoothed her peach-coloured silk dress over her hips. 'I'm not sure how long I'm going to last in these heels, though. They're killing my feet already.'

'Don't worry, I'll get you undressed in no time when we sneak off later, sexiness.' Zai flashed her his cheekiest smile. 'But for now, we can head over to the reception area so you can grab a glass of champers, find your seat, and rest those tootsies.'

Sliding her hand into his, Melody sucked in a breath while the wind brushed her waist-length curls over her back. Her eyes briefly shut in pleasure as the salty aroma gave rise to goosebumps. She wandered hand in hand with Zai to the sound of the breaking waves crashing upon the golden shore and the clip-clop of her heels on the paved pathway. As she gazed out at the horizon, the aqua blue seemed to stretch on forever; to the south, the lush green hills curved gently down to the sea; and to the north, the mountains soared into the sky, as if reaching for the heavens.

With hilarious and heartfelt speeches abounding, and copious amounts of delicious food followed by lots of music, drinking, dancing and laughter, the night whizzed past in the blink of an eye.

It was close to midnight when Melody found herself, a little tipsy and barefoot, following Zai up the plant-lined pathway that led to their ocean-view room. Once inside, she whirled herself back into his waiting arms, their bodies melting into one another's and her cheek meeting with his chest. This, right here, was her forever home. She never wanted to leave it.

'Hi there, my sexy woman,' he said, the huskiness of his voice making her shiver.

'Hi.' She angled her face to his, biting her lip in the way she knew drove him wild. 'This has been one amazing night, my beautiful man.'

'It sure has been.' A glint lit up his eyes, making them appear even bluer. 'And thanks to the three espresso martinis Tumbles got me, I'm still wide awake.'

'Well, I might have just the cure for that.' With her fingers making the motion of galloping horses up his chest, she signalled they should wander over to the bed with a slight tip of her head. 'Take me to bed, cowboy, and let me kiss you all over.'

'How could I say no to a proposition like that?' His lips slowly curling into his trademark sexy smile, he gently took her wrists and pressed her hands up against his chest. 'See how fast and how hard you make my heart race?'

His heartbeat brought her to that magical place. 'You do the exact same thing to me.' She took his hand and placed it over her sprinting heart.

They stayed like this for a few moments, drinking each other in, taking the time to connect beyond the flesh. She flushed with pleasure, her skin growing hot from the strong desire blazing in his eyes. Then, giving in to the intensity of the moment, they joined lips and kissed like two lovers who'd spent way too much time apart, their hands tearing at each other's clothing and caressing each other's soul. Melody pressed in close as he guided her towards the bed. He stopped shy of it, holding her upright, flush up against him, moving very slowly until the backs of her legs brushed against the softness of the plush doona. Wrapping his arms around her waist, he lowered her back and onto it, moving to hover above her. She was so close to losing all control. Just one more kiss from him and she'd be unable to catch her breath, she was sure …

He paused, holding her eyes with his as he brushed hair from her forehead, so tenderly it made her toes curl. 'I want to take our time, my Sweet Melody, so I can show you just how deeply in love I am with you.'

'And you wonder why I love you so much, Wellstone.' She reached for him, pulling him down to meet her lips. Hungry for his touch, she gave him every invitation to take her, to make them one. But he held back, taking it slow. When neither of them could wait any longer, he gathered her close and slowly, inch by glorious inch, slid inside her. And once he was deep within her, he stopped and kissed her, gently at first, but gradually building to ravenous. Melody lost all sense of herself as he began to thrust, unhurriedly and mind-blowingly deep. Riding the euphoric waves he was building, she cried out, begging him to take her harder, faster.

He bent into her and whispered in her ear. 'Patience, beautiful.'

All she could do was gasp.

As promised, he took his time. She spiralled at a dizzying speed, lingering on pleasure-filled clouds for a moment before he whisked her off to another, and another, each one a little higher. She closed her eyes, gripping him. She groaned and moaned from her depths as he breathed deeply above her, his body trembling. They rode the waves of ecstasy together, speeding up and slowing down, making each other wait for the grand finale, the pièce de résistance. That, right there, was the single most spectacular sensation she could ever imagine. Zai Wellstone had surpassed even her wildest of fantasies. She wanted this, and him, for the rest of her life.

Tumbling, tingling, trembling, they dove and cried out in pleasure, collapsing into each other before trying to catch their breath. No words were needed to fill the blissful silence as she rested her head against his chest and his arms came around to hold her close.

Thin fingers of dawn light were just beginning to creep into the bedroom when Melody stirred. Still wrapped up in Zai's arms, her legs were tangled with his. With her head cradled into his shoulder, she took her sweet time to wake up fully. Blinking the sleep from her eyes, she dragged her admiring eyes from him to where the opened curtains fluttered softly in the hushed inhale and exhale of the salty sea breeze floating in through the window. The sound of the waves spilling against the shore were music to her ears, as was the sound of her incredible man's heart beating against her cheek. Last night had felt different, deeper and more intense, almost as if they were sealing their lives together forever. It blew her away how they just kept getting better and better, stronger and stronger.

He stirred and his eyes flickered open. She rested her head on his bicep and tangled a leg over his to pull him in close. 'I love you, Zai, so very much.'

'I love you too, my beautiful, Sweet Melody.' He tipped her chin so he could kiss her lips ever so gently, lingering long enough to steal one of her breaths. 'And because I love you so very much, I have a surprise for you, but you have to promise to stay right here.' He threw back the covers and leapt from the bed before she could stop him.

Rolling onto her stomach, she propped her chin on her hands. 'Just where do you think you're going, hmm?'

'That's for me to know and you to find out.' He tugged on a pair of boxer shorts. 'Don't get impatient and wander out or you'll spoil the surprise, deal?'

'I'm going to miss you, but ...' She pulled a playful pouty face. '... okay, it's a deal.'

After much clanging and banging in the kitchen, and with the scent of pancakes and coffee wafting, Zai returned fifteen minutes later, tray in hand. 'Breakfast in bed for my queen.'

'You, Zai Wellstone, are a very sweet man.' Melody sat up, pulling the doona with her.

Passing her the tray, Zai carefully saddled in beside her. 'I reckon you should taste the passionfruit first, it's mind-blowingly yummy.'

She did as he suggested and plucked the top off the passionfruit. Her eyes watered and widened at the same time – nestled inside was a glittering diamond ring. Her hand covered her mouth as she brought her teary gaze to Zai's, finding herself totally speechless.

Moving the tray to the side, he took her hand in his and came onto his knees beside the bed. 'Sweet Melody, will you make me the happiest man alive and marry me?'

Unable to form words yet, she nodded.

'Is that a yes?' His intense gaze searched hers.

'Yes, yes, yes!' she finally cried, wrapping her arms around his neck.

He enfolded his arms around her, pulled her from the bed and spun her around the room. 'You've just made me the happiest and luckiest man alive.' Placing her down, but keeping his hands laced at the small of her back, he met her gaze. 'I'm going to love you like you never thought possible, and then love you some more.'

'Ditto, my gorgeous man.' She couldn't wipe the massive smile from her face. 'Thank you for believing in me. I am so blessed, being loved by a man as rare and as wonderful as you.'

'You, my future Mrs W, are the amazing one. We're going to have the most amazing life together.' He brought his lips to hers and kissed her like only he knew how.

Wrapped up in all that was him, Melody felt the final fragment of her heart slip into perfect place as he pulled her closer into his arms, and into his heart and soul. She had finally found where she belonged, and it was alongside Zai Wellstone, the man who'd taught her the bliss of deep, unconditional love.

And it was all thanks to the long and winding roads that had ultimately led her into to the heart of Australia, and into the very heart of this incredible man, beneath the expansive outback sky of her family's sprawling cattle station, Rosalee.

Take a trip

to Rosalee Station

with BESTSELLING AUSTRALIAN AUTHOR

MANDY MAGRO

It's Sarah Clarke's dream to experience the real Australian outback. Sarah is irresistibly drawn to Matt, the station owners' son – but will fate find a way to intercede?

Mandy Magro returns to the world of her debut novel, Rosalee Station, with a new tragic and harrowing story of love and second chances.

Turn over for a sneak peek ...

Savannah's Secret

by

MANDY
MAGRO

Out Now

CHAPTER
1

Far North Queensland

As the red-dirt roads finally gave way to bitumen, Ash Sullivan flicked his headlights to low-beam and turned off his spotlights. It had been a while since he'd had white lines leading the way, more accustomed to his tyres kicking up a trail of dust, and his excitement was building, knowing he was almost home.

He pressed the gizmo to squirt water over his dirty windscreen, the wipers creating a red arc that framed the progressively lusher landscape. The farmhouses were becoming more frequent, and the livestock dotting the paddocks looked a lot healthier than those he'd been mustering. And instead of flat plains with trees few and far between, neatly lined rows of avocado, macadamia and mango trees hung heavy with the year's bounty, all backdropped by soaring mountain ranges.

Australia was a place of such sharp contrast, of land both foreboding and fertile, and Ash was proud to make a living by working amongst it all.

He tapped his thumbs against the steering wheel in time to one of his favourite tunes blaring from the speakers. Hank Williams' deep twangy voice helped to make the monotonous journey a little more bearable, as did the entire packet of Minties he'd devoured, along with two cans of Red Bull. Lord knew any distraction was welcome on the five-hour route he'd travelled more times than he could count over the past seven years. Saving every penny he could, he hoped to soon bring to fruition his dream of owning a chopper-mustering business so he didn't have to continue making a living in the saddle – his back was starting to pay the price of his being a stockman.

Now back where he could get good phone service, he needed to hear his girlfriend's sweet voice, but he wasn't about to let on he was arriving home a day early – he wanted to surprise her, in more ways than one.

'Hey Siri. Call Hannah.'

Siri did as asked. The phone rang through the speakers, two, three, four times, before going to voicemail. '*Hi, you've reached Hannah, I can't get to the phone right now, so please leave a message and I'll call you back soon.*'

'Hey, babe. Just calling to say I love you, and miss you,' he said with a huge smile on his dial before ending the call.

In the distance, the soft glow of his home town caught his eye. The tiny township was going to be a welcome change from the incessant flies and barren countryside of outback Australia. He fought the urge to slam the accelerator to the floor – he'd arrive in Atherton soon enough. After almost two months away, mustering wild cattle and buffalo up the northern tip of Australia while evading crocs bigger than Ben-Hur, he couldn't wait to be back in civilisation, take his high school sweetheart into his arms and tell her how much he loved her.

Beyond the cab of his beat-up old LandCruiser, the velvet sky glimmered with countless stars, as if it too was celebrating what was about to happen. Although nervous, he was optimistic his proposal was going to be all he'd imagined it to be. He'd intended to pop the question the weekend of Hannah's sister's car accident, but had tucked the ring away. Hannah was mourning Heather, her sister, and it wasn't the time for a marriage proposal. Instead, he gave Hannah all the time and support she needed to begin to heal her broken heart. He'd been waiting for the right moment, and tonight felt like it had come. He prayed he was right.

Cruising along the quiet main street of Atherton, he saw a line of cars parked out front of the top pub – not unusual for nine o'clock on a Saturday night. He hoped Hannah wasn't in there, amongst the rowdy crowd – she loved to dance when there was a band playing. Not sounding like herself when he'd called first thing that morning, she'd said she was feeling run down, like she was possibly getting a flu, and had agreed she needed an early night. He was going to wake her with a kiss.

Passing their favourite café, then the butcher shop, Ash indicated and turned down their street. His hands were growing sweaty as he took a deep breath, running what he was going to say through his mind for what felt like the millionth time. He couldn't wait to give her the one-carat diamond engagement ring his late grandmother had left to him, her dying wish that he marry the love of his life and have a family together. He liked to believe his dear Granny Fay was watching down from heaven because, with any luck, he was about to fulfil their shared aspiration.

Pulling up in his usual spot, he killed the engine and tapped his top pocket again to check the ring box was still there. He'd get his bags and swag out later. A spring in his step, he strode down the footpath and through the side gate, plucked a red rose from the garden and crept around to the back door. The spare key was where they always left it, beneath the old gumboot that was now home to the maidenhair fern he'd bought Hannah at the local market. She had a green thumb, unlike him.

Slipping his boots and socks off and the key into the lock, he quietly turned it and stepped inside. The house was dark and the timber floorboards were cool against his feet. He sighed. It was good to be home.

The tinkle of a bell sounded as Minx, their three-year-old cat, scurried into the room and leaped up onto the kitchen bench – a place she knew she shouldn't be. Ash chuckled, deciding not to reprimand her this time. It was nice to be eagerly welcomed home. The moggy meowed urgently, as if trying to tell him something important. Wishing he understood cat lingo, he scooped the rescued tabby up and cuddled her to him, noting with a wry smile that her bowl at his feet was overflowing with dried food. Hannah had always been a sucker for strays, bless her beautiful heart, and it appeared she was overfeeding Minx too. He grimaced at something wet and sticky on the cat's coat, and wiped his hand off on his jeans. God only knew what mischief the cat had been up to. He'd clean them both up as soon as he got to lay a kiss on his girl.

In the lounge room, the sheer curtains fluttering in the gentle breeze allowed just enough silvery moonlight to filter in so he could see the dirty plates and cups littering the coffee table, with a half-empty pizza box and fully empty vodka bottle lying on the floor. Concern gripped him – it was very unlike Hannah to be so untidy. He tiptoed down the hallway, past the line of framed family photos, his ears honed. Their bedroom door was wide open, and the curtains still tied back on the windows. His heart sank at the piles of dirty clothes covering the floor, the tousled bed, and no Hannah. And the room stank of stale cigarettes. Striding over, he shoved the windows open to allow the fresh air in. An ashtray filled with stubbed-out rollies sat on the windowsill. When had Hannah started smoking? Had she been hiding it from him? And where in the hell was she? Maybe she'd gone against his advice and headed to the pub after all. He just hoped she didn't drink too much because he was sure as anything that a fight would ensue – he was worried about her, and she wasn't going to like his 'suffocating attention', as she'd put it.

Turning the bedside lamp on, he laid eyes on a curled-up ten-dollar note alongside specks of white powder. Dropping the rose, he snatched a little plastic bag from the dressing table, with traces of what he assumed was illicit drugs. It was then that he spotted the ensuite door ajar and heard water dripping. His held breath released a little. Maybe Hannah was enjoying one of her baths. She'd always liked him to run one for her at the end of a long day, and he'd always made sure to construct a mountain of bubbles for her to climb into.

With Minx still cradled in his arms, he stood, his heart in his throat – he was going to have to confront her about the mess and the drugs and the cigarettes, and he hated it. Tonight was meant to have gone so differently. He'd imagined her saying yes and then them making love all night long.

Ash cracked the ensuite door wider and, to his surprise, found the bathroom was pitch-black, with not even a flicker of a candle. 'Hannah, are you in there?'

The ear-piercing silence sent a chill racing up his spine. Minx hissed, then growled. Something wasn't right. Adrenaline jolted him, and with dread in his heart, he flipped the switch. The overhead fluorescent bulb flared to life and Minx leaped from his arms and scurried out the door.

Ash's breath caught as the sight before him chilled him to the very core.

CHAPTER 2

Sydney – six years later

Head tilted back, Kayla Robinson blinked the eye drops in, waited for her vision to clear, then glided out of her top-floor office with clear views of almost every inch of the warehouse-style building. It was a typical Saturday night at Sydney's elite nightclub, Urban Underground, and the place was jam-packed to capacity. As usual, the queue outside was filled with people hopeful to bribe the ferocious-looking doormen so they could rub shoulders with the influential. Kayla knew their plight was hopeless – she made the rules. No matter how short their skirts or how big their muscles, if their name wasn't on the list, there was no entry – no ifs, buts or maybes. The bouncers knew if they broke that rule, they lost their job on the spot. Didn't stop people from trying to get in every night, though. They were painstakingly consistent, she had to give them that.

Stepping from the glass lift, she continued to survey the crowd, ignoring a wolf-whistle from one of the boozed-up patrons. One smooth stride after the other, she kept all of her senses alert. It was that particular time of the night when things could go awry in a heartbeat. Three-fifteen am – just under an hour until closing time – but she knew from years of experience that a lot could happen between now and then. Three years spent as a barmaid followed by seven years as the nightclub's manager, dealing in secrets, lies, underhanded business deals and stupid drunken behaviour from people who were meant to be level-headed CEOs, politicians and other high-flyers – she'd seen it all.

Ducking behind the black marble bar backdropped by a matching wall studded with crystal lights, Kayla made her way over to her flatmate, the only true friend she'd had in her twenty-seven years. 'How's it going, Jaz?'

Straightening from where she was stacking a tray of clean glasses into a fridge, Jasmine Fuller rolled her pretty blue eyes, groaning. 'My feet are killing me in these bloody heels, and I don't think I can bear another hip-hop tune, but I'm hanging in there.' A blender whirred to life beside them. 'How about you?' she said, a little louder. 'You got rid of your headache?'

'Yeah, the paracetamol you gave me did the trick, thanks, babe.' Kayla leaned in closer. 'I'm so exhausted. I seriously can't wait for my head to hit the pillow. I'm going to spend my days off catching up on sleep.'

'Ha! I can't wait to bite the pillow while Jimmy has his way with me.' As she flicked her long blonde ponytail over her shoulder, Jasmine's red-painted lips curled into a wicked smile.

Kayla frowned. In hindsight, employing Jasmine as the bar manager when she'd lost her day job hadn't been the best idea.

BESTSELLING AUSTRALIAN AUTHOR

MANDY MAGRO

Novels to take you to the country...

talk about it

Let's talk about books.

Join the conversation:

romance.com.au

If you love reading and want to know about our authors and titles, then let's talk about it.